THE TRANSCENDENT GREEN

BOOK ONE

MATI OCHA

Robot Dinosaur Press
robotdinosaurpress.com

For her.

Dhise.

FRIENDLY NOTICE

This book may contain Scottish swearing, including but not limited to the following: damn, shit, shite, gobshite, fuck, bugger, bloody, arse, cunt (affectionate), cunt (pejorative), cunt (neutral), wanker, goddamn, gods damn (when one god isn't doing enough damning), bollocks, bawbag, balls, hell, fanny, piss, and pish.

Selected terms both vulgar and polite presented at intervals with definitions for your convenience and amusement.

This book has been rated as approximately three (3) blasphemies out of an unspecified number of blasphemies.

(We are capable of being reverent where it suits. But being precious about swearing is not something we're known for. If that's not for you, you have our sincerest well-wishes to find a wealth of literature that meets your every whim as well as the freedom to seek such things out. I've included this notice to save you time. Mo shoraidh leibh.)

PROLOGUE

The Transcendent Plane, one day before the end of Earth.

"Explain to me how this could happen."

The voice filled Ghilla's being, suffused every cell with the weight of its disapproval. He stood at the pinnacle of his people's power, and today was supposed to prove he deserved to be here. If he'd still had fingertips, they would be tingling with shame.

For a moment, Ghilla hovered in a strange kind of stasis, staring around him at this hallowed chamber at the highest peak of the tallest mountain in his world. The clouds blanketed the land far below, stretched out toward the curve of the horizon under the glaring buttery yellow of their star. Soon, the rotation of the planet would light those cloud-fields with gold and molten orange—if Ghilla were still alive to see the sunset.

The voice's resonance still hummed all around him as he stared into the scrying pool, its essence depleted so far, it was almost reduced to a puddle.

The longer Ghilla failed to answer, the harsher the consequences. He would answer in more ways than one.

His energies shifted, still jangled after the accident.

Accident.

Such a word to describe the annihilation of a planet.

"A failure of calculation, off by the barest fraction of trajectory," Ghilla said finally. "The guiding minds were unable to reroute it once it left the well. I take full responsibility."

He was proud that his voice did not crack or waver in the presence of the god who would judge him. Her—if celestial beings indeed could be described by mortal appellations—presence grew somehow heavier, somehow increased the gravity around Ghilla where he stood until he swayed on his feet in the full force of her displeasure.

"You do," came the voice again. "You shall. For your foolishness, you shall bear witness to what you have caused. The planet affected was not ready to ascend; its people and its creatures were *far* from ready to ascend. Your folly has forced this upon them, and they will tear each other apart. And the world that has waited for its ascension will be forced to wait yet longer. This is the price of your failure that billions will bear in your stead. For that, I must act."

Ghilla was stuck on the first three sentences of his god's pronouncement. Bear witness? Surely, she couldn't mean—

"I can, and I do." Her voice swelled in volume like the rising of the wind outside the chamber, and Ghilla shook where he stood.

Of course she could sense his thoughts, his panic.

"Please," Ghilla begged. "It was a simple mistake, one mistake in a thousand cycles of faithful service, Divine One. I didn't mean—"

Some of the pressure of her presence lifted, just enough

that Ghilla released a wisp of breath even from his only partly corporeal form, the smallest sigh, of hope, of relief.

"You did not mean it," she said, her voice softer now with the nurturing of a god rather than divine wrath.

Ghilla almost collapsed from the force of her care.

"You have indeed served us faithfully. Serve your next thousand just as faithfully, and you will be forgiven."

The light of the sun faded at the edges of Ghilla's perception as his question caught, unvoiced, at the edge of his ability to speak.

Around him, the chamber receded as if he were shrinking, shrinking, his remaining form bundled into an infinitesimal speck until all he could see before him was his own error, the pride and pooled might of his people poured out onto an unsuspecting planet.

The puddle of depleted power was replaced by a blue-green orb against the blackness of space. The orb grew larger, swirls of clouds over immense, green-and-brown landmasses. From the angle of approach, the view straddled the line of sunlight, and pinpricks of gold spread out in the shadow beyond. Even as Ghilla wept in his soul, those lights rippled. Flickered. And vanished.

Ghilla did not know this planet beyond his hasty and frantic investigation when the offering had gone wrong.

Even as he grew nearer, nearer, nearer, the shadowed side of the planet's face was plunged into true darkness.

Ghilla felt his essence traverse the Earth's atmosphere and spread out across its surface, his consciousness split like it had once been so very long ago, before the gods chose him. The sensation of billions of minds threatened to overwhelm him, and he wondered for a fragment of a moment whether this was what his gods experienced. Then it receded just as swiftly, leaving him suspended, formless, unable to feel and able only to observe.

The last thing Ghilla heard was his god's regretful words.

I hope you will learn the weight of intentions as you measure the impact of your actions.

The lifeline of her presence sheared away as if cloven by the keenest blade.

If Ghilla could have, he would have screamed.

CHAPTER
ONE

Y ou'd think it would be some kind of comfort that an arsehole intent on making my life miserable was an absolute shite speller, but for some reason, that only made it worse, because my petty comfort in his grammar fails made *me* feel like the arsehole. And in this equation, the arsehole was, undeniably, him.

Your [sic] *lucky I'm not in Glasgow—you peak* [sic] *round a corner in Dundee and I'll give you something else to smile about.*

I stared at my phone, unable to decide whether an outright threat—putting the words "Glasgow" and "smile" in a sentence like that is a very particular kind of outright threat—merited more than a stomach-turning flash of combined rage and anxiety. I leaned aside to let other passers-by get round me in the tunnel, hovering in the threshold to the beer garden out the back of the adjacent café.

I'm not sure what he thought I had to smile about now, so the threat was rubbish to an even greater degree, but if there was anything I'd learnt in the past three months since

I'd started getting these messages, it was that John Frost didn't give a toss about whether he made sense.

Shoving my mobile in my pocket, I shrugged my shoulders up to my ears and ducked out of Kelvinhall's subway station, chucking my mask in the bin on my way. It didn't ultimately matter if that absolute weapon my ex left me for couldn't tell the difference between *your* and *you're* or *peak* and *peek*; at the end of the day, he'd three inches and two stone on me, and my broken bones would mean as little to him as me spending the rest of my days like a sad imitation of a certain comic-book villain with cheeks slit up to my ears.

Dumbarton Road was busy for the hour, clouds hanging heavy over the city even though they scudded across the sky almost faster than the traffic could crawl along the streets, and I shouldered my satchel and hoofed it across Mansfield Square, up Hyndland Street toward my flat.

The days were stretching out longer after the darkness of winter, but you wouldn't know it by the dimness of the February afternoon. One street away from my flat, the clouds opened up with a vengeance, a proper spring Scottish downpour in that it skipped the drizzly mist and instead sent a curtain of rain cascading down the hill.

"Sod it," I muttered, hopping laterally on the pavement to duck under the awning of, ironically, The Duck Club.

I briefly considered going in to wait it out—they had truffle fries I'd consider going toe to toe with my ex's weapon of a new boyfriend for—but I'd food at home, so instead I burst into a trot up the hill the remaining distance to my door.

I was still soaked by the time I shouldered my way into my flat on the second floor, leaving a trail of water all the way up six flights of stairs. Immediately, I wished I'd gone into the restaurant. The flat smelled stale, despite the cleaner having come through earlier in the week—a luxury my best mate Iain had forced on me when I stayed in a sulk for two months after I found out Susanna was cheating on me with her aggressive Dundonian bampot.

"You're no spendin' it down the pub or on anything else, mate," Iain'd said. "Pay someone to clean your bloody terrarium. Even hamsters have that."

After a month of following his advice, I had to grudgingly admit he was right. I was still a pathetic hamster, but at least a pathetic hamster with a clean terrarium and fresh cedar chips or whatever.

I'd also not replaced the furniture Susanna'd taken, so the flat itself was a shell more than a home. The hall was a perfect microcosm: one rickety side table where I dumped my satchel and my keys, one loose coat hook where I dropped my coat to drip on the creaky hardwoods, one horrid painting of a rat the landlord wouldn't let me take down. I didn't know if it was his own handiwork or his wife's or his bloody ten-year-old's, but the flat had one in every room, including the entry hall, and they were all like an impressionist's nightmare. West End rats were sort of legendary both in size and persistence, but if these monstrosities were good for anything, it was convincing me more and more I ought to get a cat just in case the painted rats came to life and tried to eat me in my sleep.

In the kitchen, I threw a frozen pepperoni pizza in the oven and dug my phone back out to set the timer and go through the now-ritual blocking of John's newest burner number. I almost had to respect the dedication to harassing me. The one time I saw him was enough to suggest his little anger issues could be 'roid rage, but I still didn't appreciate being his preferred punching bag.

He got the girl, for fuck's sake. I wouldn't be surprised to come home one day and find he'd pissed on my door even so. Not sure why he thought I was a threat.

This was not a good train of thought for the twenty-five minutes I'd be waiting for the bloody pizza. I thumbed my way to WhatsApp and sent Iain a message.

Pint at the Lios Mòr, mate? Shite day.

He hopped on a moment later, and the chat showed him typing.

Naw, soz. I'm in Oban for the weekend with Mum and Meeksy. Back Sunday if you want to go then.

Damn. *Nae bother. Tell them I said hi.*

Another pause while Iain typed. *You could come through and tell them yourself, mate. Get out of Glesga for a couple days.*

For a moment, I was tempted to say yes. I could do— drive up tonight, spend the weekend with Iain and his family, come back in time to face the grind on Monday.

But my fingers betrayed me, typing the opposite. *Maybe another time, pal. Give em my best.*

Iain was still online—we both had read receipts off, but I'd known him since we were weans, and I could almost feel his eye-roll from here. He didn't respond and went offline after a moment. I shoved my mobile in my pocket and went into the lounge to see if there was anything on the telly.

By the time the timer went off on my phone twenty minutes later, I'd finally settled on watching *Hannibal* for the thousandth time, feeling restless and indecisive. I could still go to Oban. Iain and the family would be happy to see me, but they were just getting some spark of happiness back after his dad had passed away, and the last thing they needed was a Glaswegian rain cloud turning up to piss their mood into the gutter.

I settled onto my gaming chair in front of the telly

with my pizza—the whole thing—on a plate on the eight-quid Ikea table next to me. Susanna used to be disgusted that I could watch Mads Mikkelson turn humans into dinner while eating my own meal, but it's not like it was real.

When I was on my third slice of pizza, though, the telly flickered and went off, along with all the lights in the flat and the kitchen extractor fan, which cut out with a sputtering cough. I'd forgotten to turn it off, used to the drone at the edge of my awareness.

Fucking power cut. I couldn't remember the last time one of *those* had happened. The blinds were drawn, so at a glance I couldn't see whether it was just my flat or if it was the rest of the street from where I sat in now-near pitch black.

I got up, moving to the window and tugging on the cord to the blinds.

The entire street was dark. No lights whatsoever, no car headlights, no street lamps—nothing.

Even with a power cut, there should at least be cars visible from here going past me on Hyndland. It was not a super busy street, but it also wasn't dead at seven at night in the early, wobbly steps of a newborn spring.

Unnerved, I pulled my mobile from my pocket again, absently tapping the screen with my thumb.

Instead of lighting up, though, the screen stayed as black as the telly. I must have turned it off accidentally in my pocket. I pressed and held the on button, waiting for the flare of light and the Apple logo to appear.

Ten seconds. Fifteen. Twenty.

The battery had been at sixty percent. There was no way it was dead.

I looked around the lounge for something else that

could be turned on. There. My Switch in its charging dock. I picked it up, hitting the on button.

Nothing.

What the fuck was happening?

And then, just like the bloody electricity, my vision plunged into darkness.

I could feel myself flailing, but I heard no noises to indicate I'd kicked over the table with my pizza on it, and my arms didn't encounter even the rickety lamp or the window I'd just been peering out of.

My heartbeat sounded impossibly loud in my ears, as if every other sound had vanished and I'd gone blind and deaf at once from one *ba-bum* to the next.

Except the beat was more like *ba-bum-ba-bum-ba-bum-ba-bum,* because it was going for it like a maraca.

I heard of those rooms in America where they'd made them sound *absorbent*, they were so silent, and this had to be what it was like to be inside one of them.

Well. If the room existed in the bowels of the fucking planet, where there was no light in existence.

Even as I thought it, though, a fuzzy, gold-ish glow began at the edges of my vision, pulsing out of rhythm with my heartbeat.

The effect was strangely calming, and as it grew in intensity, my heartbeat slowed.

Greetings, human.

The words resounded inside my skull, echoing like my shoddy Partick lounge had suddenly transformed into St. Mungo's cathedral.

What. The. Fuck.

Due to extenuating circumstances, Earth shall begin to ascend ahead of schedule by approximately 10,329 Earth years. Because Earth is not prepared to ascend, we regret to inform you that the process is likely to cause mass casualties, as Earth had, until now, only trace quantities of spirit, and fewer than 0.005% of inhabitants display any affinity for its detection, let alone its gathering and use.

We are unable to provide assistance, as even with our advanced technology, we would arrive too late, and astral projections are incapable of providing meaningful aid.

We apologise for the inconvenience.

Ascension begins in one minute.

We wish you fortitude.

With that, the words vanished, and sixty seconds appeared, becoming fifty-nine. Fifty-eight.

As the timer counted down, the blacked-out vision grew hazier, brightening to the more washed-out dimness of my twilit flat. At least this power cut didn't, like, somehow nuke the sun. Though I reckon if it had, we'd all be much deader.

The moment I could, I peeked out the window again, hoping to see headlights, tail lights, any lights.

None.

The timer continued to tick inexorably downward. Forty seconds.

I could assume this was a joke somehow. Or hey, maybe my depression had manifested into hallucination! I didn't *think* so. The logical explanation for the electricity grid—and anything electrical at all—going dead was some sort of EMP surge. But unless someone on this planet had been keeping major secrets, the type human beings are notoriously terrible at keeping, no one had the tech to pull off an EMP and broadcasting messages into brains.

If this was some other country, I would also think they'd have a better line than "soz, you're ascending early" without any further explanation.

What the hell; might as well treat the weird floaty digital timer in front of my face as real.

Twenty seconds.

I didn't hear any yelling, also no cursing—a feat for Weegies—and to the contrary, the evening was eerily quiet. Squinting out the window, I couldn't make out the cars on Dumbarton Road even if I was sure they were there. I imagined the drivers all standing in the middle of the street scratching their heads. No point in being cheesed off about everyone stopping when your own car won't budge.

Ten seconds.

Nine.

Eight.

Seven.

Six.

Five.

What the fuck is going to happen?

Four.

Three.

Fuck-fuck-fuck-fuck-fuck. Susanna's face. Mum's silhouette. Mull in the distance.

Two.

Iain, the only brother I've ever had.

One.

Nothing.

CHAPTER

TWO

The world returned as I hung suspended in my own mind. I don't know how I could be so bloody certain that was the case, that I was somehow adrift within the confines of my own synapses, but my body felt far away.

Splayed out in front of my consciousness, though, was a ... stat sheet.

Name: Calum Green
    Age: 36
    Level: 1
    Class: N/A (Class selection at: Level 3)
    Affinities: N/A (Gain experience to discover your affinities)

Alteration:
    Strength: 8
    Dexterity: 12
    Agility: 10

Mind: 12

Regeneration:
Constitution: 11
Stamina: 9

Manipulation:
Spirit: 11
Pathos: 8
Will: 14

I'd either gone so far round the bend I was about to run into my own arse or this was real. Worse, as I stared at the numbers—my Strength and Pathos (whatever *Pathos* was supposed to mean beyond the Greek) striking me with no small amount of shame—the quantification of my life in nine different corners made me feel like I was worth sod all. Just as John Frost was so eager to remind me.

Strange that this stat sheet used a word I had just thought, which seemed to lend credence to the "gone round the bend and up my own arse" theory.

Before I could become any more of a pathetic hamster, though, more text appeared, the stats blurring into the background.

At Level 1, you are allotted five stat points and one boon to distribute. Our recommendation is to use them not according to the life you have led thus far but according to the life you wish to lead. Upon ascension, your world is subject to vast changes, and your survival, however unlikely, will depend on your abilities, your mental acuity, and the emotional connection you share with your homeland and those who share it. The simpler, non-sapient creatures will change quickly and more violently than those with control over choice and strategy. Be wary.

As a planet unprepared for ascension, your trials will be many, not least of which survival. We can offer little more guidance than this: no one, even the prepared, can survive alone. Every sentient species known to us has one thing in common, and one thing alone.

Strength is found in connection, not isolation. You will never have every skill needed to thrive.

The limits, such as they are, of your new world are far enough beyond your comprehension so as to be irrelevant. Should you survive long enough to discover them, you will have proven your own mettle and that of your planet.

Do not forget to allocate your stat points and choose your boon.

We wish you fortitude.

With that, the words faded, the stats returning.

Five stat points and one boon. Okay, fine. Round the bend or not, I'd go with it until I could wake up and prove doing otherwise was wiser.

Our recommendation is to use them not according to the life you have led thus far but according to the life you wish to lead.

That was an existential question far too great for my puny brain to deal with in the midst of this psychological fracture. What did I want to be?

I didn't want to be weak.

I hated the way John Frost made me feel, the way he decided I was a bug to squash beneath his foot as if adding insult to the injury of his trysts with Susanna was something gleeful for him. If there's one thing I hate, it's a bully. Sad thing was, I forgot the golden rule. I'd never once bothered to stand up to him in any way.

The flash of shame I felt at seeing the single-digit numbers on my stat sheet decided it for me. If I had to hazard a guess, I would say ten was the magic number of the human median, impressing upon me that in many ways, I was startlingly run-of-the-mill. I'd played enough games to know that this wasn't my wisest decision and that I really should be more strategic, but the text had told me I ought to choose according to the life I wanted.

I put two points in Strength and one in Stamina, but when I went to add the final two to Pathos, I got an error.

Manipulation resources can only be increased through usage and harvesting. Do you want an explanation of these resources?

I mean, yes? I thought the affirmative, and the screen immediately scrolled up in response, text covering my field of view.

A Primer On Resources of Manipulation

Though there has been much debate over the course of history on terminology and semantics, the lay term for manipulation is magic. *Even worlds far from ascension seek out this term; it is a reflection of their germinating ability to recognise and subsequently utilise these resources, though the learning curve is steep enough over time that entire civilisations can rise and fall before anyone lives to see the dream realised.*

All manipulation abilities stem from spirit. We distinguish between Spirit, Pathos, and Will only because it allows minds to more fully comprehend their interconnectivity. Just as steam, water, and ice are not all "water" but are all dihydrogen monoxide, so too is the functionality of Spirit, Pathos, and Will, with the latter two behaving according to what catalyses them.

Spirit, therefore, is the flow of magic. Conceptualised as mana, energy, chi, magic itself, and many other names throughout the ages, it is manipulation in its purest form. Like water, Spirit appears deceptively simple. It can lull one into believing in its simplicity just as the still surface of a pool can bely depths that will swallow an unwary walker whole. Spirit is capable of feats of enormous power. If you imagine the force of a tsunami or the inexorable carving-away of a canyon with the ages of a river, you will begin to understand.

Pathos is Spirit given heat. Like steam, it can scald and burn. Its absence can erode Spirit and Will. But when directed with intention and precision, Pathos can fuel miracles of mind and magic alike. Many people learn one facet of this force. Many others decry it as useless, to their error and peril. Others still deride parts of it while clinging to its fringes. Pathos forms through emotion; emotion itself encompasses everything from joy to grief to fury. How those emotions are used can unlock—or hobble—the efficacy of Pathos.

Will is Spirit given form. Like ice, it can be as implacable as a glacier . . . and as immense. It can level mountain ranges in time, inch by painstaking inch. Will is rooted in patience, and many have little of that to spare. Perhaps the least intriguing of the trinity of spirit, Will nevertheless is a rare and precious commodity. It is not as simple as desire, nor is it as changeable as Pathos. When nurtured, Will may be the keystone that allows the mage to transcend obstacles that would crush others.

Underestimate these powers at your peril; as your planet ascends, you will find you have access to all three. Be mindful of the laws of reactions when you act.

I tried to read on, but that was it. Five short paragraphs. Magic? If this was real, if this was not just happening inside my head—maybe I tripped over the lamp cord and bashed my skull on the windowsill; who knew—this text seemed to suggest the equivalent of handing an entire nursery full of toddlers loaded fully automatic weapons, safeties off. Here, Planet Earth, known for your level heads in the face of power shifts, have magic! All eight billion of you!

For the first time, I felt the stirrings of something beyond confusion and shock. Eight billion people on Earth —or there were yesterday.

Any more hints at what I'm supposed to do next? An instruction manual? A quest? A Holy Hand Grenade?

The system gave no indication I'd thought anything at it. Hmph.

Guide, I thought. *Information.*

Nothing.

They really did expect us to just roll over and croak.

Well, I wisnae about to do anything of the sort.

I had two more stat points to allocate, and it seemed I could not use them to increase my middling pathos. Apparently, if I wanted to channel emotions, they wanted me to . . . feel emotions.

After a long moment of deliberation, I chucked one in each Constitution and Stamina. And then my stats flashed and faded, and I was standing in my lounge at the window, muscles tense and sore as if I'd seized up for the past hour.

The sky outside was now fully dark, and sounds began to filter in, a low murmur of confusion and alarm.

The walls seemed to inch closer to me like that bloody rubbish compactor on a certain moon-sized spaceship of destruction. That scene always made me feel claustrophobic, but I wasn't used to feeling it in general. Suddenly, though, my flat felt too small.

Think, Calum.

Or maybe it *wasn't* my flat, not entirely. I shifted my shoulders, trying to stretch, and the sound of ripping fabric broke through the stillness of the room.

What the—

It was too dark for me to see. I fumbled through the room, my knee finding the table where my pizza grew cold and bonking against it with a clunking scud of almost-wood on wood.

"Bugger," I muttered.

The cupboard in the corner—there was a torch in there. Whether it would work was anybody's guess, but I needed to try anyway. If not, there were some candles.

A panicked laugh tried to burble out of my throat at the thought of being plunged back in time from the twenty-first century to the eighteenth. Would gas work? Would water?

The thought of water almost froze me where I stood. First move: light. Second move: check the taps.

Having a plan settled me a wee bit, and I found the cupboard door and opened it, fumbling about until I found the middle shelf where I thought the torch lived.

Sure enough, my hand closed around the length of it, my thumb seeking out the silicone button.

Click-click.

Nothing.

Okay, not unexpected.

I could smell one of the candles—Susanna loved floral scents even though they gave me blistering headaches—and I'd forgotten I'd shut one in here. It was on the shelf above where I'd found the torch, and next to it was a stick lighter.

At first, I almost despaired; the ignition trigger wouldn't even move. But then I shook myself. The damn things had a safety lock. That laugh threatened to return at my being foiled by a childproofing measure, but my finger found the little rough switch and flipped it, and the trigger moved, clicking once, twice . . .

A small *whumph* and there was light.

I crowed in triumph, no matter how pathetic a hamster it made me; at least now I could see my bloody terrarium.

I lit the candle, finding another, less-offensive vanilla-scented one behind it and lighting that too.

The lounge now bathed in flickering golden light, I took a breath, then held it for a moment before letting it out.

One small step for a useless Weegie, one giant leap for the apocalypse, I guess.

I placed the vanilla candle on the table next to my congealing pizza, grabbing one slice and moving toward the kitchen.

The candle lit the tiny Glaswegian galley kitchen with more ease than the larger lounge, and a wave of heat blasted me in the face. I'd left the bloody oven on. I turned it off, glad at least for the double confirmation that the gas still worked even if electricity didn't, and I set the rose candle down on the bunker to fiddle with the tap.

Water gushed out like normal, and it sounded like relief.

Maybe this was a dream after all. Maybe I'd just spaced out.

My boiler ran on gas, which meant I'd still have hot water.

Even though I knew I shouldn't leave fire sitting around, I also couldn't be sure whether the boiler would continue to work. I was pretty sure it needed electricity, which meant whatever hot water there was would be the last I'd get until the power came back on.

Light and water were a go. Third move, then: shower.

My decision made, I hurried to the bathroom and stripped off my shirt, which, as I had dreaded, was torn at the seams. I couldn't really see myself well in the candle-light, but some muscle in my shoulders must have gotten larger. The shirt wasn't loose before, but it also wasn't tight.

I'd deal with that later. I hopped in the shower by the light of that rose candle, regretting not switching it out for the vanilla, since by the time I'd washed my hair, a headache prickled at the edges of my temples.

Halfway through scrubbing my armpits, I realised I'd fucked up. Like every good soul living in existential dread of climate change, I'd set my boiler to eco, which meant it didn't continually heat water, and I was already running up against the end of it.

With a curse, I hurriedly rinsed my body as best I could before the water turned frigid, hopping out of the tub and shivering.

The water off, I could now hear what I dreaded: no boiler kicking in, no radiators clicking. Late February in Scotland wasn't exactly tropical. It was going to get cold, and I'd just gone and gotten wet.

I dried off and wrapped up in jeans and layered—larger—shirts and jumper.

A knock sounded at the door.

Grabbing the candle, I went to answer it.

The person outside was called Neil—or was he Nathan? —a neighbour from downstairs.

"Hiya," he said. "Sorry to bother, but is anything in your flat working?"

"Naw, mate," I said. "Not even the battery-powered torches. Just the water."

"Shit," he said.

He was a portly bloke, about my height—which is to say a smidge over average—and balding even though he wasn't quite my age. I'd lent them my dilapidated hoover once last month, which might have been why he decided to pick my door to knock on.

He looked around nervously. "Did you like . . . see anything weird?"

Shit, indeed.

After a moment of hesitation, I nodded. "Weird text? Blacked out for a bit? Stats and something about an ascension?"

He laughed, but it was a high-pitched, nervous laugh similar to the ones I'd choked back. "Fucking hell, mate. This some kind of attack? This is some conspiracy-theory-level bollocks."

Whatever I was about to say was lost in a scream cutting through the air of the close, echoing through the stairwell.

"Tracy!" Neil-or-Nathan yelled, turning and half-running, half-slipping down the stairs.

"Neil! Help!" came a woman's voice, followed by a sickening crack that sounded like the time Iain fell out of an oak tree and broke his tibia.

I was moving before I could think, darting after Neil down the stairs, hearing doors open around us, and through that, a hissing noise punctuated by clicks that sounded like fingernails on stone and a vibration like a rattlesnake's tail.

THREE

I almost slipped in a puddle of . . . something.

Only grabbing the bannister of the staircase kept me upright. At first I thought it was pigeon shite—sometimes the wee beasties got stuck in the close until we shooed them out into the back garden—but the glimpse I caught as I tried to catch my balance was something virulent puke yellow and gooey.

A moment later, I saw the source and almost dropped my candle.

Tracy had a kitchen chair in her hands and was using it to beat the ever-living daylights out of a creature I couldn't identify. Legs. So many legs.

Neil had frozen three steps from the bottom of the stairs, and he wasn't moving.

"Help me!" Tracy shouted at her partner.

I put the candle down on the stairs and leapt over the bannister. I couldn't exactly fight some sort of monster with a rose-scented Doodle Dandy Candle or whatever it was, but because of the pigeon problem, we kept a shovel by the door to the garden, and there was just enough light for me to grab the handle.

It was a stumpy, square-bladed thing that probably once was used to clean out the ash from a fireplace before getting relegated to scraping up pigeon shit from the pathway, but that meant it had sharp edges.

My heart pounded in my chest, threatening to choke me, but Neil still wasn't moving on the stairs, and all I could think of was this poor woman fighting for her life with a bloody *chair* of all things.

I leapt toward the creature, swinging the shovel overhead. It slammed into the creature like I'd hit a tin roof, but the edge caught on the thing's carapace. Bloody hell. This was an insect the size of a pit bull.

And the thing unfurled, spasming with the impact of my blow.

It was a sodding *centipede*.

Something flashed in the edges of my vision, but I mentally batted it away, making eye contact with Tracy over the stunned arthropod.

With unspoken agreement, she raised her chair just as I raised the shovel again, and together, we brought our makeshift weapons down on the centipede not a moment too soon. I felt the shovel blade bite into the carapace this time, heard it crunch, heard the wider crunch from Tracy's larger implement smashing through the creature's armour.

A half-second later, there came a splat like beer sloshing over the edge of a pint glass when jostled, and I instinctively cringed away from the sound. The centipede twitched, but it was the last, fading movement of something that hadn't quite realised it was dead.

"Thank you," said Tracy, panting. "Neil, what the *fuck*?"

Neil was still standing stock-still on the stairs, his eyes

open and glazed, hand half-raised and shaking. His part-ner's question seemed to snap him out of it. "It's real," he said, his voice shaking as much as his hand. "It's real. That thing was real."

"Aye, it was real, and now it's real dead, no thanks to you!" Tracy dropped the chair right side up.

One leg came down on a chunk of centipede, making the chair teeter precariously, but it didn't fall.

"I-I'm sorry," Neil stammered.

"It's all right, mate. We got it," I told him. "None of us know what the fuck is happening. You all right, pal?"

The last was directed at Tracy, and she gave a nod, swaying a little on her feet as if the adrenaline had deserted her all at once.

"Left the door open so Neil would nae have to take his keys upstairs, and I heard something scratching and opened it to find . . . that." Her voice dripped disgust, and her whole body shuddered. "Tried to bite me."

Tracy kicked out one leg, where I could see a tear in her jeggings and a bit of blood.

The sight reminded me that some centipedes are venomous.

"It didn't get its teeth or mandibles or whatever into you, did it?" I asked.

She shook her head. "Just a scrape, I reckon."

Footsteps sounded up the stairs. "What in blazes are yous up to down there?"

Shit.

All three of us froze as if we'd been caught breaking and entering.

I realised all of a sudden I was not going to be able to stay here. Not because it wasn't safe—it clearly wasn't—but because I couldn't deal with other people no matter what this bizarre new interface in my brain said.

People. Iain and his family. Bollocks.

"Hello?" the neighbour upstairs called again, the footsteps treading closer as he descended.

"Erm," Tracy said, waffling as she shifted her weight from side to side.

"No point in trying to hide it," I said under my breath, and she nodded after a beat, so I called out, "There was a monster fucking centipede. You can come see it if you like. We killed it."

"Did ye, aye?" came the voice as the sixty-something-year-old from the first floor stumped down the stairs.

I didn't think much could come close to the eye-rolling disdain of a Weegie's "did ye, aye," but in this particular case, the proof was in the centipede pudding, and the moment the old codger rounded the landing between the ground floor and first floor, he entered the pool of candle-light and stopped short.

Neil helpfully moved to the side to give the man a view, which was followed by the surreality of the older man squinting into the flickering light, then grabbing his glasses where they hung from a cord around his neck and pushing them onto his nose.

"Ugh!" he yelled, startling backward and almost running into the stairwell window. He recovered quickly, though, his eyes seeking me out. "Well. Don't see that every day."

"You could say that, aye," Tracy said, and she glanced at me again, seeming to ponder something. "Come inside, Neil. We need to figure out what to do."

With that, her shell-shocked partner darted one last glance at me, studiously avoiding the mangled centipede at my feet, though he edged around it and almost clung to the wall to miss landing in it with his feet.

Neither of them said goodbye, just ducked inside the flat and slammed the door, which was followed by the unmistakeable click of the Yale lock engaging as they released the catch that was keeping it open.

I looked up at the older man, who was peering down at the creature's remains more analytically than I could have expected after his initial reaction.

"I've seen enough in my day," he began, then stopped and shook his head. "I'm going tae bed. Too old for giant beasties and words pasted into my brain. You ought to look closer at that thing, lad. Can't claim I understand it, but there's something waiting fer ye."

With that, he was gone, back up the stairs, leaving me in a pool of candlelight and the warring odours of rose petals and viscera.

The edges of my vision still pulsed, and I wasn't sure what they wanted from me. On a whim, I concentrated on that pulse, and I jumped when another paragraph of text appeared. Before I could read it, though, a gust of wind rattled the garden door, making the candle gutter, and I hurried to latch the door against the elements. Last thing I needed was to be left standing alone in a stairwell with a centipede smoothie in the dark.

Once I was sure a rogue breeze wouldn't ruin my light, I pulled up the text again.

You have killed a giant centipede.

Caught in a wave of spirit upon Earth's ascension, this centipede mutated far faster than can normally be expected for a creature of its complexity.

Such creatures frequently contain common crafting materials such as: chitin.

I snorted at that. One material was hardly plural.

Spirit-mutated creatures also contain reserves of manipulation resources, depending on complexity. The simpler creatures contain only spirit, then spirit and pathos, then spirit, pathos, and will. A giant centipede contains only spirit, though certain subspecies may also contain pathos.

Manipulation resources dissipate into the environment quickly after death, so it behooves the harvester to make use of these stores quickly. Gathering the resource will result in temporarily increasing your capacity for this resource or refilling a depleted resource well. If the former, the resource capacity increase can be applied to increasing said capacity permanently at the rate of one percent of the total harvest. Anything beneath one full point will be lost at dissipation.

Do you wish to harvest this giant centipede?

I hurriedly thought *yes,* not expecting anything exciting but also wondering what it was the bodach—Gaelic word for old man—saw when he looked at this thing. Would I have to tear the chitin apart with my bare hands? Where would I put it?

As if in answer to my question—perhaps truly—the interface sprang up with something that made me again ask if this could possibly be real: an inventory.

My current capacity was a measly ten slots, and as I watched, the centipede glowed slightly, dissolving into motes of yellow-white light, and one of the slots was filled with chitin, a small number three in the corner.

Your spirit capacity has been increased by 13. This effect will last 12 hours.

At my feet, the mass of centipede was gone.

A momentary pang of guilt struck me as I stared at the now-clear chunk of floor. Half of that loot should have been Tracy's, but I wasn't about to knock on her door to tell her. Maybe it was shite of me; I didn't know. None of us knew the rules of this new ascension.

I decided as I retrieved my candle that I was going to pretend as if this was real and approach it the way I approached an enormous data-entry project at work. Find the entry point for the project as a whole, and then work one bit at a time, like the old adage of how you go about eating an elephant: one byte at a time.

As I hurried upstairs, I thought about the impulse I'd had standing over the carcass. That I couldn't stay here in Glasgow.

It was almost as if the centipede was a warning, a mere taste of what was to come. If that bug was a particularly precocious creature and others were to follow, I didn't want to be in the city.

Not only that, but without electricity? Who these days carried cash or could access it without power? No one, that's who. With the entire economic system upended over night, literally everything we had adapted to was gone.

My flat door thankfully had not closed all the way. This time of year, the jamb tended to swell, and I had to laugh at the ridiculous luck of not getting locked out when I couldn't exactly ring the landlord's manager to get back in in an apocalypse.

Apocalypse.

That's what this was. Fucking hell.

My flat was still and quiet, a small light flickering in the lounge where I'd left the vanilla candle, and I blew out the rose one in a vain attempt to head off the headache.

I needed a plan, and fast.

Staying here was out of the question. I apparently had nine slots in my inventory. I had a bike, some packets of biltong in the cupboard from when I was actually going to the gym and needed more protein, and a big jug I could—and should—fill with water. On a whim, I decided to test something. I went into the lounge and picked up my gaming chair, not sure exactly how sending something to or retrieving something from my inventory worked, but the moment I thought about it, the chair vanished from my hands. I let out a surprised yelp at the sudden absence of its weight, despite half-expecting it, and I pulled the chair back out, promptly dropping it on my foot.

I swore, putting it back in the inventory again.

Once it was gone and my heartbeat settled again, I took a few experimental steps.

The weight of the chair didn't seem to cause an issue.

Which meant . . . I glanced into the darkness beyond the hallway, where my bike sat in my spare room that I'd used as an office when working from home in the pandemic. It was far too dark to even consider cycling anywhere just now, but if I could put my bike in my inventory, that wasn't a half-bad idea.

That glow still pulsed in the edge of my vision. Had I missed something?

I took my chair out again and sat in it, concentrating again on that glow.

You have one boon to select.

Shit. I completely forgot about that.

It'd be just like me to bugger off out of the city without taking care of *something*, but even though part of my brain screamed at me to stay safe and hidden in my flat, the itch to get gone was far stronger, and I needed to be smart about it.

Boons, then.

I, like much of the pandemic world, had played the shit out of Hades when it came out, and if these boons were anything like the ones in that rogue-lite game of monsters and divine mayhem, I wasn't about to let one go by.

Disappointingly, also like Hades, I only had a few options. Three, to be exact, and at first glance, they appeared to be a not-so-subtle test of how I wanted to shape this new, possibly truncated existence.

Brawn

You will gain a permanent +3 increase to Strength, which will allow you to hit harder and weather others' attacks with greater resilience.

Brains

You will gain a permanent +3 increase to Mind, which will allow you to better analyse your environment and your options for survival.

Blessings

You will gain a permanent +5 increase to Will. Normally, manipulation resources can only be increased through use and harvesting.

Shit.

Brawn was right out; I didn't have enough of a wardrobe to rip through any other shirts. But the other two sounded enticing, and I had no way of knowing whether I'd get this choice again. Brains was the obvious choice for immediate effect. Survival could require it. And Blessings made me side-eye it a wee bit—despite apparent evidence of *some* sort of higher power in the past two hours, I didn't really expect this was a "blessing" of any pantheon we knew on Earth.

Ultimately, I had no idea how many stat points I would get per level, if any, and beyond that, I had no way of knowing if I could also increase my core stats by doing things. Like, if I started doing press-ups every morning, would my Strength increase? My gut told me I would get attribute points at each level up, and if this were anything like any game I'd ever played, I was likely not horribly far away from level two.

After a long moment of staring back and forth between Brains and Blessings, I winced and chose Blessings. It was a gamble, and maybe what I needed was to convince myself that I would be around long enough to experience the payoff of patience. Will was the glacial resource. I was either going to have immediate regrets or an eventual reward.

The glowing pulse around my vision finally faded away completely, leaving me with a strange sense of calm.

Iain and Meeksy and Catrìona, Iain's mum, were in Oban. People walked the West Highland Way all the time; surely, I could do the same and detour westward to the coastal town rather than going north to Fort Willy. With my inventory what it was, I could bring my hiking backpack, my tent—which was covered in dust—and enough food and clean water to last me the few days it would take to cover the ninety miles between here and there. Four days at twenty miles a day, less time if I could be on the bike, despite the highland hills.

I could do this.

I was going to get out of here.

CHAPTER
FOUR

I tried to be methodical about what I packed in my backpack. It reminded me of a daft game I'd played in German class once upon a time in school when I was doing my Highers. Ich packe meinen Koffer, und ich packe ein . . . We'd play a game of repetition, adding one more item to the list of things in our coffer, which always grew more and more ridiculous as the game went on.

But with this inventory of mine, hell.

I pack my coffer, and I put in it: a bicycle.

I pack my coffer, and I put in it: a bicycle and a three-litre jug of water.

I pack my coffer, and I put in it: a bicycle; a three-litre jug of water; and a rucksack full of maps, trail guides, non-perishable food, and pharmaceuticals.

It was like bag-ception, because I discovered—much to my delight—that I could stuff bags full of items and put the whole thing in one inventory slot. I packed a dry bag full of basics that I would carry on my shoulders—the remainder of my cold pizza wrapped in foil, protein bars and a smaller water bottle, a pair of dry socks and boxers, a bottle of hand sanitiser, face masks, and some soap.

Last thing I wanted was to give myself norovirus or something because I ate with dirty hands. I never played that nineties game Oregon Trail, but I heard enough from American mates to know that dysentery was the real enemy of survival.

Hell, for much of Earth, that never *stopped* being true.

I reckon I'd rather get murdered by a giant centipede than deal with the ignominy of shitting myself to death.

It didn't take me too long to get ready, and despite the terror of wondering what monstrosities could pop up between my neighbourhood in Partick and Iain's family home by the harbour in Oban ninety miles away, as I tucked my final item into inventory—my ergonomic pillow, because fuck it, I was nae spring chicken, and I'd the spine of my sixty-year-old neighbour—I couldn't help but feel a thrill of excitement.

I couldn't remember the last time I felt excited about anything that wasn't a half-decent jobby after a few days of constipation. *That* reminder was enough to almost thank the apocalypse. It was putting my sorry-arse life in a dismal perspective.

I still had one slot free in my inventory in case of emergency. The shovel was taking up one of the ten spots, just in case I couldn't find a better weapon, but who knew what I'd run into along the way.

If Iain was still my flatmate, there'd be a cricket bat lying around, but he wasn't, so no easy bludgeoning tool. And Susanna took the nice knife block, so aside from the Leatherman I tucked in the dry bag on my back, the other knives in the flat were only useful for spreading butter on toast.

Fuck. No more toasters. I'd always been rubbish at making toast over a campfire. Not that I'd had much practise over the past five years. Susanna hated camping, hence the layer of dust over the tent.

Right. Those particular thoughts were not gonnae get me out of Glesga.

Before I could psych myself out of it, I grabbed my keys on the very, very off chance I'd ever be back, and I stepped out my door for the last time.

I'd no idea what time it was without my mobile, but my best guess as I hoofed it toward the Kelvin Walkway was that it had to be approaching eleven.

I crossed over Dumbarton Road rather than walk along it, preferring to head straight for the River Clyde rather than try and navigate the busier street with all its silent vehicles stranded in the middle of the road. At least once I hit the cycle path, I could make better time without having to squint into the darkness. You forgot, living in a city, just how much ambient light a half a million or more people created. Even night time here was seldom really dark—until now.

The rain that had soaked me on my way home had passed, and I could actually see stars through the intermittent cloud cover. No moon. I hadn't the foggiest idea what phase the moon was in, but since it was neither visible nor lighting my way, the question was moot.

Partick felt strange as I walked, the streets silent, though some windows glowed with candlelight, and the occasional face peered out at me as I passed a row of houses on my way to the river. The Clyde was lined with new builds, high-rises that dominated the view during the day on this route, but just now, I could barely make out their looming shadows in the distance.

I was just reaching the riverside walkway when ahead of me in the bushes, amid the gorse and thistles that hadn't yet shaken off the winter, something rustled. Something *way* too big to be a squirrel.

I frantically looked around me for something—anything—that could be a more suitable weapon than the shovel in my inventory, but nothing presented itself.

When the snout of the creature broke through the brush, my first thought was that a tapir had gotten loose from the zoo.

Like the centipede, I would have assumed mammals would be too complex to have changed so quickly after the ascension, but what was it the system had said?

Caught in a wave of spirit upon Earth's ascension, this centipede mutated far faster than can normally be expected for a creature of its complexity.

The creature shifted into the dim light, and I bit back a curse.

The thing was a bloody ROUS, if the Rodents of Unusual Size in the *Princess Bride* had the agility of actual rats instead of human actors in rat suits.

It lumbered out of the bush, looking far more hale than it had any right to look in an apocalypse. It didn't appear to have seen or scented me yet, but I had few illusions that it *would*.

I hurriedly grasped the wooden handle of the shovel, yanking it out of inventory as if the old superstition of touching wood could actually ward off ill luck, and it did absolutely fuck all for my chances, because the enormous rat stopped, whiskers twitching, and turned to look right at me.

Two heartbeats passed while I stood stock still, wondering if it might be content to go on its ratly little way in a direction that was *not* aimed at me.

Then it charged.

It was as if the bloody rodent had decided to get revenge for centuries of death-by-rat-poison and I was the unhappy target of its wrath. It let out a shrill squeak that was almost a shriek as its claws scrabbled against the pavement, closing the distance faster than I could react.

I did the only thing I could think: I swung the shovel like a cricket bat. It connected with the rat's head with a loud *clang*, and the rat squealed again but barely slowed. I leapt out of the way of its renewed charge, trying to remember the very brief lessons in martial arts I'd taken in uni. Bugger all came to mind, and I smacked the rat on top of the head once more with the shovel with another *clang* that, this time, landed from above and forced the rat's head down to make harsh contact with the pavement. The crack of bone preceded another loud shriek, this one of pain.

Fuck.

Killing a giant centipede was one thing, but despite the terrifying rats in their canvases in my flat, I didn't actually have anything against real rats.

My hesitation almost cost me my life.

Driven by pain and rage, the giant rodent lunged at me, well within striking range, and despite my having broken its jaw, its teeth clamped down around my calf.

I screamed in shock more than pain, stumbling backward. My balance thrown, I fell onto my arse, barely keeping my hold on the shovel as panic rushed over me in a wave. I grabbed the shovel's handle in both hands like it was one of the clamshell post-hole diggers I'd used with my mum as a kid, and I rammed it down onto the rat's neck as hard as I could.

A loud snap broke the air, and the pressure on my calf released. I kicked the rat off of me, my leg twinging where its teeth had dug in, puncturing my jeans and the first couple layers of skin.

In the dim light, I could see the rat, dead, lying on its side, its large incisors stained red with my blood and its mouth open. If I hadn't broken its jaw, my injury would have likely been much, much worse.

The glow at the edges of my vision was quickly becoming familiar. I'd reached the cycle path now, and as I clambered back to my feet, I decided I didn't want to risk being a bipedal mammal against swifter quadrupeds, thank you very much. My expensive-as-hell light rigs for my bike were as good as junk, but the bike itself was all mechanical. I braced myself and pulled it from inventory, wincing as I put weight on my leg. The injury wasn't too deep, but it throbbed with my blood.

Meeksy was the nurse of our wee circle of friends, and he was in Oban with Iain. I remembered what he'd done when, in a spectacular drunken moment, I'd run my shin smack into the concrete ridge at the centre of Mansfield Square and managed to literally tumble arse over tit and land right side up. My shin had been bruised, and I busted it right open. Meeksy—heroically, through his own drunken haze—had escorted me home, mixed up a saline solution, and rinsed the wound before taking a clean shirt and bandaging it triage style until I could get to the chemist for proper dressings.

Salt was not one of the things I had chucked in my bag, and I wasn't about to trot home and get some. I did have soap and water, though, so I pulled out a smaller bottle from the dry bag on my back and, after a brief hesitation, used the whole five hundred millilitres to flush the wound as best I could, pausing halfway through to sanitise my hands and lather up a bit of soap, too. Water dripped into my sock and my hillwalking shoe despite my best effort, but at least I'd probably helped get *some* germs off the wound.

Sacrificing one of my older T-shirts, I bound it quickly with a torn-off strip and bundled everything else back into my bag. The soap still stung, but it was worth it.

I debated with myself for only a moment before taking a breath and pulling up the notifications. Both Stamina and Constitution had been labelled Regeneration on my stat sheet the first time, so I hoped to whatever powers had descended upon the planet that that would guard against whatever rat diseases that rodent had injected into my leg that my hasty wash missed.

My stat sheet hadn't changed since I'd last looked at it, though I felt a flash of triumph when I saw the first notification.

You have killed a giant rat.

Caught in a wave of spirit upon Earth's ascension, this rat mutated far faster than can normally be expected for a creature of its complexity.

Such creatures frequently contain common crafting materials such as: rat meat, crude pelt, rat teeth, rat claws, bone.

Do you wish to harvest this giant rat?

I immediately confirmed, only to be faced with a major problem: I only had two free inventory slots since the shovel would have to go back. The rat carcass didn't dissipate like the centipede had, and while I gained fifteen spirit —assuming the centipede had also started with that, by the time I'd harvested the bug, it had already lost two spirit —only the rat meat and the pelt fit into my inventory. I didn't get everything in the list; the carcass showed some bones remaining when I examined it closer.

I wished I had more information. Could I craft things in this new world? I wouldn't know where to start if I tried without some sort of explanation or even a vague, general direction I could aim at. On a whim, I pulled out my rucksack and eyed the shovel I'd used as a weapon twice now. It was cleaner than I'd expect for having been used as a giant bug swatter, which gave me a thought. Quickly, I inventoried it and then pulled it back out. The few rat hairs and debris attached to it were gone.

Okay, that was good to know. I peered at my bike tyres to see if they were changed at all, and they did seem to be free of any mud I hadn't cleaned off, but thankfully the chain didn't seem to have been degreased. I wasn't going to pry open the jaw of this particular gift horse to scrutinise its teeth. Nope, I'd take the good fortune and be thankful.

I quickly shoved the handle of the shovel through the mesh on the outer shell of the rucksack, thankful it wouldn't leave smears of rat or centipede, and there I was. One remaining inventory spot for the rat bones.

As soon as I inventoried them, the rat carcass dissolved into motes just like the centipede had.

Would human bodies do that? The thought was unnerving.

I still had a notification, and I already could guess what it was.

You have reached Level 2! You have three attribute points to distribute.

There was no question, not with the fact that I'd already had to fight two creatures that wouldn't have even registered as a threat to a house cat a day ago. Much as I would have loved to put my points in Dexterity or Mind or Agility, without modern medicine? Without the NHS and antibiotics readily available? Yeah, no. I put two points in Constitution and one in Stamina.

It was going to be a bloody long way to Oban.

FIVE

A s soon as I was on my bike, I felt better, and I didn't think it was just the faster movement speed.

Like ripping out of my shirt when I'd added points into Strength, adding the two points to Constitution and one to Stamina had an immediate effect. Though it was midnight, I felt ready to cycle up Ben Lomond if I had to. I kept a close eye out for the signs marking the Kelvin Walkway as I moved north. I'd made this cycle before with Iain several times, but it was a different world cycling at night with no street lamps or anything else to distinguish from the lunking shapes of houses and shops and trees.

There was no indication of time, only the slow, sludge-like crawl of that amorphous scenery slipping past me. I had to keep my eyes trained on the path ahead, because I couldn't see very far in front of the bike by starlight.

I could have shouted with relief when I reached the River Kelvin itself, because for a while, the path was as simple as cycling along the water.

But everywhere was the reminder of the dramatic shift in the world. No electricity. No lights except the dim glow of the occasional candle. And even over the whirr of my bike's tyres on the pavement, as I rode I sometimes heard strange gurgles from the underbrush on either side of me, once a loud splash, and once, a shout that ended so abruptly, it made my hands wobble on the handlebars.

My leg seemed to have either gone numb or be recovering, because it had stopped hurting as I made it to the next stage of the path beyond the old Garrioch Flint Mill, and to my huge relief, a very welcome sight crested the horizon beyond the tree line.

The moon.

Gibbous and either almost full or just past full, it rose like a harbinger of hope, immediately lighting the way ahead of me more clearly.

I was so elated by being able to see where the fuck I was going that I almost missed one of the route's trickier turns, a sharp U-turn from the river to follow the A81.

It was unsettling, the reminder that I would have no helpful AI in my ear to tell me I'd gone off course. I could end up in Balloch instead of heading toward the West Highland Way in Milngavie, and while it wouldn't be the end of the world—I winced as the thought crossed my mind since, you know, it *was* the bloody end of the world, apparently—I wasn't sure I wanted to follow the A82 around the western edge of the loch. It was mostly single carriageway, and while the danger of getting run down by motorists was nowt for obvious reasons, I wanted to stick to my plan.

With the moon rising steadily into the ever-clearer sky, I made good time, the light making the path far more familiar and easy to follow. I stopped once to scoff down a slice of pizza and drink some water, and I was just about to throw my leg over my bike again when I remembered to check my wound. Gingerly pulling up my jeans leg to reveal the bandage, I flexed my foot a little. Nothing seemed to hurt.

I untied the shoddy knot I'd looped around my calf, surprised it had stayed in place in all the cycling, but when I unwrapped the long strip of fabric, I did a double take.

The white cotton was definitely bloody—a dark stain marred it in a wide circle—but there was no trace of the rat's bite.

For a long moment, I simply stared at it.

Then I got back on my bike, tucking the makeshift dressing into my pocket and shaking my left leg to undo the bunched-up jeans I'd shoved upward over my calf.

There would be time to worry about impossibilities once I got to Iain and Meeksy.

By the time the sky started to lighten, I was finally starting to flag. I'd passed Milngavie and made it all the way through Drymen, which meant I could use my daylight to follow the eastern edge of Loch Lomond up through Inver-arnan at the northernmost point of the loch.

My good intentions lasted until a little after dawn, which I vaguely guessed to be around eight in the morning.

I needed rest, I needed food, and I needed to sit still. I'd already covered probably thirty miles of the distance, but I also knew that my ninety-mile estimate from Glasgow to Oban took the shortest driving route, not the "as the cyclist pedals" route.

Pulling my bike to the side of the path at Balmaha, just as the path converged with the edge of the loch, my legs seemed to register the exertion all at once, and I almost teetered over with my bike before I could get the kickstand in place.

Part of me wanted to ask if I was really so pitifully out of shape, but I stopped myself with a small burst of a guffaw. I'd fought off a giant fucking centipede, an even bigger rat, *and* cycled thirty miles in the dead of night.

Yeah, maybe not a pathetic hamster after all. I mean, I knew I wasn't Bruce Lee by any stretch of the imagination, but I'd made it this far.

By now, I expected the telltale glow of a notification, though I highly doubted I'd gained any experience just for spending a night on a bike.

But the notification came as a pleasant surprise anyway.

Through physical exertion, you have gained a permanent +1 to Agility and +1 to Stamina. Please note that such increases have diminishing returns as your base statistics grow.

I didn't care if it stopped paying off as much later—fuck, yeah! I guess that answered my question about the press-ups. Maybe if I could get access to a range of clothing sizes, I could give that a go too, but for now, I had my goal.

Though I hadn't stopped to think about it too much, I hoped Iain was okay. I'd just spoken to him, for Christ's sake, but if there were giant vermin in the middle of Glasgow, who knew what could be lurking in the Scottish Highlands, let alone Oban Harbour. Mutated lobsters seeking revenge on fishers? Enormous basking sharks bored of their sunbathing in the shallows of the Hebrides? Eagles plucking people off the streets?

Hopefully, it would take some time before the wildlife really started changing. I didn't think it would be as simple as a size increase. It couldn't be.

As I ate the rest of my pizza and downed some more water, I finally let myself think about magic.

According to that primer, everyone would have access to it now. I didn't know what that meant exactly, or *how*, precisely, I was supposed to do a magic. Was it like wiggling your ears and you kind of couldn't describe how to do it even once you managed it? Or was it like rolling your tongue like a taco and some bizarre facet of genetics? I'd no clue.

The area felt peaceful. Calm.

The birds were singing their normal morning songs. I recognised a few of their calls—along with a childhood and having a forager and gardener for a mum, Mum'd also rehabbed injured animals, so we got many-a songbird that had flown into someone's double-glazed window pane they'd shined to perfection.

I heard blackbirds and finches, wrens and tits, which made me suppress a rueful smile. Mum always got so exasperated when I'd snigger at the tits.

Part of me wished she was still alive—another part was glad she wasn't here to see the world end. The thought of Mum having to come up against a mutated creature she'd have to kill when she dedicated her life to saving them, well. Not something I'd wish on her.

I had a wee lump in my throat and tried to clear it, taking a sip of water as if it were some kind of substitute for the loss of a loved one, no matter that it had been eleven years. As always, I shoved it back down, locked it away, though sitting here and gazing at the bonnie braes at the edge of Scotland's second most famous loch—the first obviously being Loch Ness—I almost didn't see the point in my own repression. If you can't admit you're sad at the end of the world, when can you?

I sat there for a moment, feeling stupidly like that "is this a butterfly?" meme but with "is this an emotion?" until I could almost feel my body converting that pizza into energy and had to get to my feet again.

Pathos or no pathos, I knew one thing: I was going to get to Iain, Meeksy, and Catrìona. It might be the last bloody thing I ever did, but I was gonnae do it.

The lochside was far quieter than I would have expected, bar the birds, of course. I supposed I ought to be thankful Scotland was fresh out of large predators, and I was, but I also didn't feature the idea of getting my eyeballs pecked out by a great tit as payback for making jokes at their expense as a wean.

And let's be real, as an adult too. Bird or not, "great tit" is a delight of a name.

Back on my bike, I kicked off.

My sweat had dried on my arms, leaving me chilled, but the movement warmed me up again straight away, and soon I was sweating all over again.

The morning shaped up to be a belter—clear skies, bright sun, and warm enough I felt relieved to be in constant motion with the wind from my passage a sort of portable air-con.

Ben Lomond rose to my right, the mountain towering over the loch. Loch Lomond and the Trossachs form one of Scotland's bonniest national parks, and today was the perfect day to be here.

At the same time, having such a beautiful day to be fleeing Glasgow meant that just as I'd get settled in, just as I'd look over to admire the view—this country was a bloody revelation for scenery; no denying it—I'd remember the apocalypse.

I didn't see anyone for the first half of the day even

when I passed Rowardennan and the lodge there, but I also didn't slow down to check. The lodge itself was silent, overlooking the loch's waters with a stoic calm I envied. I wondered if there were tourists there who, upon the sudden power cut and lack of anything else to do, simply carried on with their plans to go hillwalking up Ben Lomond to bag their munro.

I wouldn't be surprised if there were.

The morning passed uneventfully, and I came upon the end of Loch Lomond so suddenly, I almost missed it. My heart gave a thud as I realised I was almost to Inverarnan. Just one more leg of the West Highland Way, and I'd be turning west toward Oban.

It shouldn't be much more than an hour even with the hills, and that bore out in truth—it was still a bit before midday at my guess when a familiar sight greeted me: The Green Welly, a Highland hub for travellers where the A82 continues north and the A85—which would take me to Oban—heads west.

I couldn't count the number of times I'd stopped there myself—as a kid with my mum any time we went back and forth between Oban and Glasgow, in my twenties when I'd road trip with my mates or bugger off into the hills to camp, and more regularly as time went on, with Iain and Meeksy to visit Iain's mum when his dad passed. Seeing it now gave me pause as if the familiar landmark could shatter any illusions I had about this really being an apocalypse. The thought of seeing it overrun with giant centipedes or rats— or, hell, mutated versions of the dreaded Highland midge— was enough to slow my approach. It was the first time in my harebrained journey I'd come across something I had a real, personal tie to.

It was also the first place I ran into other human beings.

CHAPTER

SIX

The carpark was about half full, some cars clearly stalled out halfway out of a parking space. Others, it was clear people had shifted into neutral and pushed out of the way of oncoming traffic without realising there wasn't gonnae *be* any more oncoming traffic.

Normally, at midday, there would be plenty of folk coming in and out of the Welly, the enormous green boot managing to stand out amid the green of the trees and landscape around it. Even in late February in the off season, Scotland got tourists.

Today, there was a crowd of people milling about outside the shops, smoking and talking in low voices, and I saw the exact moment I was noticed, because the entire group turned almost as one to look at me.

"Oi," called a man near the door in an English accent. "Where you coming from?"

I slowed my bike, sudden paranoia pushing me to stay on the far side of the road from the group. They all *looked* like tourists, some likely Scottish, some certainly not. As I peered about the carpark, bracing one leg on the edge of the road to be able to push off again quickly, I noticed a few others sitting in cars with the windows cracked, also watching me.

"Glasgow," I answered the bloke.

"Yeah, and I swam here from Newcastle," he retorted. "Can't cycle all that way in a morning."

"Aye, well, I left before midnight," I shot back. "Cycled through the night."

The rest of them—mostly folk of all genders and a wide range of ages, including some weans among them—looked me over dubiously.

"Power cut in Glasgow too?" a woman asked, leaning around the man's shoulder.

Her voice had the sound of Argyll, so she was either a transplant into the Central Belt or had been caught between somewhere else and home.

I nodded at her. "Everywhere, from what I can tell."

She chewed on her lip for a moment, glancing southward.

I didn't want to bring up the system or whatever it was that had been throwing text and attribute points at me unless they did, and from the tight-lipped glances they were giving each other, they weren't in any sort of hurry to start that conversation either.

"If you need food or water, you can go inside," the Argyll woman said after a beat. "I'll make sure your bike's safe. Toilets are still working, too, but ye'll no have light in the loo. Shop folks have candles, but they're trying not to use them too much."

No one seemed panicked or nervous—well, beyond the general unease that was unavoidable—and shit, the loo was a temptation. I don't mind pissing in the bushes, but it's not as hassle-free to do a poo in the wilderness.

My decision made, I swung my leg over the bike and walked it across the road and into the carpark. I went straight to the woman, and she gave me a tight smile. She was probably in her late forties, dressed in green wellies not unlike the shop's eponymous boot, and she had smile lines around her eyes that didn't wrinkle up even with her short attempt.

"I'll watch it," she said. "I'm Helen."

"Calum," I told her. "And cheers."

"No power, so you'll have to pay cash if you've got it."

"Aye, I expected as much." I didn't mention that I didn't have so much as a tuppence on me, but there wasn't really anything I needed.

I felt a bit nervous walking away from the bike—with my inventory full, I would have had to take something out right in front of them to put it in, and the last thing I needed was to materialise a pile of giant rat meat or bones or whatever in front of a bunch of strangers.

But Helen had a solid grip on the bike, and she was already in casual conversation with a different bloke who hadn't spoken, pointing eastward as if she were just picking up where they'd left off at my arrival's interruption.

I hurried to the loo first, grabbing a candle—Skye Candle Company, a strangely posh emergency measure—and lighting it with the provided matchbook.

Looking in the mirror in the flickering candlelight, I didn't look particularly haggard even without sleep. I splashed a bit of water on my face and did my business, hustling back out and blowing out the candle before going into the shop to see if there were any other options for food besides paying with nonexistent cash.

"Hiya," said the lass at the till, giving me a once-over that, any other time, I would have taken as a compliment, but she looked so tired I could barely work up the desire to be flattered.

"Hi," I said.

She was probably in her mid-twenties, pretty and slender with stick-straight hair that probably looked lovely before she had to stay up all night working.

"Let me guess," she said, "no cash?"

"Got it in one. I probably don't have anything I could trade you for a piece"—there was a case of sandwiches that was still closed and *likely* wouldn't give me food poisoning yet—"but I don't expect tae get anything for free."

The lass eyed me for another moment, then shrugged. "Honestly, I've just been giving the sandwiches away. Can't sell them if they've not been refrigerated for this long, and if you fall ill, it's your own business, but you're welcome to take a couple. Sneak a cheeky wee Bounty if you like as well."

I gave her a genuine grin and looked at the sandwich choices, settling for a BLT—bacon had to be cured, right? Surely safer than tuna mayo or prawn—and took her advice, snagging a dark chocolate Bounty and popping both into the dry bag on my back.

"Cheers for that," I said. "I'm headed to Oban—got any news I should take?"

"Nothing but the power cut," she said. "Home's in Crianlarich, but you'll no be going through there."

"Sorry," I started to say when a commotion outside burst through the stillness.

"Get off me, you useless bampot!"

Shit. That was Helen's voice, and worse, even as my feet broke into a run, I heard the unmistakable sound of tyres skidding on pavement.

I burst out the door of the shop just in time to see my

bike vanish around the corner, heading north on the A82—the complete wrong direction. Not as bad as if he'd gone south with it back toward Glasgow, but almost as bad. I wasn't about to detour to attempt to chase him down. He'd be to Fort William or anywhere else before I could reach the bloody Bridge of Orchy. A couple blokes had run after the arsehole, but they clearly couldn't outpace a cyclist and were already huffing and puffing to a stop at the edge of the carpark.

Fuck, fuck, fuck. My bloody *bike*.

Helen was half-leaning on the outside wall of the shop, and dimly, I noticed the lass from inside emerging from the door in alarm. Helen shook her arm out like she'd hurt it somehow, and when I hurried to her, I saw she had indeed —the knuckles of her right hand were already bruising.

She looked up at me to see who was approaching and then shook her head apologetically.

"I'm sorry, Calum," she began, but the bloke I'd seen her talking to from inside cut her off.

"Bugger was *fast*," the guy said. "Helen got a hell of a punch in on him, but he threw himself on the bike without warning, so he was already on it when she hit him. He managed to not go down even so and clocked her back. Sorry, mate."

At his *and clocked her back*, my eyes sought out Helen's face, and sure enough, a welt blossomed on her cheekbone.

"Nae bother," I said despite that being a total lie. "Just glad nobody's hurt worse."

"He must've been desperate," Helen said, standing up straight and wincing. "Nobody else's been that much of a numpty yet."

"Where's it you're headed?" the bloke asked me. "Calum, is it?"

"Aye," I said. "Oban."

Just like that, my ease of the morning vanished in a cloud of anxiety. I was more than halfway there, and I could walk to Oban without a doubt, but it was one thing to go ten or fifteen miles an hour on a bike and another to be reduced to three or four tops on foot.

"Grant," said the man, sticking out his hand, which I shook. "If you want to stick around here, once the power works again, I'd be more than happy to take you."

I stared at him for a moment in disbelief, taking my hand back. "You think the power's coming back?"

Grant looked at me sideways. "Why wouldn't it?"

"Yous *did* see the—" I began, and Helen hurriedly nodded.

The rest of the group had moved a bit away, though they were still murmuring and glancing over at us now and then, and Helen clenched and extended her fist a few times.

"We saw the text an' aw," she said. "Grant just thinks it was a prank."

"It had to be," Grant insisted. "The Americans or hell, the Russians—"

But he broke off when he realised Helen was watching me closely. So was everyone else, for that matter.

"You know something," Helen said as if Grant hadn't spoken.

I hesitated for only a moment before squaring my shoulders and blowing out a breath.

"It wasn't a prank," I said slowly. "Or if it was, it was the kind of prank like 'ha-ha, I nuked Frankfurt' or something, not the type of prank like stretching cling film over a toilet seat."

At Helen's expectant stare, I nodded, more to myself than to her, moving a little bit away from the group just in case anyone got freaked out to the point of deciding to jump me.

"Here goes nothing," I muttered, pulling the rat bones from inventory.

Everyone around me jumped, and a couple people yelped or cursed.

"These bones came from a rat the size of a fucking pit bull," I said.

"I don't bloody well care what animal they came from —you just pulled them out of thin air!"

This came from the English bloke who'd first called out to me, and I was strangely relieved to see he wasn't the one who'd taken off with my bike after he'd gotten me to stop in the first place.

"Have none of you even looked through the text and shite in your heads?" I asked them. "Really? None of you?"

"It just vanished after the first bit last night," Helen said slowly, but her eyes went a bit unfocused as she seemed to concentrate on something, and a moment later, they widened.

"Helen," I said. "Later. It's important, but I have to warn you about more important things first."

She blinked and nodded, the glazed-over look vanishing into acute attentiveness.

"You heard me say rat the size of a pit bull, right?" I asked the group, watching them nod warily. I shuffled the rat bones back into inventory and then removed the centipede chitin, causing the people to jump again. "This was from a centipede that was almost that big itself."

A couple muscular blokes scoffed at that where they leaned against the ramp railing up to the doors, and I fixed them with a dead-eyed stare.

"A bug's a bug," one of them said.

"Aye, well," I said. "Centipedes are venomous. You want to risk getting yourself bitten by a monster and dying without life flight or ambulances to get your sorry arse to a power-less hospital, fine by me, but I hope the rest of this lot has some brains."

"You killed it," the other muscular guy said, in what was clearly supposed to be an insult.

"I had help," I said, trying to restrain myself from cringing with the knowledge that the addition made me seem even *more* like a pathetic hamster. "And I got lucky. The woman who it attacked managed to keep it at bay with a chair long enough for me to help her, or she'd probably be dead."

At that, everyone but the two lumps-for-brains at the back of the crowd looked at me with bleak stares.

"So, what, there's like . . . monsters?" someone asked.

I nodded. "Picture a midgie the size of a normal rat and then picture a swarm of them. You tell me if that sounds dangerous."

"Real *Jumanji* shit, right there," someone muttered, and I had to agree.

"Why is it we've not seen anything like this here?" Helen asked.

I shrugged. "Population density? Dinnae ken. All I know is we're lucky it's not summer."

A bit of strained laughter filtered through the group, and I put the chitin back in inventory.

"Just . . . be careful," I said. "Read through whatever text you've got in your heads and make sure you allocate your stat points and boons, okay? It'll make a huge difference. I cycled all the way from Glasgow to Tyndrum in twelve hours without stopping to sleep."

With that, I gave them a tight-lipped smile and started to turn away.

"Wait," Helen said. "Where are you going?"

I paused, all semblance of a smile fading quickly.

"I still have to get to Oban," I told her. "And I don't blame you for the bike getting stolen, but now I've got to walk the distance."

"It's not safe alone," she said, giving me the mum-liest frown I think I could imagine, and I couldn't help but grin at her.

"Where're your kids?" I asked her instead of addressing her concern.

She snorted at my clocking her as a mum. "One's standing right there."

Helen pointed at the lass who'd been working in the shop, and I blinked.

"Other's in Crianlarich with the old man," she finished, then looked at her daughter.

"Crianlarich's close enough you could make it in an hour or so," I said to her, wondering why she hadn't left yet, but then again, I think she was currently staring at my answer. "But even if you decide to stay here, be careful, and look out for each other. This isn't bloody *Lord of the Flies*."

Helen turned back to me and cracked a smile at that. "Golding wrote that about spoilt private school boys, anyway."

To my surprise, she reached into her pocket and pulled out a wee Moleskine notebook with a pen and tore out a piece of paper, scribbling something on it. Helen closed the distance to me and handed it to me.

"That's where we stay in Crianlarich," she said. "You make it to Oban and decide not to stay there for whatever reason, you're welcome to come back through here, and we'd be happy to have you."

I stood there for a moment just holding the paper in pure surprise, but after a beat, I pulled my rucksack out of inventory, making Helen jump.

"Not used to that," she muttered with a grin.

"Just wait till you can do it too," I said to her, grinning back.

With that, I tucked her note inside a pocket on my rucksack and put the whole thing back in inventory. If I was walking the rest of the way to Oban, I'd better get started.

I was losing daylight.

CHAPTER
SEVEN

I t took about two hours of walking for it to really hit me that someone had up and stolen my bike. I hadn't been kidding when I told Helen I didn't blame her, and I hadn't been joking about the world not being Golding's *Lord of the Flies*—he really did write that to critique the entitlement of the upper classes, not as an allegory for general misanthropy—but without my bloody bike, I was moving *slow*.

In comparison, anyway.

The sky above was bright blue, almost painfully so. I preferred it to the perpetual highland mist, and I wasn't about to moan about *not* being sodden through, but it meant that every shift in light, every inch the sun sank across the sky—it all reminded me that night was coming, despite the way the days started to stretch in spring.

I moved quickly through the village of Arrivain and tried to enjoy the view of Ben Lui on my left as I made my way in the direction of Inverlochy and Loch Awe in the distance. Occasionally, there was an abandoned car I passed, including one little Peugeot hatchback about a mile out of Arrivain right in the middle of the A85. Not a soul was around, and I couldn't tell from the roadway if the car's owner had gone in any particular direction, since they didn't exactly leave tracks. The number plate was unremarkable, but there was a sticker next to it proclaiming allegiance to a football club down in the south of England, so at a guess, they weren't local. I hoped they were okay.

It seemed as good a place as any to pause, so I perched on the front bumper of the car, leaning back against the bonnet to eat the sandwich Helen's daughter had let me take. It tasted fine, though I don't reckon I would have trusted it to last to the other side of sunset. My stomach growled even as I finished, as if the piece had simply reminded it that it was mealtime.

Food was going to be a problem soon, and not just for me.

I shifted my weight where I sat, turning to look through the windscreen of the abandoned car.

Slowly shouldering my dry bag again after flattening the sandwich packet and popping it in the bag, I made my way around to peer in the car's windows.

There, in the back, was an insulated cooler.

I hadn't seen a soul in Arrivain, though I'd also been avoiding people. I could—or maybe *should*—just walk away. The car wasn't mine, and just because someone nicked my bike didn't make me entitled to anyone's food.

But then the image of the rat meat in my inventory popped into my head, and before I could deal with any further ethical questions in the eschatological situation in which I found myself, my right hand was tugging at the door handle.

It squeaked a little as I pulled, and at first I thought it was going to be locked, but almost before I could feel a flash of disappointment, the door popped open without issue.

Power locks, I thought after a beat.

Even if they'd wanted to lock the doors, it didn't seem the keyless entry would have let them. There had to be a failsafe or something, but maybe it just slipped the driver's mind.

Hurriedly, I pulled the driver's side seat forward, unzipping the cooler to peer inside. It wasn't large—enough to maybe feed a couple for a day or so—but there was cheese in there, along with a wee bag of apples and a ziplock bag of carrots and snow peas.

Never in my life did I think I'd be so delighted to see a snow pea. After a moment of hesitation, I pried my dry bag back open and stuffed the whole cooler inside. It filled the dry bag to the rim, but I could still get it closed. There was a can of salt and vinegar Pringles wedged between the front seats, and I grabbed that too.

If I ran into the car's owner on my journey, I'd make sure to beg their forgiveness.

Part of my mind whispered that maybe I should be asking myself why I hadn't seen anyone in the small village of Arrivain, but I punted that thought to the back of my skull.

Inverlochy wasn't far now, and I could look around there for some people, see if anyone had any news at all. Scotland wasn't exactly the Netherlands for cyclists, but it wasn't as if we didn't have bikes—I couldn't be the only Glaswegian to have high-tailed it out of town on wheels, and I would have to guess that some folk in Oban could do the same in the other direction if they were panicked by the state of impending—or ongoing—apocalypse.

The glen around me was almost eerily quiet. As the Peugeot faded in the distance behind me, my ears strained to seek out the noises of anything other than the wind. I couldn't hear a single bird now, and looking around, all my eyes could see was heather and bog and the River Lochy flowing alongside the A85.

That didn't seem . . . right.

I'd spent enough time in the highlands to know that they're still teeming with life. Far from the barren waste-lands devoid of settlement, they were complex ecosystems, and threatened ones. So why was this habitat so apparently empty?

I drained my water bottle as I walked, pausing briefly at the roadside to fill it again from one of the many springs and waterfalls that poured into the river. Mum had taught me from a young age how to make the best guess of what water was safe to drink, and since these hills were alive with the sound of fluid music, both runoff and spring water alike, it was far from the riskiest thing I'd done in the past day.

The road curved a bit, and as I put the bottle back, I could make out a strange hummock lying in the middle of it at a distance.

Squinting, I tried to see what it was. Maybe some rock had tumbled over the road, or a hummock of peat—any number of things could shift in a land as wet as this one. But as I drew closer, my stomach began to sink, the digesting sandwich swirling with acid as dread crept up my throat with bile.

What. The fuck. Was that.

My brain couldn't make sense of the vaguely trape-zoidal shape, but slowly, as I drew closer, my eyes processed something much more readily identifiable.

Red.

Bright red.

Somewhere in my more analytical mind, the pieces

clicked together, but the part of me that had to actually see it—and, as the wind brought it to me, smell it—shut down.

That was not a human torso, and that was not part of another one. That was not a leg, there, lying boot up in the ditched, attached to nothing.

That was not a gob of yellow fat, ripped out of its home beneath layers of skin and now sitting in a pool of blood. Those were not entrails. That was not a ribcage.

My stomach convulsed, and my eyes burned as acid crawled its way up my throat and into my mouth. It took every tiny smidgen of willpower I possessed not to vomit all over the corpse—corpses—in front of me.

I stumbled off to the side, then staggered forward, trying not to step in remains and failing. All I achieved was getting a tiny bit upwind where the smell wasn't as overwhelming.

This was worse than anything . . .

I didn't know what to think, if I even *could* think.

Without any real reason, I felt these two had to be the owners of that abandoned Peugeot. If they'd been relying on their mobile navigation—and let's face it, who wouldn't these days?—they would likely not realise Arrivain was the closest settlement, especially if they'd charted their course to go in a circuit rather than a straight line out and back.

They were likely trying to get to Inverlochy, the last place they would have seen on their drive.

And now they were dead.

Bile tried to escape again, and I stumbled forward a few more steps, grabbing my water bottle and chugging a few gulps as if that alone could ward off the sick.

It almost worked—until something obvious, something that ought to have occurred to me sooner, reared its head.

Two people were dead.

Two people were dead, and they hadn't simply keeled over.

Something—something large and dangerous—had killed them.

My feet broke into a run before I could think further, sloshing water over my hand as I tried clumsily to screw the lid back on mid-stride.

My lungs burned as I ran, half from gasping down my own bile and half from the exertion. I couldn't remember the last time I ran at top speed on purpose, and I'd never in my life run as if something could be *chasing*.

When I finally slowed enough for my mind to clear, I almost threw up all over again, this time from running on a full belly.

"Calm down, ya bampot," I said to myself, panting. "Not gonnae sprint to Oban, and there's nothing bloody chasing you."

Not sure if that counted as positive self-talk, but hey, at least it was better than staring at people who'd gotten torn limb from limb.

I didn't know if that made me feel better or worse about stealing their cooler.

Okay. I had to figure out what I was going to do. I didn't know what the fuck could have ripped two adults to shreds like that—in broad daylight, no less—but I sure as hell didn't want to find out.

Scottish wildcats were almost extinct. Foxes were a real possibility if they'd been hit with an early wave of spirit like the centipede and the rat, and something that vicious with the intelligence of a fox would be dangerous indeed. But Scotland was also home to mammals like stoats and pine martens, wee weaselly beasties that would harry a crofter's chickens or unsavvy outdoor cats. Hell, a rogue tabby mutated with spirit could easily have done such a thing.

None of those options sounded like anything I wanted to encounter. Foxes were usually scavengers, at least, but stoats preyed on smaller mammals like rats and mice, and cats of any sort, well. The *last* thing I wanted was to fall victim to a supersized moggy lying in ambush in the heather.

But even as I thought it, something else trickled into my awareness: birdsong.

It was faint on the wind, but when I looked in its direction, I saw a flutter of a normal-sized starling or three in the heather not too far away.

I let out a breath I'd been holding high in my chest.

That pulsing glow returned at the edges of my vision, and, feeling marginally safer, I concentrated on it.

Through physical exertion, you have gained a permanent +1 to Agility and +1 to Stamina. Please note that such increases have diminishing returns as your base statistics grow.

The feeling of refreshment washed over me, and I stretched my tired muscles as some of the day's exertion drained away. That was much faster than I'd gained the extra points on the bike, but maybe the combination of my mad dash away from the bodies plus having to actually move my entire body weight without mechanical help had contributed to the gains. But before I could dissect it further, I noticed that the glow remained.

Through observation of your surroundings, you have gained a permanent +1 to Mind. Please note that such increases have diminishing returns as your base statistics grow.

Observation of my surroundings? I stood there for a moment, trying to make sense of what it could mean. All I'd really done was walk . . . but another flutter of movement from the nearby lump of heather caught my eye.

The birds.

I'd noticed the silence and then noted the return of bird noises. That seemed like something far, far too simple to have any real merit, at least as far as a permanent stat increase was concerned.

"Thanks awfully," I muttered aloud, starting to move again down the road.

Except what if it was important?

I thought back to what the system had told me when it first began, about survival being unlikely but implying that it *would* still give us benefits no matter what sort of numpties occupied this misfortune-encrusted rock.

Increasing my stride, my mind whirled through the possibilities, trying to fit everything together.

If the birds were notable enough for the system to reward my notice of them, why? Birds absent and then birds present—or birds silent and then birds active. I couldn't assume the birds had completely *gone* when I didn't hear them; that would be illogical. But if they'd remained, why had they gone quiet? I'd spent a lot of time with wild birds as a wean, what with my mum's rehab efforts and all. She'd always said they vocalised for myriad reasons—to find a mate or to announce the presence of food, to stake out territory or . . . to frighten off a predator.

Something pinged in my memory, impossible to ignore now that I'd caught the edge of it.

Just like humans, birds would go quiet to protect themselves from possible detection.

Their silence, the silence I had noticed around the site of that poor pair's deaths, indicated that whatever killed them . . . was still present.

CHAPTER
EIGHT

I was running again almost before I could account for it, my feet pounding the road's surface as if with a little luck, I'd be able to spring off of it and fly to Oban myself.

My ears strained for all possible sound outside my feet against the asphalt.

As if belatedly processing—not a surprise, honestly; my brain was nothing if not excellent at delayed processing— my mind showed me images again of the mangled corpses. It had been difficult for me to make sense of them at first, while I was still far away. Even once I got closer, they were barely identifiable as two bodies.

Because parts had been missing.

There simply hadn't been enough remains to account for two adult humans, but there had been enough of two torsos even with the missing limbs.

That might have been the only thing that saved me.

My lungs burned with the exertion of running so much when I wasn't exactly a marathoner, but the increases to my Stamina and Constitution were helping noticeably; that

I was still moving was evidence enough. And since I hadn't yet tripped and fallen flat on my face, the Agility wasn't hurting either.

That might have been the only thing that saved me.

The thought returned again, and I forced myself to continue the line of thinking.

If parts were missing, that implied that whatever creature had killed those two poor sods had eaten them. Recently. The blood was still red, still wet. I obviously hadn't gotten close enough to look for any other signs that could have given me a timeline—I stuttered a gasp at the thought of checking for rigour mortis—but if the thing that had killed them had also eaten them, the one thing that saved my sorry arse was likely that it had a full belly.

Which also told me this creature hadn't killed them for fun.

Food was going to be a problem soon indeed.

I finally slowed after probably another mile or two between myself and the dead.

I didn't know whether or not their killer would follow me; hopefully, it would find some deer to prey on rather than bipedal victims.

But as I managed to slow myself out of my panicked flight and looked around at my surroundings, I noticed the hill to my right was starting to slope downward, which could only mean Inverlochy was close. That didn't help my sense of dread.

Despite what I'd said to the good folk of Tyndrum, I honestly didn't know what to expect from humanity at large. I'd seen the panic buying at the start of the pandemic, sure. The asinine assertion that everyone only had to look out for themselves. But I'd also seen the networks of mutual aid that popped up in Partick overnight—signs telling folks to check on their elderly neighbours in windows all throughout my street and signs addressed to the vulnerable themselves. I'd seen people *helping*. It had felt like the old wartime efforts, people coming together to protect the most vulnerable because it was the right thing to do. And then, of course, came the actual wartime efforts where it got a lot more literal.

I desperately wanted to hope that would bear out now.

But could I trust it would?

Almost as if I had manifested it by my dumb-arse thoughts, a noise that was *not* birdsong broke through the air.

Human shouting.

I froze where I stood, unable to decide whether to run toward it or away from it. I didn't want to run into the middle of a brawl, thank you very much, but if people needed help—

A very inhuman screech pierced through the raised voices, followed by a scream.

Shit-shit-shit-shit-shit.

I broke into a run again, the weight of my dry bag bouncing against my back all the more cumbersome now that I'd spent so much time exerting myself. Sweat stuck my shirt to my back, and I realised I had no weapon.

Fuck.

I stopped, yanking my rucksack out of inventory and grabbing the shovel, throwing the rucksack back in almost before its weight could register in my arms. The shovel clanked against the road, and after a moment of frozen indecision, I snatched the centipede chitin out, shoved it into the overflowing dry bag with a flash of heat along my palm, and inventoried the dry bag, leaving me free to run with the shovel.

The yelling was getting louder, and I wasn't quite to the edge of the village yet—but in the distance, there was a cottage at the side of the road, mostly blocked from view with a large hedge that butted all the way up to the drive, and that was the source of the screaming.

"Is there another one?" I heard someone shout in alarm, followed by the sound of a heavy impact, not unlike the way my shovel sounded hitting that rat.

Another screech.

I reached the drive and sprinted around the hedge, entering the cottage's front garden to a scene that made the corpses back near Arrivain almost look serene.

The human scream had to have come from the man who was sat slumped against the hedge, its branches covering his face. At a glance my eyes took snapshots—intestines in long ropes across his thighs, an arm torn from bicep to elbow, a knee that shouldn't have bent that way. But I tore my gaze from the dead man to where the living were fighting off . . . a fucking *seagull*.

The bird was monstrous—the things in Glasgow were big enough, as large as the average rooster and twice as mean. Once, I'd seen one scoop a pigeon off George Square by the neck and subsequently slam the hapless sky-rat into the paving stones with a sickening crack before ripping its throat out.

And this one was big enough to do that to a human.

The bird's back was to me, and even as I sprang into action, I heard the sound of its beak hitting something metal. Probably a shovel like mine. Its wings flapped, churning the air and making the sweat chill on my face. A normal-sized swan could break a human bone with its wings; I didn't want to get in range of a seagull the size of a fucking horse.

But how in any possible hell was I supposed to kill something this large? Hitting it with my shovel from behind would be useless at best, and at worst it would simply make the thing turn its attention to me.

Frantically, I looked around the garden for something that could be of some use. It was likely the people fending off the gull's attacks had already grabbed whatever was most useful, but I couldn't see what they had, and all that remained was a spooled coil of garden hose and an empty flower pot.

It was the anguished, yelling sob that did it.

Whoever was on the other side of that monster was running out of stamina—and time.

I dropped the shovel onto the drive and snatched the end of the garden hose, yanking it as hard as I could and hoping it was long enough. The spool was attached to the house, which I hoped would hold at least for a minute if my desperate plan worked at all.

As soon as I reached the end of the hose—it had to be at least twenty metres—I hurried back toward the bird, which was still beating its wings toward the person or people on the other side of it. The only thing that was saving them was likely that the hedge and the cottage walls kept the gull from opening up its full wingspan.

The hose was heavy, and the bird's head was lowered. I watched as it reached out its neck to peck at its victim once, then again, each time rebuffed with a loud clang as it connected with something metal instead.

I couldn't believe I was going to try this, but my only other choice was to hit it in the leg, which would probably just piss it off.

Not that trying to strangle it would be much better. I wound the loose end of the garden hose around my arm a few times to try and secure it, sucking in a breath. My heart pounded almost out of my chest.

The next time the monstrous gull stuck its neck out to attack, I flung the middle loop of hose at the back of its head.

For a moment, I thought it was going to slide down the bird's back, but as the gull felt it, it made a mistake: the seagull ducked its head farther to get it off . . . and the hose slid right around its neck, nestled perfectly into the clefts of its shoulders.

I grabbed the other side like reins and frantically wound the slack around my right arm. Stupid, stupid, stupid—one wrong move, and this bloody bird could break both my arms.

But the bird had hardly noticed the weight of the hose, it was so intent on its prey.

I didn't know if I could move the enormous creature, but I did know I needed to get that hose tighter around its neck.

"Hit it in the head as hard as you can!" I shouted to whoever was listening—and I took three running steps at the bird's tail and leapt.

This time the human yell was more of a startled yelp from the other side of the bird, but as my feet sank into feathers and scrambled to find purchase on the seagull's back, I didn't care about anything beyond hanging on for dear life.

My triumph at being successful with the first stage of this harebrained plan paled next to the reality of trying to hold on to two handfuls of garden hose and also somehow not fall off the back of a now-stumbling giant gull.

Or maybe I didn't need to not fall.

Maybe I just needed to fall in a useful direction. Both arms straining against the pressure of holding onto the hose, which was now pulled taut against the thrashing bird's throat, I windmilled my arms twice to wrap it even tighter and the next time the bird pitched forward, I threw my entire weight down at the base of its neck.

The seagull fell off balance, lurching forward, and I felt the impact as it hit the grass, my own impact cushioned ever so slightly by the feathered body beneath me.

Clang.

Clang-clang!

The final *clang* was accompanied by a heaving sob, and I felt the seagull spasm beneath me. I tried to scramble to my feet, hauling back on the hose and crossing them before me. The bird was still thrashing, but its movements felt weaker.

Clang.

I could finally see the source of the yelling and the clangs—a woman with frizzy auburn hair half-plastered to her face with sweat was pummelling the seagull with a spade, and slightly behind her was a much-older woman who was leaning upon a wrought-iron garden table to support herself, staring in vacant horror over the fluttering wing of the dying monster.

With a grimace, I stood on the seagull's neck and jumped. A sickening crack resulted, and the sound came with the bird jerking one last time before settling into a dying twitch.

That glow returned, pulsing in my vision, but I couldn't pay attention to it. Not now.

My eyes finally took in the face of the woman who had been fighting for her life, her open mouth wet with sweat and spittle and her chest heaving, one shoulder of what had once been a gorgeous, ivory-coloured Eriskay jumper a mess of unravelling wool and stained with an alarmingly large radius of blood.

"Calum," she said before I could recover enough to say anything at all. "What the fuck are you doing here?"

CHAPTER
NINE

Eilidh's words hung in the air for a long moment, but before I could answer, the woman beside her let out a keening wail.

"Robert!" she cried, lurching over the still-twitching wing of the monster gull and falling to her knees beside the dead man.

Eilidh's already-pale face went whiter, the smattering of freckles standing out in even starker relief as she stared past me.

"No," she said, then again. "No, no, no, no, no, no."

I stumbled out of her way as she moved past me, standing stupidly over the carcass of the enormous gull as Eilidh darted to the woman's side, throwing an arm around her.

Half-dazed, I could hear her murmuring in Gaelic to the woman.

"Ò, a sheanmhair, rinn sibh ur dìcheall, rinn sibh ur dìcheall," she said, repeating the words over and over and over as if trying to convince herself.

Oh, Gran. You did all you could. You did all you could.

Fuck.

Those tourists in the Peugeot—that had been horrible to see. But I hadn't known them, hadn't had any connection with them whatsoever.

Eilidh Macintosh, though?

I stumbled half a step from the dead bird, unwinding the hose from my arms at last. Pins and needles prickled up both arms from the return of blood flow—I hadn't even realised I'd cut off circulation so badly.

A matching wrought-iron garden chair lay overturned on the grass by a second spade—clearly it hadn't just been Eilidh fighting the seagull—and I numbly righted it and collapsed into it.

Of all the people for me to just run into in an apocalypse. Vaguely, I remembered Eilidh telling me and Susanna that she was spending the holidays in Argyll with family. She'd been brought up in Glasgow and met Susanna at Glasgow Uni. She must have come up here for the weekend only to be hit by an apocalypse.

I hadn't spoken to her in months, not since the last time I saw her with Susanna. That'd been a weird bloody night that only made sense in retrospect. Susanna'd been distant and cold all week before it, and then I'd caught her blushing from cheeks to collarbone at a text message, which at the time unsettled me, but it also flipped some kind of switch. We'd gone out with Eilidh into town for some EDM dance night—I don't even remember where, only that Susanna had gone from cold to red hot, gussied up to the nines in club clothes I hadn't seen in ages. *Eilidh* had been the cold and distant one that night, shooting me strange looks and only giving monosyllabic answers.

And now, here she was, pressing bloodied hands into a wound in her grandfather's abdomen in vain. Her grandmother's shoulders shook with the kind of sobs my body remembered from losing my mum, the kind where a formative part of your world is suddenly wrenched away and you can no longer orient yourself in what remains.

For a moment, I just stared at them from my chair. The old man was dead; he wasn't coming back. But I could still see the red spreading across Eilidh's ivory jumper. She was losing a lot of blood.

Everything around me turned to haze, like one of the three muggy summer's days we get annually in Scotland. A hum began in my bones, almost *through* my bones, as if I could suddenly feel every blade of grass, every leaf on every rose bush, every branch in the hedge behind the dead man.

Without thinking, I reached out and harvested the seagull, gaining 117 spirit—the delay must have cost me a few—and a number of other items that were useless to me right now. Feathers and talons remained in a pile, and I quickly secured them under an empty flower pot since my inventory was still full, but it also netted me sixty pathos. The more complex a creature, the more complex its rewards.

My perception of the world seemed to expand even further. The mundane, unmutated insects making their way through the soil beneath me, the smell of blood mingling with dew-drenched grass and moss and urine, the triune patter of three human pulses elevated with adrenaline and fear—all of those things came to me.

And I could *feel* the wound in Eilidh's side. The gull had taken a chunk out of her abdomen, just above her hip. It had thankfully gotten mostly skin and, in a twist of irony considering I'd previously heard her complaining about a nearly nonexistent muffin top, a beak full of fat. No major organs or arteries, but that didn't mean a wound like that wasn't dangerous.

My fingertips buzzed as I straightened in my chair, the weeping of Eilidh's grandmother now palpable in the light hint of salt from her tears. I could smell the old woman crying.

Eilidh wasn't.

Her hands fumbled on her grandfather's shoulders as if rearranging his lambswool-lined jacket would somehow fix his organs.

I couldn't do that.

But maybe . . .

Something in me reached out through that buzz in my fingertips, through the movement of grass and wind and energy and the heat of our flushed, survival-mode bodies, and it found that wound in Eilidh's side. It tasted the edges of it, found healthy flesh, and even though I was sitting, I swayed in the chair as her wound grew a crust, then a scab, filling in with scar tissue that the influx of spirit in this new world seemed to latch onto and coax into becoming healthy skin cells once more like the whispers of waves on a calm seashore.

I didn't realise she'd turned away until she was roughly shaking my shoulder.

"Calum," Eilidh said.

My eyes popped open.

Every muscle in my body ached like the time I made the mistake of working out on leg day with a bodybuilder colleague and then ran three miles to my tae kwon do class. I could barely move for a week then, and now, staring hazily up into Eilidh's face, I wasn't sure I could stand up, let alone walk.

Had I passed out and imagined healing her?

I had no idea.

"Sorry," I said. I'd no idea why apologising was the first thing I did, but it made her scowl.

The downturn of her lips lasted only a moment before faltering, and she said grudgingly, "Don't apologise for saving our lives."

I somehow managed to nod. I'd slumped in the chair when I passed out, and that put me at eye level with Eilidh's side. There was no new blood coming from her wound.

"Are you okay?" I asked.

She jumped as if startled, her hand twitching toward her side only a hair, as if she was afraid to touch it. "Aye," she said slowly. "But Seanair isn't."

Her words brought renewed sobs from her grand-mother, but I couldn't seem to feel anything about that anymore. Some cynical part of my brain told me I'd shut it out for self-preservation, but when I didn't respond, Eilidh gave me a tight-lipped smile that was more of a grimace. Susanna told me that Eilidh thought I was an unfeeling frozen mackerel. Maybe I couldn't help but subconsciously reflect her confirmation bias.

"I'm sorry I didn't get here in time to help before—"

Eilidh cut me off. "Why *are* you here?"

Just like that, I felt something—yep. That was definitely the feeling of becoming the easy scapegoat. Thing was, I couldn't bring myself to mind, all things considered.

"I was just passing by," I said, trying to stretch my shoulders and arms without looking too flippant. Gods, that hurt. Like someone took a meat tenderiser to my entire muscular system.

"Just passing by?" Eilidh said. The breeze was drying her sweat-dampened curls to her forehead, and she scrubbed the back of her arm against her skin to loosen them. "Aye, and I'm the muppet of Downing Street."

Finally, something kindled in me that wasn't just physical pain. "Have you set foot outside this cottage in the last two days? It's literally the fucking end of the world."

The quiet, shaky breath of Eilidh's grandmother's crying faded to silence.

"What does that have to do with it?" Eilidh said, her voice dangerously soft.

"You have to have seen that text in your vision, yeah?" I didn't wait for her nod before I went on. "I'm not about to try to explain it, but everything electronic is dead, there's *creatures* out there killing people, as I don't have to explain to you, and—"

I was about to snap that I'd healed what could have turned into a mortal wound with magic, apparently, but before I could, Eilidh waved her hand at me.

"I'm not stupid, asshole. We all gained a level killing a vole the size of a bloody wheelie bin last night. I'm asking you why you'd be *here*, of all places. 'Just passing by'—you live in Glasgow. What are you doing here?"

With effort, I shoved down the rising irritation.

"What's it to you?" I asked pointedly. "Iain and Meeksy are in Oban with Iain's mum, and I wasn't about to sit on my arse in Partick with the giant bloody centipedes."

Eilidh didn't even blanch at that, but she gave me a tight nod just as I heard her grandmother clamber to her feet with a small hitch in her breath and a knee that popped alarmingly loud in the sudden silence.

"Na bi mì-mhodhail, a luaidh," the old woman reprimanded her grandaughter in Gaelic, which made Eilidh splutter.

Either because the granny didn't think I'd understand

that she just told Eilidh not to be rude or just out of habit, she then switched to English with a remaining lilt of her Argyll Gaelic in her cadence. "You saved our lives, young man. Thank you for coming along when you did, whatever brought you this way. I'm Mòrag. Come inside. I'll put the kettle on."

You don't say no when a Highland granny tells you to come in for tea, no matter whether a kettle has electricity or not, so I followed after her, hearing a huff from Eilidh behind me.

The cottage was very much a grandparents' cottage. Dark wood, off-white walls, cheery crocheted blankets folded neatly on top of a sofa so puffy, I wanted to immediately face plant into its cushions. And it was warm—as I watched, Mòrag stirred up the peat fire and added another couple chunks from a tin bucket beside the fire with the easy motion of someone who had done it a thousand times.

But that moment of ease and habit soured a heartbeat later when her hand froze halfway between the stove door and the bucket, and she began to shake.

"I'll get the fire," I said hurriedly. "You should sit down, Mòrag."

"We just left him out there," she said, her voice faint. "My Robert."

"I can—move him inside if you want," I said. To my embarrassment, my voice hitched as I spoke, but Mòrag was already shaking her head.

"No, a luaidh, there's—no." She closed the stove door with a weary hand and pushed herself back to her feet, eyes distant. The old woman glanced at Eilidh, who hadn't said a word since we came inside. "I won't be a minute. You both stay here. Eilidh, put the kettle on."

Nonplussed, I stood alone in the lounge while Eilidh

vanished toward what I assumed was the kitchen, and Mòrag went outside, the door creaking closed behind her. It didn't latch.

I couldn't help myself. I walked over to the window, peering out between the floral-patterned drapes to see Mòrag kneeling beside Robert's body. She folded his hands over his chest, placing her own on top of them. The sun cut through the clouds as if on cue, lighting her in a ray of gold that caught a sparkling tear as it dripped from her chin onto her husband's shoulder.

Robert's body dissolved into motes.

She harvested him.

For a moment, I stared in shock. It took me a moment to realise that she must have been reading system text when she stood up a moment ago—did the system tell her to harvest her husband's body?

I couldn't decide if I was repulsed or merely surprised, but I thought of the seagull monster I'd killed, the centipede and the rat. Their bodies had contained their essences, spirit, somehow quantified.

Maybe, just maybe, what the system had done was give Mòrag a way to take some of her love's spirit into herself, to strengthen her for whatever was to come.

CHAPTER
TEN

Drinking tea with a new widow and her granddaughter who hated me was an experience I didn't think I'd ever forget.

From the mismatched-but-dainty teacups and saucers to the way we all pretended we didn't hear the rattle of Mòrag's clattering together every time she lowered the cup onto the porcelain, the loudest sound beyond was the crackling of the peat fire and three people's ragged breathing. Eventually, Eilidh took Mòrag upstairs with a pointed look at me that practically screamed, *Don't you dare leave before we have a chance to talk.*

It was for this reason, among others, that I decided now would be a grand time to look over my pulsing notifications —to avoid the migraine that was forming with the constant light, if nothing else.

You have reached Level 3! You have three attribute points to distribute. You may now choose your class. You have three skill points to distribute.

Through physical exertion, you have gained a permanent +1

to Agility and +1 to Stamina. Please note that such increases have diminishing returns as your base statistics grow.

Through arcane exertion, you have gained a permanent +1 to Spirit and +1 to Pathos. Please note that such increases have diminishing returns as your base statistics grow.

Through arcane experimentation, you have unlocked the Slàinte skill tree.

You have unlocked an affinity: Nature. Continue to explore the connections of the natural world to increase your affinity and your abilities. You have unlocked the skill tree: Nature.

You have unlocked an affinity: Healing. Continue to learn the ways of mending body and mind to increase your affinity and your abilities. You have unlocked the skill tree: Slàinte.

I blinked at that—my successful and impulsive attempt to heal Eilidh seemed to have an unexpected outcome. But I didn't want to get bogged down in looking at a skill tree before I figured out what class I was going to take. If my instinct was correct, my classes would have skills involved, and I had a sinking feeling that three skill points would vanish as fast as a cat fleeing the screeches of a children's chanter class.

At Level 3, you may choose your first class.

Class selection is meant to be an exploration of the way you wish to live, not a lifetime commitment. You will have further opportunities to specialise—or even to move in a different direction entirely. This is but the first step on a path to your personal ascension.

Based on your choices and strengths thus far, you may choose from the following options. You may request further options if you wish, but be aware they will not be optimised to your personal abilities and may require extensive training.

Your class options are:

Nature's Blade—A scion of the natural world, you combine

your own nature of treading lightly upon the earth with a deadly promise to any who upset the balance it requires. You will receive an immediate bonus of +2 to Agility, Mind, and Stamina as well as a +1 bonus to Will. You gain access to the Nature skill tree as well as the Combat Stealth skill tree.

Nature's Blades are silent shadows amid the dappled glens —they treat the world around them with respect and rain down its vengeance with pristine accuracy upon those who do not. Skilled in stealth and tracking alike, they are dangerous foes and can call down the wrath of animal companions upon their enemies.

As tempting as this one looked—and it *did* look tempting—I thought I would kind of need a blade to wield, and I was not sure a fireplace shovel would count. I highly doubted Granny Mòrag had a claymore or more than a sgian dubh floating around the hoose, and I'd hardly expect her to give it to me if she did.

I looked on to the next one, trying to fend off the seed of disappointment germinating in my gut.

Fiosaiche—

The second addition of Gaelic startled me—how did this system know my mother tongue? Then again, how did it know English, for fuck's sake? Not the brightest question. I read on.

Fiosaiche—Keenly observant and able to connect disparate patterns and information in order to form accurate conclusions, the Fiosaiche is a master of strategy able to turn the tide in their favour. You will receive an immediate +2 to Mind, Stamina, and Constitution, as well as a +1 to Spirit. You gain access to the Speech skill tree as well as the Hand-to-Hand skill tree.

Fiosaichean are able to navigate the currents of the natural world and of people with equal facility. Masters of the subtle arts of power dynamics in the wilds and in civilisation alike, you don't want to get on their bad sides. They are natural scouts in any environment with an uncanny ability accurately assess strengths and weaknesses to their own advantages.

This one was tantalising . . . but for someone like me whose tolerance of people in general was about as enthusiastic as the average person's tolerance for smallpox, the last thing I wanted was to choose something that would rely on me being in the centre of—or even adjacent to—human politicking.

No, thank you.

I suppressed a shudder.

I had almost resigned myself to having to dig through second-tier classes to find something that felt suited to me when I pulled up the final of the three initial options.

Hedge Witch—Perfectly in tune with nature and its many boons and dangers, the Hedge Witch is able to draw from the ambient Spirit and Pathos with an iron Will to act as the hand of the earth itself in asserting what is right. You will receive an immediate bonus of +2 to Dexterity, Mind, and Stamina as well as a +1 bonus to Pathos. You gain access to the Nature skill tree as well as the Arcane skill tree.

Hedge Witches are expert wielders of Spirit, using their emotions and their resolve to shape the world in the image of nature. Able to call upon flora and fauna alike to manifest their will, it is nigh-impossible to escape their reach. With the world as their weapon, the branches are their claws and the eagles their eyes.

Yes.

Yes.

Semantics and pop-cultural pedantry about whether it should be witch or warlock aside, I felt a thrill go through me at the thought.

I noted, of course, that it would boost my lowest

Manipulation stat, Pathos, rather than reinforcing my already-higher Will or Spirit, but the rebel in me liked that.

What the hell.

I selected Hedge Witch.

Welcome to the Hedge Witch class!

You now have access to the Nature and Arcane skill trees.

You have three skill points to distribute.

You have three attribute points to distribute.

I was champing at the bit to look at Nature, but . . . magic.

With a thought, I opened the Arcane tree. It actually was a tree, with greyed-out, star-like points amid the roots, climbing the trunk, and splaying out among the branches above it. But only one of the points, in the centre of the root system, was available to me to look at now.

Spèird—Often the first spell a mage learns, Spèird is a blast of force that can be used to fling projectiles and foes alike to buy the wielder precious time or space to manoeuvre.

Increased use of this skill allows for more targeted applications and, with the power of a true proficient, can be as lethal as a martial arts' master's fists.

I had a feeling I would come back to that to learn it, but before I did, I wanted to see what else existed.

Opening the Nature tree, I was not disappointed.

Connection—You gain a deeper affinity to the earth and its needs, and it whispers to you. With this skill, you are able to see how things around you interact, be it the tracks of a deer hunted by paw prints of a stalking cat or the passing of a band of hunters.

Increased use of this skill enables you to take in an entire scene at a glance and appropriately assess its secrets. Addition-ally, the skill will allow you to ascertain the needs of the natural world, *giving you the power to aid creatures and plants that may one day return the favour.*

It immediately made me think of the Fiosaiche class, but actually tailored to what I would find useful. I didn't have to think twice about this one—I used one of my skill points to learn it immediately. The white pinprick of light turned emerald green, twinkling like a star.

Beyond the affinity I felt with this skill already, I still had to make it to Oban somehow, and having a skill like this? It'd make that trip much easier. At least I hoped it would.

Though it made two more of the points on the Nature tree go from grey to white, I forced myself not to look at them quite yet. I still had the Slàinte tree waiting.

To my surprise, something was already illuminated in yellow—and it wasn't the initial point on the roots but one partway up the trunk.

I focused on the one I'd unlocked through experimentation.

Beannachd Shlàinte—This skill can be used once per day to heal a severe injury of tissue trauma and infection. You gain an increased affinity for Healing, allowing you to intuit what is necessary to save lives of humans and animals alike.

Increased use of this skill allows for more complex healing, including but not limited to: internal haemorrhaging, progressive disease, antivenin formulation, purging toxins, and limb regrowth. Additionally, greater knowledge of the body's anatomy and physiology makes you more effective in combat.

My brain practically exploded into thought at the words.

Not only were the possibilities phenomenal, but this was something I picked up by *accident*, merely wanting . . . what? Instinctively not to let another human being die in front of me? I didn't know if I wanted to go full-on healer, but knowing that by mere exploration of abilities I could unlock new skills and powers just by existing? This new world, whatever the cause, had given us barely any information, but fuck if I wasn't going to take the chances given me.

I looked at the unlocked skills around Beannachd Shlàinte—which meant Blessing of Health—and realised something else vitally important: not only did experimentation yield fruit here, but it also unlocked three new skills I could put points in. Three new skills beyond the fundamentals at the bottom of the roots, climbing the trunk.

I knew holding on to a couple points would be smart, but damn. This was going to be a tough choice to make.

Tempted as I was to just go ham on the Slàinte tree with my two remaining points, I couldn't shake the memory of that giant gull, of Robert's entrails hanging out of his stomach. Once, back when I was living in Inverness for a summer, a woman was eating a sandwich in front of Eastgate Shopping Centre, and a seagull swooped down and ripped half her cheek off in the process of trying to steal the food literally out of her mouth.

Those things were vicious before they were the size of a horse. If I didn't get some combat abilities soon, I was going to die bloody.

It wouldn't matter if I could heal myself if I couldn't stay alive long enough to have the chance.

With regret, I moved back over to the Arcane tree, and before I could talk myself out of it, I unlocked Spèird and looked at the two root-level skills—spells, I guess, though the system didn't seem to differentiate—that turned white when I spent the skill point.

Fuaran—Like its name, Fuaran is a skill that brings with it a wellspring of refreshment. This skill increases your spirit regeneration by a base of 20% for 3 minutes, and if comrades are within 10 meters of you, it will also do the same for them.

Increased use of this skill will increase its efficacy and area of effect and may also bestow other boons that can benefit you and your party.

That one was going to be a necessity sooner rather than later, but I stubbornly moved away from it to check out the other option, hoping fervently for something useful in combat.

Purifire—

I got as far as the name and did a mental facepalm. It switched back to English for a *pun*? I didn't think I liked the idea of this system making jokes, but I decided to look closer.

Purifire—This skill is most used in combat, instilling basic fire with the power of the arcane, making it burn hotter and brighter than typical flame—and all within the mage's control. This fire is not friendly fire in more than one way. Magic is will and intent, and it will strike only your foes. While a staff is needed for advanced use, this skill can be wielded without need for a weapon.

Increased use of Purifire allows for more complex use. Many mages utilise it with metal weapons to great effect, adding burning damage and spirit damage to physical. Others prefer a staff's elegance and the advanced precision a mage finds therein. At its heart, this skill moulds itself to its wielder, and only the mage can decide its limits.

No-brainer.

I spent my final skill point, and it was like the Hulk punched through a dam in my mind.

CHAPTER
ELEVEN

"Calum," someone was saying.

Not someone. Eilidh.

I blinked away the residual rush of the skill acquisition, looking up to meet a pair of agate-hard blue-grey eyes in a pale face blotchy from crying.

She certainly wasn't crying now, and she'd changed out of her bloody jumper into one that was moss green, which set off her auburn hair and made her eyes seem to glow.

"Sorry," I said. "Level up—got my class and figured I should sort all that."

She nodded, sitting on the sofa as far away from me as she could and pulling her long legs up with her, wrapping her arms around her knees. Even in her dark grey leggings and fuzzy sherpa socks, even in that position, she managed to not look vulnerable.

"I should thank you," she said haltingly after a moment. "If you hadn't come along—"

"You would have managed," I said.

She scowled. "Don't patronise me." She tugged at the hem of her jumper. Over where the wound had been. "I know you healed me. That fucking bird took a bite out of me and I wouldn't have lasted much longer. My bloody sword was upstairs, and I didn't dare leave Seanmhair to fight that thing alone to get it."

It took a moment for her words to process. Naturally, it was the least consequential thing my brain decided to latch onto. "Sword?"

Eilidh gave me a bland look. "Since I was a wean."

"I never knew that."

"You never asked."

Touché.

"Anyway. Thank you." She said it as if the words tasted of rotting fish, but she did say it.

"Nae bother." That sounded way too flippant to my own ears, so I hastily added, "I'm just glad I was close enough to help. This time, at least."

My mind pulled up the images of the poor Peugeot owners splattered against the road.

Eilidh had probably not let anything go past her in her life, and she didn't now. "I take it you were too late for someone else."

"Aye," I said to her. "I probably only escaped myself because whatever it was was . . . busy."

"Busy?"

"Eating," I said shortly.

If I expected her to blanch, she disappointed me. Her eyes simply grew steelier, and she stared across the room at a framed cross-stitch of an exquisitely detailed thistle.

"I'm coming to Oban with you," she said suddenly.

"What? No way—you're—"

"Look, Calum, but Seanmhair asked me to, so I'm doing what she wants. She can take care of herself, and she's got enough food here to last her a few days until I can get back.

But we've cousins in Oban, and I'm going with or without you. It's safer with, but whatever."

"Okay," I said.

Eilidh's mouth was half open as if anticipating further pushback, and it snapped close with a click of teeth. She nodded once, tension in every line of her jaw even if it didn't otherwise show in her posture.

"So what did you choose?" she asked after a moment, and at my blank stare, she went on. "Your class."

"Hedge Witch," I said. "Do you have one yet?"

"Not yet," she said, "but that gods damned overgrown parasite likely got me pretty close."

We sat there in awkward silence for a long moment. I certainly wasn't going to be the one to bring up Susanna, and it was a strange relief to feel that Eilidh clearly didn't want to either. At least we had one thing in common. Two if you count shared languages.

A moment later, Eilidh put her feet back on the floor and slapped both hands against her knees, possibly louder than she meant to because we both started.

"I'm going to go get ready. Do you have any weapons?" she asked.

I stood, pulling the fireplace shovel from my inventory. "Does this count?"

She raised one auburn eyebrow. "Erm, no. I'll see what I've got upstairs. You can't have my claymore."

Before I had the chance to say anything to that, she was swiftly taking the stairs two at a time.

Bloody hell, there actually *was* a claymore in the house.

It wasn't too long before she came back, the unmistakable long hilt of a literal claymore protruding above her shoulder and a sheathed dagger barely bigger than a kitchen knife in her hand. She had another one strapped to her belt, and to my surprise, she also wore a set of leather bracers over fingerless leather gloves, along with what had to be sparring gear. It was far more armoured than I was, to be sure.

"What?" She asked the question as if daring me to say something.

"I'm just impressed," I said honestly.

"I told you not to patronise me."

With that, she stumped down the rest of the stairs and thrust the sheathed dagger out at me hilt first.

"This isn't sharp because I used it for sparring, but I've a whetstone, and I can show you how to take care of it. Do you have a belt?"

"Aye," I said, taking the dagger.

"Put it on whichever side suits you." She gestured vaguely at me. "Not really a wrong way to wear it if you can easily draw it with your dominant hand—only way it's wrong is if you can't access it when you need it."

She said the last with a certain amount of self-reproach that I didn't dare show I'd noticed.

"Got it," I said.

Mòrag chose that moment to come downstairs, bracing herself on the banister. Her hair was neatly pulled into a bun, and she'd changed her clothing as well, into well-worn tweed trousers and a thin jumper with a knitted blue shawl over her shoulders.

"I'll see about making sure you've enough food for the journey," she said without preamble. "How long did you say it took you to get here from Glasgow, a ghràidh?"

"About a day and a half," I told her. "I was faster before someone nicked my bike in Tyndrum."

At the old woman's beckoning hand, I followed her into the kitchen, Eilidh staying behind.

Mòrag opened a large cupboard at the far end of the kitchen next to the refrigerator, and it housed a pantry. She pulled out a couple packets of oatcakes, then rummaged about and found some bags of dried fruit, squinting at one of them.

"Careful with the prunes," she said dryly. "And the apricots are chopped, but they'll still count as calories."

At Mòrag's insistence, I emptied out my inventory: the chitin, the rat remains, my rucksack with the shovel, my half-drunk jug of water, all of it. Together, we consolidated everything as best we could—she found a large burlap sack from a twenty-pound bag of rice, and we dropped all the animal remains into that, bundling them into one slot instead of the previous six.

That's also how we discovered that the rat meat remained perfectly fresh. Not so much a whiff of foul odours or decomposition.

"Will you leave this with me?" Mòrag asked thoughtfully.

"You want the rat meat?" That was unexpected.

"Yes," she said, waving a hand. "When I was a bairn, we ate whatever meat we could find. Robert"—her voice hitched at her husband's name—"built us a smoker out back. I'd like to smoke it and see how I get on."

"Be my guest," I told her, belatedly remembering the talons and feathers I'd left outside. "I'll be right back. I forgot the stuff from the seagull."

The old woman gave me a startled look, but after a moment, her chin dipped in a tight nod of assent.

Eilidh was nowhere to be seen when I walked back out through the lounge and into the front garden, for which I was thankful. Of all the people to run into in rural Argyll.

The pot was just where I left it, the terra cotta slightly spattered with dew from the grass, and the feathers didn't seem too bedraggled from having a pot sitting on them. They were massive feathers, one pinion easily as long as my arm, and the talons were nasty things, each of them a similar length and girth to my fingers. I shuddered at the thought of taking one of those to torso.

Pulling out the bag Mòrag and I had just repacked, I fit the talons into that, but the feathers had to go into their own slot, leaving me with four slots remaining. If this system was giving us feathers and bits of things, there had to be a reason. Was there crafting? Where would one even begin to ask that question?

In a burst of nihilistic futility, I asked into my own mind. *Crafting information.* Nothing. *Help with crafting. Crafting rules. How to craft. What the ever-loving fuck do I do with this shit clogging up my inventory?*

Nothing. Nada. Zilch.

Bugger.

Feeling surly, I remembered I needed to add my attribute points, so I pulled up my character sheet. I had three to work with—and along with that, a welcome surprise.

You have gained a permanent +1 to Spirit due to harvesting the resources from an enemy.

Name: Calum Green

Age: 36
Level: 3
Class: Hedge Witch (Further class selection at: Level 9)
Affinities: Nature (Level 1), Healing (Level 1)

Alteration:

Strength: 10
Dexterity: 14
Agility: 12
Mind: 15

Regeneration:

Constitution: 14
Stamina: 16

Manipulation:

Spirit: 12 (+117 capacity for 12 hours)
Pathos: 9 (+60 capacity for 12 hours)
Will: 19

After a moment of thought, I put all three of my new attribute points into Mind, bringing it up to eighteen and making it my new highest stat. If I was going to focus on magic abilities, I'd need the capacity to do that, and while I couldn't directly affect that by adding points to Manipulation stats, I'd already figured out that just by doing things, I could grow those. And if I was right, increasing my Mind stat would make me more effective.

"More screen time?" came Eilidh's voice behind me.

"I didn't get a chance to add my attribute points earlier. Figured I better do it before we leave." I half expected her to come up with some sort of snide response to that, but instead, she just pressed her lips together. "You really know how to use that thing?"

The question fell out of my mouth, and I winced. Why couldn't I ever keep my foot out of there around her? Maybe it was the disapproval she practically radiated from the earliest days I knew her, or maybe it was just that she seemed the type of person who didn't let anything faze her *except* me.

"Yes," was all she said, though, and she turned on her heel and went back into the house.

I followed behind, wondering if I'd survive the trek to Oban—and not because of any potential monsters.

CHAPTER

TWELVE

Mòrag was stoic as she saw us off an hour later, with Eilidh murmuring to her in Gaelic low enough that I couldn't hear what she was saying. The language has been nearly driven to death in most of Scotland, but hearing Eilidh and her grandmother speak it so naturally to one another gave me a pang I didn't want to acknowledge. Reminded me of my mum—I learnt Gaelic at her knee, as we say, and now she was gone.

Before too long, Eilidh and I made our way back onto the road, heading westward towards Oban.

We remained in silence all the way to Inverlochy, about another mile up the road from Mòrag's house. There's more than one Inverlochy in Scotland, and this one was very literally the place where the River Lochy met the River Orchy, and not much else.

Unfortunately, the break in the quiet did not come from either of us.

A panicked whinny tore through the air from just north of the A85 where we walked. There was a car in the middle of the road ahead of us, door ajar and no sign of its occupant, but in the field just at the side of the road, I could make out a horse in the distance where it reared violently, hooves hitting the earth with thuds that took a second to reach my ears.

"What is that?" Eilidh breathed, staring at the horse's feet.

Something moved through the sheep-trimmed field, but I couldn't tell what. In fact, it barely looked like anything beyond a shimmer, like roads gave off on a rare hot day in summer.

"I don't know," I said, "but that horse is terrified, and it's not safe to get closer unless you want me practicing more healing on you."

"I *know* that, you—"

She broke off with an irritated huff, eyes still glued to the horse in the field.

I didn't know if I was close enough to use my force spell, but I tracked the disturbance where the horse still reared, half leaping to the side to avoid whatever was out there.

Something felt . . . off. As if anything didn't this week, but as I concentrated on that patch of heat-like shimmer in the air, I began to think the horse had the right idea trying to trample it.

"Here goes nothing," I murmured.

Unlike with the healing, there was no gentle swell of spirit, no sense of plucking one strand in a spider's web and feeling it resonate through the rest. No, where that had been delicate, intricate, this was gulping in a breath to scream.

Spirit flooded me, and for the blink of an eye, it felt like it might drag me down to drown.

Then it exploded out of me again, charging across the intervening meters of the field.

The horse danced sideways away from it, but the force didn't strike it.

I had my gaze set on the disturbance, so I saw the precise moment it struck. Watching something barely visible fly through the air was an experience I didn't think I'd ever forget.

"Jesus Christ," Eilidh said under her breath. "What *is* it?"

The horse had taken the opportunity to flee, running towards the farthest side of the field. I felt for the creature —there was only so far she could go to escape. She was fenced in on all sides.

"I don't know," I said, bracing myself as alarm pinged me, "but I think it's coming our way."

Eilidh must have already come to the same conclusion, because before I finished my sentence, she was already pulling her claymore from the sheath on her back with a steely whisper of metal on leather. If I'd had any real doubts of her ability to handle a weapon like that, the fluid motion and practised ease would have disabused me of them in from one breath to the next.

"Stay away from the pointy end," she said to me.

"I was planning on throwing myself on it to see what would happen," I said sardonically. "There goes my entire experiment."

I could feel the pulse of my spirit—my use of Spèird hadn't taken much out of me, much to my surprise. Why wasn't there some sort of bloody indicator or something? All I wanted was to have an idea of whether or not I could use several spells without, I don't know, keeling over or whatever would happen if I overextended my spirit capacity.

But then I remembered the seagull—I hadn't really thought through what the increased capacity meant.

"Oh, fuck yes," I breathed, tracking the bizarre bubble of distorted air. Thirty meters.

"What?"

"Get ready. I'm going to try to hit it from above," I said. Twenty meters.

"*What?*"

"I'm going to try to smash the bloody thing to the floor so you can stick it with the pointy end!"

Ten meters.

I drew on my spirit again, watching Eilidh brace herself out of the corner of my eye.

Five meters.

With everything I had gathered, I slammed the spell into motion, and this time, I didn't direct it laterally. I used it like a piston to crush whatever the fuck this thing was into the gravel strip at the edge of the A85, and as I did, I saw the bizarre way the thing ballooned out, almost like trying to smush a jellyfish.

Eilidh exploded into motion.

The claymore whirled through the air with precision, using its weight and momentum to fuel the strike as she brought it down directly on top of the jellyfish thing—and it rebounded right off like she'd struck a rubber ball with a cricket bat.

"Fuck!" She yelled the curse, quickly adjusting, but the unexpected reaction of the substance had already thrown her off balance.

Reaching for my spirit, I kindled Purifire.

Having never used it before, I had no idea what to

expect, but heat pooled between my palms, and my hands glowed blue-green, flames licking off of them and spilling from my fingertips in little drips and sparks.

I released the spell, my every intent on stopping this thing in its tracks.

The Purifire hit with a hiss like a pressure cooker releasing steam, and it rose in pitch to a keening wail like a hundred people dragging inch-long talons down a hundred chalkboards.

The spell ballooned out from the point of impact, racing over the entire surface area of the jellyfish thing and covering it with blue-green fire.

"That sound!" Eilidh yelled over the din.

In the distance, I could see the horse fleeing farther away from the noise, and for a moment, I felt sorry for the poor creature. She was having a *terrible* day.

Eilidh, perhaps realising that a slashing strike wouldn't work, gripped her claymore in both hands, bringing the point down upon the shrieking being.

It pierced through the Purifire—and something unexpected happened.

The fire raced up the blade of Eilidh's sword, sheathing it in light that lit her face like ripples in a pool. She yelped, but she kept her grip on the sword and drove it into the creature.

The jellyfish screamed.

Triumph flared in Eilidh's pale face, and I drew on my spirit again, adding to the spell.

I was just about to cast Spèird again to hold it in place when Eilidh drew back to stab it again, and the creature took the opportunity to wrench itself off of her blade entirely.

Before I could react, the thing froze, and I had the

distinct impression that I'd just been perceived, weighed, and measured.

And found to be a threat.

Then the thing flashed into motion too quickly for me to track, soaring over the grasses in the direction the horse had gone.

I could see its path only because of the sharp jerk of a thistle at the edge of the field—it had veered away from the horse and into a stand of trees.

It was gone.

Eilidh let out an explosive breath. "What the *fuck* was that?"

My heart pounded in my chest, and I felt something I never expected to feel when in mortal peril—I felt alive.

"I don't know," I said shakily. "But it didn't look like it was running for its life."

I don't know what made me say that beyond instinct—or maybe it was the sudden flashing pulse in my notifications.

Eilidh stared after the thing as if willing the trees to part and reveal its trail. Then her eyes went distant for a moment.

"I think you might be right," she said blandly. "You might want to check your notifications."

That made my heartbeat give a little stutter before resuming its frantic pace, though it began to slow, if glacially.

As gingerly as such a thing was possible, I summoned my notifications.

You have discovered a quest!

What.

I held off on reading more long enough to glance over at

Eilidh, who gave me a tight-lipped smile that most definitely did not reach her eyes.

Her tone was bleak when she spoke again, only three words. "It gets worse."

Well, shit.

THIRTEEN

Quest discovered: *The Hills Have Eyes*

Upon ascension, people adapt and survive in different ways. Part of the ascension for all worlds is achieving a balance of power that allows them to take their place in the universe—and part of that achievement inevitably involves some who think the path to power lies in seizing it by any means necessary.

Though your world has only just begun this journey, Earth was unprepared. A world of inequality, greed, and destruction is not one that, in universal history, has ever been selected for ascension. Because of that, some in your world have already begun to clench their fists.

This is unacceptable.

I stopped reading, my only-just-recovering heartbeat turning round to start a frenetic rhythm all over again.

You have discovered a simulacrum. Simulacra are used most frequently as communication entities. Nominally alive—they are closest to a fungus, in Earth terms—they are connected to their summoner with threads of spirit and will that allow them to relay information. They are not, however, intelligent, nor are they autonomous. They must be clearly directed, and if not, they will cause alarm quite by accident.

The one you found is new, and its summoner is yet unversed in the particulars of such magic. Simulacra are not suited for combat, though as you experienced, they are quite difficult to harm if the summoner attempts to use them to attack.

Whatever harm does *befall a simulacrum rebounds on its summoner.*

You have made an enemy today.

Objectives:

-Investigate the simulacrum's origin

-Find out the summoner's name

-Find out the summoner's purpose

Rewards:

-Experience (commensurate with current level progression)

-1 skill point

-1 item (as ascension permits)

-All cooldowns reset

I blinked myself out of my notifications, feeling sick.

"What the fuck," I said. "So that wasn't just some *thing* attacking us, but a *person* was behind it? What fucking cunt would terrorise a goddamn horse?"

"That might be the most emotion I've ever seen you display," Eilidh said dryly. "Good to know you have one, at least."

"Clearly you'd know all about emotions, since you don't seem to have any. At least I have the one, I guess."

"Congratulations. You found me out."

"Are we going to talk about this quest or are you going

to continue to attempt to hurt my feeling, singular?" I asked her, shoving my anger down into a box.

"We're *going* to go to Oban," she said. "Also known as the entire reason we're out here in the first place."

"Fine, then let's go."

I didn't wait for her to respond, only turned down the road towards Dalmally.

After a moment, I heard her footsteps follow.

My mind whirled through the information the quest had thrown at me. Not only was Earth apparently not supposed to ascend or whatever, but it seems like whoever or whatever entity controlled the system information, they didn't have a high opinion of humanity. To the contrary, it seemed like they might have a higher opinion of ticks.

That thought stuck in my craw.

I've never been hugely positive on humanity as a whole, but I've also never been a horrible misanthrope. Humans are capable of monstrous things, but we're also capable of spectacular acts of bravery and kindness for the sake of itself. But this system seemed to think we were all going to destroy each other.

Sure, with the past few years on Earth, things had seemed pretty dire, and there were undoubtedly certain subsets of the population who wanted to watch it all burn while they had space races that doubled as dick-measuring contests—with literal penis-shaped rockets, no less!—but that wasn't *all* we'd done as a species.

If this quest was right, though, there was someone nearby who had decided to take advantage of the apocalypse to . . . do what, exactly?

I hoped Iain and Meeksy and Catrìona were okay in Oban.

I didn't let myself glance back at Eilidh, whose foot-steps still let me know she was following.

Whatever harm does befall a simulacrum rebounds on its summoner.

You have made an enemy today.

We'd set out in the afternoon, so we didn't have much daylight left by the time we made it to the end of Loch Awe, and we weren't alone.

Kilchurn Castle's ruins lurked out in the middle of the loch, a shell of what had once existed, but for the first time since Tyndrum, I saw people—and they were all working together to move cars out of the road. A couple women and a man were braced against the boot of a Honda hatchback while a teenager sat half in and half out of the driver's seat with the door open, foot taking steps on the road while he steered the car into the carpark at Kilchurn Suites, an old Edwardian house turned self-catering.

"Hiya," I called as we approached.

One of the women glanced over her shoulder, still pushing the car, which was almost into a spot.

"Make sure you put the parking brake on," the man called to the kid.

"Ugh, I *know*," the kid called back, and even from where I stood, I could hear as he wrenched on it, making the man wince.

The woman who'd looked back at us straightened up, rolling her shoulders. She was average height, with middle-aged plumpness and the no-nonsense expression of High-land women. Her skin was naturally pale but pink from exertion—something told me this wasn't the first job they'd been at today. "Hiya, yourselves. Where you coming from?"

"Glasgow for me," I said, deciding—probably prudently —not to speak for Eilidh.

"Inverlochy. My grandparents are Helen and Robert Gregory."

The woman made a clucking sound. "I'm Diana Beaton. Are they all right, then?"

"My granny's fine," Eilidh said shortly. I saw her face darken out of the corner of my eye. "We lost my grandfather today."

Diana's eyes softened, and the others at the car stilled in their movements and turned towards us. "Och, I'm—so sorry to hear that, love. We knew Robert well."

I took the other woman to be the teenaged boy's mother. A younger blond with skin far too tan to be real, she reached out to her son, pulling him closer into her. The kid squirmed in typical teenager fashion. He probably wasn't older than fourteen, his near-white skin dotted with spots over his chin and forehead.

"Yous need a place to sleep?" The older man spoke up gruffly. Like Diana, he had the plumpness of middle age, but with a bigger beer belly and a build that just looked sturdy. "We've got suite three open. Take it yous are headed to Oban?"

I nodded at the same time Eilidh said, "Aye, we are, and that'd be grand, thank you."

"It's only one bed," Diana said, glancing between us. "I'm sorry for that—the others are occupied."

"I'll sleep on the floor—it's more than fine," I said hastily. "Inside is better than bedding down with the ticks by a mile."

"Aye, it is at that," the man said, then walked over and stuck out his hand to me. "Donald."

"Calum." I shook his hand.

"Eilidh," said Eilidh.

I could almost feel her glaring at the back of my head. Not sure what I'd done now—I didn't want to share a bed with her any more than she probably wanted to share one with me. I wouldn't be surprised if she went out and found every tick she could possibly gather up to dump them on me in my sleep.

"Anna," said the teenaged boy's mum. "And this is Andy."

Andy, predictably, was staring at Eilidh. Not in a teenage horndog way—at the claymore strapped to her back. He pushed a shaggy bit of dirty blond hair back from his face. "Why do you have a sword?"

Eilidh and I exchanged a glance, both of us breaking eye contact the moment we made it as if it burned.

"Things have changed out there," I said at the same time she said, "We've seen some scary stuff in the past couple days."

"I think you'd better come inside," said Diana, wiping her palms on the knees of her jeans. "No power, but we've got the fire on, and we'll have some soup for tea you're welcome to share."

"We've got food to share too," I said without hesitation. "I'm afraid we don't have any cash."

Both Diana and Donald waved a hand at the same time with the practice of a long-married couple.

"Never mind that," Donald said, gesturing at us to follow him towards the house. "I expect you've got stories we need to hear, and that's worth more than a few quid."

The next few hours were spent with both Eilidh and myself going back and forth, telling the tales of the past couple days. While we waited for tea, I told them about the centipede and the rat—and trotted out my bag of trophies, no less—and Eilidh shared about the vole and the seagull, though the latter she related in a wooden tone no one pressed, only greeted with grim nods of understanding.

They hadn't seen anything of the like yet, so they were all still level one. I didn't know if that was good news or bad; something in my gut told me without them reaching at least level three, if something *did* turn up, they wouldn't stand a chance.

We told them about the quest, too. If someone in the area was going to cause problems, they deserved to know.

By the time we sat round the table with soup, candles blazing down the table runner in the centre, the mood had turned sombre. Almost as soon as he was done, Donald got up from the table and excused himself, returning a few minutes later with a rifle, which he began to disassemble and clean with Andy looking on, eyes nervous and darting between the gun and Eilidh's sword, which was leaning against the windowsill behind her chair.

"So this quest," Anna said. She'd been quiet through most of the meal, listening and occasionally looking at her son with concern. "You're just going to ignore it?"

"We need to get to Oban," Eilidh said stubbornly, looking at me without blinking.

"I—yeah," I said after a beat. "Oban first to make sure our friends and family are okay. We'll go from there."

"What if it's too late by then?" Donald asked without looking up from his rifle.

Alarm pulsed through me. "What do you mean?"

"You said this system or whatever—it told you the simulacra are not supposed to be used in combat but whoever summoned this one did exactly that." Donald did look up then, dark brown eyes boring into mine. "And whatever you two did to the thing, it hurt him. Her. Them —whoever summoned it."

"Aye," I said.

"All I'm saying is you were given a pretty explicit warning," Donald continued. "Might be prudent not to ignore it."

A line of cold worked its way down my spine. I glanced over at Eilidh, who was frowning.

"We don't know they'll come after us," she said, but at the end of the sentence, she chewed on her bottom lip.

Her lips were full and pink, and for a moment, I just stared at her delicate face, pale skin and freckles turned golden by the candlelight. Then I shook myself. She hated my guts, and I wasn't much fonder of her.

"Simulacra 'are connected to their summoner with threads of spirit and will that allow them to relay information,'" I quoted, fixing my gaze on a safer target—the candle in front of me. "I reckon we'd be stupid to assume that information wouldn't be about us."

Again, I could practically feel the weight of Eilidh's glare, but after a moment, she sighed. "Fine. But where do we even start?"

"Fuck," I said, remembering something. Then I glanced at Anna's raised eyebrow. "Erm. Sorry. I just—I have a skill I haven't used yet. It's called Connection, and it might help me track the thing."

"Track it how?" Diana asked, pushing her bowl away from her with a clink of the spoon on the edge of it.

"I'm not sure," I admitted, pulling it up in my mind.

Connection—You gain a deeper affinity to the earth and its needs, and it whispers to you. With this skill, you are able to see how things around you interact, be it the tracks of a deer hunted by paw prints of a stalking cat or the passing of a band of hunters.

Increased use of this skill enables you to take in an entire scene at a glance and appropriately assess its secrets. Additionally, the skill will allow you to ascertain the needs of the natural world, giving you the power to aid creatures and plants that may one day return the favour.

On a whim, I triggered the skill right there.

My vision shifted, and small swirls and currents appeared in the air, weaving between the family around us. There were strong ropes of it between Donald and Diana, with similarly strong ones from Diana to Anna but, oddly, less so between Donald and Anna. Anna's line to Andy was like a mooring line. Following the impulse, I glanced at Eilidh before the skill ran its course.

To my surprise, there was a cord between us. Flimsy and weak compared to the weight of family, but it was there.

"I think the skill will help," I said after a moment. Eilidh was watching me, her expression perfectly schooled into stillness. "At first light, we should go back to that field, and I'll use the skill to try to track the thing from there."

"And what are we going to do if we find it?" she asked. "Kill its summoner? Just up and murder someone?"

Everyone around the table went still.

"I don't think anyone's saying that," I said finally.

"No, no one is saying that," Donald agreed, and Diana nodded, speaking up herself after a moment.

"We need to know if there's danger," she said. "We can't be prepared if we don't know what to prepare for."

We talked until we finally had to give in and stumble to our respective sleeping areas, where I collapsed on the floor, too exhausted to envy Eilidh her bed.

I slept like the dead—until a scream tore me from my slumber.

FOURTEEN

M y mind still carried the heaviness of sleep, and I flailed once until I remembered I was on the floor in suite three.

It was pitch dark except for the single ribbon of moonlight that threaded between the heavy drapes, and I heard Eilidh thrash on the bed.

A second voice joined the scream.

"Fuck!" I scrambled out from under the duvet, fumbling for my shirt in vain. I vaguely remembered taking it off in a half-asleep daze after overheating, but now I didn't have time to find it.

My belt with the dagger Eilidh had given me, though, was on the ottoman at the foot of the bed, and I grabbed that, slinging it around my waist without a thought.

A loud thump made the bed shudder against the ottoman, followed by a spat "Sodding—*shit*."

"All right?" I asked, but before she could answer, the scream came again. "Fuck, come on."

I threw the door open, not bothering to grab shoes, and

heard Eilidh patting at the wall where she'd leaned her sword before we went to sleep.

"Where's my sword?" She hissed the question through her teeth, and I felt a flash of pity for the evident pain in her voice. Must have stubbed her toe hard.

"It was right there a few hours ago," I said.

"I know it was right—oh, that wee numpty!"

I remembered the way Andy had been eyeing the claymore at tea the night before, and I sucked my lips against my teeth.

"Want my dagger?" I asked her.

"No," she said grimly. "I want my sword."

With that, she squeezed past me, taking off down the corridor. I followed as quickly as I could, hoping neither of us would take a dive head first down the two flights of stairs we'd climbed the night before.

On inspiration, though, I pulled on my spirit, kindling Purifire in my hands without directing it. It bathed the corridor in vibrant blue-green light, and Eilidh let out a surprised noise as she glanced back at me once, then took the stairs downward two at a time. I hurried to catch up.

The sound of yelling seemed to be coming from the family area, which was blocked off by a door telling guests to ring the electronic bell, which obviously wouldn't work now.

Eilidh wrenched on the door the moment she reached it, her disheveled face reflected in the polished wood in watery blue.

It didn't budge.

"Stand back," she said to me.

"I think it opens out—"

"I *said* stand back!"

I took a leaping step backward as she quickly gauged the distance, braced herself in a practiced stance, and planted a side kick right beneath the handle with unerring aim.

There was a crunch of wood at the impact, and when she retracted the kick and yanked on the door handle once more, it swung open towards us, the entire locking mechanism barely hanging on by some splinters.

Jeezo. Someone put some points into Strength.

Without a further word, she leaped through the door, with me fast on her heels.

What we found was utter chaos.

The family's lounge was a mess of overturned furniture with enormous gouges taken out of antique stuffed sofas and carved armrests alike.

Donald and Anna were nowhere to be seen, but Diana was backed into the far corner with Andy in the middle of the room, struggling to raise Eilidh's claymore against a simulacrum.

Just as we skidded to a halt inside the door, he got it above his head, swinging it downward.

"No!" Eilidh yelled, but it was too late.

Like had happened with her, Andy's unskilled sword blow struck the simulacrum hard and rebounded with a sickening crunch as something in his arm took the bulk of the force. The claymore clattered to the floor, landing half on a plush carpet and the other half with a clunk on once-pristine hardwoods that now bore a sizeable dent.

I was already readying Spèird, positioning it as I had before to strike the thing from above as Eilidh scooped up the sword, grabbing Andy by the back of the shirt and yanking him backwards.

The moment I had enough space, I slammed my spell downward on the simulacrum, channeling my held Purifire at the same time. This time, I didn't release the spell, only kept the thing pinned and wreathed in blue-green flame that licked outward without further damaging the carpet.

Diana briefly closed her eyes and blew out a breath before drawing another as deeply as she could. She pried herself out of the corner, making a beeline for her grandson, who had collapsed in a pile of gutted chair stuffing and was moaning in pain.

"I'll heal him after we deal with this!" I said through gritted teeth. The strain of keeping two spells trained on this blob pulled at me, and Eilidh circled it warily, glancing at me.

"Deal with it *how*?" she asked acerbically. "Best we can hope for, it flees again—if this is even the same one we saw before."

"Give me a second," I said.

This time, I remembered to trigger Connection. The additional pull on my spirit staggered me—literally—and I could feel my ability to control three spells fading. Fast. Without the increased capacity from that fucking seagull, we'd be toast right now. I had to find a way to permanently increase my spirit capacity—and quick.

As Connection blazed to life, I almost recoiled from the jellyfish thing. Instead of a jellyfish, in the view of the spell, it looked like . . . well, you know when you're in school and they make you do sex ed? You know how the egg looks when it's swarmed with wriggling sperm trying to fertilise it?

Yeah. It looked like that.

That was an image I didn't think I'd get out of my head for a while.

"Anything?" Eilidh asked. "If you don't come up with something soon, I'm going to stab it again."

Beyond the lounge, I could hear others moving upstairs —what had taken them so long to get up was anyone's guess. What kind of person heard screams and just rolled over in bed?

"Hold on," I said, trying to shake off the sudden wooziness.

Something that quest text had said.

Nominally alive—they are closest to a fungus, in Earth terms—they are connected to their summoner with threads of spirit and will that allow them to relay information.

Just before the spell flickered out, I saw it, and I used one last pulse of Purifier to light it up. "There! Slice there!"

Eilidh didn't hesitate, bringing the sword down in a wide arc that looked like it would take off an inch or two of simulacrum—but instead, I *felt* as her blade ignited with Purifire again and severed what I had seen: triune threads of spirit longer than the other waving fronds that held taut where all the others dangled, wriggling.

The moment it was severed, the simulacrum flopped to the carpet like a deflated jellyfish after all.

Eilidh sucked in a ragged breath. "What did I just do?"

"You cut the strands of spirit the summoner was using to control it," I said, exhaustion hitting me like a wave.

I half walked, half lurched to the torn upholstery of the sofa, collapsing on a pile of fluff and ragged fabric.

Diana had Andy cradled to her chest, and tears ran down her cheeks. "You said you could heal him?"

She asked the question with a break in her voice, like tectonic plates had cracked down the middle.

"I'll need to wait a minute," I said to her. "That—took a lot out of me."

Andy whimpered in her arms, his right shoulder at an unnatural slump, hand dangling limp. Dislocated.

My head throbbed—I must have come dangerously close to bottoming out even my hugely increased capacity. My notifications pulsed gold in my peripheral vision, and in the haze of the blooming headache, I craned my neck, wishing fervently I had some sort of indicator for my spirit usage. Every game I'd ever played had a heads-up display, a HUD, and this wasn't a game, but it was enough like one that it seemed stupid not to have some sort of indicator. I futilely tried to will one into existence.

Maybe not so futile. Just like that, a blue bar appeared in my vision.

"What the—" I breathed out the words, then winced. The bar was nearly empty even after having a bit of recovery time, pulsing an angry rhythm that screamed *danger*. "Might need more than a few minutes. I've almost no spirit left."

Eilidh, on the other hand, had remained where she stood, her sword still in her hands and her eyes fixed on the far wall.

"What is she doing?" Diana asked. "Can't she help with Andy?"

"I don't think she has the healing spell I do," I said apologetically. "And I think she's probably just hit level three and is choosing her class."

I had to admit, I was curious to see what she would pick, but now that my spirit bar was recovering infinitesimally, my mind had cleared enough to take in Diana's face. Tears.

The way she clung to Andy—and the way he shook quietly from pain.

Suddenly, I didn't think it was the pain from his dislocated shoulder.

"What happened before we got here?" I asked slowly.

Diana's throat bobbed as she swallowed, and when she spoke again, her voice cracked. "My Donald—Anna—"

She broke off, and my heart crunched. *No. Please no.*

"Grandpa tried to shoot it," Andy burst out. "He tried to shoot it, and the bullet—and the bullet—"

I thought of the way the sword had just bounced right off the damn thing. Like flinging a rubber ball against a fucking trampoline with the explosive force of a rifle behind it.

Fuuuuck.

"Both of them?" I asked quietly.

Diana drew a shuddering breath. "The gun didn't work at first, but he must have figured out how to make it go off with his magic. I wish he hadn't. The first round ricocheted and hit Anna—neither of us even . . . neither of us even saw at first. His second was dead on and rebounded to hit him right in the heart."

I let out an explosive gust of air. "I'm so sorry. I'm so, so sorry. This—this is our fault if it followed us here."

Shaking her head violently, Diana turned a flinty gaze on me, and again, the no-nonsense Highland woman was back. "Don't you dare take this on, son," she said. "You had nowt to do with it."

Eilidh chose that moment to come out of her notifications haze, and she turned to look at the room, her gaze taking in the tears at a glance. Inexplicably, she looked to me, a question in her eyes. I gave her a curt nod.

"Whoever sent that thing," Diana said after a moment, "wasn't just looking for you two."

"What makes you say that?" Eilidh asked slowly.

"Because it went straight for my Donald." Diana met my gaze. "Like it was looking for him."

FIFTEEN

I told the others about the HUD once my spirit recovered enough to heal poor wee Andy, who took it like a champ with a grimace and an alarming crack of his joint, but then he relaxed in relief. I was just thankful my level up had allowed me to use it before the twenty-four-hour cooldown ticked down.

Diana and Andy both spaced out for a moment after that as they clearly tried to add their own spirit bars—and I added a health bar as well, red per what I'm used to—but Eilidh just raised an eyebrow at me.

"You didn't know that?" she asked, bemused. "Seanmhair figured that out the first day."

"It's not like this goddamn system comes with an instruction manual," I said, irritated. "There's not *actually* a tutorial or anything."

Then I realised maybe I should be watching the swearing, since Andy was probably thirteen—not that I thought *he'd* care, but Diana also didn't seem fazed. I guessed a few curse words were far less important than the immediate grief of losing her husband and daughter.

Fuck.

"You should check your own notifications," Eilidh said after a moment, changing the subject. She frowned, her eyebrows pressing together in a pensive expression.

That didn't sound good, but she was probably right. I was growing even more curious about her class, but since she didn't seem to be eager to share, I let it lie.

Quest updated: The Hills Have Eyes

You have discovered a second simulacrum. Simulacra are used most frequently as communication entities. Nominally alive—they are closest to a fungus, in Earth terms—they are connected to their summoner with threads of spirit and will that allow them to relay information. They are not, however, intelligent, nor are they autonomous. They must be clearly directed, and if not, they will cause alarm quite by accident.

The summoner is yet unversed in the particulars of such magic. You have managed to sever the second simulacrum you found from its summoner, defusing the threat and buying yourself some time. While this causes no immediate harm to the summoner, they will *know they have lost their connection to one of their entities, and they will likely not be happy with you.*

Additionally, because of the nature of the relationship, it is very likely that the summoner knows your location. Prudence would advise you make haste to remove yourself from your current whereabouts.

I stopped reading at that, muttering a "motherfucker" under my breath. Distantly, I was aware of Eilidh murmuring to Diana and Andy, likely filling them in.

Objectives:
-Investigate the simulacrum's origin
-Find out the summoner's name
-Find out the summoner's purpose
Rewards:

-Experience (commensurate with current level progression)
-1 skill point
-1 item (as ascension permits)
-All cooldowns reset

Hmph. Nothing new there, though that wasn't particularly surprising.

There were more notifications.

Through arcane exertion, you have gained a permanent +2 to Spirit and +1 to Will. Please note that such increases have diminishing returns as your base statistics grow.

Oh, thank the gods.

You have disabled a simulacrum.
While such things cannot be harvested, because they contain no resources, they can be useful to study in and of themselves. Perhaps a closer look is merited.

Didn't have to tell me twice.

I shook myself out of my notifications, concentrating on the simulacrum. I triggered Connection again, surprised to see that the unnerving sperm-and-egg impression was still there—all it was missing was the tether of spirit that had connected it to the summoner.

Part of me was curious to see if I could take it over, but

my first attempt slipped off of it like a sheep's buttered hooves on ice.

But Connection showed something else, something intriguing.

Just as I had suspected when we discussed going back to the horse's field to track the first simulacrum, the place where Eilidh's sword had severed the threads of spirit maintained a . . . disturbance, for lack of a better word. The wriggling tails of the simulacrum all seemed to avoid that one part.

I wondered . . .

Gingerly, I stepped towards the thing, ignoring that Eilidh's voice broke off at my movement.

I didn't really want to touch it—and I wasn't sure if it would be dangerous to—so I summoned my Purifire again to coat my hands as a buffer. Maybe overkill, maybe not. My spirit bar, which had been climbing past sixty percent, dropped back to forty.

"This had better be worth it," I muttered.

I reached out and picked up the simulacrum. About the size of a half-deflated football, it felt like picking up a sticky ball of slime. Or whatever that borax mixture is that my mum made for me when I was in school, but softer and more . . . bouncy.

There seemed to be no ill effects.

I moved slightly in the direction where the tether had stretched.

A flare of triumph went through me.

The wriggling threads of spirit? They parted down the middle of the simulacrum, drawing an unmistakable straight line in the direction of the summoner.

· (ᘓ) ·

"You want to do what?" Eilidh said once I placed the squishy not-a-fungus back on the floor and told her and the others what I'd seen.

"Track the thing from here," I said shortly. "We need to leave anyway—you saw the quest update—and Diana and Andy aren't safe here either."

At that, Eilidh nodded. Grudgingly, but she nodded. "They can go to my seanmhair's," she said. "Safety in numbers."

"You said you have other guests here?" I asked this of Diana, and her answering nod was tight.

"Aye. They didn't see fit to come down to help, it seems, but I'll not leave them to face one of those things alone."

The shock seemed to have finally hit Andy, who was looking back and forth between me and his grandmother with wide-eyed fear. "We're leaving?"

His pubescent voice cracked, but he didn't seem to notice.

"We've got to, love," Diana said to him. "It's not safe."

"I wish I could tell you Seanmhair's is safe," Eilidh said, "but I can't promise that either. What I can promise you is that she knows the land better than anyone in a ten-mile radius, and if anyone has a shot at getting through this mess, it's her."

"Aye, I've known her for most of my life," Diana said. "We've fallen out of touch in the past ten years or so, but you're right. Not right for her to be alone right now, anyway. We'll leave at first light."

I nodded, seeing Andy's tears spill over, though he blinked them away, scrubbing at his cheeks with the back of his hand.

Diana squeezed his shoulder—the left one, though the

right one was healed now—and glanced at me. "I'm going to go wake the guests," she said, ice entering her tone.

"If they give you any trouble, let us know," I said, surprised as much by the steel in my own voice as by the sudden sharp nod from Eilidh.

"Yes," Eilidh said. "Do."

"I'm sorry I took your sword," Andy blurted out. "I—I just wanted to look at it."

"What did you learn?" Eilidh asked him.

"What?"

"What did you learn about it?"

The kid blinked, looking at me as if for help, but I'd no idea what she was asking, so I just shrugged.

"It's heavier than it looks," he said. "And swinging it is *hard*."

"Anything else?" She asked the follow-up question blandly, but a smile tugged at the corner of her mouth.

"It's more effective against sofas than . . . those sim—simile—"

"Simulacra," I supplied, stifling a chuckle. "And yes, that is a fair assessment."

The world seemed to crash back in on the kid with that, and he darted a glance at Eilidh, then back to me. "I should —I should go get ready to go."

With that, he fled, leaving me and the tall, auburn-haired woman alone in the wrecked lounge.

"This was our fault, no matter what Diana says," Eilidh said after a beat. "We led that thing here."

"I know." I glanced out the window, where the sky was starting to turn grey with the approaching dawn. "So we better fix it."

· ‹ ⟨⟨⟩⟩ › ·

I did not love hauling the simulacrum with me. It felt like it was going to turn to jelly in my hands, but as we walked, it functioned like a compass.

A really, really gross compass.

One that, naturally, pointed straight out over the waters of Loch Awe, which meant wherever we were going was on the other bloody side.

"You can really see where we're supposed to be going in that—that thing?" Eilidh blurted out an hour into the trek, just as the sun was starting to cast shadows across the hills.

"Aye," I said, grimacing as I shifted the thing in my hands.

At least it wasn't heavy. Even so, walking through the highlands and holding something out in front of me was getting old quick, preternaturally enforced strength or not.

When I didn't elaborate, Eilidh scoffed, an irritated sound that in turn irritated me.

"What do you expect me to say? You don't have the skill, so it's kind of pointless for me to say anything. And it's not like you're being particularly forthcoming—you've not even mentioned your class," I said.

Maybe it was the lack of sleep, the rude awakening, or just the fact that I'd ended up tramping through the bloody mountains with someone only slightly above my ex's shit-stain of a new boyfriend on my list of people I wanted to spend the apocalypse with: my ex's best fucking friend.

I could almost feel her gaze sharpen into literal daggers. If she picked a class that allowed looks to actually kill, I reckoned I was about to find out in three . . . two . . . one . . .

But I didn't drop dead, and she also didn't say anything, so instead, I just continued walking and wishing for the ground to open up and swallow both of us whole.

We'd been moving steadily away from Oban, circling

around the head of Loch Awe in the opposite direction to the one I wanted to head in, which was not taking the sour edge off my mood.

Another hour put us directly opposite Kilchurn Suites, and I caught Eilidh doing the same as me: casting a glance over the water to see if, by some freak of magical eyesight, she could tell if Diana and Andy had gotten away okay. Smoke rose from the chimney, but that wasn't anything particularly unusual. I doubted Diana had invited the guests to come along, so it was likely one of them who'd started a fire.

Eilidh doggedly looked back to the road when she saw the path of my own gaze.

Only to stop short as I triggered Connection again, nodding in the direction it wanted us to go.

"Shit," she said.

"What?"

"I know where it's going."

I stared at her. "How would you possibly know that?"

She pointed overland in the direction I'd nodded. The heather and gorse were all still winter browned, the meagre forests not much better looking.

"There's only one place that way before you hit Lochan Shira, and if money still meant anything at all, I'd bet you a hundred quid it's the manor."

Oh, no.

Eilidh's cheeks were flushed with the exertion of our quick walking pace, but I thought it was anger that mottled the pale skin of her neck, and this time, I was in complete agreement.

"Lord Bawbag," I muttered.

"*What?*" Eilidh sputtered in reply.

"Lord Edwin Thomas Sackington, fifth in his line of

absolute cuntwaffles, also known in absolute revulsion as Lord Bawbag."

The guffaw that escaped her had to be the first time I'd heard her make anything resembling a laugh in ages—I think the last five times I saw her before the world ended, she looked like she was attending her mother's funeral.

The thought made me wince.

Her laugh was short lived, though she shook her head after a moment. "I can't believe I'd never heard that before."

"Catrìona hates that man so much, I half expected her to set fire to his house the last time he tried to buy up more land around Oban," I said. "I think it was her idea."

"He's actually Satan."

"He's worse. He's a Scottish landlord."

"Careful, a Chaluim," Eilidh said. "Your feeling is showing."

I rolled my eyes, stifling the strange pang that came along with her using the Gaelic address. She didn't seem to even notice she'd done it. "I'll try to bottle it up tighter."

"In this case, by all means, let it fly free."

It was my turn to let out a dry laugh. "If that's the enemy we've made, what do we do next?"

"I'm not saying I'm more inclined to murder him, but I'm not *not* saying that either." Eilidh's fingers looked like they were itching towards the daggers on her belt.

Where to start with Lord Bawbag's crimes? The fact that he'd made it nearly impossible for anyone who wasn't a millionaire to build a home in driving distance of Oban? The fact that he strutted about in a kilt whenever he had the chance but actively campaigned to further depopulate the Highlands so he could build golf courses? The dirty money? The fact that he never paid his taxes? The laundry list of accusations of sexual harassment? The way he told us our language was useless? The reports of his corporation actually using slave labour in Kazakhstan? How somehow, *just somehow*, any actual prosecution of his crimes magically vanished at the wave of his powerful, nepotistic pals' hands?

Yeah, if it took killing the bastard, I'd roast him on a fucking spit.

CHAPTER

SIXTEEN

T hat, as it turned out, was a little more difficult than it might sound.

After our few minutes of cathartic shared rage—possibly the only emotion Eilidh and I had ever shared in the entirety of our acquaintance—we formulated a simple plan: reconnaissance.

Which *was* simple.

Embarrassingly simple.

So simple, we made it all the way up to one of the manor's side doors with no one the wiser . . . only to discover the place was absolutely *teeming* with people we didn't actually want to murder.

One glance through the window showed at least five or six people, all of them moving, all of them busy. None of them, thankfully, were paying any attention to the windows, and in another second, I figured out why.

It was only with my instinctive activation of Connection that I caught the tripwire of spirit threaded right up against the hedge we were about to sneak behind, and I grabbed Eilidh by the claymore on her back and yanked, juggling the simulacrum in my other hand.

Thankfully, Eilidh had the presence of mind not to make more than a scuff on the gravel beneath our feet, but I'd barely gotten her back from the thread of spirit when footsteps crunched just around the corner of the house.

Eilidh's blue-grey eyes widened, and, after a quick glance, she bolted in the opposite direction, where a pristine Hummer sat, polished and utterly useless, at the edge of the drive.

She dived behind it, and I followed, heart racing.

Looking for one shithead wannabe feudalist was one thing. Facing him and a fucking army was something else entirely.

My mind sorted through that glimpse into the manor. It looked like what would have been the old servant quarters or something of that ilk, and it was full of weapons.

I'd known Lord Bawbag had a hard-on for guns, but I guess I'd been too naïve to realise he'd have an entire illegal arsenal.

Reckon the whole "makes his fortune on illegal slave labour" ought to have been a clue.

"Bad enough the bastard's suddenly got creepy spy jellyfish magic, but who the fuck does he think he is? Alan Rickman in *Die Hard*?" I whispered the words barely above a breath, and Eilidh rolled her eyes.

"You know he'd think he was Bruce Willis," she murmured in response.

Touché.

An idea struck me.

"Watch for anyone coming," I said. "I want to try something."

A quick glance around told me no one was nearby

except a pair of starlings, who sat on the edge of the perfectly manicured grass not far away from the Hummer's front bumper, cocking their heads at me and occasionally chirping to each other.

Eilidh's terse nod said she was paying attention, and I sucked in a deep breath, holding the simulacrum in both hands. The thing had an odd sort of weight, not unlike I'd imagine a jellyfish to feel if it had more density.

Drawing on my spirit to cast Connection, I looked carefully at the simulacrum. Holding it with Connection active was a bad idea—those wriggling threads of spirit that looked so much like worms were now fanned out around my fingers, and I had to fight the impulse to fling the thing into the grass.

I rotated it slightly to expose the bit I was looking for. Still visible amid the other squiggles was the frayed cord that had tethered this thing to Lord Bawbag.

We were making an assumption that that was who was responsible for it, but I didn't think it was the wrong assumption. This was his home, and the flag peeking up above the eaves said the family was in residence, and I couldn't imagine he would have ceded control to anyone. As much as the guy worshipped the status quo, I wouldn't put it past him to toss the late queen herself out on her arse, not to mention the son that succeeded her.

And knowing this guy's reputation, he'd probably cop a feel even with royalty, though it didn't seem like his tastes ran to the likes of kings.

As I probed at the simulacrum, I could almost catch an edge of the man's magic, like an undefinable odour at the back of my nose. I've never been able to stand incense because it has always struck me as smelling of death. Some ineffable, cloying heaviness beneath the frankincense or patchouli or resins, something that clung to the scent receptors in my nostrils and wouldn't be dislodged.

This felt like that.

And just like that cloying odour, it escaped my clumsy, grasping spirit.

I wasn't sure it was even possible to recreate the connection—so maybe it would be best to try to forge my own.

I reached out gingerly with my spirit, triggering Connection again to act as a guide. Trying to picture the way the weave had looked before we severed it, I felt my well of spirit dip as I spooled together threads of magic in an attempt to replicate it, reaching out from my centre to the entity in my hands.

For a moment, I thought it had worked. The threads mingled with the frayed edges of the cut cord like an anemone rippling with the presence of its resident clownfish.

But then it discovered I wasn't the clownfish, but an intruder.

The edges of the cord I had stretched out to the simulacrum stung like I'd touched a bug zapper with my bare fingers—or with a guitar string that conducted that zap straight into the core of my being.

I bit down hard on the inside of my cheek to keep from yelling, fighting a wave of exhaustion as my spirit whooshed out of me like a spilled pint, sloshing around the simulacrum before soaking back into the surrounding aether.

Eilidh's head had turned sharply with my movement, and now she stared at me, lips parted, but she didn't say anything. I stared back for the space of a breath or two, forgetting in my sudden dizziness everything except the fullness of her bottom lip and the way her mouth turned downward with concern.

I shook myself out of it and gave her a tight shake of my head to say my attempt hadn't worked.

A chirp behind her made her jump, and I peered over her shoulder to see the pair of starlings watching us, now barely a meter away. One cocked its head at us, and I felt a ripple of spirit.

"No way," I breathed.

Like the simulacrum, when I used my still-recovering spirit to trigger Connection one more time, I saw the starlings' own threads of spirit. But unlike the simulacrum, which wriggled and squirmed, theirs flowed. Cohesive. Controlled.

On instinct, I reached out with my own, feeling where that indiscernible spot in my chest still buzzed with the aftershocks of the last attempt's recoil, but this time, something reached *back*.

With a trill, the closest starling launched into the air, swooping towards me fast enough that I felt the brush of its wingtips against my unruly hair, and the wind of its passing followed.

And then the world fell away.

The sensation unnerved me. I was still crouched next to the ridiculous Hummer with Eilidh, could feel the warmth of her presence beside me even as I saw her below me, blue-grey eyes turned towards the sky—towards the starling.

With a blink and the flutter of wind, it was like my consciousness divided. As the starling soared out of sight above my head, I *saw through its eyes*.

The bird flitted to the window, where one of the people inside glanced at it briefly, then away again as they realised it was just a bird.

Soaring upwards, the starling curved around the first floor of the manor, then banked yet further to climb towards the second. It swooped around to the front of the manor house, coming to rest on a wrought-iron widow's walk in front of an open pair of French doors.

Gauzy curtains whispered in the breeze.

My focus was so wholly on the bird's vision that I almost missed Eilidh's none-too-gentle poke into my deltoid.

"What just happened?" she hissed.

I shushed her with a finger to my lips, pointing to the house. "The bird lent me its eyes."

She just mouthed *what*?

I ignored her.

Lord Bawbag sat on an ottoman at the foot of an enormous four-poster bed, peering into a basket at his feet with a smirk on his face.

The man was, among his many horrid traits, known for his outward attractiveness. He'd graced the cover of many a fashion magazine, because he had that sort of square-jawed symmetry that threatened to slice you open with the angles of his face. If he weren't so putrid inside, he'd likely have actually managed to marry a supermodel, but the last one he dated was, as far as I knew from office gossip discussing it, the latest in the very long list of his accusers and had been forced into seclusion by his stans after they got her SWATted.

Real mensch.

Naturally, as the starling's eyes darted about the room, that meant they showed something completely out of character.

In the basket he was preening over? A tiny tabby kitten.

CHAPTER
SEVENTEEN

"Okay, what the fuck," I muttered—too loudly, judging by the elbow I took to the ribs from Eilidh.

As soon as she was satisfied I wasn't going to make any other noises, she edged over to the front of the car, peering around the bumper.

I tried to keep my words lower than the whisper of the wind. "All he's doing is sitting up in his room with a kitten in a basket."

At that, Eilidh turned to look at me over her shoulder. "A kitten."

"A tabby kitten," I murmured. "Big eyes, much floof, typical number of ears and a little stick tail, so it's very young. Probably just old enough to have its eyes open."

A crunch of gravel smashed through my calm, and Eilidh scrambled back half a step. How she managed not to make any noise herself, I'll never know.

Still, she leaned around the front end of the car, and I saw every single muscle in her neck tense at the same time.

Shit.

I still had the double vision—the literal bird's eye view

upstairs along with the rigid tension in Eilidh's posture—and when she reached back a hand and frantically mimed backing up, I acted as quickly as I could, though there's no world in which scuttling backward in a crab walk is smooth or graceful. It'd take more than magic to not look like a horse's arse.

The starling still sat there on the balcony upstairs, and I shunted it out of my mind for a moment, though I could still feel the threads of spirit that kept a low drain on my reserves, sort of like carrying a rucksack all day.

I'd just made it behind the Hummer's rear bumper when Eilidh practically landed on my lap. I craned my neck backwards to see if there was anyone in my line of sight. No one, though in front of us, the crunch of gravel continued as a burly man walked across the drive towards a stone path, carrying what looked like a large lump of fur in his left hand, obscured by his body.

The grating of boot on rough rock faded as he stepped onto the smoother slate of the path, heading for an outbuilding that lay just a bit further down, visible just before a small grove of trees rose up beyond.

Eilidh looked back at me once, then as soon as the man disappeared through the door of the outbuilding, she darted forwards.

I cursed to myself, following and all too aware that she somehow made less noise on the gravel than I did.

She avoided the stone path, sticking to the grass, but there was no cover here. Anyone who so much as peeked out one of the side windows of the house would see us moving—the one thing we had going for us was that there were a lot of people around. Hopefully a couple unfamiliar faces wouldn't cause an attack-on-sight sort of impulse.

The outbuilding was a shed about the size of a normal

person's garage, though it clearly wasn't meant for cars. It had no windows on this side except for the one in the door, which showed light within.

I followed Eilidh around the side of the building, crouching to avoid the one medium window on the southern wall.

"What are you doing?" I whispered to her once we'd stopped and my breathing had resumed a more normal pace.

"I want to know what *he's* doing," she said after a beat where I thought she might not even answer. "He's got— ugh, I don't know. Something's *wrong* with him."

"What do you mean?" I asked her slowly.

She shrugged, shifting her shoulders as if trying to dislodge a knot and tucking a lock of her wavy auburn hair behind her ear. Eilidh was perspiring a bit, either from exertion or nerves—or both—and her hair had curled away from her scalp to form a tiny ringlet just in front of her ear, which her movement had missed.

First her lips, now a curl. *Get it together, you useless hamster,* I thought to myself viciously.

"It's a class thing," Eilidh muttered after a moment, her pale cheeks flushing pink. "Just . . . trust me on this."

I was momentarily distracted by the starling on the balcony, which shifted in a small flurry of movement, and instantly, I was tugged back to its view. Lord Bawbag was standing now, gesturing imperiously at the kitten in the basket.

A young woman, probably barely out of secondary school, stood a few feet away from him, holding . . . a baby bottle?

After an apprehensive moment where both Bawbag and the woman said something I either couldn't clearly hear or just couldn't understand through the ears of a bird, the woman moved over to the basket, deliberately taking up a spot on the opposite side to Lord Bawbag.

Why the fuck would he have a kitten too young to be weaned? He did not strike me as the rescue type.

The sharp thwack to my shoulder smacked me back to my own point of view.

"Look," Eilidh said, practically grabbing me by the scruff of the neck like I was a kitten myself.

I shrugged off her hand, rising just enough to peek over the edge of the windowsill.

The man had the lump of fur on a wide workbench—and a knife with a blood-red smear on the blade. Facing towards us was a long, plush, blunt-tipped tail capped with black.

My mother worked in wildlife rescue and rehab—because of that, while she was alive, I got to see all sorts of Scottish animals up close and personal. And one of them in particular was nearly extinct—the last remaining indigenous feline in the isles.

Eilidh said it before I could. "That's not just any kitten Lord Bawbag has. That's a Scottish wildcat."

I was too shocked at what I was seeing to register that she had also managed to identify the cat. Due to cross-breeding with ferals, it's notoriously difficult to tell at a glance, but the biggest giveaway was the tail. Domestic cats' tails generally taper to a point unless the cat is long haired; Scottish wildcats are sleek and plush, and their tails are wider at the tip than at the base. Even from the window, I could see the lack of the dorsal line, the distinct black banding on the tail, and the telltale—telltail?—black tip.

The man spun the dead creature around with a practised ease.

I knew the exact moment Eilidh saw the wound to the cat's skull, because she hissed in a breath at the same time I did.

It was the fucking apocalypse and this scabbed-over pustule was shooting critically endangered cats for sport? With an arrow, no less. There was a still-bloody arrow on the workbench as if waiting its turn to be cleaned.

For a bare moment, the world faded to static and rage, that in a world where I'd seen humans pulped on the road in the middle of the highlands by some untold monster, humans were still trying to fuck things up even more.

Footsteps crunched on the gravel behind us.

Both Eilidh and I jumped, and she hit her head on the corner of the windowsill even as I practically clothes-lined her to shove her around the back corner of the shed.

I couldn't see over towards the house, and as Eilidh rubbed her head, both of us froze when another unmistakable sound joined the footsteps.

Hooves.

The steady *clop-clop* of a horse walking across the drive.

I threw myself into the connection with the starling, which had already left the balcony, and I soon saw why: Lord Bawbag was on the move.

As the starling flitted back towards us, the man emerged from the house, sleeves rolled up on his two-hundred-quid shirt, looking as if he'd been waiting his whole life to punt the world back into the nineteenth century.

He carried a riding crop in his left hand, and around him scurried a handful of people, clearly servants.

He said something to them, and again, maybe because everything I was interpreting came through a literal bird-brain, I couldn't understand the words that came out of his mouth. But he mounted the horse with practiced ease, taking the reins and setting off immediately at a good clip, heading down the drive away from the house.

"Shit," I muttered to Eilidh. "Bawbag's leaving on horseback."

Ironically, with our new Strength and Agility, we might very well be able to catch up, but watching the starling soar above the winding drive, I realised the folly of that thought. The same magic that had twisted and mutated some creatures had clearly acted upon the horse—and likely the starling too. Humans weren't the only animal to grow hardier, as I saw when the horse picked up speed.

Lord Bawbag let out a whoop, clearly exulting with the rhythm of the horse's movement. The horse itself was a gorgeous Arabian, an oak-brown mare with a smooth gait, and that was about all I knew about horses in one glance.

Seeing the asshole happy on an afternoon ride in the highlands made me want to scream.

I mean, sure, even horrible human beings could take pleasure in good things. In fact, there was a war-mongering dictator to the east who was known to have a penchant for endangered cats and horseback rides himself, for fuck's sake.

Maybe Lord Bawbag was just emulating a hero.

Ugh.

Tempted as I was to have the starling continue to track him, I could feel the small bird's interest and energy waning, and I released the thread of spirit, feeling a residual burst of emotion from the bird that I could only conceptualise as *happy-help-hungry* as it flew away to find something to eat.

The dual-vision sensation faded, leaving me feeling strangely bereft. I turned to Eilidh.

"He's gone for now. What do you want to do?"

Glancing around us, I could see no other movement. The stables seemed to be in the other direction, but due to the trees that cradled the shed we hid behind, I could barely make it out a couple hundred meters away.

I thought of the kitten, up in that house in its basket, its mother drawn and quartered on the other side of the wall.

Eilidh looked pensive and a bit unmoored, not so different to how I felt.

A shout broke the air, and both of us spun towards it.

Then something blasted into me from the side.

My head slammed against the wall of the shed, and I knew nothing.

CHAPTER
EIGHTEEN

The first thing I smelled upon waking was blood and offal.

Eilidh sat against a wall—fuck, we were inside the shed we'd been hiding behind—half slumped with a trickle of blood running down her left temple. On the wall was a sick imitation of a Rorschach test where she'd apparently pressed her bleeding head against the wall, leaving an imprint of her skin and eyebrow.

Her bottom lip was fat and swollen on the left side, and her left eye had the painful blue-red of a fresh shiner, which had to mean we hadn't been out long.

I couldn't feel much that indicated I'd been treated as roughly, and when I met her eyes, I saw no relief in them— only pure, unbridled rage.

"What happened?" I asked her. A stupid question, but considering all I knew was that I'd gotten knocked out, she seemed to at least have slightly more information by virtue of having been smacked around with it. I winced, adding hastily, "Are you okay?"

"Peachy," she said, her tone about as warm as a glacier. "We were captured."

"Aye, that much I worked out, thanks."

Rope cut into my wrists, and my shoulders felt tight where they'd been wrenched back to bind me while I was unconscious. The dagger at my waist was gone, and Eilidh had been relieved of her claymore and blades alike.

The room smelled like death.

When I looked over, the wildcat pelt was stretched on a tanning rack, its tail dangling, lifeless.

"They knocked you out with one punch," Eilidh said after a moment. "To be fair, it was a hell of a punch—for a second, I thought they'd crushed your skull. The bloke who hit you was built like a brick shithouse and not half as cute."

The corner of her mouth twitched, pulling at the swollen lip, but she didn't seem to notice the pain.

"I took a couple chunks out of him before his friend tackled me," she said fiercely.

Something about her seemed different. I didn't think anything worse than getting beaten up had happened to her in the time I'd been knocked out, but the tension I'd seen building in her as we'd clumsily snuck around the manor had crystallised.

"They're keeping us here until Lord Bawbag comes back to 'deal with us,'" Eilidh added. "Much as I wish I were able to absolutely fuck these assholes up from captivity, if you've any ideas for how we can get my sword back and be anywhere *not* here when Bawbag gets here, I'm all ears."

"Aye, it'd be nice to pull a Rorschach," I muttered, gaze pulled to the inkblot of blood beside her head.

Eilidh twisted to see where I was looking. After a moment, her blue eyes met mine, unblinking, and a tight smile drew back her lips. "I'd love if I could confidently say we're more dangerous to them than they are to us, but that feels a little overly optimistic."

At that, I felt a mirthless smile tug at my own lips. She'd clearly gotten my reference without missing a beat. I'd forgotten she loved graphic novels—that was one of the few things I'd learned about her from Susanna, though from Susanna, it'd come as teasing that in retrospect did not seem like the friendly type.

"Well," I said, shaking myself from my concussion-induced reverie. Sure, we'd call it that. "They seem to have thought that dagger was my only weapon. And they clearly forgot something."

"What did they forget?"

"It's a brave new world," I said. "We may not be super-heroes, but I *am* a weapon."

Now that I'd woken up and my high Constitution had helped heal the concussion, my brain started to clear.

Whoever these bampots were before the apocalypse, they were clearly as out of their depth as we were. It'd only been a handful of days since things went to shit; they clearly were neither used to nor expecting magic.

Which meant that the ropes they used to bind us? Yeah, just normal ropes, and my Purifire burnt through them with ease.

Both of us took a few minutes to stretch once we were free. Enhanced healing or not, being thrown unceremoni-ously in a shed with your limbs bound together roughly was not pleasant on the joints.

As we regrouped, Eilidh told me they'd taken the

weapons with them and had said something about wards, which meant someone around us *did* have some magic ability, but I highly doubted it was much. There just hadn't been enough time for people to become really adept with things. If I were to trust my hunch, it would say that Lord Bawbag was the most studious of them—that he'd commanded the simulacra said enough, but even that was clumsy and untrained.

This was probably as equal as things were going to get from here on out, which meant we had a small window to do something while we had the chance.

First up was checking our blaring notifications.

Quest updated: The Hills Have Eyes

You have discovered the source of the simulacra. Lord Edwin Thomas Sackington seems to have taken to the ascension with alacrity, using it to immediately consolidate his local power.

Until Earth, all ascending worlds were subject to a rigorous approval process, initiated by the inhabitants themselves, in which they would need to prove that they could meet intergalactic standards for access to the power ascension inherently provides. Part of this is living peaceably with one's own species—and with the wider world. Contrary to popular belief, abuse of power is not inevitable—and ascending worlds know this.

Earth, however, is an anomaly and a cosmic accident of epic proportions. Unprepared and unvetted except for the certainty that your planet was not and is not qualified to enter the universal community, the ascension has created a dangerous phenomenon that, in time, could prove to be a threat to the peace of the universe itself.

Lord Sackington is a ready example of such a danger.

In the pre-ascended world, he made sport of his fellows, treated humans like worse than animals and treated animals like toys. A being such as him in an ascended world must not be allowed to grow in power.

You must discover his purpose and thwart him at all costs. This quest has become an evolving quest, subject to change upon completion pending results.

Objectives:

-Investigate the simulacrum's origin (Complete)

-Find out the summoner's name (Complete)

-Escape captivity

-Regain your weapons

-Find out the summoner's purpose

-Rescue the Scottish wildcat kitten (Optional)

Rewards:

-Experience (commensurate with current level progression)

-1 skill point

-1 item (as ascension permits)

-All cooldowns reset

Balls.

I knew if I started ruminating on that information, I would probably spiral into a fucking mess, so I hurriedly pulled up my other notifications.

Through arcane exertion, you have gained a permanent +2 to Spirit and +3 to Will. Please note that such increases have diminishing returns as your base statistics grow.

. . .

Through arcane experimentation, you have unlocked the Tàthadh skill tree.

Through analysis and application of observation, you have unlocked a new ability: Tàth.

Goddamn. This was the second time I'd managed to unlock a new ability without using a skill point, and I could not wait to see the new skill tree. The Gaelic word meant to bond, to solder, to connect. It had to be what I'd done with the starling. Had to be.

The tree expanded in my view, and it brought with it a small flare of disappointment.

I hadn't managed to unlock something up the trunk of the tree this time, but seeing one of the root skills highlighted was still gratifying.

Damn, I wished I had a skill point. Tàth was obviously the one that was lit up, but the others also looked amazing. One of them in particular, Caidreabhas, seemed like actually bonding an animal companion. Permanently.

It wouldn't immediately be super powerful, but it was a bond that would deepen with time, and that was so tempting it practically made my brain itch.

I forced myself to pull away from that tree. What was it Iain and Meeksy would say? They were both into meditation and existing in the present moment. Abundance over scarcity—concentrating on what they had here and now.

I could do that. I looked at the next notification.

. . .

Through diligent use, you have increased the level of your skill: Connection (Level 2), Tàth (Level 2).

Tàth (Level 2)—This ability allows you to form a consensual bond with an animal, giving you the power to see through the animal's eyes and guide the creature's movements where necessary. These bonds, once created, will bring a consistent drain on spirit until released, but the benefits far outweigh the sacrifice. Tàth comes with a one-time bonus of +1 to Pathos.

Continued usage will improve the usefulness of these bonds, providing a symbiotic balance for both you and your companion. You gain eyes and ears and mobility—they gain intelligence, protection, and, in rare cases, special abilities.

"Holy shit," I muttered, quickly reading the changes to Tàth.

Your use has granted you a bonus to working with birds. While they still will not understand human language, they will now project their instinctual reactions to what they observe. This bonus is more effective the higher your Pathos.

Damn. My mind practically exploded with the pure potential of this growth—though that last bit filled me with dread. Pathos was the area I was weakest. I didn't want to think about that, so I eagerly moved over to Connection.

. . .

Connection (Level 2)—You gain a deeper affinity to the earth and its needs, and it whispers to you. With this skill, you are able to see how things around you interact, be it the tracks of a deer hunted by paw prints of a stalking cat or the passing of a band of hunters.

Increased use of this skill enables you to take in an entire scene at a glance and appropriately assess its secrets. Additionally, the skill will allow you to ascertain the needs of the natural world, giving you the power to aid creatures and plants that may one day return the favour.

Your use has granted you a bonus to clarity. Your ability to see and identify patterns has increased, and you are now 5% more likely to spot items of import, foes in stealth, and escape routes.

My mind fixated on those last two words.

I was starting to formulate a plan.

CHAPTER
NINETEEN

E ilidh still had that look of crystal clarity about her, face set and resolute.

"I think I have a skill that can help us now," she said after a moment, getting to her feet but staying away from the window. "I don't think they're guarding us."

I cast Connection, my vision immediately flooding with the new, level-two version.

It almost took my breath away. The differences were subtle, but they were profound. Where before I'd had to really squint and focus to see the flows of spirit around me, now they appeared to glow.

"They're not guarding us," I said, turning in a slow circle. "They're relying on the wards."

Like everything so far, they were crude, similar to the tripwire of spirit I'd pulled Eilidh back from at the manor. But now with Connection levelled up, I could see more than its mere existence. Threads of will wove in with the spirit, just small ones, barely enough to give it form and structure.

It ran around the whole of the shed like a one-ply single string around a parcel and about as useful.

The ward was just above knee level, and if my thought was correct, it had to be actively broken for it to signal the caster.

And even better? They'd cast it *outside* the walls. The door opened in.

A chuckle escaped me, and I shook my head, looking back to Eilidh, whose foot tapped impatiently.

"What's funny?" she asked blandly. "Or would you like me to share how I can help, since you were previously so critical of my failure to be forthcoming."

"By all means," I said, biting off a retort, though from her sniff, she had taken my reply as a retort anyway.

"It's a class skill," she said.

"You levelled up?"

"No." Eilidh gave me an irritated glance. "I saved a skill point when I chose my class just in case something went wrong, so I could pull something out of a hat in a pinch."

"Ah," I said.

"We need to figure out what Lord Bawbag plans to do, yeah?" She didn't wait for me to affirm it. "The skill is called Dearg-Fhìrinn. It means—"

"Whole truth," I said, irritation creeping up. "Tha Gàidhlig agam, for fuck's sake."

She blinked at me as if that were news that I spoke Gaelic, and while we had more important things to talk about—like a need to get the fuck out of here—for some reason, this of all things wedged itself under my fingernails like a splinter.

"Dh'ionnsaich mi aig glùn mo mhàthar i," I said sharply. "Mar a dh'ionnsaich thu fhèin i, tha mi creid'."

I learnt at my mother's knee. Just as you did, I believe.

For a moment, her face softened, but in a heartbeat, the stoic disdain was back. When she spoke again, she still spoke in English, going on as if I'd not interrupted, which dug that splinter in a bit further under my nail. "The skill makes me a—a magnet of truth. It's obviously at its lowest level, and with more use, I'll be able to *compel* the truth from people, but even as it is, it makes it harder for people to lie to me. Which means if we can get hold of one of Lord Bawbag's people . . ."

"We can find out his plan," I finished, and she gave me a grim nod. "Without resorting to torture."

I added the last bit with a sarcastic smile I hoped communicated that I wasn't actually considering torturing people, and she rolled her eyes.

"Torture literally doesn't work anyway. You almost never get the truth from it—they just tell you what you want to hear or feed you innocent people's names to make you stop the pain."

"Thank you, I had no idea," I said flatly.

"You're welcome."

Fucking—ugh.

If I had to spend much more time with this woman in an enclosed space, we might be more likely to become a danger to each other than anyone else. Which would be a Rorschach moment, of sorts, just the least useful of possible reenactments.

"So we get out, try to find your sword and the daggers, and then we try to catch one of Lord Bawbag's pet wankers," I said.

"Aye," Eilidh replied, "though if the shed's warded, that's your territory, if you can figure out how to get past their magic."

The doubt in her voice was far too obnoxious.

Instead of responding, I walked to the door, peeked out

the window, and, seeing no one, I cast Connection again to look at the lock.

Disgust warred with triumph.

It was only a fucking Yale lock. That's it. No deadbolt, no bar in front of the door. They had literally stuck us in a shed and closed the door and that was it.

I couldn't decide if it was pure folly or just a gross underestimate of our capabilities. I landed on both, like that *Road to El Dorado* meme. *Aye. Both is good.*

All I needed was pressure applied in the right way. I didn't need to pick the lock or anything.

And will was my strongest Manipulation stat by a mile.

I barely even had to think of it—no sooner had I formed the wedge of spirit and will when the lock clicked, and I yanked the door open and stepped over the ward line.

"You coming?" I said to Eilidh, unable to keep the snide bite from the words. "Make sure you step up and over or you'll set it off."

She looked about ready to vibrate into another plane of existence, and the now-yellowing bruises just made her look even more cheesed off, but she moved fluidly to the door and stepped over the threshold far more gracefully than her boiling fury would indicate.

"That was too easy," she muttered.

"Yes. It was." I gestured towards the manor. "That's the hard part."

"We should just fucking leave," she said. "To hell with this quest, these assholes, all of it."

But her voice had no real conviction, and she looked at me as if to dare me to say so.

I got it, though. "This isn't exactly how I wanted to spend my weekend either, don't worry."

When neither of us moved, I sighed.

"Look," I said. "I don't want to hurt anyone to finish this quest, and I don't love the idea of going after people just because we're told to. But I will defend myself if it comes to it."

"You think I won't?" Eilidh's eyes flashed dangerously.

"I didn't say that." I swallowed. "We already know at least a few of them aren't opposed to hitting first, asking questions later. We can stand around here debating ethics all day, but I'd rather *not* be here when Lord Bawbag gets back, and I think he's the most powerful of the lot. This is our shot to at least find up what he's up to, so at least we can tell others who might be able to help stop him."

From the frustration on her face, I thought she knew I was right and hated it. After a moment, she nodded, but then she glanced over her shoulder.

Without a word, she stepped back over the ward, moving into the shed and out of sight. Eilidh emerged again a moment later, taking the same amount of care not to trigger the ward, and she pulled the door closed behind her. The Yale lock engaged again with a *snick* of metal.

"What did you do?" I asked her.

At that, a sardonic smile crossed her face.

"Stole his trophy," she said, and for the barest moment, a flash of striped pelt and black-tipped tail appeared in her hand before vanishing back into her inventory. "Figured he doesn't deserve to keep it."

With that, she motioned to me, and I followed as she stalked towards the manor.

I couldn't quite suppress the flare of admiration—and the view of her purposeful stride from behind didn't hurt.

This time, we approached the manor from the side, under cover of the trees.

With a little luck, it would take them a while to realise we'd waltzed right out of their little cage. Until then, though, we waited, watching the house.

I pulsed Connection each time my spirit recovered to full again, seeing the eddies of it in the house. I didn't know how many people were inside, but I suspected at least twenty. When we'd come in, there had been six or seven in the one room we saw alone. Eilidh said it had been two men who attacked us, and they were likely the bruisers of the bunch. From her description, they were hired muscle and had probably punched every one of their new attribute points into Strength. I nursed a wee hope that that meant they'd neglected Constitution or Stamina or Mind, making them into glass cannons at best or barely active brain cells in a pinch, but I knew we couldn't count on that to save us.

Add to it the young servant I'd seen with the kitten as well as He Who Skins Cats and that was already over ten. We'd be stupid to bet on fewer than fifteen and foolish to assume it was fewer than twenty.

Twenty to two? Not exactly terrific odds.

"Chances of getting in there and finding what we need without being seen?" Eilidh asked.

"Slim to none."

She nodded, letting out a long sigh. "I think we can count on them being weaker than us for the most part, and I highly doubt Lord Bawbag would surround himself with servant fighters when he's such a dickweasel."

I snorted a laugh. "Probably an accurate assessment."

"That he's a dickweasel or that they're likely not all fighters?"

"Yes."

This time, it was her turn to snort a laugh.

"We could really use some kind of distraction," I muttered.

My gaze roamed over the surrounding estate, falling on the stable in the distance.

Eilidh followed my line of sight, then glanced curiously at me.

"I have a really bad idea," I said.

We both felt the press of time as we made our way to the stable through the woods, keeping out of sight as best as possible. I didn't think Lord Bawbag would be back in the immediate future, because magically enhanced horse or not, literal horsepower was no match for an engine, and anywhere he was trying to go would be at least a couple hours away.

Still, the longer we took, the more likely someone would pop out to the shed to check on us and realise we were gone.

I cast about with Connection as we approached the stable, the earthy smell of manure and animal musk filling the air with the breeze that drifted our way.

"Literally no one here," I said with satisfaction. "Five horses and the corral out back."

"What are you thinking?" Eilidh asked. "I don't think anyone would notice if we just let them all out."

"They might if we let them all out and then set the stable on fire," I said, kindling Purifire in my right palm and giving her a smirk I could feel was lopsided.

We reached the side door of the stable, and the knob turned easily in Eilidh's hand. I followed her in, watching as her thoughtful gaze settled upon a gorgeous grey-white Arabian gelding that had to be eighteen or nineteen hands tall. Absolute monster of a horse.

"Calum," she said absently. "I don't suppose you can ride, can you?"

"It's been a while," I said. "Like . . . twenty years a while."

"What do you weigh? About thirteen stone? Fourteen?"

"Smack in the middle of those two," I answered, nonplussed.

Eilidh nodded with satisfaction. "He'll be able to carry us both."

"You want us to steal a horse."

"I *want* us to get away from that asshole once we have what we need, and you can Doctor Doolittle this beauty into being our getaway car."

The horse snorted as if he was as offended at being called a car as I was to being called Doctor Doolittle.

But Eilidh did have a point.

"Okay," I said. "Let's do it. Here's the plan."

I ran her through my idea, and she barked a laugh once, poked a hole in a weak spot twice, and finally gave me a grudging nod of respect when I was finished.

"Don't take too long," she said over her shoulder as she set off deeper into the stable to do her bit, which was gathering as much flammable tinder as she could find in five minutes.

"I'll signal when it's time," I told her.

Once she was busy at her work, I took a deep breath, approaching the grey-white gelding with a little trepidation. What I hadn't mentioned to Eilidh was that the last time I was on a horse, the bastard had thrown me into a wall. I broke three ribs and tore a ligament in my back, which is partially why my mid-thirties arse had the spine of a sixty-year-old.

Or had before this apocalypse fixed it.

That thought was a little more heartening. At least if the horse threw me into another wall, I'd probably heal a lot quicker this time.

The horse watched me warily as I entered the stall with him, tossing his head but not retreating.

"Easy," I said. "You'll almost certainly prefer Eilidh to me, but I could use your help, if you're willing."

I took a deep breath, reaching out with spirit and weaving it into the shape my mind identified as Tàth. Something told me I wasn't supposed to use the more permanent bond here anyway even if I had spent the skill point for it, which I hadn't. I only needed enough to work together for now.

Like with the starling, I triggered Connection and could see the glowing energy that surrounded the horse. He was agitated, but not because of me—he practically burst with strength and vitality, a pent-up need to run dominating his being.

"I can work with that," I murmured, closing the distance between us.

I showed him what we wanted, projected the image of fire in the stable but all of the horses safely running into the hills, of him waiting for me and Eilidh amid the trees.

Unlike with the starling, there was hesitation. The bird had flitted to me on impulse, ready to take a chance, eager and curious. The Arabian gelding, on the other hand, felt tempted to the partnership but was uncertain—even the assurance that his herd would be safe was not quite enough.

And then, to my utter surprise, an image filled *my* mind

from the horse: the walnut-brown mare Lord Bawbag had taken.

I cursed internally.

The gelding would help us—on one condition.

We had to also steal Lord Bawbag's horse. It was the whole herd or none.

Which meant we would have to hide after phase one of our plan until the sentient bog scum returned.

For now, though, it was time for arson.

After fifteen minutes, we were ready to go, though both Eilidh and I shifted our weight uneasily as we got to the point of no return.

"It'll definitely get their attention," she said, "but who knows if it'll get *enough* of their attention to clear out the house."

"That's why I'm going to make it impossible to ignore," I said flatly.

"Oh, god, what are we doing?" Eilidh groaned, looking a little queasy.

"Brave new world," I said again. "Haven't you ever wanted to absolutely raze an arsehole's shit to the ground before? Think of this as your chance."

"Thank you," she said dryly. "Fantasising about calling down my wrath on the wanker elite and actually doing it are definitely the exact same thing."

"Glad I could help."

"You're so gracious. But that still doesn't count as a second emotion."

I feigned horror, and she rolled her eyes.

"Light show time," I said. "Let's go."

"You're sure the horses will get out of here?" Eilidh eyed the stalls as we walked back into the stable.

"I'm sure. The grey gelding wants the herd safe and free more than anything."

"At the extreme least, Lord Bawbag seems to take good care of them." Her eyes darkened as she glanced over her shoulder towards the manor. "Not that it's actually him taking care of them at all—but someone has shown them love."

Through the threads of spirit between me and the big grey, I felt a sense of fondness, the image of a few faces in my mind. People who brought him carrots and apples, people who brushed every inch of his coat, got a sharp rock out of his hoof, kept him warm in winter.

That thread also told me that those people weren't here. For some reason, that filled me with a certain amount of relief, which ricocheted back from the gelding's mind. He would have been less keen to help if there was any threat to his caretakers. His loyalty was something earned, and I hadn't earned it yet—but when I pictured the handsome Lord Bawbag with distaste, that came back tenfold. Though I couldn't see that he'd ever mistreated the horses, they distrusted him. A moment later, I got an image through the link of Bawbag battering a young lad senseless in view of the corral.

The sight left me queasy . . . but it also left me resolute.

"Ready?" I asked Eilidh, half including the gelding in the question.

"Aye," she said.

Without another word, we separated, walking down the middle of the stable and opening each gate to the stalls as we went. The grey was on my side, and he came out first, nudging my shoulder with his snout. He had to lean down quite a bit to do it. Massive beast.

"Thank you," I murmured to him.

He snorted, sending a small puff of hay-scented warm air past my nose.

One by one, we opened the stalls, and when we reached the big door that opened into the corral, all nine of the horses followed. Eilidh kept looking over her shoulder as we hauled the main doors open together.

"Unreal," she said under her breath.

Out in the corral, there was one large gate on the far side that opened into a pasture and the woods. I didn't know if there were fences beyond, but I didn't think that would be a problem for the horses. Humans on foot couldn't exactly outrun a cantering quadruped, let alone nine of them.

The sound of hooves made a staccato rhythm as we made our way to the gates, and I could feel the humming tension of the herd through the bond. Since the gelding could sense it, so could I. A small whinny or two rose from them, and Eilidh swung the gate wide.

We both hurriedly stood back as the horses tossed their manes, a few of them pawing at the floor with palpable excitement.

"That's you lot free," I said quietly. "Stay out of sight as best you can—and thank you."

Eilidh gave me an unreadable expression, watching the horses press out of the corral with a hint of wistful longing flashing into being for barely a moment before her features again smoothed themselves out into placidity again.

For someone who always accused me of having no emotions, she was hardly one to talk. Though perhaps that old saw was correct—what we react to in others is simply reacting to seeing our own reflection.

I didn't know what that said about either of us, and right then, I didn't care.

"I'm gonnae start a fire," I said, then began humming Billy Joel under my breath as I stalked towards the stable.

It began with a lick of blue flame and a curl of smoke, tracing a seam up the back corner of the stable as if I'd laid down a thread of kerosene and touched a match to it.

The pull on my spirit was negligible—it wouldn't take much. Normal fire would be eye catching enough. Magical blue-green fire, though? That ought to also metaphorically light one under their collective arses.

Eilidh walked with me through the stables as I touched stall after stall with spirit, kindling it into flame that quickly began to fill the upper reaches of the building.

"Won't take long for them to notice," she cautioned me. "We'd better hurry and get out of sight."

"That's the plan," I said, and as we passed the pile in the centre of the space where she'd layered old straw, dry hay, cardboard, wooden crates, and anything else that appeared flammable, I walked around it in a sun-wise circle, this time letting the Purifire drip from my hands.

It caught immediately—and it began to race.

Behind us, blue flames billowed from every stall.

"Get to the door," I said to Eilidh. "I need to hit the front."

She was moving before I finished speaking, her footsteps increasing in speed.

I trotted to the front of the stable where the big doors

remained closed, and with my spirit dipping below half, I laid down a line of fire from one corner to the other, not unlike the trip-line they'd used to attempt to ping if we escaped.

Unlike that clumsy ward, however, my fire would not be simply stepped over.

As soon as it was done, I turned and ran after Eilidh. Smoke clawed at my lungs, and I stifled a cough.

My last move was to throw up a veritable *wall* of flame over the small side door we had used as our escape. Panting with the arcane exertion, I took a deep, steadying breath.

I'd barely turned away from the stable when I heard a gurgle off to my right and turned to see Eilidh—with one of the big bruisers' arms clasped tight around her neck.

Fuck.

Fuck fuck fuck fuck fuck.

Her hands pried at his arm, but despite her solid Strength stat, I was certain she'd also put points into something else, and this bloke? I think he'd gone min-max and dumped *everything* into that one.

"You're going to pay for that," he said, jerking his chin at the stables, which were beginning to billow smoke from the eaves. "In every possible way."

Eilidh's pale face was blotchy and red, her eyes bulging.

I was vaguely surprised to see that the bruiser had hair —and a lot of it. It was pulled back and clubbed at the nape of his neck, and he also had a massive amount of facial hair with long moustaches that curled out on either side of his face and glistened with oil.

I had barely enough spirit to trigger Connection, and while it was regenerating, it wouldn't be very useful right now. But I had one thing this piece of shit did not. Two, actually.

I'd put points in both Agility and Dexterity, and with my Stamina? I could run circles around his sorry lump of an arse all day.

Eilidh didn't have time for that.

Without further thought, I sprang into motion, feinting right and then darting back left even as he spun, his free hand fumbling to pin Eilidh's right arm—or maybe he was going for the knife at his belt. *Her* knife, I realised even as I leapt behind him with a flare of rage.

I had barely any spirit left, and this was a gamble, but it was a gamble I couldn't afford *not* to take. Even as I gritted my teeth and pulled on my magic, exhaustion hammered at me, pain blooming in the base of my skull as I dredged up just enough spirit to cast Purifire.

On the bruiser's hair.

I wasn't prepared for the effect the oil had—I'd likened lighting the stable on fire to setting a match to a trail of kerosene, but his entire head went up with an audible *whumph*, and it caught the curled ends of his moustaches at the same time.

He let out a bellow, practically flinging Eilidh away from him. She collapsed to her knees with a gasp, her auburn hair singed at the back. I flew to her, swatting it out with a few thumps against her shoulder, wincing as I realised we'd have to cut off a chunk of it that had melted together.

Better she lose a few locks of hair than her entire head.

"Thanks," she gasped.

"Nae bother," I told her as I gulped breaths, trying to steady myself. Eilidh did the same, her fingers clawed into the mossy floor of the forest's edge.

Bruiser over there was stop-drop-and-rolling, his flailing frantic and desperate. After a moment, Eilidh stumbled to her feet, staggering towards him, where he was pressing his face into the damp moss.

Flames licked from the walls of the stable now.

"We've got to go," I hissed to Eilidh, hearing a shout from somewhere out of sight.

"One moment," she croaked.

She shifted her shoulders as she approached the still-smoking guard, and just as he noticed her arrival, her foot snapped out, catching him in the side of the face.

There was a crack of bone, and he spasmed and went limp.

Eilidh dropped to her knees again, unbuckling the man's belt and taking the whole thing, dagger and all. It also had a Leatherman attached to it, and the belt was far, far too large for her, but she threaded the long end through the belt buckle without a thought, pulling it around to make a knot.

Her hands were shaking as she turned back to me.

"I think he's dead," she said faintly. "I killed him."

The breeze brought with it the smell of smoke, of burning hair, and of one more thing I'd smelled once before.

Once was enough to identify it.

Bowels and bladder void when we die.

Eilidh was right.

"He's dead," I agreed. "Come on. We need to move."

CHAPTER
TWENTY-ONE

"I didn't think I could kick someone hard enough to break their neck," she said as we slipped through the trees. Her voice was distant, numb.

"Until the apocalypse, you probably couldn't," I said, but I didn't think that helped.

I also didn't think she'd even noticed I'd spoken.

"He just died," she said.

"He was going to kill you," I told her, and this time she did hear me. Her eyes snapped to me like metal drawn to magnets. "He would have killed you, and he would have killed me, and if you hadn't killed him, I would have."

I realised as I said it that it was the truth. I would have done the same. And I would have done it on purpose.

Moreover, I would have thought it was the right thing to do.

Eilidh didn't speak for a long moment, some of the numbness bleeding away to leave her eyes brighter, alert.

We could both hear the yelling now—we'd passed the shed where they'd tried to keep us captured and now were circling around the edge of the manor's park to where we could see the front of the house. Shapes poured out of the back, and in the back of my mind, I counted. Fourteen. Seventeen. Twenty-one.

That had to be most of them.

"If we're going to go, we need to go now," Eilidh said.

It was as if a brick wall had slammed down over whatever she'd been feeling, and that more than anything else that had just happened left me reeling.

It was all I could do to nod in agreement.

My spirit had recovered enough that I could cast Connection, and I did that as we approached the front corner of the house. The flows of spirit all led to the stable out back, all but two upstairs, one of which was very small but bright as a beacon.

"Front window," I said after a moment. "We'll have to break it."

Eilidh gave me an exasperated look that at first I took to be about the window—until she strode past me, stripped off her jacket, wrapping it around her arm, and punched through it with the explosive sound of shattering glass.

She watched me as she calmly shook her jacket out again and put it on.

"Yes, thank you," I said, voice drier than the Sahara.

I didn't think anyone except the person upstairs would have heard the sound over the roar of the fire—which I could hear from where we stood—and the shouting of Bawbag's scrambling servants, but I honestly didn't care.

I climbed through the window, managing to scrape my palm on some glass despite taking pains not to, and I shook the blood off my skin. It knitted back together in moments, the laceration fading to pink, then to normal skin.

Eilidh scrambled through behind me, cursing lightly as

she snagged a trouser leg. That wouldn't heal like my skin had.

"We should split up," she said. "I'll get the weapons, you get the kitten."

"You want to split up again?" I asked incredulously. "You almost got killed!"

"Fine, but weapons first."

Without waiting for me to reply, she stalked towards the back of the house as if daring the very walls to try to stop her.

Gods, how had I ended up stuck with this woman?

I followed at a distance, checking on the bond with the gelding to get a feel for where he and the rest of the herd was. They were close enough to see and smell the smoke, but they were well out of sight—not that the humans would notice. They were too preoccupied with arcane fire-fighting, which I doubted was going well.

But when Eilidh and I made it to the room we'd peeked into upon our arrival, we both stopped short in the threshold.

"Jesus H. Christ," she said, pointing. "That's a fucking military-grade sniper rifle."

The sight of the thing set a chill tingling up my spine. "How do you know that?"

"Parents were—are—both Marines," she said shortly, her face dark. "The one thing they really had in common was what they knew about guns."

I noticed she didn't correct the past tense a second time. I glanced around the room as she moved towards the pristine weapon, a familiar shape catching my eye.

In two long strides, I reached it. "Got your—"

A creaking screech cut me off, and I spun on my heels to see that she had picked up the sniper rifle and *bent* it.

Holy shit.

Her eyes fell on the sword, and she gave me a nod, dropping the rifle and picking up an AR-15 instead.

With a quick pulse of Connection, I located one of her other daggers, the one I'd had at my belt, though the third was nowhere to be seen. From the wisp of spirit that flowed under the door towards the stables, someone else had claimed that.

The air groaned each time Eilidh picked up another gun and broke it.

"Do you think we should take any of them?" I asked.

"Do you know how to shoot?" she countered.

"Nope. Do you?"

"Aye." She pointedly did not pick up any of the holsters, instead moving from rifle to rifle, shotgun to shotgun, pistol to pistol.

Some she bent like the first rifle—others she broke off the triggers.

"It'd be stupid to think some of them don't have guns on them," I said, feeling the creep of time. "We need to go."

"Anything I disable now is something they can't kill us with later," she said stubbornly. "Go get the fucking kitten."

I sucked in a tight breath as I turned away, my original thought of not splitting up shattered by the absolute burr under my skin that was Eilidh MacIntosh.

If she wanted to get dead, fine.

I found the stairs easily and took them two at a time, thankful to the starling for giving me a basic idea of where I could find Lord Bawbag's bedroom. It was on the top floor of the house, and when I reached the last of the stairs, it quickly became evident that the entire top floor was his domain. Not that the rest of the house wasn't, but the corridor that spread out before me was lined with sculptures. On closer inspection, I realised they were ivory.

All of them. Every single one. And there were a *lot* of them.

Despite my mother's profession, I've never been against hunting. We'd get venison from local hunters—the deer in Scotland can get to proper pest level since we killed off all their natural predators—but there was a difference to me between killing to save your own life, whether in defence of it or for sustenance, and killing just for the sake of it. And killing things just because they existed, just because they were big and it made your cock feel bigger in your pants, well. I don't fucking know.

Elephants were intelligent. Emotional. Hell, they had more emotions than I did, I guessed. They mourned their dead and returned to the sites where they'd lost members of their families. Braver than me, in that regard.

Looking around the corridor of ivory splayed out before me, I couldn't help the sick coating of bile that rose up in my throat.

I suddenly wanted to burn this entire building to the ground, too.

But that wasn't what I was there for.

The door to Lord Bawbag's suite was easy to spot. An enormous double door of polished mahogany, even that was inlaid with ivory, the designs clearly his Bawbag family crest.

I pushed them open, hearing a small squawk from inside.

The young girl I'd seen through the starling's eyes scrambled back from where she'd been sitting on the floor by the basket, her eyes wide and her skin going a paler shade of mayonnaise.

Her eyes were peat brown, and her hair almost the same colour, plaited down her back in a scraggly tail.

"Who are you?" she blurted out. "Get away from me!"

I thought about giving her a fake name for a moment in case she passed it on to her boss, but then I decided I didn't care. He already knew my face.

"I'm Calum," I said. "I'm not going to hurt you. I just want the kitten."

At that, she stared at me for a moment before starting to splutter.

"I'm not going to hurt the kitten, either, not like Lord Bawbag killed its mother. I'm not a fucking cuntwaffle like he is. But I'm also not going to leave it with him for . . . whatever he was going to do with it."

I thought I might have scared the girl into insensibility, because her mouth was moving, but no sound was coming out.

But then she sucked in a deep breath and blurted out, "Only if you take me with you."

Her brown eyes were wide and terrified, and I had a moment of clarity imagining how I might look to her. Thirty-something-year-old man with a solid foot on her in height and nearly the same in shoulder width, barging into her employer's bedroom where she was alone in a crisis.

The *guts* on this kid. She couldn't be older than nineteen.

Before I can say anything, though, she kept going, scrambling to her feet.

"I know what he wants to do," she said all in a rush, the words practically tripping over each other as they poured over her lips. "I'll tell you everything. Just—just get me out of here. My family's in Connel, and I just want to go home, but he wouldn't let me, and—and—"

"He hasn't hurt you, has he?" I asked, alarm rising with her every gulped breath.

"No," she said, after my question stopped her mid-tirade, but then she added, almost too quietly to hear, "not yet."

And that did it.

"Yeah, I'm not leaving you here," I said without another moment's hesitation, catching her just as she heaved another breath to continue her pleading.

She let the breath out with a burst of air. "Really?"

"I wouldn't leave a venomous snake with that man unless I was certain it'd bite him in the carotid artery before he could make it into boots," I told her. "Logistics might be rough, but we've got a horse—we, erm, stole a horse—and if nothing else, you and Eilidh can ride and I'll make my own way."

That was all it took for the girl to fly into action.

Within a minute, she had fled from the room with a hurried "be right back!" and left me alone with the basket.

And the kitten.

The Scottish wildcat had been sleeping, I thought, as I'd been talking to the girl, but as I walked over to the basket and knelt beside it, it stirred.

My brief impression through the eyes of the starling had been correct; the kitten was barely old enough to have opened its eyes, and it was small and clumsy as it pushed itself to unsteady paws and wobbled with a tiny, plaintive mew.

"God, what was he going to do with you?" I muttered to the little ball of floof.

"He was going to make her do things for him," said the girl's voice from the doorway. She held a small duffel in her arms, practically a messenger bag, though the top of it was covered in breathable mesh that looked hand sewn.

When she caught me looking at it, she scuffed her foot sheepishly. "I was—I was going to escape."

If I hadn't been sure about taking her with us, that would have done it. "It's not safe out there alone," I said quietly. "I'm glad I found you."

She came over, though I noticed she still stayed on the opposite side of the basket from me. I couldn't really blame her. Cooing, she scooped up the kitten and bundled it into the bag, which I noticed contained a nest of an old, soft towel at the bottom as well as pockets packed with baby bottles along the outside.

The kitten made another wee mewp from the inside of the bag when the girl zipped it, but that was it.

"I should take that," I said. "If you need to run, you shouldn't be carrying anything."

She hesitated for a moment at that, but then she held the bag out to me. I slung it carefully over my back, feeling a small weight shift as the kitten squirmed, then settled against my spine, a tiny ball of warmth.

"You said he planned to make the kitten do things for him," I said then. "What do you mean?"

The girl darted a glance towards the door as if she was afraid Lord Bawbag would come sauntering through at any moment.

"He's been . . . making these *things* that he sends out to spy for him, which was creepy the first day or so," she said, "but then he—"

She broke off suddenly as a loud crash cut through the air, along with a series of alarmed shouts.

"Shit," I said. "We need to go. Now."

The girl gave me a terrified nod, and we bolted from

Bawbag's suite, leaping down the stairs. The kid was young, but she was *fast*.

So fast, she almost ran head-long into Eilidh as the older woman met her coming up the stairs from the first floor.

"Where have you been?" Eilidh demanded, catching herself on the bannister. "The whole stable just collapsed, and they're—"

A door slammed open with a loud report.

"—coming back," Eilidh finished grimly.

"Follow me," the young girl gasped, grabbing Eilidh's hand without hesitation and yanking her towards the rear of the house. "Servants' stairs."

"Who is this kid?" Eilidh mouthed to me, and I just waved a hand at her.

"I think you need to tell me what Lord Bawbag did after the simulacra," I said to the bobbing brown plaited ponytail in front of me as I followed the teenager, grateful to see the familiar sight of Eilidh's claymore back between her shoulder blades.

The girl reached a nondescript door at the north-western corner of the corridor and shoved it open, sticking her head in to listen for a moment before letting out a relieved sigh and beckoning at us.

When she shut it silently behind me, she looked up at me through a sweat-dampened brown fringe.

Her eyes darted from me to Eilidh and back again before she answered, swallowing hard. "He started practicing on people."

CHAPTER

TWENTY-TWO

Neither I nor Eilidh had time to process that as the
still-nameless girl led us at a frantic pace down the
servants' stairs.

In my mind, I tugged on that thread of spirit connecting
me to the grey-white gelding, relieved at least that he
hadn't unilaterally broken it. At the ripple in the line, I
could feel him in the distance as he sprang into action.

"The horse is coming," I said as we reached the bottom
of the stairs—just as the door out of the stairwell flew
open.

The person in it was a middle-aged man who looked
like he could spit bullets hard enough to pierce bone.

At the sight of him, the girl veritably squealed, leaping
back up four stairs in one go even as he registered that he
was staring at the probable culprits of the stable fire.

There wasn't time or space in the cramped stairwell for
Eilidh to unsheathe her claymore without hitting walls or
flesh.

But my spirit had recovered.

Without a thought, I had a ball of Purifire between my palms, and I threw it at his face.

I wasn't trying to set him on fire, not like the bruiser who'd almost strangled Eilidh. I was more counting on the fact that if a giant, blue-green ball of plasma flies straight at your eyeballs, the biggest human instinct is to duck—or at least flinch.

Whether he was too thick or just too slow, I didn't think I'd ever know.

The fire took him right in the face with the force of a punch from a fist far bigger than mine.

His head slammed into the door that was still swinging closed, impacting right on the skinny side, and he bounced back off and slumped to the floor, unconscious.

Eilidh had her dagger unsheathed and was moving towards him, but she stopped when he hit the floor.

"Not bad," she said with a glance at me.

"Let's *go*," I said.

The girl scrambled back down the stairs, stepping gingerly over the now-sleeping man.

She hesitated at the door, though, then with a guilty look at me and Eilidh, spat on his face.

With no explanation offered, she pulled the door open and darted through it, forcing me and Eilidh to break into a run to catch up.

"What's your name?" Eilidh asked her as we hurried through the corridors, noises in the distance telling us the house was no longer deserted, though the commotion outside made it abundantly clear people were still fighting the fire.

"Rhona," the girl said after a short hesitation.

At that, she waved a frantic hand at us, looking both

ways up and down the corridor before throwing open a door and practically shoving Eilidh through it.

I pressed myself in after her, with Rhona shutting the door on both of us. She'd pushed us into a cupboard—it smelled of moth balls and a whiff of Dettol, but despite those strong odours, all I could really smell was Eilidh. Somehow, she smelled of heather and grass, a hint of lilac. Some sweat, of course, from all the exertion, and that had a tinny undertone to it that melded with my own—I wasn't sure if I was actually smelling our fear, but pressed up against her with a doorknob digging into my arse, I adjusted the kitten carrier on my back so as not to squish it and tried to concentrate on the soft fragrance of heather.

There was no light in the cupboard except what crept under the door, and I heard footsteps outside.

The sudden thought that Rhona was about to betray us crossed my mind.

"What's happening?" I heard Rhona ask, and that was punctuated by the sound of Eilidh swallowing.

She was close enough that her heat enveloped me, close enough I felt her breath stir the air between us.

My own breath came shallow, and I was struck with the sudden, irrational fear that it stank. Wasn't like any of us had had the time to brush our teeth in a while.

"Those freaks set fire to the stable," a woman's voice said to Rhona with an accent from down south. Way down south, like Sussex south. "Nothing's putting it out. Lord Sackington should be back soon—that smoke has to be visible from miles away on a day like today."

Shit.

"Oh, good," Rhona said lightly. "I'll make sure his chambers are ready."

"You do that."

I could almost hear the older woman's eye roll as the footsteps faded down the hall, washed away by Rhona's quavering sigh.

She threw the door open a moment later, the solid wood against my back vanishing so suddenly I jumped, and without a word, we were scurrying through the house again.

If there was one thing luck favoured us with, it was that giant manor houses had lots of ground-floor doors.

One more hurried run down a corridor, and we spilled out onto the northwestern lawn, a modest entrance likely meant to give easy access to the kitchen.

I tugged on the threads of spirit to the horse. He was almost here.

"When he gets here, you two be ready to ride," I said.

"What?" Eilidh said. "What about you?"

"Two grown adults would be a lot for a horse. Three might hurt him even with extra strength." I didn't love the idea of being on my own again, but it couldn't be helped. Rhona was the priority, and Eilidh had at least as much of a chance of protecting the kid as I did.

A shout pierced the air, and I spun to see a trio of Bawbag's men rounding the corner.

"You two go! The horse will meet you!" I said to them.

I didn't see whether they listened, because my entire world narrowed to one sight: a pistol pointed directly at my chest.

Almost in slow motion, I saw the man's trigger finger tighten. Heard the click.

Waited for the bang.

It didn't come.

"What the fuck?" The man clicked the trigger again, glancing at the bloke on his right.

These guys looked more rangy than the bruisers. Trigger Finger was the tallest of them, about my height with dirty blond hair and rugged stubble that would make Robert Redford's jawline cry in envy.

The other two were both dark-haired, brothers by the near-identical unibrows, and they moved with a grace that spoke to training—training I sure as hell did not have.

Too late, I remembered the kitten on my back, but I didn't dare look behind me to see if Eilidh and Rhona had left.

The horse was close and gaining on us, but not fast enough.

I pulled on my spirit, all too aware that I had notifications waiting but couldn't do shit with them now.

Purifire glowed in my hands, but instead of cowing the men who rushed me, it seemed to anger them more.

"This asshole's the one who burned down the stable!" The blond man pointed at me as if there was a need to demonstrate who he meant. "Fuck him up!"

As if to punctuate his sentence, the first of the goons—who I mentally dubbed as Thing One for the oversized fuzzy caterpillar on his brow—dropped his weight to his front foot, and too late I realised why and missed releasing my fire.

Instead of slamming into one of my foes, my fireball cratered into the lawn at Trigger Finger's feet.

Thing One used the force of his momentum to unleash a vicious spin kick right at my head.

With no real training in hand-to-hand combat, there was no way I knew how to block, but my enhanced Agility and Dexterity got me enough out of the way that the kick glanced off my shoulder on the way down rather than hitting me at its peak strength.

I still lurched off balance just in time for a left hook from Thing Two to catch me straight in the jaw.

I felt something crunch, and a scream behind me told me Rhona had *not* actually fled—nor had Eilidh, who came charging into my peripheral vision a heartbeat later.

Fuck.

I wasn't used to this. The punch had dazed me, and my wasted spirit was still recovering, but if I didn't use magic —the one weapon I really had—I was going to end up a bloody pulp.

With a furious growl, I gathered as much spirit as I dared once more, half jumping and half staggering out of the way of another kick from Thing One even as I saw Eilidh rush Trigger Finger with her claymore.

Thing Two twitched, and instead of trying to punch him or kick him, I aimed a full-palmed slap at the centre of his chest just as he swung his right arm around in another hook.

With almost half my spirit in a maelstrom of Purifire in the palm of my hand, the impact sent Thing Two *soaring* backwards, where he collapsed on his back in the perfectly manicured grass, limbs akimbo.

I didn't have time to think about the way he flopped or the crunch of bone that had accompanied the force of my palm striking his sternum.

Only a brief widening of Thing One's eyes told me he felt any concern for his brother, and he let out a roar of rage, leaping for me.

I danced backward, ignoring the throbbing of my jaw and shoulder. I heard a mew from my back and had to ignore that too, though it made me even angrier. That poor kitten had been through enough already, for fuck's sake.

Eilidh existed in flashes at the corner of my eye, her

auburn hair, the glint of diffuse sunlight off of her blade, and as I tried to stay out of range of Thing One's feet, there was a flash of red.

Blood fountained from Trigger Finger's neck, and Rhona, off to my left, bit down on her fist to avoid a scream.

And I fucked up.

Thing One feinted, darting to my left, and I reacted instinctively to dodge—which was born from reflex, not training.

Some part of my logical mind told me it was a feint, but that part didn't control my fast-twitch muscle fibres.

Sharp pain punched into my side, and I staggered, wondering how a punch could make my skin . . . wet.

I didn't see the blade until he danced back from me, blood glistening from the edge of the knife.

Fucker stabbed me.

There was barely enough time for the sentence to zap through my mind when a sound registered a split second before a horse's whinny pierced through the air and the smell of musk and fur melded with the heat from a lathered flank by my side.

Thing Two shouted as the grey gelding's hooves caught him in the chest.

I took a wheezing breath and coughed, which made me double over from the belated pain from the stab wound in my side.

"Calum!"

I heard Eilidh's alarmed voice as she sprinted away from the still form of Trigger Finger.

Dimly, I knew this whole thing had only taken a few seconds.

"Rhona, get on the horse!" she bellowed at the kid.

"Kitten," I managed to get out as Eilidh grabbed at me.

"How hard did he stab you?" she said, throwing one arm around my back and missing as I lurched away. "Fuck, there's blood on your lips. He must have nicked a lung."

"Kitten!" I gasped, coughing again. "On my back! Careful!"

"Oh, mo chreach sa thàinig. Amadain."

I didn't have enough spirit to heal myself, and as the grey gelding lowered himself to the floor to let me on, I dimly wondered what horse Rhona had gotten on or if I for some reason just couldn't see her. I clambered onto the horse, feeling Eilidh behind me and hearing her still muttering Gaelic insults at my back. *Fool* was probably the least of them, but I couldn't really be arsed to care.

Blood oozed down my side, and the rolling movement of the gelding getting to his feet again did not help. I gritted my teeth against the pain, forcing myself to look over the bodies we'd left behind us.

A column of blue smoke rose into the air behind the manor house, and a spray of red coated the grass where Trigger Finger lay, his throat wet. Thing One's skull was crushed.

I swallowed hard as we started to move.

"Rhona?" I got out.

Eilidh's hands went to the kitten carrier across my back, and she tugged on the strap until it rotated around to my stomach, thankfully passing my left side and not the right one with the wound. A mew came from the bag. Gods, maybe the creature would have been better off left alone.

But then I remembered Rhona spitting on the unconscious face of that first man we'd encountered. What she'd said about Bawbag.

Eilidh's arms tightened around my waist. I hadn't even

realised they were there, but now I did. Her right hand pressed into my wound, and I bit off a yell.

"Sorry," she said. "I need to put pressure on it until you can heal yourself. You almost there?"

The horse's gait quickened, and this time I bit down hard on the inside of my cheek, replying through a clenched jaw. "Few minutes."

"Just hold on."

I didn't think I had a choice.

But the sudden softness in her voice contrasted with the pain of her hand pressed so hard into my side.

TWENTY-THREE

The smoke *was* visible from miles away.

That filled me with dread as we made our escape from Lord Bawbag's manor.

After about ten minutes of excruciating cantering, I healed enough that I thought I stopped coughing blood. I'd pushed it as far as I could; the chance that I'd need my one use of Beannachd Shlàinte for someone else kept me from using it on myself. The pain dulled but didn't abate, its reminder pulsing through me with every hoofbeat and heartbeat.

Rhona was on a palomino a bit ahead of us, which I saw pretty quickly once we got moving, and I sent a thread of thanks through the link with the grey gelding. The horses saved our lives, I think.

Even as we moved away from the manor, Eilidh told me —quietly, so Rhona wouldn't hear—that Bawbag's men had raised the alarm and were in pursuit.

We were just lucky we had the only means of transportation, and our pursuers fell off quickly.

From Eilidh's sudden silence, I figured she was going through her notifications.

I thought I'd better do the same, though I first reached out with a probing tendril of spirit to the horse, asking him to alert me if there was need.

The first glance at the notification brought a surge of relief. The second made the stab wound in my side feel like the least of my troubles.

Quest complete: The Hills Have Eyes

You have completed the first stage of The Hills Have Eyes.

Free will is paramount in ascended worlds, and any being who seeks to thwart that is punished severely. But because Earth is an anomaly, far from the judicial reach of the Ascended Alliance, beyond system communications, the power to safeguard this tenet of society lies with the people of Earth alone.

As the third human group to discover an evolving quest, you have stumbled into an integral role in your world's ascension; if your people hope to survive and become part of the alliance, you will need to ensure that you fight for the ideals of the alliance— and that means rooting out those among your kind who believe other sapients and sentients exist to be their puppets.

Lord Edwin Thomas Sackington has shown that he is among them. While you have yet to see direct evidence of this, Eilidh has discerned that Rhona's report is true and has also discovered additional information about Lord Sackington's pre-ascension criminal activities.

At that, I had to pause. I guessed she hadn't had enough time to give us a rundown between being smushed in a closet and fighting off Bawbag's goons.

I went back to reading.

This quest has become an evolving quest, subject to change upon completion pending results.

  Objectives:

  -Investigate the simulacrum's origin (Complete)

  -Find out the summoner's name (Complete)

  -Escape captivity (Complete)

  -Regain your weapons (Complete)

  -Find out the summoner's purpose (Complete)

  -Rescue the Scottish wildcat kitten (Complete)

  Rewards:

  -Experience (commensurate with current level progression)

  -1 skill point

  -1 book: A Guide to Woodcraft in an Ascended World

  -All cooldowns reset

  Bonus for completing optional objective:

  +1 to Nature affinity

You have reached Level 4! You have three attribute points to distribute. You have three skill points to distribute.

Through physical exertion, you have gained a permanent +1 to Agility and +2 to Stamina. Please note that such increases have diminishing returns as your base statistics grow.

Through arcane exertion, you have gained a permanent +2 to Spirit and +1 to Will. Please note that such increases have diminishing returns as your base statistics grow.

.   .   .

Gods, it felt like ages since I'd levelled.

I'd accumulated a fair amount of points just from the ongoing disaster of Eilidh's and my explorations of Lord Bawbag's estate—there were an additional four Spirit, four Will, and one Pathos from earlier, not to mention the added point to my Nature affinity.

And apparently, that had gone up another from my massive amount of arson.

You have increased your affinity: Nature (Level 2)

You have increased your affinity: Nature (Level 3)

Through diligent use, you have increased the level of your skills: Connection (Level 3), Purifire (Level 3), Tàth (Level 3).

Oh, thank the gods. I was a little disappointed that Beannachd Shlàinte hadn't levelled up, but I guessed I'd missed an opportunity by allowing both myself and Eilidh to heal "naturally" with the ascension's innate boost to our usual processes.

As it was, though, my intensive use of both Purifire and Connection had gotten a boost—and making friends with the horse we were riding had also clearly helped.

I *really* wanted to see what adding two levels to Purifire had done for the spell.

.   .   .

Purifire (Level 3)—This skill is most used in combat, instilling basic fire with the power of the arcane, making it burn hotter and brighter than typical flame—and all within the mage's control. This fire is not friendly fire in more than one way. Magic is will and intent, and it will strike only your foes. While a staff is needed for advanced use, this skill can be wielded without need for a weapon.

You have discovered the utility of this offensive skill in using it not only against your opponents but also to control your environment. As such, you have gained the upgrade Ring of Fire, which you can use to encircle your foes.

Additionally, you have used Purifire to strike a blow of force, unwittingly drawing upon the spell Spèird to bring extra power to bear upon your enemies, clearing the path for you. Continued experimentation—with both skills—may lead to further discoveries.

Increased use of Purifire allows for more complex use. Many mages utilise it with metal weapons to great effect, adding burning damage and spirit damage to physical. Others prefer a staff's elegance and the advanced precision a mage finds therein. At its heart, this skill moulds itself to its wielder, and only the mage can decide its limits.

Oh, for fuck's . . .

I'd completely *forgotten* about Spèird. Apparently my Mind stat didn't make up for being a useless hamster, but in my thick-headed, smooth-brained fart noise of a failure, I'd at least done something interesting by accident.

Go me.

Before I could beat myself up too much, I went to look at Connection.

· · ·

Connection (Level 3)—You gain a deeper affinity to the earth and its needs, and it whispers to you. With this skill, you are able to see how things around you interact, be it the tracks of a deer hunted by paw prints of a stalking cat or the passing of a band of hunters.

Increased use of this skill enables you to take in an entire scene at a glance and appropriately assess its secrets. Additionally, the skill will allow you to ascertain the needs of the natural world, giving you the power to aid creatures and plants that may one day return the favour—as you have now discovered with the horses you freed who came to your aid in your hour of need.

Your use has granted you a bonus to clarity. Your ability to see and identify patterns has increased, and you are now 7% more likely to spot items of import, foes in stealth, and escape routes.

Well. That was something, anyway.

Tàth (Level 3)—This ability allows you to form a consensual bond with an animal, giving you the power to see through the animal's eyes and guide the creature's movements where necessary. These bonds, once created, will bring a consistent drain on spirit until released, but the benefits far outweigh the sacrifice. Tàth comes with a one-time bonus of +1 to Pathos.

Continued usage will improve the usefulness of these bonds, providing a symbiotic balance for both you and your companion. You gain eyes and ears and mobility—they gain intelligence, protection, and, in rare cases, special abilities. In conjunction with your harmonious use of Connection, Tàth has connected you with an additional being with the blessing of your horse companion. Remember that promises made to your companions should be kept; "once bitten, twice shy" is a good guiding prin-ciple to remember when working with sentient species—espe-cially those the ascension could elevate to sapience.

Your use has granted you a bonus to working with birds and equine creatures. While they still will not understand human language, they will now project their instinctual reactions to what they observe. This bonus is more effective the higher your Pathos.

My mind reeled with the level of interaction between these skills. I doubted they'd play off each other as well if I was throwing together things that seemed wildly disparate, but as it was, I suddenly felt overwhelmed. I was going to have to figure out where I wanted to aim my build, for lack of a better term.

I needed to look over my attributes, but I had three skill points to spend, and I had three different skill trees to poke at.

Starting with Arcane, I braced myself to have to make some hard choices.

One, at least, was a no-brainer.

I'd bottomed out on spirit over the course of our escape, and that was *with* the capacity boost, which I couldn't count on all the time—they only lasted twelve hours.

That meant it was time for Fuaran.

Fuaran—Like its name, Fuaran is a skill that brings with it a wellspring of refreshment. This skill increases your spirit regen-eration by a base of 20% for 3 minutes, and if comrades are within 10 meters of you, it will also do the same for them.

Increased use of this skill will increase its efficacy and area of effect and may also bestow other boons that can benefit you and your party.

I didn't think that Eilidh was going for a spirit-heavy build, but that didn't mean she wouldn't benefit from the area-of-effect buff. And I had no idea what Rhona was going to be in terms of class or how long she'd even be with us.

With Spèird—I couldn't believe I'd forgotten about an entire fucking spell!—Purifire, and Fuaran, that filled in the roots of the Arcane tree. I noticed that Purifire, with its upgrade, now pulsed a little brighter and had a smaller, star-like dot orbiting around it. The roots had opened up the first trunk-level spell, which I zeroed in on immediately.

Cumhachd—This spell is one of the most versatile in the hedge witch's arsenal. By tapping into the ambient spirit that surrounds you to augment your own, you are able to form missiles based upon your environment. Not only does this spell shift dramatically from mage to mage, but it also enhances your acquisition of points in Spirit. This ability is bolstered by and best used within your existing affinities, but it also rewards creativity.

Continued use may unlock additional benefits and upgrades. As with all things in an ascended world, the limits are your own imagination.

That was vague as fuck.

I wanted it immediately.

Without letting myself second guess the instinct, I unlocked it with a skill point. That would allow me to work with my surroundings, and my mind immediately shot to the idea of fists of stone from rocky ground, spears of wood in a tangled forest, any number of things. Imagination was the only limit? The thought was terrifying . . . and exhilarating.

That left me with two more skill points to spend, and with the frequency we were getting hurt, I figured the best bet would be to look at the Slàinte tree.

Before I could, though, a thought struck me. "Missile" was not the *friendliest* of words, but did "bolstered by existing affinities" mean that I could, like, create a health-based missile that would target someone and heal them? The thought was a little hilarious; the slapstick image of someone's head wound getting walloped with a wad of sticky plasters in the heat of battle glomming onto my tired brain.

Creativity, eh? Eilidh might never forgive me if I hit her in the forehead with a wad of . . . literally anything.

Not that I'd try.

That particular line of thinking was unhelpful.

Hastily, I opened up the Slàinte tree, wishing for a moment that it came with a bloody pint or three to wash out my brain.

I wasn't a huge drinker, but even I had to admit the apocalypse could do with a dram.

Or, you know, a bottle.

Or a distillery.

The yellow star on the trunk of the tree still illuminated Beannachd Shlàinte, which communicated clearly that it wasn't the basis of the tree—and I had to hope that meant that the roots would, for lack of a better metaphor, ground my abilities. Maybe that was why the skill hadn't levelled up with the others. Were there prerequisites?

Gods, what I wouldn't give for a fucking instruction manual.

I had to snort when I saw the name of the central root-level ability: Freumhan.

Literally Roots.

Freumhan (Passive)—While many might assume a spell named for roots would belong best in the Nature tree, this arcane spell is more metaphorical in nature than something to immobilise one's enemies. Freumhan taps into your innate spirit system, granting you an awareness of the rivers and streams through which your arcane abilities flow—and how to nurture them.

Holy shit.

I blinked at that, thinking of what Connection had revealed about the flows of spirit in animals, how they had a direction, movement, life.

It was like Eastern concepts of chi, though I got the feeling that the ascended worlds' conceptions of it would not map onto qigong or any other Earth practises. Sure enough, when I continued reading, it confirmed just that.

As an arcane practitioner in an ascended world, you must understand your own systems in order to use them effectively. Freumhan is the foundation upon which you will grow.

While Freumhan will not increase in levels as active spells will, your understanding of magic will, on occasion, trigger evolution.

. . .

Just as I was about to look at the other options, I felt an alarmed tug through the thread of spirit that tethered me to the horse.

I slammed the skill point into Freumhan—far better to give myself any possible advantage than not, and at least I'd seen this one.

No time for my attributes. Fuck.

TWENTY-FOUR

My head was still clearing when I felt Eilidh's heat slip away from my back.

We were on an outcropping of a hill overlooking Loch Awe—the horses had made good time, without a doubt—and in the other direction, the smoke at Lord Bawbag's manor still rose into the sky, ominous and dark.

But that wasn't what struck fear into me.

Lord Bawbag himself sat astride his walnut-brown mare, energy crackling in his hands and a phalanx of three simulacra forming an arrowhead in front of his horse.

The magic was strangely translucent, not unlike the simulacra themselves, like the magic Lord Bawbag wove was made of spun threads of molten glass.

As I watched, the threads sank into the simulacra, and all three of the bizarre, jellyfish-like automatons jerked like he'd yanked on marionette strings.

When he spoke, his accent was meticulous Received Pronunciation, each syllable pronounced with perfect, king-approved enunciation.

"I suspect, because of the way you are fleeing with my

stolen maid, that you are the interruption that has caused me to return home rather than completing my plans for the day," Lord Edwin Thomas Sackington said as if we were three annoying midges swarming about his face rather than a trio of human beings. "And, it seems, you have also stolen my horses. Theft. We've become quite lenient on thieves in recent years, wouldn't you say?"

And in the midst of that final rhetorical question, he struck.

All three of the simulacra lurched forwards.

Maybe it was the rap on the knuckles I'd gotten from forgetting my force spell Spèird; maybe it was the new passive Freumhan. All I knew was that from one heartbeat to the next, I drew breath, and with it, drew in spirit from the back of the horse where I sat, and when the gelding whickered and pawed at the ground, Spèird exploded out of my raised hands like a tsunami of pure, raw energy.

I had forgotten what my interface had said about friendly fire, but in no way would I ever intend to attack a horse merely for the diseased barnacle attached to her back.

The wave of Spèird slammed into the simulacra, hitting the one at the front of the phalanx a split second before the two flanking it, and Lord Bawbag had that much time to yank on the reins of his horse, making her neigh and dance backwards—to absolutely no avail.

Spèird scraped the wannabe medieval lord from his mare as if the horse didn't even exist, and, in a moment that would be comical if the man wasn't a literal villain, his legs held the shape of being astride while he flew backwards through the air before the downward arc of his trajectory veritably spiked him into the ground.

"Yeet," I muttered.

Bawbag hit with an explosive gasp as the impact stole his breath.

His walnut mare immediately bolted towards us, overshooting both Eilidh—who had her claymore drawn and was standing warily on guard—and myself on the gelding. I felt a surge of relief from the link with the grey horse, and my notifications flashed. Great. More things to dig through.

Not far away, I could see Rhona on the back of the palomino, both the girl and the horse looking as twitchy as someone who'd just been zapped with lightning.

But Rhona's eyes were locked on Bawbag where he lay struggling to draw breath on the turf. The simulacra were lumps of so much jelly in a haphazard smattering nearby.

"You'll see," Bawbag got out as he shoved himself to a sitting position, craning his neck first one way, then the other. For someone who'd just been thrown off his horse, his smirk was unnerving. "Once I'm ready, there will be no one in this land who will be strong enough to stand against me. It's survival of the fittest, you thieving cur, and I have farther to go than you know. If you're lucky, I'll let you serve me once I break you."

My brain had stuck on the word *cur*.

Jesus.

Eilidh advanced on him warily, though I could see her hesitation.

Neither of us were counting on Rhona.

Her shrill voice rose behind me. "I am not—your—property!"

The world seemed to narrow to one tiny tunnel.

Three things happened at once.

One.

All of the simulacra jerked from their resting places,

translucent jelly jiggling and rippling as they flew through the air—directly at Eilidh.

Two.

Bawbag launched himself to his feet on a wave of spirit, those gossamer threads of glass-like magic crackling, sharp and thirsty for blood.

Three.

Rhona erupted.

It was the only word I could think of to describe what happened. The young woman's yell had been shrill, but someone had added an extra number to the dial, because she turned it up to eleven.

Her piercing keen exploded from her small frame where she sat astride the palomino, and she threw back her head as absolute tsunamis of spirit flowed through her and tore outward.

Just hearing it was enough to make me think my eardrums were going to bleed, and the fact that she clearly didn't intend to hit me is probably the only reason I didn't have blood gushing. Something flashed in the sky, and a fork of lightning lanced through the spotty cloud cover above Rhona's head.

Eilidh swung her claymore like an enormous cricket bat, her enhanced Strength keeping it level as she smashed it into a simulacrum.

But Rhona's otherworldly shriek was not the only thing I heard.

From the southeast side of the loch, from the slope of the hill that rose with Ben Lui in the distance, a lower rumble.

It was a thrum of bass almost too low a frequency for human ears to pick up, and it made my skin vibrate.

That alone would have been an unnerving counterpart

to the frozen tableau that seemed to spring into battle in slow motion, like Lord Bawbag, his simulacra, Eilidh, Rhona, myself, and the trio of horses were all surrounded by crystal-clear jelly.

Like crystal-clear jelly if that jelly was the ambient spirit. As I instinctually triggered Connection, deeper, wider waves rolled towards us to clash with Rhona's high-pitched wail.

"Shit," I said aloud.

Only heartbeats had passed, and Lord Bawbag took my belated expletive to mean I was afraid of him.

"You've seen nothing," he roared.

But his yell was pitiful compared to Rhona's, and compared to that bone-deep thrum?

I'd leap into the poncey bastard's arms if I thought it'd let us escape whatever was coming.

"Eilidh!" I yelled. "We have to go!"

To her credit, she didn't turn to look at me, only kept playing Whac-A-Mole with the simulacra as Bawbag started toward her, blood dripping from his nose and ears.

He appeared not to notice—not the blood and not the rumble in the distance.

Something clawed into my back, and I yelped.

The kitten.

The sodding *kitten*.

With a frantic glance towards the real danger, I didn't expect to actually see anything.

But I did.

It was still far away, but it was gaining fast.

It appeared like a heather-brown blur, camouflaged in the foliage but visible against the scattered trees at the edge of the loch.

I knew without any shadow of a doubt that this was the

thing that had eaten those people and left their torn-apart, bloodied remains on the A85.

The world seemed to darken around me, and when a rumble of distant thunder boomed, I realised that wasn't just my imagination. Lightning flashed to the west, a sight that would be remarkable in February if I weren't in a magical standoff.

My quick glance westward had cost me precious seconds. For a moment, I thought I'd lost the beast, but then I saw it again, rippling forwards, so fast and undulating that my immediate thought was that it was a mutated adder.

It had closed a remarkable amount of distance in the blink of an eye, and it was gaining. Fast.

"Eilidh, we need to go! Now!"

"I don't think so," said Lord Bawbag. A cruel smile twisted his lips, and he flung his molten glass magic at Eilidh's heart.

My Ring of Fire.

I felt my spirit plunge as I cast the new spell, but I wasn't quite quick enough.

The ring sprang up in a perfect circle around the asshole of a lord, becoming a column of flame that rocketed skywards. It caught two of the simulacra and Lord Bawbag within it—and part of his attack.

I watched as the bulk of his magic hit that perimeter and vanished. Vaporised. It exploded like glitter, light refracting off of millions of tiny motes of glass dust.

But it wasn't enough.

Eilidh's left shoulder jerked backwards with the impact of the spell, whatever it had been, and I launched myself from the back of the grey gelding as quickly as I possibly could. She hit the floor before I could reach her, and it was only pure dumb luck that the simulacrum left outwith the circle had again collapsed into a gelatinous sludge. The levelled-up Purifire had severed it from Lord Bawbag's control.

Inside the circle, I could see him raging, veins pulsing in his neck.

But I didn't care.

That rumbling thrum, that marrow-deep terror—he was a puny, squalling child compared to the thing that had heard our racket and come running.

Eilidh had collapsed to the ground, and with utter dismay, I heard Rhona's screech die off, leaving her slumped atop her palomino.

My own spirit was aching, recovering faster than it had before, but not fast enough for me to do much but tug on my link to the gelding. *Help!*

Blood seeped from Eilidh's chest. Her left breast seemed totally soaked in it, and the sight of the wound made me blanch.

As if he'd made a fist of glass needles, Lord Bawbag's magic had *shredded* Eilidh's shirt with a thousand punctures the size of toothpicks. What pale flesh peeked through was only visible through the Swiss cheese texture of her shirt, and it looked like raw, bloody mince.

"Fuck, fuck, fuck, fuck, fuck," I said, terrified to move her but more terrified not to.

The beast was gaining, and I was out of time. There was no way—none—I could face that thing.

As the grey gelding lowered himself to the ground so I could lift Eilidh onto his back, I saw Lord Bawbag's raging face through the fire.

Pure hatred.

I thought I had held him in contempt before, but the

absolute repulsion I saw etched in every line of his arro-gant, picture-perfect jaw put my puny angst to shame.

The ring of arcane fire around him contained his sound as well as his person, and I returned his spiteful fury with grim resolve.

If the beast that was coming was mindless, if we were very, very lucky, Lord Bawbag would be a tempting treat.

Wrapped in a pretty parcel. Beyond the grey, his walnut mare—ironically the only horse with us with a saddle and without a rider—reared, tossing her head violently.

Through the link with the gelding, I felt his encroaching fear.

Tearing my gaze from the man in his fiery prison, I swung my leg over the gelding's back, holding tightly to Eilidh. Her head lolled back against my shoulder as the gelding stood.

"Rachamaid," I murmured in Gaelic.

Let's go.

I only hoped the horses could outrun a monster.

CHAPTER
TWENTY-FIVE

I *felt* rather than heard when the creature reached Lord Bawbag.

Its roar had a grating hiss to it, a whisper of death and hunger.

I didn't have a clue if the thing could penetrate Ring of Fire, and as the horses' hooves thundered around us, my heart pounded at least as fast as their relentless rhythm.

Despite the centipede, the rat, the monstrous gull, the goons, the simulacra—for the first time in my life I felt what it meant to be *prey*.

The sensation crawled through me, echoing around in my body. I didn't have a word strong enough to describe how much I hated it.

Lord Bawbag's poisonous glare didn't even scratch the surface.

Part of me was desperate to wheel around, to return and face that creature head on.

But as Eilidh's blood trickled over the back of my hand that grasped her waist, I knew we couldn't.

We were no match for that thing—whatever it was.

Rhona had come to and was clinging to her palomino for dear life, and I couldn't account for how I was managing not only to hold onto the grey but do it whilst cradling an insensate human being to my chest. Maybe it was the link, maybe magic of another kind. I didn't know or care.

The moment my spirit had recovered enough, I cast Beannachd Shlàinte on Eilidh.

And gasped.

The addition of Freumhan had honed my initial instincts that had healed Eilidh once before, and as my spirit sank into her skin, it pierced my mind with the damage.

Not only had Lord Bawbag's magic *looked* like threads of glass, it practically was. And they had broken off inside her body.

Some had lodged in her ribs; others had penetrated into her lung.

I felt sick.

A few had scraped the edges of the pericardial sac around her heart, but thankfully, her own innate healing had been enough to repair that before it got worse.

Eilidh gave a strangled groan that wheezed and crackled through her battered lung, and I tried to hold her steady despite the rolling gait of the horse beneath us.

I could feel a thousand phantom pains in my own left pectoral region, feel a thousand ghosts of needles as my magic pushed Lord Bawbag's horrific arcane weapon back out of Eilidh's body.

I cast Fuaran for the first time, thinking of the way the Gaelic word felt cold like its meaning, a perfect highland spring in the mountains, crisp and life-giving. Soothing after a long hike, the relief of water on parched lips.

It rippled over the both of us, making me shiver, and, to

my surprise, the horse too. His hackles rose, but not in alarm, and he tossed his head as he renewed his speed with greater vigour.

We weren't heading northeast but southwest, down the southern banks of Loch Awe. We could still reach Oban this way, but it would probably take longer—though admittedly needing to backtrack around the loch head to the north to go through Taynuilt could very well be a similar amount of time.

The dark clouds I'd seen above us had dissipated, and I got the eerie feeling that Rhona's wail had summoned them —just as I thought it had alerted the monster to our presence. That made me shudder.

The sun was sinking to the west by the time the now-lathered horses slowed their pace. Their increased Strength and Stamina showed in how long they'd managed to keep up that ground-eating pace, especially the gelding doing it with two riders.

I could just see the ruins of another castle in the distance—Innes Chonnel, I thought, from my vague memory of visiting with my mum—and I jumped at the sound of hooves. Lots of hooves.

When I turned, I was surprised to see more horses gaining on us.

The rest of the herd.

They'd *followed*.

Eilidh stirred enough to swear at me under her breath in Gaelic when I helped her dismount the horse, but the moment I lowered her to a small patch of grass, she practically passed out again.

Her cheeks were drawn and pale, her smattering of freckles even looking sallow and less defined. Her body was burning through an enormous amount of energy, I realised. We'd need to feed her—and soon.

Rhona was in better shape, but the moment her feet touched the road as she slid down from the palomino's back, her knees almost gave out, and she had to brace herself on the horse's flank, which the mare bore gracefully with only a minor toss of her head.

Loch Awe was serene and smooth beyond the shore, the lines of the castle ruins breaking the view along with its overgrown ivy and moss. There wasn't much where we were, only the road and some rocks amid the foliage, though we'd passed through a small settlement right before we'd stopped. I gave myself a minute to stretch, watching as Rhona did the same.

"All right, pal?" I said to the girl cautiously.

"Aye, I'm fine," she said, though her eyes blinked in the way I thought people meant when they said *owlishly*.

Pulling the bag of food from my inventory made Rhona's eyes go from owlish to bugging out. I rooted around in it until I found one of the bags of dried apricots and held it out for her. Carbs and sugar would probably help.

"What did you—how—" she spluttered, her fingers quaking as she took the proffered fruit.

"How did you screech like a banshee loud enough to make Lord Bawbag's nose bleed?" I asked her dryly, then waved my hand in a decidedly unmagical gesture as I popped the bag back into my inventory, minus a packet of peanuts. "Magic."

She blinked again at that, her pale face colouring under

her dark fringe. I opened the bag, dumping a mouthful of peanuts onto my tongue.

Clearly not ready to deal with more discussions of magic, Rhona glanced at Eilidh. "Is your girlfriend okay?"

I inhaled a peanut directly into my trachea.

Coughing and choking, I flailed an arm, which made Rhona come running, slapping me hard on the back.

I wasn't sure if it was that or the force of my own cough, but the offending legume rocketed from my windpipe and smacked the palomino in the arse.

The horse merely twitched her tail.

"*Not* my girlfriend," I managed to wheeze out.

My eyes burned, and I very carefully chewed my next mouthful while Rhona looked on in bemusement.

"I'd recommend not asking her a similar question," I said once I'd recovered. "You might not wake up the next morning."

"Wow, okay," Rhona said. She tore the bag of apricots open with her teeth, which made me grimace, as I sort of wanted to have some of those myself, but not if there was spit on them.

Then again, with my new and improved Constitution, maybe it didn't matter if I got Rhona germs. Or, you know, 'rona germs.

My brain was not up to the task of apocalypse epidemiology.

We chewed in silence for a long moment. I could almost feel my body breaking down the fats and proteins and carbs into useful little chunks of glucose and ATP. I'd never tasted anything as good as those fucking peanuts, the one that had tried to kill me notwithstanding.

When both of us were a bit steadier on our feet, I decided to ask Rhona about her experience since the apocalypse. Eilidh was still flat out, but a quick poke of spirit told me she was recovering, just exhausted, and if we were going to be travelling with the kid, I wanted to know more about her than her name—and also see if I could, you know, point her in the direction of *not* bringing terrifying monsters down on our heads next time.

We might not be so lucky to have bait.

To my surprise, Rhona relaxed at my initial prodding and launched into her tale.

"I've worked for Lord Sackington—"

"Bawbag," I interjected, and this time *she* nearly choked on a handful of apricot chunks.

"He *hates* that people call him that," she said.

"I'm delighted to hear it, both that he's aware and that it gets under his skin," I said smugly.

Rhona snorted. "Anyway, I've worked for *Lord Bawbag* since I was sixteen. My uncle's his groundskeeper, but he wasn't there when the—when the thing happened."

"Is your uncle in Connel with your family?" I asked, and Rhona shook her head.

"Naw, he's in Inveraray. He looks after some of the holiday properties there in the off season for some extra money." Rhona frowned at that, then blew out a breath that ruffled her stick-straight fringe. "I wasn't supposed to be at work that day myself, but the lord'd called me in to look after the kitten."

The kitten.

Jesus fucking Christ, I'd forgotten I had a kitten attached to my back. Aside from the once it had dug its little needle claws into my scapula, it had barely made a peep.

Rhona seemed to realise it at the same time, and she gave me a strangled look.

I hastily pulled the makeshift cat carrier around to my front again, unzipping it gingerly to see the tiny creature squinting up at me balefully as I let more light in.

"It's fine," I said, relief suffusing me.

"*She's* fine," Rhona said with a small harrumph.

She set the half-empty bag of apricots on a large stone and came over to me, pulling one of the bottles from the bandolier-type pockets on the side of the satchel and busying herself digging in the end pocket for a nipple.

The sight reminded me oddly of my mother—I'd seen bottles like that so much when I was growing up. Sometimes Mum'd get fox kits or baby hedgehogs, the occasional bunny or hare, sometimes feral domestic kittens, so there was always an array of wildlife feeding mechanisms in the house.

Rhona made a sound of displeasure that the bottle was cold, and I held out my hand.

"Let me," I said.

"Are you sure you know what to do?" She asked the question dubiously. "It's not like feeding a baby."

"I know more about feeding baby animals than baby humans," I told her dryly. "My mum was a wildlife rehabilitator."

"Was?"

"She died."

Rhona shifted her feet uncomfortably, her hands retracting to chest level. "I'm sorry."

"It was a long time ago."

She reached out with the bottle after a moment, and I took it, spooling the tiniest bit of spirit into Purifire to warm it, and, on impulse, to cleanse the milk in the bottle in case it had spoilt.

I tested the temperature on the inside of my wrist, which Rhona watched in nonplussed approval.

The kitten seemed to smell the milk, and she came alive, her tiny mews breaking the silence. The horses shifted around us, seemingly content that such a pitiful sound would not possibly arise from something dangerous, but one or two did raise their heads to look at us in curiosity.

I lowered the bottle into the satchel, watching the kitten's clumsy steps and little splayed paws as she closed the distance. Her claws were needle sharp and so tiny. Her little whiskers were already bushy, puffed forwards as she latched on to the bottle, and the sounds of her suckling away were almost painfully cute.

Those paws kneaded the rumpled towel, translucent claws digging into the terrycloth.

Rhona peered in at her with a satisfied smile. "I guess you do know what you're doing."

"I'm not a completely useless hamster," I muttered.

"What?"

"Nothing."

"You're not useless at all," Rhona said, as if I needed reassurance.

"Thanks?"

"I mean, you got us out of there, away from that—thing."

At first, I thought she was talking about Lord Bawbag again, but then I see her looking over her shoulder with a haunted expression on her face.

"You saw it?" I asked.

"I—" She broke off. "It's weird."

"Try me. Do I look like a little weird is going to surprise me at this point?"

"I felt it," she said softly. "Like it was inside my spine, the way it feels to stand right in front of a speaker when the bass drops, but without the joy—only pure terror."

"Yep, that's the one," I said, adjusting my hold on the bottle as the kitten aggressively went for the nipple. Its little cream-coloured muzzle had gained little tufts of milk-wet fur.

"You got us out of there," Rhona repeated. "I don't know what *he* would have done to me if I'd stayed or if he'd taken me back, but that thing? It would have made mulch of us."

"You're right there," I said, thinking of that poor couple smeared upon the asphalt.

"Why does that make me think you've seen it before?"

"I haven't," I told her shortly. "Just its . . . leftovers."

Rhona paled at that, so I hastily changed the subject.

"You were telling me what happened when the ascension hit."

"Ascension," she said slowly, as if remembering something through the fog of a dream.

She went through her experience, from the initial screens to her immediate orders not to engage with the system. How Lord Bawbag meant to tell was beyond me, but from the way Rhona kept looking over her shoulder when she spoke of him, I was starting to think that working in his employ was a dystopia of nanny cams and surveillance drones even before he could enchant giant land jellyfish to spy for him. So maybe him saying he would know was believable enough to scare her off of it.

And from there, I was able to believe without so much as a whiff of doubt—the manor had been attacked by two of the giant seagulls, and they'd killed three of Bawbag's men before he killed one with an axe to the skull and the other by hobbling its wing first and whittling it down until it died.

Then he'd killed his other two injured men.

Though Rhona didn't yet know about experience gains and levels—she hadn't even allocated her initial points yet *or* chosen her boon—from what I could glean from her report, Lord Bawbag had gained an insane amount of experience from taking down the two monstrous gulls and two humans in cold blood, rocketing him easily into level three.

Where he'd gained his class.

Rhona obviously had no idea what class that was, but I would bet my stolen bicycle it let him summon the simulacra. And that was day *one* of the apocalypse.

He'd quickly realised he could grow via murder and mayhem, so he'd essentially killed anyone who so much as sniffed at mutiny.

No wonder Rhona had wanted to get out of there.

I'd started to worry that perhaps us flying in there as unprepared as we were was, I don't know, morally questionable, to say the least. But hearing what she had to say, seeing the way she jumped at every noise, instead a bleak resolve settled into my stomach. We'd done the right thing by trying to stop him, and if that monster tore him to pieces? Good fucking riddance.

I hoped to every god and lucky star above that he was inside that thing's belly. I'd rather deal with a mindless monster any day over a human one.

The monster, for all its terror, wasn't evil. It would do what it would do: hunt, kill, feed, repeat.

But a human monster?

Those ones would hurt you because they could and laugh at your pain. And they'd do it in full belief of their own superiority, their own right to treat their fellow humans like chattel.

Belatedly, I remembered the words Lord Bawbag had used about Rhona. Not "you kidnapped my maid" but that we had *stolen* her.

Rhona's account had trailed off as the kitten finished her bottle, suckling in vain at the rubber nipple as if she could will more milk into existence. Her round little belly was fat and full, and I couldn't help but marvel at this furry wee creature, alive despite . . . everything.

"Right," I said softly to the young woman next to me. "We're going to walk you through this new world and help you protect yourself. And when Eilidh wakes up, we'll decide where we go next."

TWENTY-SIX

With the horses around us giving me enough assurance of warning in the event of danger, I finally opened my notifications again, doggedly deciding to pick up where I had left off instead of starting with whatever wanted my attention now.

I'd spent two skill points to unlock Fuaran and Cumhachd, and I couldn't wait to experiment with the latter, but I still had one skill point to spend.

I decided to revisit the Nature tree, since I had yet to look at that one to see what could come next after Connection, which had proven so useful.

Most of the other skill trees I'd seen had three root-level spells, but Nature had five. Had it always? I couldn't be sure. Five was a lot, and I only had the one remaining skill point, so I was already grumbling to myself about needing to choose between four different options. That was going to be an entire two more levels' points just investing in the Nature tree to reach the first trunk-level option—and that made me both desperate to be able to unlock it and terrified it would suck.

Okay, show me what you've got, I thought.

I aimed my intent at the root farthest to the left.

Immediately, I sensed a wider theme at play.

Gu h-Àrd (Passive)—You gain an understanding of all things above the earth: the currents of the air, the patterns of the clouds, and those that make their home therein. You receive an immediate +2 to Mind and a bonus to calling upon the powers of weather, wind, and creatures of the heavens. With experience, you may also summon the storm.

While Gu h-Àrd will not increase in levels as active spells will, your understanding of magic will, on occasion, trigger evolution.

Holy shit.

Again, there was nuance in the Gaelic that seeped into me. The name of the skill was written as an adverb or a prepositional phrase that felt more active than simply "above" might in English.

If my hunch was correct, there would be a complementary phrase . . . there.

I moved my concentration to the right-most point of the roots, satisfaction blooming as I read.

Gu h-Ìosal (Passive)—You gain an understanding of all things below the earth: the waters that flow, the roots that grow, and those that make their home therein. You receive an immediate +2 to Mind and a bonus to calling on the powers of flora and earth-bound fauna. With experience, you may also free the forest to do your bidding.

While Gu h-Ìosal will not increase in levels as active spells will, your understanding of magic will, on occasion, trigger evolution.

At the phrase *free the forest to do your bidding*, I was sold.

It took all of my willpower—and every point of my Will stat—not to immediately drop that last skill point into Gu h-Ìosal. I just knew it would also enhance my Tàthadh skill tree, which made it a sensible choice, but beyond that, it simply *called* to me.

I needed, however, to see the other options before I made a choice.

There were two left in the Nature tree, and I had to smile at their Gaelic names.

Taobh a-Staigh (Passive)—You gain an understanding of the intrinsic qualities of all life and its relationship to spirit. Rooted in Connection, this skill grants a permanent +1 to Mind and +1 to Pathos, and you receive a bonus to all spells and skills that deal with things internal: healing, buffs, and your understanding of your own spirit.

While Taobh a-Staigh will not increase in levels as active spells will, your understanding of magic will, on occasion, trigger evolution.

Unsurprisingly, after the skill that governed within came the one that took things outwith the internal world.

. . .

Taobh a-Muigh (Passive)—You gain an understanding of the relational qualities of all life and ecosystems as well as their place in the web of spirit. Rooted in Connection, this skill grants a permanent +1 to Mind and +1 to Will, and you receive a bonus to all spells and skills that deal with things external: bonds, brawls, and anything that acts upon the outside world.

While Taobh a-Muigh will not increase in levels as active spells will, your understanding of magic will, on occasion, trigger evolution.

Fuck. At this point, I didn't even care if the first trunk-level spell in the Nature tree was to let me lick my own elbow or clean my belly button of lint hands-free. All four of the other root-level skills were passives, but the bonuses? If I got all of them, that would be an additional six to Mind, one to Pathos, and one to Will, and I knew I would need to eventually spend the skill points to do just that.

Gritting my teeth, I forced myself to look at the Tàthadh tree, the one of bonds.

I got a small glow seeing the improvements to Tàth— but now I finally had the potential to unlock Caidreabhas, the one I'd briefly seen when I didn't have a point to spend. I looked more closely at it now.

Caidreabhas—This skill is a foundational one in the Tàthadh tree, but it is not one to be used lightly. Caidreabhas, like Tàth, forms a consensual bond with an animal companion, but unlike Tàth, this bond is permanent and will persist until your death or that of your companion.

Many animals in an ascended world stretch past their previous limits, often ranging from sentience to outright sapi-

ence, in time. Caidreabhas encourages such growth in your companion, bolstering the animal's natural strength and adaptability as well as their intelligence.

Unlike most active skills, Caidreabhas will not level, as for it to do so would cause first bonds to eventually lose their appeal with the ability to form more complex bonds. Instead, Caidreabhas evolves—with each animal you bond, your relationship with your companion will shift depending entirely upon what you invest in it.

Your current abilities allow you: 1 companion

Fuckles.

I wanted that skill so much it made my skin itch.

The Tàth link to the grey gelding was still in effect, but I didn't think it would last forever. With Freumhan, my awareness of the animal had deepened, and I could feel respect from the equine beast, as well as echoes of the same —if grudgingly—from the others in the herd. They carried some little resentment for being taken away from ample hay and shelter, but the wildness of the land was calling for them—that dampened any nostalgia they would have for a stable.

More, I realised that I wasn't sure I wanted to make the bond with the grey permanent. He was a cracking good ally, but bonding him would mean taking him from his herd, and I felt certain that was the wrong choice to make.

As if he could hear my thoughts, I felt a nudge of his curiosity as if he'd bumped his soft, horsey nose against my shoulder. I tried to project my gratitude, and after a moment, his presence abated.

If I could feel that much with the simpler, temporary

link Tàth created, how much *more* would Caidreabhas give me? Give the animal?

But there was no animal I thought I could offer that sort of permanent relationship. It was basically like getting married, for fuck's sake, just . . . without the sexual side. At least I *hoped*. That was a terrifying thought. If animals were going to become sapient—oh, god, it was only a matter of time. Not for me, personally, but I was a product of the internet age. Rule Thirty-Four was a thing for a reason.

For a moment, I was deeply, deeply relieved there was no longer an internet. I had no desire whatsoever to see magical apocalypse porn. Too soon. Way, way too soon.

I shifted my brain—with some effort—back to the subject at hand, leaving the Tàthadh tree in favour of checking out Arcane again, wondering if there was such a thing as a magical brain bleach.

No such luck.

I was a bit surprised to remember that I'd already sunk four skill points into Arcane. With Fuaran as a buff, Spèird as a multipurpose force spell, Purifire as offence, and Cumhachd as offence and who knew what else, I wasn't sure what to expect from the next spell up the trunk from Cumhachd.

After reading it, I still wasn't entirely sure.

Keen Eye—This ability allows you to examine an item, foe, or location, and in conjunction with Connection, it can reveal secrets or vital clues that will push you towards helpful information. Keen Eye comes with a one-time bonus to Mind of +1.

Continued usage will improve the complexity and usefulness of the information Keen Eye provides.

· · ·

Okay, I knew I'd been whinging about not having an instruction manual for the apocalypse, and on the surface, this felt like it would be useful—approximately four hours ago.

I would have loved to use it on Lord Bawbag and see what the fuck his deal was, but there was no way to do that now without getting back in his orbit. If he was even still alive.

Also, the beast or monster thing. Hell, it would have been useful with the simulacra, anything we'd fought.

Just knowing the skill existed was a useful tip, because if I'd gained access to it, pretty much anyone could, potentially.

That it was the fifth skill in the Arcane tree was telling. It must have been powerful, and as tempted as I was to get it, I just couldn't quite justify it to myself. Not yet. Not when Gu h-Ìosal could allow me to use the land itself to our benefit.

And that, I realised, was my decision made.

I went back to the Nature tree a bit reluctantly, still feeling pulled in multiple directions at once.

As soon as the skill point was spent, it was like someone took a too-tight belt off of my brain.

The only word I could use for it was *expansion*.

Like Freumhan had done for my internal sense of spirit, Gu h-Ìosal shifted my entire perception of the spirit around me. No more were the channels and tributaries of spirit inside me simply discrete entities from the ones beyond my skin—it was like everywhere I made contact with the world opened me up to harness it.

I almost lost my breath.

I could have lost *myself* for hours if I wasn't careful. The sensation of spirit circulating through me like blood but also entering from the environment like breath, exhaled back into the ambient energy? It filled me with a sense of joy and wonder that could almost qualify as ecstasy.

Was this what it meant for a world to ascend?

Was this what awaited us?

All I knew is I wanted more—I wanted to see what I could do with this new world.

Before I could completely get swept away, I needed to dig into my attributes and assign them.

But there were heaps of notifications waiting for me. Most weren't really surprising. I'd increased Beannachd Shlàinte a level, which had reset my uses—something for which I was fucking grateful—and I suspected that had to do with unlocking Fuaran as well as being close enough that Eilidh's healing had tipped me over that ledge. I was pleased to see I'd also finally increased my Healing affinity to level two. And I'd increased my skill Tàth to level three, and I was delighted to discover that I'd managed to gain a point in Dexterity, Constitution—a first without using a point!—and, my favourite, an entire three points to Spirit. That left my stats looking . . . surprisingly un-pathetic.

I had three attribute points to spend, and I decided to put one in Agility, one in Mind—which would add to the two I'd gotten with the expenditure of my skill point on Gu h-ìosal—and one more in Stamina.

Things were shaping up nicely.

Name: Calum Green
    Age: 36
    Level: 4
    Class: Hedge Witch (Further class selection at: Level 9)
    Affinities: Nature (Level 2), Healing (Level 2)

. . .

Alteration:
    Strength: 10
    Dexterity: 15
    Agility: 13
    Mind: 19

Regeneration:
    Constitution: 15
    Stamina: 17

Manipulation:
    Spirit: 19
    Pathos: 10
    Will: 23

Losing the temporary bonuses to Spirit and Pathos hurt, but then I realised something else—we hadn't harvested the humans we'd killed.

The thought of it was macabre.

I wasn't sure I *wanted* to have done that, but the idea of absorbing humans' spirit and pathos and will felt kind of . . . vile.

It hadn't seemed horrible when Eilidh's grandmother had done so to Robert, but the sudden image of someone like Lord Bawbag slaughtering people wholesale to siphon their magical energies and boost his own capacity—gaining him permanent points at one percent of whatever he got, no less—made my skin crawl.

What would stop someone from doing just that? Was this system really so broken that it would lay out that sort of temptation for the worst type of people?

The thought made my head reel.

Thankfully, Eilidh chose that moment to wake.

TWENTY-SEVEN

I hadn't finished with all the notifications—there was probably a quest update in there—but as soon as I sensed from the grey gelding that Eilidh was stirring, I tore myself out of my own head.

Rhona had the glazed-over look that said she was away with the ascension fairies, and I didn't want to disturb her. Instead, I went to Eilidh's side, pulling the bag of food out of my inventory and digging through it to find whatever I could that was high calorie and as easy to eat as possible.

Probably not the prunes.

Last thing Eilidh needed was to get the outrageous shits in the middle of sodding backwoods Argyll.

There were still bags of nuts and apricots in there, but instead, I went for the oatcakes, opening up a box and tugging apart the plastic.

"All right, there, Eilidh?" I asked her.

She swallowed where she lay, propped up on her right elbow very gingerly as if still afraid to put any weight on the healed shoulder.

"Water?" She croaked the word, and I immediately

grabbed my dry bag out of inventory and dug out a water bottle, passing it to her.

I was about to warn her not to drink too fast, but it didn't seem I needed to. She pushed herself up to sitting, grimacing as she sipped a little from the bottle. Eilidh crossed her legs, tucking the water bottle by her ankles after another few sips and reaching for the oatcakes.

"God, I'd kill for a burger," she muttered around a mouthful of oats.

"Mood," I agreed. "Low-key wishing I hadn't left the rat meat with your gran."

"*Rat?*" she asked, then shuddered. "Never mind. I don't want to know."

She finished one oatcake, then another. Then the other three in that sleeve, looking at me as if daring me to tell her she couldn't have more. I handed over the other sleeve from the box, flattening the now-empty cardboard and shoving it back in the bag with the plastic she passed back from the first.

"So that sucked," she said.

"You mean taking the equivalent of a thousand needles made of glass to the chest and then having to escape on horseback was somehow unpleasant?"

For a split second, her forehead tightened with what I thought was instinctive outrage, but then it smoothed out again. Guess we were not quite up to friendly banter from blatant animosity.

Gods, what I wouldn't have given for a Dragon Age-esque approval notification. *Eilidh greatly approves! Eilidh slightly disapproves.*

Why did I even care? It wasn't like there was anything here. She hated my guts, and it was hard to like someone who'd probably dump a bucket of water on Nigel Farage before me if we were both on fire.

"You healed me. Thank you."

The words sounded like Eilidh had to pry them out of her own larynx with a backhoe and a few metric tonnes of leverage.

"Do you honestly think I was going to just let you die?" I asked her incredulously before I could stop myself.

At that, she blinked. She opened her mouth. Then she shut it again. When she opened it a second time, I waved a hand at her.

"Never mind," I said curtly. "It doesn't matter. I wouldn't have, for the record. Obviously."

Rhona was still in screen-time mode, but I suddenly wanted to be anywhere but here. I dropped the bag of food by Eilidh.

"You should probably look at your notifications. I'm also leaving the kitten with you, so make sure she doesn't escape." With that, I deposited the kitten carrier in Eilidh's lap and walked away, my feet taking me towards the castle on the side of the loch.

Innes Chonnel Castle wasn't really on the shore but on a small island a short ways out into Loch Awe. I didn't fancy swimming in February most of the time, but Iain and Meeksy were both huge into wild swimming, and they'd dragged me enough times to convince me of the lie that it was pleasant. Gods, I hoped they were okay. Oban was just over the water and a few hills—it felt so far away.

I'd swim there if I thought it would go faster, cold be damned.

But now we had preternaturally enhanced Constitution and Stamina, and the likelihood of drowning due to the body going into hypothermic shock had lessened considerably. I wasn't going to *actually* swim to Oban, but I could swim the handful of meters out to the castle to clear my head.

Plus, I was a sweaty mess.

My nonexistent kingdom for a simple cleaning spell.

Mind made up, I cast Connection. Now that I wasn't in the heat of battle, I could truly appreciate the changes my new attributes and levelling up the spell had wrought.

Before, it was like watching currents by squinting at the waves of spirit and trying to make sense of them. The first level up had taken that to visible patterns, like the world had been overlaid with flows I could follow.

Now, though, with Connection sitting at level three, it was like those flows came to life.

Perhaps it was that in combination with Gu h-Ìosal, the skill that allowed me greater understanding of all things below the sky, I could simply parse what I saw better. I wasn't sure. All I knew was that staring into the peaty waters of Loch Awe, waters that were too murky to see more than a meter or so in front of my face, suddenly there was a whole new world.

Spirit lit up gold where fish swam, their movements making swirls and eddies from their fins displacing the water. Motes sparkled throughout, bits of sediment and peat, decomposing materials, algae, microorganisms.

I would have thought that being able to discern all of that with my naked eye would gross me out, but instead it drew me closer. It was like knowing how the human body was home to billions of other organisms, from gut flora that were now known to affect everything from cravings to mood and back again to the tiny mites that lived on our skin and eyelashes.

Connection, I thought.

We were as dependent upon our hitchhikers as they were on us, a symbiosis millions of years in the making.

Without taking off my clothes—though I did undo my belt to tuck that and the dagger into my inventory—I stepped into the water.

Perhaps it was the fact that my body and equilibrium had changed, but it didn't feel uncomfortably cold. Sure, there was a shock of a chill at first, but then my body adapted, and in the space of a few breaths, I dove under.

I immediately regretted my clothes, but I didn't try to strip them off. There was a full day of fighting and fear practically forged into them by now, and the short swim to the wee island worked wonders to dislodge the built-up sweat and dirt.

Hovering in the water a bit, I triggered Connection again. The last thing I wanted was some enormous, ascension-enraged beastie nibbling at my toesies when I could barely see past my waist.

With the sun going down, visibility was even worse.

But there was nothing there except normal fish. I idly wished I had that Keen Eye skill. I could barely tell a perch from a pike unless it was filleted and slapped with a label in a Sainsbury's fish counter.

After a few minutes of treading water and jostling my armpits enough to feel slightly less soaked with BO, I made my way to the island's shore. It was more a mess of reeds and rocks, but I clambered out onto the small chunk of land.

The wind was cold outwith the water, and while I didn't have a cleaning spell, I did have fire.

I channelled Purifire, just a trickle of it, and then, thinking of Freumhan and the veins of my body that circulated spirit instead of blood, I imagined the Purifire travelling those same waterways.

Blue-green flame ran from my hands all the way up my arms, racing across my chest. It brought with it a sense of renewal, of purification, of warmth.

Within a few moments, my clothes were bone dry and smelled . . . fresh.

Holy shit.

Purifire, a surprisingly effective cleaning spell I'd wished for. I wondered if I could use it on anyone else. The sudden picture of Eilidh or Rhona going up in flames chased that impulse out of my brain.

That question was a bit moot for now.

I picked my way up through the overgrown underbrush that surrounded the castle ruins.

What wasn't moot was that I *still* somehow had notifications to go through. Was this going to be the rest of my life? Just staring vacant-eyed into the abyss for an hour a day?

Then again, considering the screen time notifications I used to get on my iPhone, maybe I should just shut the fuck up and be grateful. I shuddered at the memory of the time it told me my average screen time had gone down . . . to eleven hours a day.

Yeah, an hour of post-apocalyptic meditation was probably better on the eyeballs. And mental health.

Though after reading the first one, I wasn't too sure about the mental health thing.

You have discovered a quest!
 The Hills Have Eyes: Part II

In completing the quest The Hills Have Eyes, you have found further mysteries to unravel, and your quest has evolved.

While you discovered the source of the simulacra and the tip of the proverbial iceberg of Lord Edwin Thomas Sackington's plans for Argyll, do not grow complacent thinking that he perished in your Ring of Fire at the hands—or jaws—of the mysterious beast.

You have deduced that those with little regard for humanity appear to be at a startling advantage in an ascended world. Be assured that Lord Sackington is seizing that advantage as fully as he can, but you have also understood that the ideals of the Ascended Alliance do not brook such things. It is up to you to discover more about this seeming oxymoron.

With the destruction you wreaked upon Lord Sackington's estate, even he will need time to recover and regroup. Be aware that whatever enmity you awoke in him with the initial destruction of his simulacrum has grown exponentially with the insult you visited upon his home.

Remember the prime directive of the ascension and take time to recover and regroup yourselves.

You will need to prepare.

Objectives:

-Create a weapon (Calum Green only. Tip: use the item you received as a quest reward for Part I)

-Craft the following items:

-Basic armour x3 (chest plate, greaves, boots, bracers, pauldrons, helmet)

-Basic upgraded daggers x3

-Basic upgraded claymore

-Basic sheaths x3

-Forage food

-Nettles x10

-Alexanders x10

-Dandelions x20
-Sweet Violets x10
-Velvet Shank Mushroom x10
-Wild Garlic Leaves x10
Rewards:
-Experience (commensurate with current level progression)
-Unlock The Hills Have Eyes: Part III
-1 item (ascension dependent)
-All cooldowns reset

As this is a shared quest, it cannot be completed alone. You must work together if you are to have any hope of successfully progressing. Remember the ascension directive.

I reread the entire thing twice, fascination and terror warring in the pit of my stomach. Take that, Eilidh. That was at least two entire emotions.

The terror part I had to engage with first, if nothing else to name it and then punt it back into the recesses of my mind where it could rear its head at the most inopportune moment when I'd been repressing it into a none-too-sturdy bottle.

Lord Bawbag was alive, enraged, and had escaped the beast.

That was bad.

But we'd bloodied his nose—literally and metaphorically—and here was the system telling us we had time to regroup.

How much time was anyone's guess, but beyond that, if *we* were getting quests about him, I'd be stupid to assume he wasn't also getting a quest about us.

Did it work that way? I had no fucking clue.

Remember the ascension directive.

Clearly, the system thought that was important enough to say twice, as was the explicit warning that this quest couldn't be completed alone. I thought back to the first text the system had scrolled past my face, in my flat a million years ago—or, more accurately, last Friday.

With a thought, I was able to pull it up.

I took an irrational moment to be thankful that if this system wasn't giving us a handbook, at least it was providing us with the means to sift back through what it said to us, like an internal browser cache we could scour with a thought.

And there it was.

As a planet unprepared for ascension, your trials will be many, not least of which survival. We can offer little more guidance than this: no one, even the prepared, can survive alone. Every sentient species known to us has one thing in common, and one thing alone.

Strength is found in connection, not isolation. You will never have every skill needed to thrive.

The ascension directive had to be that one piece of guidance they highlighted there.

There were clues there that hovered at the edge of my consciousness, just out of reach.

They'd have to wait.

As I processed through terror into fascination, I also got a healthy kick in the nuts: chagrin.

I'd forgotten the goddamn item reward from the last quest.

Worse, it appeared to be a fucking instruction manual.

CHAPTER
TWENTY-EIGHT

A *Guide to Woodcraft in an Ascended World.*
That was the name of the thing.

It sounded like a book, gave off the *feel* of a book, yet it was purely inside my head, a figment of synapses and magic and whatever the fuck had ended my world.

It only took a moment of concentration, and those same synapses all seemed to fire at once.

My brain shorted out as it flooded with images, sensations—wood grain and balance, the density of oak versus the punky sawdust of an old deadfall, the springy bounce of willow and the timeless patience of yew.

In moments, it was as if my hands lived a thousand lives of woodworkers that had built tables and chairs, powerful recurves and clubs, the perfect polished arc of a lintel and the utility of a simple wheel.

And beyond that, something else.

Something I needed.

A mage's staff.

My mind hadn't managed to put together the concept of crafting in this ascended world.

I'd been thinking of it purely as apocalypse, the end of something, the return to the Stone Age or the Bronze Age or anything I could easily map onto my understanding of the loss of all human technological advances at once.

It hadn't occurred to me that this might be something entirely *other*, something for which I couldn't hope to be prepared.

And with the almost gamification aspects of the ascension system, quests and experience and rewards and all that, I thought part of my mind had just assumed this would be like being yeeted into a massive campaign of Dungeons and Dragons where the stakes were real life.

What if that was wrong too?

For a long moment as the woodworking knowledge and experience shaped the malleable twists and turns of my brain, I sat back on my heels in an emotion I hadn't really let myself feel in so long I couldn't even begin to guess the last time it had touched me.

Wonder.

Beyond the fact that I could use magic, touch magic, shape fire from my hands.

Beyond the miracle that Eilidh was still alive after a wound that, a week ago, would have killed her almost instantly.

Beyond the marvel of, say, looking at those first images from the Webb telescope in the third year of the pandemic hellscape and seeing billions of years back in time. Beyond anything my puny human brain had experienced up until this moment.

For the first time, the system's words sank in.

The pure potential, the pristine possibility.

What would ascension look like for a world that was ready for it?

I could imagine the celebrations, the excitement, the joy —where instead Earth, war-torn and warming Earth, plagued by pandemic and human greed alike, had received only terror and grief.

My own universe seemed to expand as I considered our losses. I couldn't guess at how many casualties there had been already—I'd fled Glasgow too quickly to know. But places where cars had suddenly stalled out at high speeds on the motorways? Planes in the sky? Where the first monsters they encountered were beasts like that terrifying creature up the glen and not simply a centipede or a rat?

God.

And this system, this Ascended Alliance, they didn't expect us to survive.

Which meant there was no way, none, that they expected us to *thrive*.

To go through this accidentally and do it blindfolded with our hands tied behind our backs with *zero* preparation or knowledge on how to so much as greet these challenges, let alone overcome them?

I felt like I stood in an endless starscape in my own mind, inky black peppered with the smudges and swirls of distant galaxies, the clouds of nebulae writ large in infrared. I couldn't have explained why this book, a wood-craft manual of all things, had sparked this sort of expansion.

Ultimately, the why didn't matter.

I came back to myself in pieces, first with tingles as I twitched my fingertips, then with a breath that seemed to pour rejuvenation into my lungs.

Our ascension had been an accident, but that didn't mean we had to meekly roll over and die.

If Lord Bawbag and people like him the world over were

going to gain power by murder—they always had, but the system made it all the more literal now—so be it. I couldn't stop them.

Not yet.

But as I looked around the darkening sky and the shadow of Innes Chonnel Castle beside me, I realised I had something they didn't.

I knew they would lose.

No matter what they did, no matter how many humans they sent to hell, the Ascended Alliance wouldn't suffer the bastards to survive. Once they were able to reach Earth when the dust settled?

Yeah—those sons of bitches were cosmic toast.

That alone would be a certain amount of nihilistic comfort. The problem was, it would be way too late for the rest of us by then. No one was coming to rescue us—the Alliance would just be cleaning up the mess.

I conjured a small globe of Purifire in my left hand, making a circuit of the tiny island.

The book had reinforced everything my mother had ever drilled into my reluctant brain about trees. The island was mostly deciduous, oak and birch, a beech or two.

With Freumhan at work, I could feel them, and when I triggered Connection and relaxed into the flows of spirit that surrounded me, for a moment I almost felt like I was one of them.

"All things below," I muttered to myself.

There was an old oak near the centre of the island, its flows of spirit less busy than the younger birches that flanked it. It had been here a long time; it knew its place.

The woodcraft in my mind whispered to me, and a smile quirked the corners of my mouth.

I knew what to do.

Maybe for the first time in my forsaken, fucking pathetic hamster of a life.

Threads of spirit still wove through me, keeping Connection active, drawing on the ambient spirit around me and, for another first time, tugging on what I recognised as the blood-red pathos and gold-tinged will.

The will was stronger; it dwarfed the pathos.

As I reached out to the old oak, though, the tree reached back.

The world lit up around me, colours melding into white that left prismatic images dancing across the inside of my eyelids when I blinked.

My hand found what was offered—a proud, straight length of hardwood topped with a perfect hollow sphere that swirled with the grains of the oak.

I lost track of how long I worked there, drawing magic from the eager birches, the busy beeches, the life in the ground beneath my feet.

But when I was finally finished, I held in my hand a weapon.

A staff.

As I finally released my hold on my dwindling spirit, a wave of exhaustion threatened to tip me over. I braced myself on the staff, which felt as solid as the oak it had come from.

Everything in my mind that had led to this moment seemed to focus in the sensation of the staff meeting earth.

Help would come too late for us—I knew in my marrow that the Ascended Alliance had already written us off as lost, an unfortunate casualty of a cosmic accident.

But that was the thing about humans.

We could be horrible. We could cause harm to one

another for any number of asinine reasons. Human history was written in blood and cruelty.

But in the midst of all that? We sent a ship to another world with a little robot we called *Curiosity*. We set foot on our own moon. We reached out a million miles from home and cried out for the stars to get just one glimpse of the universe we sprang from.

In the darkest moments of our history, the ones so full of malice they scarred places like Auschwitz forever, people risked everything to save one life. To help someone who wasn't like them.

To look into the eyes of this planet's most noxious cunts and then send those fuckers straight into the pits of hell where they belonged.

Our ascension was an accident—but that didn't mean we had to roll over and take it.

Humans were too stubborn for that.

I was too stubborn for that.

One hand on my staff, I felt my spine straighten with the thought. Clarity like crystal for one shining moment.

Lord Bawbag thought he'd won something.

We'd show him what we were made of.

I took one last look at the oak.

I couldn't see any indication on the tree that I had carved away its trunk, but in the residual glow that emanated from the staff itself, I did see something else that hadn't been there before.

Every tree on the island of Innes Chonnel was covered in spring buds.

For the first time since the world had ended, I felt something like the kindling of hope.

World first!

Calum Green of Scotland has crafted the first living weapon on Earth.

An ascended world is the pinnacle of possibility and potential, and he has discovered one of the richest boons the ascension has to offer.

The chances of crafting a living weapon are exceedingly rare, but improving your crafting knowledge and ability—as well as your connection to manipulation resources—can make such things more likely.

He is the first, but he won't be the last.

Will you be the next?

The notification almost made me inhale a lungful of water.

It came as I was two-thirds of the way through the short swim back to the mainland, and I flailed in the darkened loch, spluttering at the sudden flash of gold in my vision.

What the actual fuck?

That was what I got for not examining the staff before I popped it into my inventory. I didn't know how long I'd been gone, but I figured Eilidh and Rhona were likely getting antsy.

The tone of that message had been decidedly . . . announcement-y. The thought that it had gone out globally made me consider inhaling a lungful of water on purpose.

Thanks for putting a fucking target on my head, O illustrious Ascended Alliance assholes, I thought as I dragged myself out of the loch and used my slowly refilling spirit well to dry myself with Purifire again.

I picked my way through the underbrush back to where the others waited, orange-gold light dancing across their faces from the small fire that burned in a hasty pit between them.

"Antsy" was not, perhaps, the correct term for what they were feeling when they caught sight of me emerging from behind a hedge of bramble.

"What the *fuck* did you do?" Eilidh burst out, startling a couple of the drowsing horses into wakefulness.

"I don't know," Rhona said blandly. "That shining golden PSA seemed to put a pretty fine point on it. He went off and created a living weapon without us."

Oi.

The exhaustion from working so much with magic tugged at my temples, bringing with it the unfortunate bloom of a headache.

"I didn't exactly mean to," I said. "I got a woodcrafting book as a quest reward, and I was just trying to make myself a weapon. I didn't expect the fucking tree to lend a hand. Branch. Whatever."

Both of the women just stared at me.

"Right," Eilidh said finally after a long moment of silence. "You're going to explain. Right now."

CHAPTER
TWENTY-NINE

Explaining, as it turned out, took a *while*.

Rhona was still brand new to how any of this worked, and while Eilidh clearly enjoyed rubbing my face in everything I didn't know, she was little better off than I was. I started with the horror of my realisation about how people like Lord Bawbag could gain seemingly infinite spirit capacity by just fucking up everyone and everything they encountered, and that was enough to set both Eilidh and Rhona to angry spluttering for a solid five minutes. I couldn't really blame them; I hadn't taken that particular epiphany well either.

But they both shut up when I got to the next bit.

I watched the same helpless rage I'd felt play across both their faces, along with the same spiteful satisfaction as we collectively acknowledged that aye, the cunts might win, but they'd get annihilated by the Ascended Alliance in the end.

We'd just all be dead long before that ever happened.

And then I explained the staff, pulling it from inventory. I mean, I explained as well as I *could*. I still wasn't sure what had happened; there were so many variables at work in that moment that I couldn't have pinpointed any one of them as the point of success or avoided failure.

That gave me the chance to actually look at the staff.

I was feeling the sharp edge of self-recrimination for not having the Keen Eye ability—I really wanted to see what made this staff so special—but even without the ability to examine the weapon, I could *feel* it.

Brac-Meanmna.

The words came to me unbidden, and they seemed to click into place. It felt right.

Brac, in Gaelic, meant several things—it could be an arm, the curve of a breaking wave, the branch of a hart's antlers.

And meanmna was, at its heart, spirit. It was what we'd been given with this ascension, but as with many Gaelic words, "spirit" simply didn't cover it. It also meant mettle. It meant desire. It meant imagination and will and courage. The boldness to do what must be done.

In my first moments post-ascension, I'd stupidly chucked a couple points into Strength, fearing my own stupid conceptions of what it meant to be strong.

I'd misunderstood what the system whispered. Or maybe I'd just buried every longing I'd ever had so deeply that I'd conflated it with muscle mass. Who could say?

But watching as Eilidh and Rhona passed the living weapon back and forth, their fingers tracing the whorls of wood grain that formed the hollow, delicate sphere at the end in awe, I had what felt like the hundredth epiphany of the day.

What if strength was as simple as doing the next right thing, no matter how scary or hard?

I hadn't realised I'd spoken aloud until Eilidh's arm

went still, half extended as she reluctantly held the staff out to me.

"That's always been true," she said softly. "The assholes of the world always think it just means who can punch the hardest—they forget or never knew that it's more the ability to take a punch and get back up. Or to get knocked out and try again. To keep going, to endure, to work *with* people instead of simply running roughshod over them. That's far harder than simply throwing temper tantrums."

I wanted to argue with that—to tell her that of course I knew that. John Frost, my erstwhile Dundonian bam of a nemesis, was the asshole type who thought intimidation and tantrums were how to throw his dick around.

But hadn't I been the one whose first impulse had been to play on his terms?

I took back the staff, unsure of what to say.

Rhona, though, seemed to know exactly what to say.

"We can't let them win," she said fiercely. "And Lord Sack—Lord Bawbag isn't gonnae stop. He's going to keep killing people, keep getting stronger. Yous can be as philosophical as you want to be, but philosophy won't stop him from fucking *murdering* people."

"Neither of us are proposing we do that," Eilidh said to her, rolling her eyes. "Does it look like we just stuck out our necks for him to cut our throats?"

Rhona faltered at that, and even in the ruddy cast of the firelight, I could see the pinkish blotches blooming on her cheeks and neck.

"We're not saying we let him win," I told her. "We're saying the opposite of 'let the cunts win'. But what we *are* saying is that the three of us can't stop him alone. The ascension directive."

"The what now?" Eilidh asked.

"'Strength is found in connection, not isolation. You will never have every skill needed to thrive,'" I quoted.

"The quest did say to go to Oban," Rhona said slowly.

At my startled look, she gave me a wry smile.

"Guess I'm officially on Team World First," she said, to which Eilidh gave a snort and rolled her eyes. "I got the quest too—it seems to have added me to your last one before you completed it, so I got—I mean. Ugh, back up, Rhona. I think—I think the foraging part is for me. My quest reward was *Ascended Survival: Foraging Amid the Ascension's Flora and Fauna.*"

"And I got *A Guide to Crafting in an Ascended World,*" Eilidh said, suddenly all business. Her blue eyes turned shrewd as she met my gaze assessingly. "You got woodworking. Rhona got foraging. I got crafting."

"Message received loud and clear," I muttered. "Guess we're stuck with each other."

"Team World—" Rhona began only for Eilidh to burst out with an emphatic "*No* fucking way."

I couldn't help it. I burst out laughing.

"What—is—funny," Eilidh said, her gaze turning flinty.

"Absolutely nothing," I said. "You pick the name. I'm going to sodding get some sleep."

It probably stood to reason that since I bowed out of the "name the team" discussion, we ended up with something that made me want to facepalm.

It wasn't as if Team Wildcat was *bad*, per se, but to me it sounded vaguely like an American sports team and therefore, to me, sounded entirely alien.

What was more surprising than the name, however,

was that its inspiration had been perched upon my chest when I woke up the next morning.

And she hadn't left my side since I got up.

Rhona seemed perturbed by this development, especially since the kitten was slippery enough to squeeze right out of her hands when she went to retrieve her so I could go off into the bushes to have a wee.

I ended up having to piss into a blackthorn bush with a tiny kitten perched on my shoulder, which would have been less than ideal even if she didn't insist on digging her razor-sharp little death claws into the tender flesh at the base of my neck.

"You're awfully chipper all of the sudden," I said to the kitten as I made my way back to the women.

She mewed in my ear in response.

The horses were still milling around, and I noticed that someone had unsaddled Lord Bawbag's walnut mare and given her a good scratch down in the absence of grooming implements. There was a small pile of things upon the saddle itself that seemed to have been pillaged from the small-sized saddlebags that accompanied it.

The kitten's carrier was over by that, so I made my way to it and set about adding water to the kitten formula in one of the other bottles, which did not encourage said kitten to retract claws. Instead, she used them to clamber down my chest, introducing me to what it felt like to have one's nipple stabbed with tiny needles.

I tried to bear it stoically, but after the third poke with one of her hind paws, I yelped.

Naturally, that startled her, and she dug in more.

"Having trouble?" Eilidh asked dryly.

I hadn't seen her come up.

"I'm fine." I gingerly settled myself on a boulder so the

kitten could sit—hopefully non-violently—in my lap for her breakfast.

Giving the bottle a healthy shake, I channelled a thread of Purifire into it the same way I had yesterday while Eilidh looked on, nonplussed, when I tested the temperature on the inside of my wrist.

The kitten got to her duty with alacrity, attacking the nipple with such vigour that for a moment I felt relieved it was made of rubber and not feline flesh. But that just reminded me all over again that Lord Bawbag had murdered this wee endangered floof's mother, and anger kindled.

"Fascinating," Eilidh said. "If I didn't know any better, I'd say you just displayed two emotions in as many seconds. That's actually plural."

"I hope I learn from this experience and that I grow," I deadpanned. "Just wishing Lord Bawbag a very hearty fuck off into the sun."

"We definitely agree on that."

Just as she said that, I felt a tug through the link with the grey gelding. I was somewhat surprised he hadn't broken it overnight, but I knew as soon as I felt him stir that he was about to.

I took a deep breath.

We probably could have convinced the horses to take us to Oban, but I didn't want to. Not only were they free and gaining strength for the first time in their lives, but they had more than fulfilled their part of the bargain we'd made. It would be unfair to ask more of them, especially when bringing them into human civilisation could put them at risk.

It was with some reluctance that I looked up at the grey. The kitten still suckled at the bottle, her paws kneading the inside of my right thigh, and the horse was a short distance away.

Eilidh was saying something I couldn't hear.

The grey sent me one last impression through the bond, almost a thought. It was a thanks, a proud one, and with it came a sense of the same from the rest of the herd.

Grateful. Free.

Eilidh broke off when the horses began moving away all at once, some raising their heads from the grass with bits of green still dangling from their lips.

"What's happening?" she asked, just as Rhona hurried up to our small camp from the bushes where I presumed she'd gone to pee.

"They're leaving," I said.

"What?" Eilidh spun to look at me. "We need them!"

The grey pawed at the ground at that—I wasn't sure if he could really understand the words, but her meaning seemed to have gotten across loud and clear.

"We'll be fine," I said. "If they come with us, they might not be. Let them go."

Eilidh turned on me with an inscrutable expression, looking like she wanted to fight, but between the nursing kitten on my lap and a stable full of horses making their way to the southwest, something seemed to stop her.

"If they're leaving us," she said after a moment, "we've got a long walk ahead. Ten minutes."

For a moment, I thought we were going to have to leave the saddle where it sat. Rhona had not been peeing like I thought, but foraging, and her inventory was mostly full of nettles and wild garlic. It stacked, but each plant still took up its own slot. Gods, I hoped our inventories would increase in size.

Eilidh hesitated for a second, glancing sideways at me almost guiltily, and then dropped a wooden crate from her inventory onto the floor. A gust of wind blew a lock of her auburn waves into her face, and her sudden batting at it distracted me long enough that it was Rhona's "What the fuck?" that got me to actually look at the crate.

It was full of grenades.

"What the fuck?" I said incredulously. "You stole *grenades*?"

"Meep!" said the kitten, who was perched again on my shoulder.

"I didn't want *them* to have them, so aye, I stole grenades!"

"Do they even work?" Rhona peered at them as if the

crate contained a full nest of hungry, angry adders instead of war-time munitions. "The guns didn't work."

"One gun didn't work," Eilidh said matter-of-factly. "We don't know that all guns have stopped working. Well. Except the ones I personally broke."

"You broke their guns?" Rhona's entire face lit up. "Oh my god."

"Only one way to find out," I muttered, picking up one of the grenades.

"Don't you dare," Eilidh said.

She snatched it out of my hand, gave it a quick glance, and then expertly grasped the spoon with her left hand, held the thing against her chest, pulled out the pin with a quick twist and tug, and lobbed the grenade with perfect follow-through—up over the loch and pretty much straight up in the air.

I don't think any of us had quite prepared for the additional Strength stat boost.

The chunk of explosive weaponry *launched* at the sky, and all three of us stared at it, dumbfounded, as it torpedoed over Loch Awe.

It finally hit the zenith of the throw what looked like a couple hundred metres up.

If anyone had been watching the three of us standing there, they'd probably say we looked cartoonishly stupid, three adults and a kitten staring at a speck of black metal as it arced back towards the water's surface.

And fell, and fell, and fell.

I couldn't have been the only one who was counting off seconds. I thought grenades usually exploded within about five, but my inner timer was well past seven by the time the thing dropped past the ridge of mountains and became harder to see.

All three of us jumped when it hit the water in the distance with a barely visible and very anticlimactic sploop.

At least that was the sound I imagined it making, since even my ascended ears couldn't pick it up.

"Do we assume the others will also not work?" I asked dubiously.

"Is anyone else wondering how Eilidh clearly knew how to *throw a bloody grenade*?" Rhona burst out, far more explosively than the literal explosive.

"Her parents are Marines," I said absently at the same time Eilidh said, "My parents are Marines."

We looked at each other and both hurriedly looked away again.

"My da's in the bloody air force, and he didn't teach me how to fly a bomber!" Rhona said. "What on earth—"

"You know how some parents are normal?" Eilidh said, eyeing the remaining grenades.

"No," I said.

"No," Rhona said. "I mean, I assume somewhere out there, some parent is normal, whatever that means, but I wouldn't know about it."

"Mine are extra not normal," Eilidh muttered.

She picked up another grenade and repeated the motion. Grasp to chest, twist, pull, yeet.

Again, we watched the thing soar in an overpowered arc into the sky and counted off eight seconds—I counted, anyway—until it again hit the surface of the loch with no boom, just sploop.

Rhona looked sideways at Eilidh, clearly thinking of how the older woman had yanked the grenade out of my hand, and she picked one up with her left hand, imitating what Eilidh had done.

"Lefty?" Eilidh asked with a sigh, apparently resigning herself to us wanting to play too.

Rhona nodded.

Eilidh did take the grenade from her, but this time, she just flipped it upside down in her left hand with the spoon facing out and the pin down instead of up.

"Like this," she said. "But do *not* pull that pin out until you practice throwing a couple times. Preferably with something that has less chance of exploding. Or zero chance of exploding, ideally."

I'd thought we were going to leave in ten minutes, but there was something strangely cathartic about instead standing on the shores of Loch Awe and chucking fist-sized rocks into the air as hard as we could—which was pretty hard, though Eilidh's Strength stat blew me and Rhona both away.

Not literally.

By the time Eilidh was content with our ability to time a pin-pull and and be human grenade launchers, we were all laughing.

Together, we lobbed a volley of three grenades into the air, counting off the seconds aloud. Rhona's hit the water first, six seconds in. Then mine at nine, and finally Eilidh's at eleven.

When we were done, and the crate was finally empty of potential boom, we all sounded a little breathless.

"That was fun," Rhona said. "I wish they'd exploded, though."

"I don't," Eilidh said. "But that is better data than a couple flukes. So now I'm wondering *why* nothing explosive seems to explode, except with magical help like the rifle at Kilchurn."

"Maybe this Ascended Alliance doesn't like violence," Rhona mused.

"Nah," I said. "They're plenty happy to let us kill each other. Or at least they assume we will. It's probably more likely that the infusion of spirit somehow altered the chemical composition of gunpowder along with the way it affected electrical systems. Might not have even been *much*, just enough that it would no longer create the reaction it used to."

Both Eilidh and Rhona stared at me, Rhona with confusion and Eilidh with appraising thoughtfulness.

"Astute," she said after a long pause. I thought that might be the first time she'd ever paid me a compliment.

It was a strange feeling, and one I didn't really like. I didn't want to care what she thought of me. When I'd been with Susanna and Eilidh had hated me, I'd just kind of taken it. And now here we were at the dawning of some brave new world, and I didn't know how to feel about the tingles that inhabited the backs of my arms—of *all* bloody places—at her praise.

"Aye, well," I said after too long of a pause, "I work in IT. Anyone can tell you how one stupid change fucks everything else up."

Rhona's face had gone from confusion to assessing as well as she looked back and forth between the two of us.

"I'm perfectly happy to live in a world where it's less convenient to murder people, personally." The young woman waved her hand dismissively. "Humans will obviously find a way, but it's different when you have to at least look someone in the eye or feel their breath when you stab them."

"That is . . . very specific. But also true," Eilidh said after a moment.

Silence took over the morning until the kitten moved on my shoulder—I'd almost forgotten she was there.

"Right," I said. "We should get moving if we ever want to get to Oban."

I couldn't help feel that this little interlude had just been us stalling—who knew what we'd find when we got there?

The empty crate ended up being a boon, if not a boom.

Before we started off, Rhona took all her foraged items out of her inventory and arranged them neatly in the crate, then tucked the whole thing back into its pocket dimension —or whatever our inventory space actually was. I wasn't about to hypothesise about quantum mechanics.

The kitten, thankfully, agreed to go back in the carrier, which I passed to Eilidh with some reluctance. I couldn't figure out why I wanted the wee beastie with me, but handing her over was surprisingly difficult.

There was a chill in the air as we made our way south past the castle on its island and onward, following the southeastern shore of the loch.

The chill wasn't out of character for February in Scotland, but something about it felt . . . wrong.

As the sun crept higher in the sky, obscured behind a blanket of low-hanging cloud that washed in from the west, I found myself triggering Connection almost constantly, eyes always moving. Every hair on my body seemed to be on high alert, and by the time we paused for lunch, my shoulders and neck ached so much with the tension that I had to stand still for ten minutes for my inherent healing to soothe it away.

The others didn't seem quite as on edge.

While we polished off some of the food Mòrag had given us, I skimmed through my notifications.

There was a welcome boost to Stamina from the trek, but I was disappointed not to see another level up for Connection, considering how much I'd been using it.

I was, however, pleased by the quest update.

The Hills Have Eyes: Part II

In completing the quest The Hills Have Eyes, you have found further mysteries to unravel, and your quest has evolved.

While you discovered the source of the simulacra and the tip of the proverbial iceberg of Lord Edwin Thomas Sackington's plans for Argyll, do not grow complacent thinking that he perished in your Ring of Fire at the hands—or jaws—of the mysterious beast.

You have deduced that those with little regard for humanity appear to be at a startling advantage in an ascended world. Be assured that Lord Sackington is seizing that advantage as fully as he can, but you have also understood that the ideals of the Ascended Alliance do not brook such things. It is up to you to discover more about this seeming oxymoron.

With the destruction you wreaked upon Lord Sackington's estate, even he will need time to recover and regroup. Be aware that whatever enmity you awoke in him with the initial destruction of his simulacrum has grown exponentially with the insult you visited upon his home.

Remember the prime directive of the ascension and take time to recover and regroup yourselves.

You will need to prepare.

Objectives:

-Create a weapon (Calum Green only.) (Complete)

-Craft the following items:

-Basic armour x3 (chest plate, greaves, boots, bracers, pauldrons, helmet)

-Basic upgraded daggers x3

-Basic upgraded claymore

-Basic sheaths x3

-Forage food

-Nettles x10 (23/10 Complete)

-Alexanders x10 (3/10)

-Dandelions x20 (31/10 Complete)

-Sweet Violets x10

-Velvet Shank Mushroom x10

-Wild Garlic Leaves x10 (13/10 Complete)

Rewards:

-Experience (commensurate with current level progression)

-Unlock The Hills Have Eyes: Part III

-1 item (ascension dependent)

-All cooldowns reset

As this is a shared quest, it cannot be completed alone. You must work together if you are to have any hope of successfully progressing. Remember the ascension directive.

Eilidh'd been slacking.

I knew she'd gotten the requisite item she needed to learn how to craft, but I'd no idea if she needed something else too. A workbench? A hammer? Literally any tools whatsoever?

Just because I'd crafted a staff without needing to carve it myself didn't mean she could make three entire sets of armour, I guessed.

But the one thing the ascension had taught me about

their quests was that they didn't seem to give us anything that was impossible.

I wanted to ask her, but I didn't think we had created that comfortable of a truce, and she had far too many sharp objects close to hand.

"What the fuck is that?"

Rhona's sudden outburst shook me out of my screen time. She was standing a short distance from where Eilidh munched on some walnuts, her back to the both of us.

I moved from where I'd been leaning against a tree to see what she was looking at.

It looked like . . . goo. Like translucent jelly, not unlike a jellyfish that had washed up on the seashore.

Loch Awe, however, was a freshwater loch, not a sea loch.

Now I *really* wished I had Keen Eye.

"I don't suppose either of you have Keen Eye as a skill, do you?" I asked them, and from Rhona's blank look, I deduced that was a no from her.

A scuff of shoes told me Eilidh was approaching, and she peered over Rhona's shoulder at the jelly.

"Duilleag nam beann," Eilidh said after a moment.

"I don't speak Gaelic," Rhona said. "What's it mean?"

"Star jelly," I said after a beat, my mind digging through Mum's stories to find a suitable translation, if not a literal one.

"Maybe I don't speak English either. What *is* it?" Rhona craned her neck to look over her shoulder at Eilidh.

"Legend says it's something that falls to Earth in a meteor shower," Eilidh said slowly. "There was a hill somewhere in Scotland that had a heap of it in 2009."

"I thought it was more . . . I don't know, faceted," I said. "This looks like someone boiled a simulacra into flubber."

Eilidh came round to the other side of the thing, frowning.

"I don't think it's the remains of a simulacra," she said after a beat.

"I still don't know what the hell either of you are talking about." Rhona looked about ready to stamp her feet.

"Well, whatever it is, it's nothing to worry about," Eilidh said dismissively. "It's a phenomenon that's been documented for literal centuries, so it predates the apocalypse. Ascension. Whatever. Sir Walter Scott wrote about it. 'Seek a fallen star,' said the hermit, 'and thou shalt only light on some foul jelly, which, in shooting through the horizon, has assumed for a moment an appearance of splendour.'"

Now it was my turn to stare. First grenades, now quoting Scott verbatim?

Eilidh shifted her shoulders uncomfortably. "What, I can't have layers?"

"It's not going to kill us, then," Rhona said. "Because it's cosmic star shit."

"Aye," I said. "Or something."

On impulse, I cast Connection, and the world blazed to life. The cosmic star shit—or duilleag nam beann—lit up like a star itself, threads of it flowing toward the loch.

I followed the flows of spirit, only to see a ripple in the surface.

Something rose out of it, peaty waters flowing from a grotesque, green-grey face crowned by a Mohawk-like crest of deep green that dripped and sprang up to stand straight.

Fuck.

I froze for half a heartbeat, then practically snatched my new staff out of my inventory, which made Rhona and Eilidh both swivel to look at me. I nodded to the loch.

THE TRANSCENDENT GREEN

"The star shit won't kill us, but that might."

THIRTY-ONE

I sprang into action, ignoring Rhona's fearful yelp. Fuck me, but I'd not had any time to actually practise with my new staff, so I hoped it made some sort of difference anyway. It wasn't like I'd done HEMA like Eilidh—I had no idea how to wield a glorified stick.

Connection showed this creature glowing ominously with red pathos that seemed to take over the otherwise golden spirit. Where spirit generally flowed, pathos on this monster seemed to drip from it like water, pooling on the surface of the loch like oily blood.

"What the ever-loving fuck is it?" Eilidh breathed.

"It's cheesed off is what it is," I said.

"Can we outrun it?" Rhona asked.

I noticed that, at some point, Eilidh had given her a dagger, and I wished I'd given her mine, too. From the quest log, it seemed like that was what the system had been hinting at.

Keen Eye had suddenly skyrocketed to the top of my list of skill priorities. Maybe if we managed to kill this thing, I'd hit level five and have a couple points to spend. And I guessed if it killed us instead, it wouldn't matter. *Should have gotten Keen Eye* could be my epitaph.

The thing blurred into motion so quickly I almost missed it. I reacted instinctively, throwing a third of my spirit into Spèird to shove it back into the loch.

Almost too fast for my mind to process, the monster slashed a brutally clawed hand with a flash of red pathos— and *sliced right through my spell*.

I felt a tearing sensation as Spèird was cloven down the middle, and the remnants of the spell exploded off to the sides of the attacking creature with force enough to carve massive furrows into the shore. Foliage and rocks alike split and rocketed into the loch, and the monster was still coming.

"Fuck!" I said, bracing my staff against the dirt.

Like it had last night, the sensation grounded me even as Eilidh moved.

Her claymore was unsheathed, and while her face was pale with fear, she set her stance with competent confidence, muscles remembering how many times she'd done it in practice.

I wished I had even a fraction of her training.

If this thing could cut through Spèird, what could I do?

If this monster were a Pokémon, it'd almost certainly be a water type, which would douse my Purifire with super-effective glee. But this was not a Pokémon, and I'd no fucking clue what the rules of ascended monster fighting actually were.

I didn't dare test another spell with as much spirit as I'd used the first time.

Instead, I pulled Purifire into my staff. If I'd been in any other situation, I would have marvelled at the way the entire length of the staff illuminated, but I didn't have time.

The beast would close with Eilidh in heartbeats. As it neared, the wind brought with it a horrible stench, as if despite the creature's habitat in the loch, it was putrefying beneath the waters, fat turning to adipocere. It smelled of rotten pork and algae blooms.

It was humanoid, like a creature from an early black-and-white monster film, but that was where the resemblance ended. This was far too real. Every drip of slime, every fold of fetid flesh, every spine of that crest that ran down its back. This was in no way an ascension-mutated creature. This was something *other*.

I held my staff high and released the Purifire.

It struck the monster with a hiss of popping fat just as Eilidh's claymore swung in a wide arc towards the thing's midsection.

Despite being on land, the creature moved faster than I thought possible, its spine arching back as it avoided what could have been a mortal blow from the sword.

Purifire ran up and down the length of the monster, fizzing and sizzling but otherwise causing no observable impact.

Fuck.

Then I remembered Cumhachd.

The spell name literally meant power, and I wanted to kick myself for not remembering it sooner.

By tapping into the ambient spirit that surrounds you to augment your own, you are able to form missiles based upon your environment.

Yes!

I reached for the spell, watching as Eilidh warily circled the beast, which was more hesitant now, if still spitting mad.

Unlike my other spells, Cumhachd drew from my

surroundings, not just from my own well of spirit, and time seemed to stretch out.

I couldn't see Rhona; I was too concentrated on the threat in front of us, but then suddenly, she was behind the monster in a ripple of shadow and light, dagger slashing into the creature's side.

The monster roared in pain, and I *yanked* on the threads of spirit that flooded into me as the Thing from the Peaty Lagoon spun to face its young attacker.

Cumhachd exploded out of me, bringing with it the scent of loam and roots and rock. The missile of green magic struck the exact spot Rhona had stabbed.

I tugged Connection into being, triumph flooding me as I saw the monster's spirit and pathos reserves flooding to heal the sudden damage.

It had worked. Both Rhona's blade and my magic had damaged it.

At the same time, Eilidh did something I'd not seen her do before.

She planted the point of her claymore in front of her, clasping both hands upon the pommel, and with Connection actively overlaying my vision, she suddenly *blazed* gold with spirit.

Eilidh lit up like the sun, and the monster screamed.

The moment it threw back its head in agony, she spun into action, her hands adjusting and gripping the sword as if it were a feather and not over a meter and a half of steel.

My spirit was below half now, but I'd enough to help.

I drew deeply on my remaining reserves, bolstering it with the ambient energies around us like drawing a deep breath from oxygen-rich air.

Eilidh's claymore flashed gold as she pivoted, bringing

it in a massive swing to connect with the monster's left arm.

Had it been human, that swing would have shorn straight through bone, but this monster seemed to have titanium for a skeleton.

The creature roared again, slashing out with the claws of its uninjured hand.

And everything went wrong.

Rhona had dropped back into the shadows—she must have unlocked some sort of stealth ability, and I hadn't even talked to her about her choices yet—and in doing so, she had positioned herself to make mince of the monster's uninjured right side.

But she hadn't anticipated Eilidh's swing or the monster's reaction.

Everything seemed to move in slow motion as the creature's claws took Rhona in a sharp diagonal from her right pectoral muscle all the way up to the left side of her neck. Blood spurted out in what was undeniably arterial spray.

I was a heartbeat away from releasing Cumhachd, and in that instant, I forgot everything about the monster, which Eilidh was already spinning to reengage with shout of rage erupting from her throat.

My spirit reserves were down to fifteen percent, but I didn't care. I threw all the intent of Beannachd Shlàinte into Cumhachd and shifted my mental target to Rhona.

The spell hit her full in the chest, and the triple claw wound lit up like blue fire.

And she *rocketed* backward with the force of it, flying straight into the loch.

"Fuck!" I screamed just as the monster spun and dived after her.

We could barely fight the thing on land—in its natural habitat of the loch? We'd have no chance. None.

I didn't care.

I was running before I could think.

Eilidh shouted something as I passed her, but I was aiming fully for the spot where Rhona had hit the water and gone under.

If part of me hoped the monster would have fled and gone to nurse its wounds in the depths of the loch, I was immediately disabused of the notion.

A flash of movement told me it, like me, was making a beeline for Rhona—and it was a faster swimmer with webbed feet, not an encumbered human with a giant fucking stick.

Gasping as big a breath as I could, I plunged under the water.

Opening my eyes did almost nothing. The water was golden brown with peat, and I could see barely a meter in front of my face. Just enough to see a plume of red blood that was definitely human, fading towards the deep.

I didn't know if water would douse my Purifire, but I had to try.

My spirit was low, throbbing in time with my now-pounding heartbeat, but I had enough to spin a thread of it into my staff, lighting the brown water with a blue-green glow.

Just a trickle, low enough that my natural regeneration returned it and then some.

I may not have been the swimmer that Iain and Meeksy were, but my ascended Strength and Agility carried a lot of weight, and even with my staff in my hand, I was able to kick myself deeper into the loch, using my free hand to propel me.

A flash of movement.

Almost too quick to notice, but it was far too big to be a fish.

And an explosion of bubbles burst upward from directly below me.

Rhona.

I didn't have time to get another breath; I wasn't even sure I could get to her. Even with the creature dragging a human being, it was faster than I.

But then light bloomed.

Maybe bloomed wasn't the right word. It crackled, and my body seemed to light up all at once as it reached me, my brain catching the realisation like the lightning strike it was.

I had enough spirit to trigger Connection, and I could see flows delving deeper. I followed.

Had I been hit full-force with the charge, I was certain I'd be dead, but that I hadn't gave me hope—Rhona was still alive, and she was fighting to stay that way.

I dove deeper.

My legs kicked as hard as they could, and even with my ascension-boosted attributes, I was going to need to breathe.

Just hold on, I told myself, not sure if I meant myself or Rhona.

Maybe both.

As my spirit returned, I funnelled more into my staff to light the way as daylight dimmed overhead. It already could barely penetrate the peaty waters through all the floating sediment, but the deeper I swam, the worse it got.

Another pulse hit me, diffused electricity rippling through the water.

Weaker.

Shit. I was running out of time.

And I was running out of air.

I couldn't *see* anything.

An idea struck me, one I didn't know was even viable for sure.

With my spirit just edging over forty percent, I drew it into my staff, weaving it together as finely as I could.

Spèird normally didn't take much time to come together, but I wanted this to be a finer mesh than cheese-cloth, something delicate. Something that water could get through but bigger things couldn't.

A net of force.

I didn't think I could catch the monster in a net; that felt like too much to ask.

But if I could clear that sediment...

I released the net of spirit with as much force of will as I could muster, aiming it down before me and reinforcing the light in my staff at the same time.

It hurtled out before me, cutting a beam of pure, clear water lit with Purifire like a spotlight.

And it found Rhona.

The monster had her pinned on the silty bottom of the loch as she struggled weakly, only a few small bubbles escaping her now.

It took all of my concentration not to yell and waste what little oxygen was left in my lungs.

I threw all but five percent of my spirit into Cumhachd, imbuing it with, of all things, the memory of Lord Bawbag's punch of glass needles, thinking of this young woman's bravery to go up against someone she'd seen murder her colleagues.

Cumhachd erupted from my staff.

It struck the monster in the back, dead on, and the thing spasmed, floating away from Rhona.

The silt was rushing back in after my net of Spèird had gone through, and already my visibility was vanishing.

With a massive kick, I closed the remaining distance to Rhona, wrapping my left arm around her.

The monster had been trying to tie her down.

The thought chilled me like the old stories of the each-uisge, the water-horse, that beguiled folk and dragged them into the water to drown.

I didn't have enough spirit to further attack the monster, but as it hovered, still, beside me, I oriented my feet onto the loch's bed and with underwater slowness, I jammed the butt end of my staff into the open wound I had blasted through it.

My vision was starting to go fuzzy. I barely had any time, but I knew if this thing caught us on the way back up, it wouldn't matter.

I flailed my staff inside its abdomen, drawing weakly on my regenerating spirit to strengthen the blow.

And then the creature started to glow.

Oh, shit.

THIRTY-TWO

For the space of three sluggish heartbeats, I almost panicked.

But then something flashed in my vision, something I couldn't dismiss, and my heart flooded with relief even as my lungs burned.

You have killed a fuath.
While the ascension triggers . . .

I didn't have time to look closer. I thought *yes* with all my might, and as my spirit resurged with the influx of the harvested monster's manipulation resources, I wrapped my arm more tightly around Rhona and cast Spèird right at our feet.

We rocketed upward through the murky waters so fast that when we breached the surface, we erupted out of the loch like we'd been shot out of a cannon.

My notifications were going wild, but I'd take the flashing gold over drowning any day.

I gasped a breath, feeling like half of it was water, and coughing and spluttering, I cast Spèird again, this time to propel us to shore.

We'd drifted terrifyingly far from Eilidh, who was standing up to her waist in the water, barely in view.

When she caught sight of us coming from the south-west, she let out a strangled yell that might have been half sob.

The second we were in reach where she could still touch, she grabbed Rhona from me. The girl was conscious, somehow, coughing up loch water and wheezing, but alive.

The horrific wound from the fuath's claws had healed without a scar, and the loch's waters had washed away the blood, but I knew without any shadow of doubt that physical scars were the least of what Rhona would take from today.

Together, Eilidh and I dragged her from the loch, and I collapsed on the rocky shore, half in the bracken that grew out of the dirt, one foot still in the water.

"I tried to follow," Eilidh said, her voice anguished. "That thing was too fast. You were too fast—by the time I got into the water, I couldn't see either of you."

"I almost lost her," I managed to get out in a gravelly voice, coughing and spitting out loch water and mucus alike. I couldn't even care if it was rude. "I gambled like all of my spirit on a stupid idea that happened to work—and that was only because Rhona kept trying to electrocute the fucking thing, which was like a beacon."

Rhona struggled to a half-sitting position, pushing herself up on her elbows. She wiped the back of one hand across her lips with a grimace, and her bracing arm shook with the effort of holding her upright. After a moment, she collapsed backward and closed her eyes.

"I was just trying to kill it," she said after a long pause, and then she was hit by another coughing fit, and Eilidh rolled her over onto her side so she could spit.

"Well, it worked like a flare," I told her weakly. My whole body ached.

My spirit was still low, but I had enough for what I needed—I cast Fuaran on all three of us. I had used up my one usage of Beannachd Shlàinte for the day, but I hoped the rejuvenation properties of Fuaran would shore up our inherent healing enough to patch us up.

"We need to be ready in case it comes back," Eilidh said suddenly, her gaze trained on the now-still waters of the loch.

"It's not coming back," I said at the same time Rhona said, "It's dead."

"It's dead?" Eilidh asked. "You're sure?"

"Calum killed it," Rhona said. "Got the notification right before he yeeted us out of the water."

She sounded stronger already—maybe Fuaran was indeed doing its magic.

"I guess that really was a yeet," I said to her, and Rhona gave me a tentative grin. "I was only able to do that because I harvested it without looking—I'm sorry."

"Pfft," Rhona said. "I got the loot too."

"What?" I asked. "You harvested it too?"

"No," she said. "But we all damaged it, so we all got the loot."

With that, Eilidh frowned, and her eyes went distant before widening slightly. "Huh."

"You didn't see the notification that it was dead?" I asked her.

"I was a little preoccupied, and maybe if you're not in a certain range, it doesn't do the forced popup thing? I've no idea how this works." Eilidh shrugged, then looked at Rhona appraisingly. "Was it enough?"

"Enough for what?" I asked.

This time, Rhona's eyes went distant, and then she grinned, scrambling to a sitting position. "Aye, it fuckin' was!"

"For what?" I asked again, starting to feel irritation taking the place of adrenaline and desperation.

"For me to hit level three! That means I get a class!"

Part of me had assumed she'd already gotten one, so Rhona's words came as a bit of a surprise. Much as I wanted to know what her options were, she had to go through them first, which meant Eilidh and I had time to sort through our own notifications, though we made Rhona promise she'd tell us what her options were. She seemed all too eager for our input, which was surprisingly endearing.

I started with the notification that I'd blinked past.

You have killed a fuath.

While the ascension triggers mutations in indigenous beings, the concentration of ambient spirit, pathos, and will is also known to make manifest whatever awareness of magic existed in the ascending planet.

The fuath is one such creature, steeped in the local folklore of Scotland and is, despite the general agnosticism of the local populace, a still-prominent tale of caution and memory.

Known mostly from tales in Sutherland, a fuath is a creature of extreme hatred, most frequently reported near bodies of water. Like its name, which literally means hatred, *the creature seeks nothing but the suffering and death of humans, most often by drowning.*

Unlike the each-uisge, which has been known to fall in love with humans, the fuath wants only their demise.

Such creatures frequently contain the following crafting ingredients: plasmic jelly, fuath claws, fuath skin, fuath teeth.

Ascended creatures also contain reserves of manipulation resources, depending on complexity. The simpler creatures contain only spirit, then spirit and pathos, then spirit, pathos, and will. A fuath contains spirit, pathos, and will.

Goddamn.

I checked my character sheet to see how much of each, and I almost jolted back to the world for the sole purpose of falling over. There wasn't time for me to quite process that I'd apparently also levelled up—I'd come back to that later.

Name: Calum Green

    Age: 36

    Level: 5

    Class: Hedge Witch (Further class selection at: Level 9)

    Affinities: Nature (Level 4), Healing (Level 3)

Alteration:

    Strength: 10

    Dexterity: 15

    Agility: 13

    Mind: 19

. . .

Regeneration:
    Constitution: 15
    Stamina: 18

Manipulation:
    Spirit: 24 (+221 capacity for 24 hours)
    Pathos: 13 (+387 capacity for 24 hours)
    Will: 24 (+102 capacity for 24 hours)

That was the first time I'd ever seen one of the secondary manipulation resources top spirit—the fuath must have been *made* of rage. Jeez.

No wonder we torpedoed out of the water like that.

The massive influx of manipulation had refilled my well like breaking a dam, for fuck's sake. The fuath had been by far the most complex enemy I'd faced, and my brain wasn't quite ready to face the implications of running into a literal myth in the wild. I mean, a giant sky rat of a sadistic seagull was one thing. That nightmare from the depths of the loch? Give me Niseag any day.

Fuck.

Niseag—or, as anglophones called her, Nessie—could very well be real now.

Man, if someone killed her, I'd fucking riot.

Then again, maybe she would be like this fuath and utterly feral. But I'd never heard tales of Niseag killing anyone, just of her chilling in Loch Ness, doing her thing. Maybe she was already real. Who could say at this point?

I shook myself out of my contemplation of Scottish folklore come to life.

Notifications first, existential crises later. Yep.

But the next one did not help.

You have been honoured with a Mark of Esteem.

For being the first person on Earth to create a living weapon from scratch, you now bear the Mark of Life.

This will be visible to all who have access to your information, whether by ability or your choice to share. A Mark of Esteem distinguishes you among your people as one who has taken vital steps on the path to ascension.

Should you survive, your name will be recorded in the Halls of the Ascended Alliance for all time.

The Mark of Life also grants you the following bonuses, which you must accept to receive:

- A permanent +10 to Mind

- A permanent +5 to Spirit, Pathos, and Will

- A specialised affinity of your choice from the following options based on your existing affinities: Earth, Water, Air, Fire, Wild, Rising Tide, Lifesaver

- 1 skill point

- +1 to all attributes

- 3 attribute points

Do you accept this Mark of Life and its requisite rewards along with the ramifications of renown that accompany such esteem?

I had to stop and read it twice.

The bonuses were *wild*, and I didn't mean that as a pun on the specialised affinity, whatever that meant.

I'd been scrounging for points in manipulation resources, and a plus five in all three would be a huge boon. On that basis alone, I didn't think I could say no.

But I also couldn't ignore the unspoken warning in that last sentence. The ramifications of renown, as they'd put it. My name had already been broadcast to the world, it seemed, so that particular cat was out of the bag.

With sudden alarm, I snapped myself out of my screen time to look around for the kitten, grasping around on my back for the carrier in a panic as Eilidh and Rhona still sat in their own minds, doing their own thing.

Had I drowned her by diving under water with her? Panic threatened to submerge me, but then I saw the carrier over by Eilidh. Oh, gods. Right. I'd handed her over to Eilidh before we started out, and . . . phew.

I couldn't see the kitten, but with a small tendril of spirit I reached out with instinctively, I could tell she was safe—she was even contentedly purring in her carrier.

I went back to the task at hand, mollified that I hadn't drowned a nearly extinct cat in a sack after trying to rescue her.

The Mark of Esteem.

The idea of knighthoods and peerage had never sat well with me, but this didn't quite feel like that. Even so, new world or not, it would carry with it the connotations people brought to it—and knighthoods and medals and peerage would be what people thought when they saw it.

Could I say no?

If I'd had just a bit more spirit, if I'd been a bit less tired, would that fuath have managed to take Rhona down to drown?

Would I put up with being perceived under this Mark of Esteem if it meant an easier path to survival?

It wasn't even a question.

. . .

Do you accept this Mark of Life and its requisite rewards along with the ramifications of renown that accompany such esteem?

Yes.

I felt as all the attribute increases took hold, my body going rigid.

It seemed to take longer this time, and I felt almost as if my mind was pried apart at the seams of my brain, making room for more information, more synthesis, more magic.

When it was done, I took a shuddering deep breath, coming back to myself just long enough to try to ground myself in the world again.

Three long breaths, in and out.

Might as well get the rest of it over with.

You have reached Level 5! You have six attribute points to distribute. You have three skill points to distribute.

You must choose a specialised affinity from among the following options:

-Earth: Gain access to the Earth skill tree. All Earth-based skills, including those that pull from other skill trees, gain a 10% bonus to efficacy. Earth governs: plant life, animal life, manipulation of the land, and crafting domains of woodcraft, foraging, and hunting.

-Water: Gain access to the Water skill tree. All Water-based skills, including those that pull from other trees, gain a 10% bonus to efficacy. Water governs: all freshwater and saltwater bodies, plants and animals that make their homes therein,

manipulation of water, and crafting domains of alchemy, brewing and distilling, and plumbing.

-Air: Gain access to the Air skill tree. All Air-based skills, including those that pull from other trees, gain a 10% bonus to efficacy. Air governs: wind, storms, animals that inhabit the skies, and crafting domains of windcatching, smithing, and wind engineering.

-Fire: Gain access to the Fire skill tree. All Fire-based skills, including those that pull from other trees, gain a 10% bonus to efficacy. Fire governs: flame, lightning, fire-based lifeforms, and crafting domains of smithing, cooking, and pottery.

-Wild: Gain access to the Wild skill tree. All Wild-based skills, including those that pull from other trees, gain a 10% bonus to efficacy. Wild governs: chaos, ascended magics, seanchas, mythic creatures, and crafting domains of enchantment, spirit-infusion, and world-weaving.

I had to stop there, because I needed a sodding glossary.

The general elemental affinities felt fairly straightforward, aside from a few head-scratching terms like windcatching and wind engineering, but the Wild affinity stumped me. Chaos? World-weaving? What the hell was that?

My lone clue seemed to exist in the form of the single Gaelic word: seanchas.

Seanchas was a term that most generally referred to lore and storytelling, particular oral traditions so long rooted in our culture. But it also meant conversation, talk. Saying craic might be a bit cheeky for the gravitas of the word, but where it fit into magic? I didn't know.

But at the same time, it was like this stupid system knew how to hook me. That word—it felt like mine.

The remaining two specialised affinities had to refer to the Healing affinity, and when I looked, I wasn't disappointed.

-Rising Tide: Gain access to the Rising Tide skill tree. All Rising Tide-based skills, including those from other trees, gain a 10% bonus to efficacy. Rising Tide governs: group buffs, group healing, community blessings, and crafting domains of alchemy, cooking, and communications.

-Lifesaver: Gain access to the Lifesaver skill tree. All Lifesaver-based skills, including those from other trees, gain a 10% bonus to efficacy. Lifesaver governs: targeted buffs, targeted healing, targeted blessings, and crafting domains of healthcraft, alchemy, and spirit infusion.

I felt torn. Part of me thought that I was getting nudged towards a fork in the road. On one side, there was a clear healer path. I couldn't deny that my frantic use of Cumhachd as a healing missile had saved Rhona's life, but I wasn't sure I wanted to be a healer.

The memory of how I'd plunged after her into the loch kept playing in my mind.

It hadn't been as a healer—it had been a different instinct. A protective one, one that couldn't bear the thought of someone I'd rescued perishing at the bottom of a peat-darkened body of water. A fighting instinct.

It was an instinct I didn't want to ignore. Healers could be fighters; I had no doubt in that. And I'd known enough combat medics over the years to have enormous respect for their vocation, their calling, and their commitment to saving lives.

I just wasn't sure that was *my* calling.

At least not that way.

I'd intended to go through all of my notifications, but I found myself stalling, unable to decide.

When I blinked myself back to the side of the loch, Rhona and Eilidh were quietly talking.

"Finally," Rhona said, giving me a wobbly smile. "Calum, should I choose nature's blade or wraith?"

THIRTY-THREE

"A what or a what now?" I asked.

Rhona rolled her eyes. "My class! I also got offered the tracker class, but that sounds boring. Here, I'll show you."

Before I could ask *how* she intended to show me, my vision filled with text.

"What the—" I cut off, peering through the text at Rhona's amused face. Eilidh just studiously looked at the kitten, who was sitting in her lap.

All right, then. Guess I was reading.

Nature's Blade—A scion of the natural world, you combine your own nature of treading lightly upon the earth with a deadly promise to any who upset the balance it requires. You will receive an immediate bonus of +2 to Agility, Mind, and Stamina as well as a +1 bonus to Will. You gain access to the Nature skill tree as well as the Combat Stealth skill tree.

Nature's Blades are silent shadows amid the dappled glens —they treat the world around them with respect and rain down its vengeance with pristine accuracy upon those who do not. Skilled in stealth and tracking alike, they are dangerous foes and can call down the wrath of animal companions upon their enemies.

Wraith—Normally not offered until level nine's class specialisation, due to having already unlocked the Wraith skill tree through the Vengeance affinity, this class is an option for you at level three.

A shadow day or night, the Wraith can slip through nearly any obstacle unnoticed. If that alone did not make a deadly foe, Wraiths are as skilled in magic as they are in blades, using their skills to disorient, disarm, and disable their opponents. You will receive an immediate bonus of +2 to Agility, Dexterity, and Mind as well as a +1 bonus to Pathos.

Wraiths are the spectres of the battlefield and the tingling spine of the guilty. They move through more than one world at once, spinning their shadows to extreme effect. Suited to both spycraft and assassination, Wraiths are hardly limited to the underworld. They can also embody justice incarnate and righteous fury, exacted with exquisite precision and razor-sharp focus.

"Holy hell," I said when I finished reading. "You seriously have to ask me?"

"I mean, I know what *I* want," Rhona said, preening slightly. "But Mam always said I'm too impulsive, so I figured I should at least ask."

I looked at Eilidh. "Not even a contest, right?"

Eilidh shook her head, though the look she gave Rhona was a little apprehensive. "It sounds frankly terrifying, but the kind of terrifying we would be lucky to have on our side. I'm certainly not going to be sneaking around in the shadows with my giant knife."

"Just lighting up the battlefield like a sun," I said without thinking, and then my cheeks warmed when Eilidh's blue-eyed stare fell on me.

"What did you just say?"

"Nothing," I muttered. "Just—your class skill, or whatever you did with the sword right before I accidentally blasted Rhona into the water."

Now Eilidh's pale, freckled cheeks turned pink. "Oh. That. You could see that?"

"I had Connection active. It was like you'd swallowed a star."

Rhona was eyeing back and forth between us like she was watching a particularly confusing tennis match. "Right, you two are very cute, but can we get back to me?"

Both our heads snapped towards the younger woman, and she shrugged as Eilidh took a sip of water from a bottle I hadn't seen by her leg.

"Sexual tension you could cut with that big-ass knife," she said, and Eilidh sprayed water out of her nose, which Rhona pretended not to see.

I pretended to be very, very interested in a small tuft of moss growing between two rounded rocks by my left hand.

"*Anyway*," the teenager said, "if you're both sure I'm not just being impulsive, I'll take the wraith class."

"Do that," I said, my voice cracking embarrassingly. I cleared my throat. "Seems like too good an opportunity to pass up, especially if you'd otherwise have to wait till level nine to see it again."

"Exactly," Rhona said. Eilidh was still coughing, but she waved one hand to—I presumed—show agreement.

Rhona's confidence faltered then, and she bit her lip a little bashfully. "I don't know if yous noticed my sonic ability."

"Noticed?" I asked blithely. "You mean the one that almost ruptured every eardrum in a ten-mile radius? That sonic ability?"

Rhona grinned. "Aye, that's the one."

"I think we noticed," Eilidh said, finally recovering herself enough to take another gulp of water. She had me fixed in a baleful glare.

Of course she was pissed off about the sexual tension comment. Ugh. Probably reminded her how much she hated me.

"What about the ability?" I prodded Rhona, mainly to focus anywhere else but Eilidh.

"Oh. It's part of the Vengeance tree, which I didn't quite understand at first except to guess that it was due to really not liking Lord Sa—Lord Bawbag. Lord Bawbag." Rhona repeated the name as if drilling it into her head would remind her that she didn't have to worry about him catching her using it anymore.

At least I hoped she didn't.

With her decision, she retreated back into her own brain to sort out her class and skill points, leaving me and Eilidh sitting awkwardly together.

"Did you get through everything?" She asked the question almost warily, as if she were afraid to hear the answer.

"I got stuck. Apparently my whole living weapon thing gave me a whole heap of bonuses, and one of them is a choice of specialised affinity."

"Wait, what? You got bonuses for that?" Her voice rose slightly in pitch.

"Would you rather I turned them down?"

"You . . . could do that?"

"Aye," I said, "but it didn't seem practical."

"What sort of bonuses were they?" Eilidh asked suspiciously.

I hesitated for a moment, then decided she probably couldn't hate me any more than she already did—an uncharacteristic stab at pure optimism, that—and told her.

Her face darkened with every line, and I finally gave up and just willed the choices of specialised affinities over to her to look at.

By the time she was done reading, I half expected lightning to flash from her eyes.

"You got all that for making a fucking stick?"

"I literally didn't ask for it," I said. "I was just trying to make a weapon. Which I now don't even really know how to use, so bully for me."

At that, she actually started to splutter.

"Why the hell do you hate me so much?" I burst out after a minute. "I never did anything to you. Or Susanna. If you recall, she's the one who fucked off to Dundee with that sentient curd of smegma. Who, I have to stress, she started seeing *before* she and I broke up. By, like, months."

"I don't want to talk about this."

"Neither do I, but I also don't want to be your verbal dartboard the whole way to Oban, so if you've got something to say, just fucking say it, for Christ's sake." My words came out without any vitriol. I watched her fume for a moment, her pink lips slightly parted, her eyes flashing grey-blue in the overcast light. "I didn't do anything to deserve being treated like I'm the sentient curd of smegma."

"Oh, god, stop saying smegma."

With that, she got to her feet and practically hit warp speed heading north in the direction we'd come from.

I stared after her.

My clothes were still wet from the loch, and the last thing I needed was chafing from hiking all day in wet trousers, so I used my Purifire trick to dry myself.

It didn't do much to fix my mood. What was *wrong* with that woman?

Of all the people I ended up braving a bloody apocalypse with.

Feeling reckless, I decided if she wanted to literally run away, two could play that game.

I still had choices to make.

But before I went back to my notifications, I went over and picked up the kitten in her carrier and placed the strap over my shoulder, settling her into my lap.

She gave a small and happy purr inside her wee nest, which I took as vindication.

I probably should have been more thoughtful about what I was choosing, but Eilidh had left me in a hell of a mood, so I just went with my gut and chose Wild as my specialised affinity.

I had six attribute points to distribute and three skill points, and I really needed to spend those skill points. With the massive bonuses from the Mark of Life I'd received, I decided to use that as my cue. I put three more of my free points into Mind, and then due to the way my lungs still remembered what it was like to almost run out of air, two in Stamina and one in Strength, hoping the single point wouldn't make me bust out of my clothes.

First order of business in Oban after finding Iain, Meeksy, and Catrìona would be finding some new stuff to wear. Loch bath or not, I felt like by the time we reached Oban, they'd need to be burned.

Name: Calum Green
   Age: 36
   Level: 5
   Class: Hedge Witch (Further class selection at: Level 9)
   Affinities: Nature (Level 4), Healing (Level 3)
   Specialised Affinities: Wild (Level 1)

Alteration:
   Strength: 12
   Dexterity: 16
   Agility: 14
   Mind: 36

Regeneration:
   Constitution: 16
   Stamina: 21

Manipulation:
   Spirit: 29 (+221 capacity for 24 hours)
   Pathos: 18 (+387 capacity for 24 hours)
   Will: 29 (+102 capacity for 24 hours)

The sight of how far I'd come in a few short days almost floored me. We'd been in survival mode all this time, and it hadn't really sunk in just how much of a jump this was.

That plus *ten* to Mind? My spirit capacity had gone up thirty-three percent! Not that I wouldn't notice the bonuses for harvesting the fuath on top of that, but suddenly those bonuses made a lot more sense. Once my Manipulation resources increased past the starter levels, those bonuses would be a lot less of a boost.

That was somewhat of a comfort, considering the awful reality of Lord Bawbag and his ilk using murder as a way to boost the hands-off stats—at least that route would have diminishing returns.

Eventually, anyway.

I hastily steered my brain away from the thought that he'd just have to murder more people at once. That was not the way for me to calm down.

Before I let myself look at the Wild skill tree I'd unlocked, I went straight to Arcane.

Keen Eye was an absolute must.

Keen Eye—This ability allows you to examine an item, foe, or location, and in conjunction with Connection, it can reveal secrets or vital clues that will push you towards helpful information. Keen Eye comes with a one-time bonus to Mind of +1.

Continued usage will improve the complexity and usefulness of the information Keen Eye provides.

That could have helped us with the fuath. It could have helped us with any number of things, but especially that. If I'd been able to identify a weakness? It could have saved Rhona from nearly drowning—or the trauma of having her torso slashed from nipple to neck.

There wasn't time for recriminations, though.

I spent the skill point and moved on.

The other two felt more fraught.

I wanted to at least look at the Wild skill tree, but there was one from the Nature tree I felt like I needed to get. All of them, really—the remaining three at the base of the tree were all necessary if I wanted to climb above the basics in the Nature tree. But one in particular I needed now.

Taobh a-Muigh (Passive)—You gain an understanding of the relational qualities of all life and ecosystems as well as their place in the web of spirit. Rooted in Connection, this skill grants a permanent +1 to Mind and +1 to Will, and you receive a bonus to all spells and skills that deal with things external: bonds, brawls, and anything that acts upon the outside world.

While Taobh a-Muigh will not increase in levels as active spells will, your understanding of magic will, on occasion, trigger evolution.

This skill would work with Connection, which would in turn work with Keen Eye, and I needed to tie those skills together. I spent the skill point.

And then I finally allowed myself the treat of opening up the Wild tree.

It seemed to spring up beside the Nature tree when I concentrated on it, and I could suddenly imagine all of the skill trees as a forest, how they might work together, each playing a part.

The thought was full of excitement, wonder.

Maybe my sudden jump in Pathos was giving me more feelings than the usual one.

There were three root-level spells, but only one of them

was available. I was almost thankful for that—I didn't think my brain was up for any more choices.

Tairm—This spell calls upon the land around you to respond, which it will, based on your affinities and your own intent. As this is wild magic, the results are difficult to anticipate for the caster, though if that is true, it is all the more confounding for the targets.

Be clear in your need, and nature will respond to your call.

I was hitting it with my remaining skill point before I could even finish reading. Could there be anything more suited to a pathetic hamster who hated making decisions? *Gods, yes, bring on the nature chaos to rain down upon my foes.*

Once the new skill points had taken hold, I sorted through the rest of the notifications. Most were of the usual level of consequence—notifications of increases of Spirit and other attributes that explained my stats' jump—but one was something I wish had shown up higher in whatever method the system used to prioritise.

You have discovered a personal quest!

Having created Earth's first living weapon—two others have since joined you in this distinction, one in Kenya and one in Thailand—you as yet have little comprehension of what you have done.

Myriad factors contribute to the creation of a living weapon, not least of which is luck. But most ascended worlds agree that the ability of a crafter to create a living weapon increases with experience not because the experience itself increases the likeli-

hood but because, through experience, the crafter must by neces-
sity learn to connect with their crafting materials.

This means understanding, intuiting, and actively forming
a relationship with the world around them, something that is an
insurmountable feat for many or most people, even in tradi-
tional ascended worlds.

Some believe living weapons respond to need; others believe
it is the soul of the crafter. The statistics with which we describe
the chances of creating a living weapon are, therefore, not the
same for everyone—they are merely the most logical expression
of what we find in ascended worlds across the known universe:
that the ability to connect with one's world is precious and rare.

Yours is the first in your world. As such, it is already a
legend, though it is new and untried.

You must get to know it the way you would any other mind:
with diligence, patience, and an open heart.

Objectives:

-Commune with your living weapon (What this means
varies—first you must listen to it)

-Practise with your living weapon for three days (1/3)

-Name your living weapon

Rewards:

-2 items (ascension dependent)

-Affinity: Staves

Holy shit.

Now we were talking.

A s much as I wanted to get right on that new quest, there wasn't time.

Eilidh stomped back into our wee circle not long after I shook myself out of my screen time again, and I barely had time to offer to dry Rhona's still-sopping clothes before Eilidh insisted we start moving.

We made good time for the rest of the afternoon, and several times I scouted ahead, my Stamina and Agility giving me a significant advantage and more energy than the others had.

Twice, we encountered ascension-mutated animals and were forced to kill them. One was a mutated stoat the size of a badger, and the other was a hedgehog bigger than a rugby ball that had, among other terrifying developments, learnt to throw its quills.

Aside from the vole and the seagull Eilidh had seen, these were her first experience of animals that had been caught up in the waves of spirit.

The rewards from both were meagre—pelts and teeth and not enough spirit or pathos to increase an attribute permanently. I was particularly annoyed about the pathos bit, because now my bonus was sitting at 397. Literally three points away from another boost.

I wasn't sure how the system calculated the times of these bonuses—the stoat and the hedgehog didn't add to the original twenty-four hour bonus from the fuath. Maybe it wouldn't unless something bigger came along. I also wasn't sure I wanted an answer, since it probably would come at the price of having to fight something more terrifying than the goddamn fuath.

When we finally stopped for the night, daylight already faded into gloom, Eilidh was half limping and pretending not to. I didn't think her clothes had managed to dry before we'd gotten caught in a drizzle that didn't let up sometime between stoat and hedgehog o'clock.

She was clearly experiencing the chafing I'd dreaded.

More impressive was that it seemed to have outpaced her ascension healing.

I still had my tent in my inventory, but when I went to grab it, I got a small shock.

My inventory had increased by five spaces.

It must have hit at level five, but I'd not been expecting it. It was really, *really* good to know it could increase.

I got the tent set up while Rhona and Eilidh gathered wood for a fire. Despite boosted Constitution, it was still February in the highlands of Scotland, and a wet night was a cold night.

"God, what I wouldn't give for a hot meal," Rhona griped as I used my Purifire to dry out the wood they'd collected.

"There's a whole loch of trout right there," Eilidh said. "And no way to get to it."

"O ye of little faith," I said without thinking, considering how I'd used Spèird to filter out the sediment from the water so I could find Rhona when the fuath took her.

"If you're going to splash around chasing fish, I have to see this," Rhona said, but then she cast an uncertain look at the water. "But I think I'll stay back a ways."

I couldn't blame her. She didn't seem to blame me for the fact that my panicked healing spell had punted her right into the drink where the fuath could take advantage and drag her underwater, but that didn't change the fact that was exactly what had happened.

Moving down to the water's edge, I cast about with Connection first. I really, really didn't want to disturb another fuath or any monster. Last thing we needed was a kelpie or an each-uisge raining down vengeance for its monstrous brethren.

But all there was down there was Loch Awe's famed brown trout, some char, and a confused salmon. The salmon was young, and I'd prefer it get to grow up to be a full-grown salmon someday, so as I structured my spell with the same intent I used under the water, I purposely threaded it between the trout and the salmon.

It was dusk, and the fish were closer to shore than they might have been during daylight. Most of the fishers I've known throughout my life—growing up in a coastal town, you meet a lot of those—were those who worked on the sea, but I'd met enough who also enjoyed going inland.

I thought about just getting one of them, since there was a big one in there probably close to the top of their weight range at fifteen kilos, but after a moment of consideration, I decided two things.

First, none of us had had a hot meal in a while, and while I could keep us relatively warm in the drizzle with the fire and the tent, some protein and heat wouldn't go amiss in the belly.

And second, Scotland had a long and glorious tradition of hot-smoked fish—salmon, trout, mackerel, you name it. I hadn't the faintest idea how to go about it, but if I kept fish in my inventory, they wouldn't spoil. Mòrag had reminded me of that with the rat meat.

Maybe someone in Oban would know how to smoke them.

I gathered up six trout in my net. The ease of it was almost terrifying. Because I was working with my mind and magic, I could basically just draw a wobbly sphere around them and close it up, a spirit-based net with no possible escape.

When I pulled them out of the water, though, I felt the net strain a bit against them. At least one of the fish seemed to have been caught in the ascension, and in my ignorance, I'd grossly underestimated its weight. The thing was *huge*, nearly as long as Rhona and probably weighed twice as much.

"Maybe I didn't think this through," I muttered even as Rhona herself clapped delightedly behind me.

"Jeezo," said Eilidh, coming up to stand beside me. Then, after a moment, her voice turned dry as she continued with, "I take it you forgot you have to kill them somehow?"

I really didn't want to dignify that with a confirmation, but she was right. "Any suggestions?"

She gave a long-suffering sigh. "Let me."

"Let Rhona help so she gets some experience," I said absently, sweat beading on my forehead with the strain of holding the giant fish and its non-mutated friends above the water.

"I know," Eilidh said, tone curt.

Ugh.

And then Eilidh did the sword thing again, drawing her claymore and planting it tip-down in the earth. I didn't have Connection active, but I felt the pulse of spirit that went through her as it exploded out, stunning all six of the fish in the net.

"Pull it over, quick," she said.

I obeyed, watching in bemusement as she and Rhona got to work beheading them.

Give a pathetic hamster six fish, he'd eat for a night. Teach a pathetic hamster to magically fish, and, well. Guess we'd eat for a while.

I had to stifle a moan when I bit into my fish a while later.

The kitten was *wildly* interested in the fish, but thankfully after a full bottle of kitten formula, she settled down in her carrier again.

The trout was unseasoned except for the wild garlic Rhona had chopped up to rub it with, but it was still probably the best thing I'd tasted in the course of my life.

We'd cooked three of them, thinking we could save what we didn't eat for breakfast, but as the three of us tucked in with our ascension-boosted metabolisms in full swing after days of surviving on nuts and chopped apricots and the occasional prune, I wasn't so sure the fish would make it that long.

My body seemed to *yearn* for the protein, and I wasn't sure if it was just a passing fancy or not, but it felt as if I could sense my digestive system greedily grabbing for it.

Half of my ten-kilo fish was gone within half an hour, and I still felt hungry.

"Bet this would actually taste good with stewed prunes," Rhona mused.

"You might actually be right," Eilidh said, wiping away a smear of grease from the corner of her mouth.

None of us had given a shit about making a mess—I didn't think any of our little trio had realised just how ravenous we were. We were expending more energy than we ever had, and we hadn't been replenishing it. I hadn't really thought about it, but even in the past few days since the ascension, my clothes had started to feel a little loose. I'd attributed it to constant wear, but maybe that wasn't all of it.

We had some stoat and hedgehog meat in inventory as well, though I think we were all a bit put off by the idea. One thing I couldn't quite wrap my mind around was the fact that we hadn't had to actually clean the fish or butcher any of the animals—the system provided anything useable from them with the kill. Including, somewhat disconcertingly, a pile of trout skins and worse, an inventory slot taken up by trout oil, which was apparently an alchemical ingredient. How it was contained in the inventory was anyone's guess. How we'd get it *out* without ending up absolutely soaked with fishy grease was a mystery none of us were eager to solve.

Some bit of stress eased off with the meal. As a kid for a short while, Mum and I had been reliant on food banks. She'd lost her job, and the cuts to universal credit had made it extra hard for her to feed us. For a while after that, I became obsessed with food. Put on a lot of weight that my growth spurt eventually ate up, but I hadn't realised the burden the past few days had edged onto my shoulders.

Food insecurity was no joke, especially when we apparently needed so much more sustenance than we used to.

My ears perked up when Rhona said, "You haven't told us what *your* class is. That stun skill or whatever is wicked."

Eilidh kept her eyes trained on her trout, chewing and swallowing before she answered. I got the feeling she didn't really want to talk about her class for some reason, but I'd be lying to say I wasn't burning with curiosity.

"Dìonadair," she said after a long pause. Her eyes flickered in my direction without actually reaching me, as if she were trying as hard as she could *not* to look at me.

"Again with the Gaelic. Why is your shit in Gaelic? Mine's all in English."

"It's my first language," I said at the same time Eilidh said, "It's my mother tongue."

Again, the flicker, and again the sensation that she was wrenching her eyes away from me.

"Most of what I see is in English," I said. "I'm not going to debate the philosophy of that, but the Gaelic fits better for some of it."

"Okay, fine, but what does"—Rhona stumbled over the word she'd only heard once—"Jee-un-a—what does it mean?"

"Dìonadair," Eilidh said again, enunciating carefully. "It means defender."

Now it was my turn not to look at her, instead watching the fire burn merrily, blue-green flames giving off a cheery heat.

"Sounds like a warrior class," Rhona said, and at my raised eyebrow, went on. "What? I played RPGs back when such things existed."

"It was last week," I said with a chuckle. "Besides, we could get a *D and D* campaign going if you really missed it."

Eilidh's lips tightened. I had a vague memory that she and Susanna had had a long *Dungeons and Dragons* campaign with some uni friends—like a *decade*-long campaign—that had ended during the time I was dating Susanna. Susanna had always said it was because of "group drama," but yet again, it seemed like I'd inadvertently kicked one of Eilidh's sore spots without meaning to. I suddenly wasn't sure if I could trust any of Susanna's assertions about anything at all.

"I just want to know about Eilidh's class," Rhona said bullheadedly. "C'mon. I showed you mine . . ."

Eilidh had just shoved another chunk of fish into her mouth, but she managed to scowl around the huge bite and just waved one greasy hand.

Words appeared.

Dìonadair—The paragon of combat, a Dìonadair is the bulwark in the face of even the most intimidating of foes. They are able to draw any eye, and indeed, this is their goal. Empowered by their steadfast confidence and sense of duty, the Dìonadair is not one to trifle with. They may be slow to anger, but once awoken, their fury is as implacable as their advance is relentless.

With abilities that range from crowd control to issuing unignorable challenges, a Dìonadair is a force to be reckoned with alone or as part of a team. They will often be the last to fall in any fight once trained. This is a rare class, as it requires extreme dedication, honour, and valour. It will not be offered again. As a Dìonadair, you will receive an immediate bonus of +3 to Strength, +2 to Constitution, and +1 to Will.

The Dìonadair is the beacon in the fight, a source of strength and will to rival heroes of legend. They do not brook injustice, nor will they shy from a fight when what is right is on the line. Cross them at your peril.

Bloody hell. Here I was with a hedge witch class, and these two were getting rare level-three classes and early level-nine ones? And Eilidh'd been jealous of *me*?

"Your turn," Eilidh said blandly to me when I closed out of the screen.

"Only fair," Rhona agreed.

I sighed and showed them my earthy little normal class.

"Okay, that's badass," Rhona said after she read it.

For a while, she chattered on about affinities—she had Vengeance and had apparently just unlocked Stealth, while Eilidh had Nature and Broadsword—and I finished the second half of my fish, slipping dangerously close to a food coma.

"We should set up a watch," Eilidh said suddenly. Or at least it seemed sudden, but I realised the small camp had gone quite a bit ago.

"Since Calum's about to pass out, I'll take first," Rhona said. "But I don't know how this works, so just tell me when to wake you up, I guess?"

"The system will do that if you ask it to," Eilidh said, shooting me a sideways glance. "Just tell it to ping you in two hours."

"Only two?" Rhona said.

"Better to be safe on your first watch. Any sign of danger, and you wake us. No screen time or you might not see something coming." Eilidh spoke sternly, and I was glad at least one of us knew what to do, though I was beginning to have some serious questions about her parents' childrearing style.

With that settled, I clambered into my tent with the kitten carrier. The tent itself was supposedly a four-person one, but like every tent ever invented, this was woefully optimistic.

I wasn't sure how even three of us would fit into it, and once I was inside lying in my sleeping bag with Eilidh crawling in beside me, I realised exactly how close she was about to be.

Which is to say: very.

Rhona *could* fit between us, if only just, and if we all had giant hiking rucksacks instead of a magically convenient pocket dimension for inventory? Yeah, no.

Without needing to discuss it, Eilidh and I both wedged ourselves as far against the opposite walls of the tent as we could. Her sleeping bag was identical to mine, down to being the same colour. I'd slid my staff beside me, which in theory was in case I needed to grab it quickly in the night but in actuality was the stupid impulse to put some sort of literal barrier between me and Eilidh's venom.

"I'm taking second," she said. "You should get some sleep."

With that, she rolled over, and I lay there on my back.

Get some sleep, she said.

As if that was going to happen.

THIRTY-FIVE

Sure enough, I spent the two hours of Rhona's watch staring at the ceiling of the tent and listening to the *pat-pat-pat* of drizzle and the little raspy rumble of the purring wildcat kitten beside my head.

And then when Eilidh got up, I spent the next two hours dreading her wake-up call with Rhona snoring lightly sprawled upon Eilidh's sleeping bag.

I was the opposite of rested when Eilidh did come to get me, and I brought the kitten with my sandy-eyed self as I forced myself out of my cocoon of warmth.

"Nothing happened," she said in a near whisper.

Then she seemed to realise that Rhona was occupying her sleeping bag—that kid could sleep through another fuath attack, I thought—and that she'd have to lie down on mine.

I left her to that without comment, going over to the fire.

The drizzle had stopped, thank goodness, and the magical fire didn't seem to care much about the rain anyway, because it still burned merrily.

Inside the carrier, the kitten mewed.

There wasn't much to do for the next couple hours, but staying awake was going to be a challenge, so I decided to try something.

I wasn't about to cast Caidreabhas on the kitten, but I did want her to be able to exist outwith that carrier without the fear of losing her, so I tentatively reached out with Tàth instead.

To my surprise, the little furry creature responded with alacrity, her sleepy kitten spirit rousing to the point that she practically pounced my offered threads.

My skill had levelled up with the horses, so it was now level three, and already that connection felt firmer.

A kitten, however, was not an adult horse—nor was she an adult starling.

Nope, a kitten was a literal baby, and like a literal baby, the connection brought with it a chaotic mess of feelings, impulses, and distractions. I couldn't help but chuckle at her as she batted at my fingers. She really was an adorable little thing, still clumsy, but slowly gaining some control of her wee body.

On inspiration, I reached over and grabbed a length of willow that had escaped the woodpile—probably because it was the relative size and shape of a switch and not a log.

The kitten's whiskers immediately puffed forwards, and her eyes dilated as a leaf on the end of the willow switch dragged along the grass.

"Och, I've your attention now, have I?" I murmured.

She half scrambled, half fell from my lap, stalking towards the leaf on wobbly paws.

Through the very light bond I maintained with her, I could feel her concentration, the instinct to ambush this leaf.

I twitched the switch, and the kitten sank into a crouch, her little bum beginning the wiggly dance someone once told me was how cats calculated the trigonometry of their pounce trajectories.

The thought of any creature doing trigonometry with their arse was hilarious enough, but a tiny kitten? There was a reason the internet loved cat videos.

With a stuttering jolt of motion, she launched.

"Launch" was only the most generous of words—it was more she jumped, slightly at the wrong angle, and surprised herself in the process, so the moment she touched down again, she bolted up into the air like she had four tiny jetpacks strapped to those wee paws, back arched and stubby tail poofed.

She skittered around in a crescent to look at the offensive piece of foliage side on, and then she approached it from that angle, this time toddling straight at it and collapsing atop it with a vengeance.

"Gods, I wish I had my iPhone to record this," I muttered. "It'd hit a million views on TikTok, easy."

Because I was exhausted, I continued to pull on spirit to cast Connection as I watched the kitten play. It had been probably a couple days since she'd been able to work out any energy, and she seemed overjoyed for the opportunity.

A solid hour went by before she finally got tired and cushed down in what had to be the most adorable loaf I'd ever seen. She could have fit in the palm of my hand.

"This is coming with us," I told her, letting the willow switch vanish into my inventory, though the few leaves it had once carried certainly hadn't survived the continuous assault.

The stick was worth a slot, for sure. Rhona, at least, would lose her mind at the chance to play with the kitten.

A kitten's best friend, the willow.

I sat back, leaning on my hands. Ha. Just like that, I had a name for the wee beastie.

Sailean. The Gaelic word for a willow.

As I thought it, a flash of gold told me that was significant.

Your party has gained an animal companion. Though not permanently bonded, because the Scottish wildcat Sailean is both endangered and vulnerable due to her age, she will remain with you until she is old enough to survive alone—though be prepared that she may not wish to leave.

She has gained a permanent +3 to Mind and has learned the ability: Pounce.

Pounce—A fundamental attack for an ambush predator. Currently most effective against slow-moving flora.

This ability can evolve.

Oh, my god.

This was almost worth waking everyone up for.

I quickly closed the notification, but not without a surge of—dare I say it?—affection for the tiny cat. A moment later, it was washed away with the anger that Sailean's mother's pelt was still in Eilidh's inventory.

While a lot of people might not agree what he'd done was terrible, for me it was one of those heinous choices that displays the true cruelty of a person: to kill something precious and rare just to see it dead, no matter who it hurts.

Especially in this new world where the animals around

us were gaining intelligence and strength with every passing minute, those choices could, quite literally, come back to bite people.

And when it came to Lord Bawbag, I was happy to be the teeth.

Boosted Constitution and Stamina or not, the next day kicked my arse.

Maybe at higher levels, ascended people wouldn't need more sleep than approximately zero, but level five was apparently not that day. I got through the first part of the day in a haze as we worked ourselves to the end of Loch Awe and then up the A816 north towards Oban.

We hadn't made it far the previous day due to the fuath incident, but by noon, we'd made it into view of a sight I hadn't realised how desperate I was to reach: the sea. Or, more precisely, a sea *loch*, Loch Craignish, but in my mind, we'd made it. To the coast, at the very least.

The clouds had scattered as we walked, moving at a steady pace across the sky, which meant that on the horizon I could see the islands of Jura and Scarba and Luing rising from the sea. It had been too long. Something about the sight of the Inner Hebrides tugged at me, like I was just waking up and for the first time in years, I was alive and I was home.

We made good time. By unspoken agreement, we paused only briefly for lunch when the sun broke through the clouds, and we ate fish I flash roasted with Purifire and some of Rhona's gathered greens.

None of us mentioned the fact that we'd traversed over twenty miles of road and it was barely midday—nor that we were about to do another twenty that would take us to Oban.

We were so close.

Just as we were about to get back on the road, though, Eilidh stopped short, cursing under her breath.

"What?" I asked, tugging a web of Connection into being to search for threats. Nothing.

"I think the system wants me to do my part of the shared quest before we get to Oban," she said slowly. "It just basically threw it in front of my face and wouldn't let me get rid of it."

"What?" The thought made the hair on my arms stand up straight.

"That's no' creepy at all," Rhona muttered.

"I don't know how I'm supposed to do anything with a sword without a forge, and even if I had one of those, I wouldn't have the faintest idea how to improve a weapon," Eilidh said. "For fuck's sake. What does it want from me?"

"Have you read the book it gave you as a reward for part one of the quest?" I asked the question as carefully as I could.

"No," Eilidh said.

Both Rhona and I stared at her.

"You should read the book. Like yesterday," Rhona said, making no effort whatsoever to be delicate. "When I read my foraging book, it literally made the plants I needed glow so I wouldn't, like, feed you guys hemlock or something."

"Yeah, mine pretty much data-dumped an apprenticeship of magical woodcrafting into my head Matrix-style," I said. "I'm not saying making my staff was as easy as picking up a fallen branch and whittling the bark off of it, but . . ."

"But he's not *not* saying that," Rhona finished.

Eilidh started to turn red. "Both of you got quest assignments that seemed simple. Gather some plants, make a long, magical stick—"

"That's what she said," Rhona muttered.

"—and *I* got 'make three entire full sets of armour and upgrade existing weapons with no gear'," Eilidh went on as if Rhona hadn't spoken, but she glared at the younger woman, who merely gave her an impish smile.

"Eilidh," I said after weighing the odds of making her more pissed and deciding there was probably no way to not fail that saving throw even if I rolled a natural twenty, "it's not giving us anything impossible. You've been roasting fish over a blue campfire. You basically brain slapped said fish from five yards away last night. If the system's telling you to make the armour, read the book and figure out how."

For a moment, there was dead silence.

And then I heard a sound that almost terrified me more than if she'd flown at me shrieking.

Eilidh MacIntosh burst out laughing.

Rhona seemed as unnerved as I felt. "What—what's funny about that, aside from the obvious, which is Calum's use of the phrase 'brain slapped', I mean."

"Magic," Eilidh wheezed, half stumbling over to a boulder that lay half buried in a hummock of dirt and grass. "Magic is what's so funny. Nothing makes sense."

With that enigmatic response, she plonked herself down on the rock, put her head in her hands, where her sweat-dampened auburn hair fell over her face in a curtain, and she went rigid.

"Reckon that's her reading the book?" Rhona whispered.

"Reckon that's her reading the book," I whispered back.

"Should we . . . maybe give her some space? Or at least get out of range of her brain slap?" Rhona sounded deadly serious, and I didn't blame her. "Is she going to be cheesed off at us for being right? Is she dangerous when she's angry, or—never mind. I already know the answer to that."

With that, Rhona prudently stepped about fifteen paces away from Eilidh's boulder, then beckoned at me to follow.

"She doesn't hate you, you know," Rhona said when I got her. She pitched her voice so low I could barely hear her.

"Erm," I said, "that is unlikely to be true."

"I'm right," the teenager said stubbornly. "She doesn't hate you. I think she hates herself."

I looked sharply at her, but she just turned away, her gaze trained on the northern tip of Jura. We couldn't see Corrievreckan—the enormous whirlpool that haunted the waters between Jura and Scarba—from where we stood, but I suddenly wished the bloody maelstrom would come closer so I could jump into it and let it swallow me whole.

THIRTY-SIX

When Eilidh snapped out of her book haze, she pretty much demanded the daggers Rhona and I carried, along with any pelts we had, and I turned over the entire burlap sack Eilidh's gran Mòrag had helped me stuff all the animal remains into, which, frighteningly, made Eilidh practically snatch the thing out of my hands with an eagerness well beyond reason.

After that, she told us to go away and come back in an hour.

Rhona and I walked southward down the coast with Sailean in her carrier.

"What if something comes to attack her while we're gone?" Rhona asked, looking over her shoulder.

"I pity the creature who interrupts Eilidh MacIntosh while she's working," I said.

"That's . . . a good point."

When we got to the narrow crescent of beach halfway down the road to Craobh Haven, we stopped.

"What do you think we'll find in Oban?" Rhona asked as I prepared a bottle for Sailean.

"I honestly have no idea," I said. I'd been avoiding thinking about Iain and Meeksy and Catrìona, mostly because if I let myself dwell on it, I'd not be in a state to do anything but fret. "But it's the biggest town or village I've seen since Glasgow, and I reckon it'll be the most people I've seen in one place since Tyndrum."

Gods, that seemed so distant, now. What was the woman's name who'd helped me there? Helen. Somewhat ironically, that was the English translation of Eilidh.

"I've only been at the manor," Rhona said slowly. "What was it like seeing other people?"

Rhona had greeted everything we did with such bravado so far that I'd sometimes forgotten she was still a kid. Nineteen years old. Just starting out in the world.

"Really weird," I said after a beat. "Most were great. One nicked my bike and punched a woman who was guarding it for me. And then I found Eilidh right after a giant bloody seagull tore her grandfather's guts out."

Probably shouldn't have said that.

Rhona's eyes widened at that, and she swallowed.

Then she seemed to pull herself together as I tested the bottle temperature and opened Sailean's carrier to feed her.

"Did you get the notification about the kitten?" I asked suddenly as the kitten herself began to hungrily tuck in to her lunch.

"About her joining our party? I didn't know we had a party, but yeah, I got it. Not sure why you named her Sailin', though. You spelled it wrong."

I let out a chuckle at that. "Not *Sailin'*, daftie, *Sailean*. It means willow in Gaelic."

"More Gaelic."

"I am what I am," I said. "If you want to have a go at

road signs or something though, take it up with your local councillor, if you can manage to find them."

"What? Road signs?"

"Nothing. Just . . . Gaelic world in-joke."

Rhona looked at me as if I was the single strangest thing she'd seen in the apocalypse.

"Just teach me how to say her name right," she said after a minute.

I walked her through it, careful to coach her on the short vowel so she didn't accidentally call the kitten Inlet by making the A too long, and then I fished out the willow switch that had given me the idea for the kitten's name.

Which, naturally, led to an entirely different form of catfishing than the internet had made us used to, because even though she'd just eaten until her furry wee belly was round, Sailean's entire mind lit up at the sight of her erstwhile victim.

Before long, Rhona was laughing delightedly at the kitten's pounces across the beach, each of which sent up tiny sprays of damp sand.

"It's a little sad she's going to be domesticated," Rhona said when the kitten finally tired. "She's supposed to be wild."

"Aye, I know," I said. "But she'll have a choice when she gets old enough to understand."

"She's a cat," Rhona said, eyeing me askance.

"Didn't you read the notification?" At Rhona's sheepish shrug, I snorted. "She's an *ascension* cat," I told her. "She got a hefty boost to her baby Mind joining our party, and she'll stay with us until she's old enough to choose for herself. If she wants to leave, she can go into the hills and find others like her. If she wants to stay, though, she'll be welcome."

At that, my warm little glow of affection returned, and I

realised I already knew what I hoped. This little kitten had been a source of laughter—a precious commodity even before the ascension kicked our world down the hill arse over tit.

Rhona was quiet as she processed that, and through the Tàth with Sailean, I felt more than heard her little purr.

"We should probably head back," I said.

I bundled the kitten back into the carrier, which she accepted with an almost eerie magnanimity. I'd never met a cat in my life that enjoyed being stuffed in a bag, no matter how cosy.

The sun had vanished behind the clouds again, and as the horizon to the west drew my gaze, I winced. More at what I didn't see than what I did. I should have been able to see Mull in the distance beyond Luing, but the largest of the Inner Hebrides lay under a heavy, blue-black shroud that promised not only rain but a full-on monsoon once it hit the mainland.

"Aye, let's go," I said to Rhona. "Quick. If she's not done, we may have to tell her to wait—we should get as far as we can before *that* hits us."

But Rhona wasn't looking at me as we reached the road once more. She was facing eastward.

"I don't think the rain is our biggest problem."

At first, I couldn't be sure what Rhona was talking about, but when I turned to follow her gaze, I saw it. Or, more accurately, *them*.

Three men sat astride enormous stags, far larger than any Scottish red deer I'd seen in my life. Right then, they were facing away from us, about a hundred meters down the road and pointing farther to the southeast.

One of them was the one who'd skinned Sailean's mother.

And that wasn't all.

The men were not small men—they had clearly over-loaded their Strength stats, but that wasn't what stood out.

The stags.

They were . . . *wrong*.

Their fur was desaturated, almost grey, and it grew lacklustre and ragged, rubbed raw in places where it seemed the animals had scratched themselves with their own hooves as if chasing an impossible itch.

Not only were they mahoosive creatures, but their antlers grew like gnarled blackthorn branches, complete with forbidding, two-inch-long spines.

Their eyes, normally deep brown and warm, had flat-tened to dull black, filmed over with silvery grey.

I cast Connection and almost lost my footing.

Where most living beings had flows of spirit around them, these were covered in wriggling, worm-like threads. Just like the simulacra.

"Those are Sackington's men," Rhona said urgently. "They're the *worst* of them."

Belatedly, I realised one of them was also the one she'd spit on, the one I'd knocked unconscious accidentally blending Spèird with Purifire.

"Do we run or fight?" I asked her.

"I don't have any weapons! Eilidh's upgrading them!"

Fuck.

"But you can hide," I said, unslinging Sailean's carrier and passing it to Rhona. "Use your stealth ability and get to Eilidh."

"What are you going to do?"

"I'm going to be your early warning sign if they come your way," I replied, my voice full of grim resolve. "Watch your six."

I didn't have to tell her again. I simply blinked and Rhona was gone bar a shimmer in the air and a whoosh of wind.

There were only three trees on my side of the tiny single-track road Rhona and I had taken down to the beach, and I made use of them immediately.

With a little luck, the men weren't looking for us. I didn't like the idea that they were looking for anything or anyone, but they seemed so intent on the direction they faced that it seemed unlikely they'd been tracking us directly. Not impossible, but not likely.

Small blessings.

Even as I thought it, one of them gave his stag a kick and started down the road in the direction they were looking.

I cast Connection again and then kicked myself.

The one Rhona'd spit on was the one who'd rode down the A816, leaving only the other I'd seen and one unfamiliar bloke I hadn't caught a glimpse of at the manor.

With the first spell still active, I reached for more spirit and cast Keen Eye, targeting the cat skinner.

Raymond Campbell
 Level 9 Bloodhound
 Affinities: Dual Daggers, Tracking

Fuuuuck.

Level *nine*? And that class had to be an unlocked specialisation—Rhona had mentioned the tracker class, so maybe it came from that, considering his affinities.

Maybe they were tracking us after all, but I didn't think so. Not if he had that class, unless it was total shite.

Bracing myself for more bad news, I cast Keen Eye again. My spirit dipped below seventy percent, and I winced. That was *with* the upgrades. Either this spell was just that expensive to use or it took more spirit the higher levelled the target was. Judging by the bloodhound being level nine, the latter seemed likely.

Puppeted Hart

This stag has been robbed of its will, which has been replaced with the will of another. The animal will fight to the death if it deems anyone a threat to its master or its riders, though it is still conscious within the confines of its own mind.

Puppeted beings frequently experience crawling sensations under their skin, causing them to inflict scratching wounds upon themselves, which may fester and turn septic, but if they are healed frequently, they are difficult to kill.

A swift end will be seen as a mercy for these creatures.

Under the laws of the Ascended Alliance, such use of sentient beings is an abomination.

Double fuck.

That was more of an explanation than I'd gotten for Raymond Campbell. Gods, what were the odds it was a Campbell, with Scotland's notorious history? This bloke would make that surname infamous for another several centuries.

I wished I could hear what they were saying to each other, but with the wind blowing in from the sea, there was no way in hell.

Instead, I grimaced and cast Keen Eye on the other man, bracing myself for the worst.

Steven Brown
  Level 10 Amhasg
  Affinities: Broadsword, Grappling

They were twice our levels. I'd be a fool to assume Sir Spat-Upon was any less formidable, and despite Raymond Campbell's existing status in my brain as someone I'd happily set on fire, this Steven Brown had a class that made the back of my neck prickle.

It *could* mean mercenary—but it could also mean something wilder, boorish. Like a reaver.

We had likely no chance against these men if it came down to a fight. We were so close to Oban. So close.

I had to do something.

Something that would cause a big enough distraction that they would go haring off to deal with it.

Something . . . chaotic.

If Steven Brown's class meant he was a wild man, well. Two could play that game.

My spirit was recovering more quickly than I expected, and I hoped it would be enough. This system didn't indicate how much of my spirit or pathos or will something took, only did the thing. I was a bit afraid to find out what would happen if I overextended.

But now wasn't the time to worry about that.

I crept closer, chancing the risk of crossing over the small road into the much-bigger copse of trees that waited on the other side, which also shaved off about ten meters of distance from the blokes.

Concentrating on the land beneath my feet and how it connected to the road beneath theirs, I reached out with all three of my manipulation resources for the first time. Spirit as the mist to float around them, pathos as the rushing river, and will—the implacable resolve of a glacier.

I triggered Tairm.

And all hell broke loose.

THIRTY-SEVEN

The road between me and the two mounted men split down the middle with a jagged line, the sharp report reaching my ears a half second after my eyes registered it.

I was too stunned, marvelling at the fact that I'd broken a *road* in half with my mind, to register what else was happening. And dazed. The spell had taken all but fifteen percent of my spirit, and it left me wobbling.

It wasn't my will that had broken the road—it was a wall of roots that sprang free from that crack as if they'd been lying in wait for a hundred years, and maybe they had. They rose and curved like a cresting wave.

Normal deer would have startled, bolted.

The stags those two men rode did nothing of the sort. They stood there, eerily still, as that tsunami of roots reached out above their heads and the two men kicked at them ruthlessly to get them to move.

And Tairm apparently wasn't done.

Above the men, the sky seemed to break open as if the storm to the west over Mull had teleported directly onto their heads, and it dumped a flash flood of rain straight down on them in a terrifyingly precise three-meter radius that followed them as they spurred their harts down the road in the direction Sir Spat-Upon had ridden.

That was my cue if I ever saw one.

I turned and bolted.

I didn't dare trust the road, which would put me in plain sight if either of those men looked back.

Instead, I took off through the trio of trees I'd first hidden behind and ran at a sprint through the field beyond. There was a farmhouse ahead and to the left, and smoke from the chimney told me it was occupied, but I couldn't stop. Better if they didn't know anything.

I gave it a wide berth, using more brush and trees along the road for cover.

What had seemed like an easy stroll with Rhona now seemed to take an age, despite my awareness that I was running faster than I'd run in my entire life. Faster than I'd fled the monster days before the first time I encountered its carnage, faster than I'd have ever thought possible.

When I reached the headland and caught a flash of Eilidh's auburn hair, I finally slowed, coming to a stop.

"What did you *do*?" Rhona asked from beside her.

"Distracted them," I said with a gasp. If I'd managed to run fast enough to get out of breath, I must have been practically flying. "We need to go. Now. Finished?"

All I could manage was that level of questioning, but Eilidh nodded. "You'll have to check your notifications later, but it's done. All Rhona needs is sweet violets, and we'll have completed the quest."

"Then let's get out of here."

I'd expected chaos, but I'd not expected *that*.

The more I thought about it as we ran northward, the more I realised it hadn't really been as intense as I'd first believed. While, aye, it'd been impressive, everything Tairm had done was incredibly localised over that three-meter radius.

I'd wanted to distract the bastards—the spell seemed to have taken that to heart.

To say the least.

Once we were a few miles up the road, we finally slowed to a jog, and I told them what I'd gotten from Keen Eye. The news that both Campbell and Brown were above level nine with specialised classes made both of the women look as green as I'd felt.

The landscape around us slowly became more familiar. Kerrera appeared off the coast to the north of us, its long, treeless form a bulwark that protected Oban's harbour from the punishing gales blowing in from the Minch.

Just like was happening right at that moment.

Mull still lay obscured in a heavy bank of clouds and rain, and the three of us pushed on with mounting dread. It wasn't that we feared getting wet—Scots laugh in the face of soggy socks—but the noise and the lack of visibility would make it harder for us to spot if we were being chased.

Which, naturally, meant things were about to get worse.

We had just reached the tiny village of Kilninver, only a few short miles outside of Oban itself. The sky above us was dark and forbidding, and sheets of rain now sluiced just beyond the rise that blocked the view of the sea, about to make landfall.

The quiet was eerie, but at this point, it was familiar.

One lone car sat abandoned in the middle of the A816, heading in the opposite direction to us, and the fields that stretched out on either side of the road were trimmed down to the quick by the herds of grazing sheep.

It struck me that until that moment, I couldn't recall seeing any other sheep—something that turned the general eeriness of the ambience up a few degrees. If you've not seen a sheep yet in rural Scotland, something must be terribly wrong.

But the sheep seemed to be their normal placid selves, a few startling at the sound of our rapid footsteps on the tarmac of the road.

At least until they turned around.

If the harts had been a shock, the sheep were like comparing those near-zombified deer to malamute puppies.

I stopped short in the middle of the road, staring out at a lump of white wool, which was officially the only familiar thing about the creature staring at me with baleful red eyes. Its formerly soft, cleft-lip mouth had been twisted into a hideous beak, blade sharp and black like obsidian.

And worse, it dripped red.

That particular sheep had not, as I'd assumed, been grazing on green grasses. On the field in front of it lay instead a lump of carcass I could only guess was some unfortunate rodent.

"Caora nan sìthichean," Eilidh muttered darkly beside me.

"I never heard the fairy sheep were *carnivorous*," I hissed back.

"Well, a few days ago, loch monsters were a myth. Have an open mind," Rhona said with aplomb. "Besides, it's not attacking."

Out of the corner of my eye, I saw Eilidh shut her own eyes tight.

"Now you've done it," I said to Rhona.

"What?"

From up the road on the right, a series of screams pierced the air, as if on cue. Every monstrous sheep in the field—at least a hundred of them—went rigid like a goddamn pointer.

I groaned.

"That wasn't me!" Rhona protested.

"Yes. Yes, it was." Eilidh resolutely unsheathed her claymore. "We better get to—"

That was all she had time to say before every sheep in the field bleated like the sound of a hundred hooves on a chalkboard and burst into a frenzied gallop.

"Run," I said, taking off towards the building the scream had come from.

I didn't need to wait to see if the others followed; I could hear the sound of their feet slapping the tarmac.

A small sign at the front of the building's carpark said "Kilninver Primary School."

And the screams weren't stopping—worse, they were high-pitched and unmistakably children.

As we flew into the carpark and around the front corner of the school building, I could hear the horrid, churning *clo-clop-clo-clop-clo-clop* of the entire herd behind us, and I cast Fuaran over the three of us to hopefully help us keep our stamina and spirit ready for a fight I wasn't sure we could win.

The sheep behind us weren't the only ones.

There were three of them at the side door of the school, and they beat their cloven hooves against the half-open door, leaving long furrows of blood and scratches. The screams sounded like pure terror.

Whoever was trying to close that door wasn't going to last much longer against that onslaught.

Without another thought, I practically flung Spèird from my staff.

Against a large foe, it could throw something. Against sheep? All three of them went flying away from the door, and the door slammed shut with a loud bang and a startled yelp as the person who'd been holding the door suddenly had no resistance.

"Stay inside!" I yelled through it.

Eilidh was already moving, and her stun burst out at the three reeling monster sheep, which scrabbled and flailed against the gravel to right themselves.

The one that had managed to struggle to its feet stumbled as Eilidh's spell hit it, and then Rhona was there, materialising behind the thing with both daggers flashing.

I reached through the flows of spirit in the air, drawing deeply as I cast Cumhachd. A missile like a fist of gnarled root and stone flew from my staff and hit the second sheep right in the horrifying beak with the force of cannonball. The sheep's head *exploded*.

The rest of it collapsed, twitching.

Behind us, the sound of hooves was getting louder, and Eilidh swung her claymore with perfect aim, cleaving the final sheep's head from its body with a splash of viscous red blood, so red it looked like it might come to life.

"Plan?" Eilidh barked.

"Crowd control," I said, moving behind Eilidh when she strode ahead to meet the coming onslaught. "Spèird, Purifire, whatever your stun is called."

I triggered Connection, not wanting to risk overspending my spirit on Keen Eye, but the spirit around us seemed to draw back like the ocean pulling water outward from the shore before releasing it in a punishing wave of death.

Rhona looked a bit sick, but she straightened her shoulders. "I can help with crowd control."

Then just as the sheep barrelled into the carpark, Rhona threw back her head and wailed.

I didn't think I'd had Connection active the last time she'd used that ability—the one that had unlocked the Vengeance tree for her—and her voice rose into an ear-splitting shriek so suddenly that I almost forgot to cast Spèird.

Every sheep within ten meters of us screamed in response, their legs going stiff for a moment before they recovered, but they'd already faltered, and the sheep farther behind ran smack into their arses.

There was a moment where I half expected the lot of them to topple like dominoes—a few in the front stumbled enough to fall on their faces—but what actually happened was worse. The ones in the back immediately turned on their fellows, shiny black beaks flashing out as they bit deeply into the flanks of their fellows, bright red staining the still-white wool pink.

At the last second, I drew deeply of my spirit, weaving together Spèird and Purifire as I'd done at Lord Bawbag's manor. This time I was more conscious of what I did, and I imagined it like a cone, gaining strength with every inch that took it farther from me.

It blasted into the ravenous horde like I'd clothes-lined them, and the Purifire component of the spell ignited.

Sheep produce a lot of lanolin. It's what keeps them protected against the constant mist, among other things.

And lanolin is highly flammable.

The first line of them went up with a loud *whumph*, followed by more ear-rending bleats of pain and rage.

Just ahead of me, Eilidh positioned her sword point down again, and this time I felt the build of her spirit, her will. It gathered in her like a breath drawn to roar. When she released it, it slammed into the rampaging monster sheep like a wrecking ball.

I'd no idea how many of them were dead. I'd no idea if they would mindlessly stay intent on slaughter. No idea if they'd eventually break.

I had to assume they wouldn't.

Eilidh let out a yell and charged the line of sheep, Rhona a blur of shadow on her heels. I couldn't let them get overrun.

My spirit was about half gone, and I braced myself as I called out to the earth, tendrils of spirit reaching, coaxing, building into the insistent summoning call that was Tairm.

Along the road, dividing it from the primary school's small carpark, was a bramble hedge. It was still dormant for winter, but when my spirit flashed out of me and bid its aid, the thorny branches undulated like a pit of startled snakes.

The vines sprang forth with alacrity, seeking out the tender flesh of the ascension-twisted sheep with single-minded fury.

They didn't try to wrap the sheep in a cocoon of thorns; they simply ran them through.

If there were a hundred sheep, there must have been fifty vines in a tangle of pure chaos—or so it seemed to my horrified eyes.

Their tips struck with terrifying viciousness. They pierced sheep's eyeballs and burst out again from the shoulder blade; they snaked into ears and came out the nose.

Rhona's banshee scream had faded, but the bleating screams of dying sheep took over the air. Eilidh's claymore took down two or three with every swipe, and Rhona's double daggers were at least as efficient as she ghosted through the now-stumbling and confused horde. My vines harried their flank, reaching farther and farther, each thorny finger skewered like a goddamn woolly shish kebab and splattered with brains and gore.

But my vines didn't reach the far flank, and a quintet of the horrible creatures broke off from the herd, giving Eilidh and Rhona a wide berth and heading straight at me.

Three of them had blood and dripping pink wool dangling from their hideous beaks, and the other two looked like they wanted to make sure they matched—by adding my flesh to their own.

I had enough spirit to continue to fight, but I was suddenly struck with just how squishy I'd be without any further melee ability.

Channelling Purifire again, this time I poured it into Cumhachd, trying to create a firebomb to blast into their midst.

It struck the foremost sheep in the face, making it veer off from the others, and it caught the one on its right side as it did. Purifire leapt from one to the other, igniting across their wool like I'd lit a fuse.

But it wasn't enough, and I knew Spèird would take me to the end of my limits.

Sailean still sat in her carrier against my back, and all I knew was that I'd be damned if I let her get eaten by fucking *sheep*.

That was the last thought I had time for.

I struck out with my staff, slamming it down onto the head of the nearest sheep the moment it came into range.

There were still two more—and one flew at me faster than any dumpy quadruped had a right to move. Its horrible obsidian beak clamped down on my thigh just above the knee.

I screamed.

CHAPTER
THIRTY-EIGHT

I f I expected the flash of a sharp knife, like the time I'd been slicing carrots with a mandolin slicer and took the skin off the whole of my thumb knuckle, I was immediately disabused.

That beak tore into the meat of my leg and *ripped*.

Blood fountained from the wound, and I jammed the butt of my staff into the sheep's eye, or tried to.

Spèird was now out of the question, because with the strength of this monster's jaw, I was afraid blasting it away from me might take my entire knee with it.

The other sheep had only not yet attacked me because it seemed to want to go for the same leg as the one that had latched onto me.

I gritted my teeth, my head going dizzy with the pain and the loss of blood.

Enough for Purifire—I had to hope I'd enough.

I screamed again as I cast it at point-blank range, blue-green flames exploding in the face of the sheep.

It didn't let go.

Even as it went up like dry tinder doused with kerosene,

even as the fire leapt from its back to the other bloodthirsty monster that was worrying at it's hindquarters, the goddamn thing held on with the force of a bloody alligator.

A wave of lightheadedness went through me. I was aware of Eilidh and Rhona still fighting, of the cracking and squelching of my vines still at work, but I could feel blood soaking my leg in a torrent.

I brought my staff down upon the sheep's head again. And again. Each strike made the beak tear deeper into my leg rather than dislodging it, and as I heard Eilidh cry out, barely a shadow visible in my peripheral vision, I greedily reached for my last dregs of spirit, forming a missile from pure will, aimed right at the beak. Cumhachd allowed me to fuel the spell with the ambient spirit around me—I had to hope it would be enough.

It didn't have to be enough to launch the sheep across the carpark, just enough to get it off me.

I released the spell.

For one ponderous moment, I wasn't sure if I'd succeeded.

I had just enough time for the blessed feel of relief to hang there in the air as the fist of spirit obliterated the sheep's beak and half its face, and then my leg went numb, and everything bled out to grey.

"I think he's coming around," an unfamiliar voice said.

Someone was crying in the background—a child, it sounded like.

I blinked my eyes open, which was a mistake.

Eilidh and Rhona were both staring down at me, their

faces barely visible through the dual curtains of their hair—Eilidh's auburn and Rhona's dark brown.

"I'm around," I rasped, pushing myself into a sitting position. "Where's Sailean?"

"She's safe," Rhona assured me, moving so I could see the kitten carrier slung over her shoulder.

Thank every lucky star in the sky I hadn't fallen on her when I lost consciousness.

I was on the floor of a classroom. All the desks had been shoved against one wall, and as I leveraged myself against the tile of the floor, I felt terrycloth. Someone had put a rolled-up towel under my head.

"I guess we won," I said.

"Thanks to you," Rhona said. "God, that was awful."

She shuddered, stepping back a bit as Eilidh motioned at her to give me some space.

There were a few adults in the room, a middle-aged woman with blood drying on her hands and a younger one with the same who looked like she regretted being born. A stick-thin man with tortoise-shell spectacles sat half perched on one of the desks. I couldn't see any of the children who'd been screaming, but I guessed maybe they'd not wanted them in the room with someone bleeding to death.

My notifications were flashing in my vision, a golden strobe I wished would go the fuck to sleep before it gave me a headache.

"We got them all?" I asked Eilidh faintly.

"Aye," she said. "No idea how, but we did."

"That spell of yours—" Rhona broke off, shuddering again.

I was beginning to think her *God, that was awful* was

more in horror about my wild magic than the monstrous mutant sheep.

God, the nightmares that were going to plague my sleep.

My leg still ached, but I studiously did not look at it.

My spirit had recovered enough for me to cast Bean-nachd Shlàinte, but something told me not to. I only had one use a day; wasting it did not seem prudent if I was not dead.

And if I was dead, well. Then it'd be moot.

The younger woman ventured towards me with two wee bottles of Fruit Shoot.

"It's all we've got to drink, I'm afraid," she said hesitantly.

She was probably just a bit out of uni, likely a new teacher, and she was very pretty. Her hair was chestnut waves just past her shoulders, and her eyes were enormous, warm brown with long eyelashes that didn't so much hint at a need for mascara.

I took the bottles from her with what I hoped was a grateful smile. It felt lopsided.

I winced as I bent my right leg—no way was I going to try to bend the left one yet—and settled for the awkward sitting position of right leg curled in and the left leg extended. The slight movement of air in the room felt cold on the blood-wet jeans I wore.

Cracking open the first of the Fruit Shoots—blackcurrant and apple—I downed it in two gulps.

"Thank you," I told the woman.

"Ronald would probably be dead without your help," she said. By the way the skinny, bespectacled man on the desk shifted his weight uncomfortably at that, I assumed that was Ronald. "He'd gone out to get the emergency kit from his car boot, and those three sheep came at him when he was halfway there. He barely even managed to get the door partially closed before they hit it."

"I'm just glad we came along when we did," Eilidh said, speaking for the first time since I'd woken. Her voice sounded as hard edged as usual, but it had an undercurrent of something I couldn't parse.

"You're telling me," the teacher said.

"Are the kids okay?" I asked.

"Traumatised," said the middle-aged teacher from the other side of the room. "They're with a couple of the parents who accompanied them to school. I suppose this is what we get for trying to go on like normal in a—in a whatever this is."

"Ascension," I said.

"Between pandemics and war and God knows what else, these children deserve a break, not more horror."

"You're not wrong," I said, draining the second Fruit Shoot. "I just don't know that any of us get a choice."

"Yes, well," said the man—Ronald—speaking for the first time. "By the looks of you three, you've got a story to tell, or at least you can give us some news of what's going on out there."

"I suppose we can do that," I agreed, grimacing again at the throbbing pain in my leg.

With that, we started exchanging information. All three of the teachers jumped when I said I'd come all the way from Glasgow, and their faces darkened considerably at the mention of Lord Bawbag, who I hastily referred to as Lord Sackington after one syllable, which got me the first grim snort of laughter from the teachers.

The tension in the room grew as we talked, describing everything from the giant seagull to the fuath and what we'd learnt of this new world. The sheep had been their first encounter with monsters—something I found nigh-on unbelievable, but they just shrugged and told me everything had been quiet.

I didn't know what to make of that. The herd had apparently been docile, normal sheep that morning. What had happened to change them so quickly was anyone's guess.

All of the people here were level one.

That was almost more terrifying than the sheep.

Alison, the younger teacher, told us that the children had all been granted an ability called Shield that did just that—it cast an impenetrable weave of will and spirit over them that would last one hour—but none of them had yet needed to trigger it. It also apparently would self-cast.

That brought up a whole other question of how the fuck children were supposed to survive in an ascended world. What if a threat lasted longer than an hour? Could they level up? Gain experience? The notion of an army of child soldiers facing off against mutant sheep sent a chill ricocheting off every vertebra in my spine.

It felt thoroughly against the ascension's general ethos, but how the fuck would we know?

The older woman was called Mairead, and she, oddly enough, seemed less out of her depth than the other two.

When we finished exchanging our—frankly bewildering—deluge of information, it was Mairead who peered at us through keen grey eyes.

"What do you propose to do?" She asked the question carefully. "You lot are going to Oban, but what then?"

"I don't know," I said honestly. "But Lord Baw—erm, Sackington—is not a threat that will just evaporate."

"He was a stain on Argyll before he got magical

powers," Mairead said, her voice thick with disgust. "You truly believe he's that dangerous?"

"He is," Rhona said quietly. "I watched him kill two injured men in cold blood after they defended him with their lives. And Calum and I just saw three of his goons riding possessed deer that were the scariest thing we'd seen today before those bloody sheep."

"Let's put it this way," Eilidh chimed in. She pointed at me. "He's level five, and so am I. Maybe higher now after that mess outside—probably, actually—but Rhona's level four. You saw what we can do. Those goons? They're levels nine and ten, with a third who could be beyond even that."

The room went deathly still.

"And we're all level one," Alison said uncertainly.

Ronald, who I had assumed was listening all this time, cleared his throat uncomfortably. "Actually, I'm level two."

"What?" Alison said, and he scratched at his sandy blond hair somewhat sheepishly.

Fuck. That word was going to take on a whole new meaning after today's sheep. A gruesome one.

"I guess hitting them with a door a few times counted for something," he said. "I was reading my—my notifications while you were all talking."

"Glad we had your attention," Eilidh said, her voice totally deadpan.

The man blanched. I couldn't say I blamed him.

"Either way." I cut in hastily, trying to diffuse the sudden tension. "Level two against a level ten is no contest."

"That brings us back to my question," Mairead said, sounding like she was trying to wrangle primary schoolers rather than adults. "What do you propose we do?"

I glanced uncertainly at Eilidh. When she didn't say anything, I blew out a breath.

"One thing the system keeps hinting at—not very subtly—is the ascension directive." At their blank looks, I summarised it. "Safety in numbers, basically. The Ascended Alliance or whatever is insistent that no one can survive without a community, which sounds like basic common sense, but ..."

"Common sense is far from common," Eilidh finished dryly. "In Oban, there should hopefully be enough of a community to begin to defend ourselves."

"You haven't encountered *that* many monsters, have you?" Alison asked, her brown eyes wide and earnest and completely focused on me.

"Erm, I think we've encountered enough," I said, slightly uncomfortable under her intense gaze. "And more than that, everything we've seen so far was things caught in the tumult of the first wave of the ascension. Now everything's had time to ... steep."

"Now it's not just some giant rats or voles or seagulls," Eilidh said quietly. "The ascension changes *everything*. And those changes are only going to compound."

"Like the sheep?" Ronald asked. He had his thumbs through the belt loops of his slacks, and he nervously drummed his fingertips against the seam of his pockets.

"None of us really know," I replied. "We're all just sort of taking stuff as it comes."

"And you think we'll be able to do that better in Oban," Mairead said.

"None of us are saying you have to come with us," Eilidh said, irritation colouring her voice.

"I think we should," Alison murmured, still looking at me.

"What we are saying is that nowhere is safe," I said, looking up at Mairead. "Against a fuath? Against that *thing* we tried to sic on Lord Bawbag? Hell, against his thugs? Anyone who isn't actively levelling up is a sitting duck. Not everyone needs to be a fighter, but *some* people need to be, or everyone else is just chewed-up meat in something's belly."

That may not have been my best inspirational speech.

Then again, I wasn't sure I'd ever made one before. Guess I had to start somewhere.

The teachers left us after that to go speak with the few parents and staff who were in the other classrooms. Alison cast not-very-subtle glances over her shoulder as she followed Ronald and Mairead out of the room.

As soon as we were alone again, I groaned and slumped backward onto the tiled floor, my head landing half on and half off the rolled-up towel. I adjusted it, wincing as I shifted my weight.

"Why don't you just heal it?" Rhona asked, peering down at me.

"If I do, I won't be able to heal anything else for another day. Someone else could need it more before then. It is healing. Just slowly."

On a whim, I cast Fuaran, in a vain hope that doing so might speed up my inherent healing a bit, but I couldn't tell if it was doing anything.

"We're not going to make it to Oban before dark now," Eilidh said. She did not sound happy about that.

"I know," I said. "Sucks."

"Yes," she said, and I could almost hear the eye roll. "Sucks."

"Very . . . suck-cinct, both of you," said Rhona.

I groaned again, but this time not from the physical pain. No, this pain was purely emotional from that terrible pun.

"You love it." Rhona gave my shoulder a playful kick.

"False." I closed my eyes. "So now what?"

"You're not going anywhere on that leg," Eilidh said. "So right now, we wait for you to heal. We should probably all dig through our notifications. Maybe with a little luck you'll, I don't know, get a better healing spell or something."

"Good point." That *would* be nice. And if we really had killed a hundred sheep, maybe I'd levelled up.

Sure enough, that was the first notification I saw—and it wasn't just one level.

You have reached level 6! You have three attribute points and two skill points to distribute.

You have reached level 7! You have six attribute points and four skill points to distribute.

Bloody hell, I guessed I must have been close to level six or something already—either that or the sheep were just that big a deal.

That actually made me feel less freaked by Lord Bawbag's goons' levels. I still didn't want to have to take them three on three with the gap we had, but I definitely liked that gap being narrower.

Assuming they were not slaughtering their way through Craobh Haven and jumping up to level fifteen as we sat there in that tiny primary school.

Nothing I could do about it if they were.

You have killed an ascension-twisted sheep (113).

Caught in a wave of spirit upon Earth's ascension, these sheep mutated far faster than can normally be expected for creatures of their complexity, and moreover, they did so en masse. Had they been left to grow in strength, their danger would have been far more formidable.

It is unusual for such things to occur during a controlled ascension, but due to Earth's anomalous situation, your ascension has been more violent. Most worlds who are gifted with ascension are prepared, both by the sapient species' awareness and by naturally having higher tolerance and understanding of ambient spirit and its effects.

Such creatures frequently contain common crafting materials such as: wool, mutton, sheep bones, mutated sheep beak, cloven mutated sheep talons.

Sheep harvested.

A brief peek into my inventory showed a *lot* of wool. So much wool. So. Much. Wool. I assumed Eilidh and Rhona had also gotten similar amounts, but what the hell were we going to do with thirty fleeces each? I guess that was a problem for our resident crafter—and this was the Scottish highlands, anyway. In terms of likelihood of finding someone who could turn fleeces into jumpers, our odds were probably higher here than if we were in central London.

I also glanced at my stats sheet to see how much my Manipulation resources had shifted, and I wasn't disappointed. While individually, the sheep hadn't been that impressive, collectively, they packed a punch. And I'd gained two points in Mind, as well. I went ahead and added my attribute points while I had it open—the sheep beak incident made me all too conscious of my own mortality, so I added two points to Constitution before I could change my mind. I also added two to each Dexterity and Agility, since those stats were already a bit higher, and I wouldn't have to worry as much about bleeding if I could, you know, avoid getting hit. Or bit, as it were.

Name: Calum Green
> **Age: 36**
> **Level:** 7
> **Class:** Hedge Witch (Further class selection at: Level 9)
> **Affinities:** Nature (Level 4), Healing (Level 3)
> **Specialised Affinities:** Wild (Level 1)

Alteration:
> Strength: 12
> Dexterity: 18
> Agility: 16
> Mind: 38

Regeneration:
> Constitution: 18

Stamina: 21

Manipulation:
Spirit: 37 (+801 capacity for 16 hours)
Pathos: 24 (+614 capacity for 16 hours)
Will: 30 (+109 capacity for 16 hours)

Holy hell.

I was starting to get a vague feeling for how the system did this—it seemed to have added in the bonuses for the sheep to the existing bonuses and then subtracted what had already been permanently added, but no matter what, that was a massive jump. And while it was clear there were magic-heavy builds as well as hack-and-slashy ones like Eilidh's, what was also evident was that ascension brought magic to *everyone*. I had to assume that Eilidh and Rhona (and to a lesser extent, Ronald) had gotten similar boosts from the sheep, and it made sense.

If Rhona was a classic stealthy stabby rogue, she still used magic to hide her movements, and that banshee shriek she had was most *certainly* . . . otherworldly, to say the least.

The next thing I looked at was simultaneously fantastic and maddening.

The Hills Have Eyes: Part II
In completing the quest The Hills Have Eyes, you have found further mysteries to unravel, and your quest has evolved.

While you discovered the source of the simulacra and the tip of the proverbial iceberg of Lord Edwin Thomas Sackington's plans for Argyll, you know of more threats, including the myste-rious beast.

You have managed to observe Lord Sackington's flunkies doing something on the west coast near the village of Craobh Haven, and more to the point, you did so without being observed.

Furthermore, you came upon the village of Kilninver and rescued fifty-three of its inhabitants from a herd of ascension-twisted sheep. Most frequently, entire herds do not succumb to such sudden changes, but it is not unheard of.

Remember the prime directive of the ascension and take time to recover and regroup yourselves.

You will need to prepare.

Objectives:

-Create a weapon (Calum Green only.) (Complete)

-Craft the following items:

-Basic armour x3 (chest plate, greaves, boots, bracers, paul-drons, helmet) (Complete)

-Basic upgraded daggers x3 (Complete)

-Basic upgraded claymore (Complete)

-Basic sheaths x3 (Complete)

-Forage food

-Nettles x10 (23/10 Complete)

-Alexanders x10 (21/10) (Complete)

-Dandelions x20 (31/10 Complete)

-Sweet Violets x10

-Velvet Shank Mushroom x10 (11/10)(Complete)

-Wild Garlic Leaves x10 (13/10 Complete)

-Defeat the horde of ascension-mutated sheep (Complete)

-Escort those who choose to leave Kilninver to Oban (Optional)

-Ask Kilninver's adults about Lord Sackington's pre-ascen-sion activities in Argyll

Rewards:
-Experience (commensurate with current level progression)
-Unlock The Hills Have Eyes: Part III
-1 item (ascension dependent)
-All cooldowns reset
As this is a shared quest, it cannot be completed alone. You
must work together if you are to have any hope of successfully
progressing. Remember the ascension directive.

Part of me wanted to scream that we had been ten sweet
violets away from completing the quest only to now have
new objectives, but I supposed that was what an evolving
quest did—evolved.

I had four skill points to distribute, which felt like a glut
of them, but I knew *that* feeling wouldn't last beyond a wee
wander through my forest of skill trees.

But with four skill points and having already unlocked
Keen Eye, I knew where I needed to start, which made the
first decisions easier.

Gu h-Àrd (Passive)—You gain an understanding of all things
above the earth: the currents of the air, the patterns of the clouds,
and those that make their home therein. You receive an imme-
diate +2 to Mind and a bonus to calling upon the powers of
weather, wind, and creatures of the heavens. With experience,
you may also summon the storm.

While Gu h-Àrd will not increase in levels as active spells
will, your understanding of magic will, on occasion, trigger
evolution.

. . .

Taobh a-Staigh (Passive)—You gain an understanding of the intrinsic qualities of all life and its relationship to spirit. Rooted in Connection, this skill grants a permanent +1 to Mind and +1 to Pathos, and you receive a bonus to all spells and skills that deal with things internal: healing, buffs, and your understanding of your own spirit.

While Taobh a-Staigh will not increase in levels as active spells will, your understanding of magic will, on occasion, trigger evolution.

Those two skill points finally finished the root-level spells for the Nature tree.

Which meant the first spell on the trunk opened to me as soon as I confirmed them. I had to take a minute for the now-familiar-yet-still-awe-inspiring sensation of expansion in my mind—each of the passives that formed the foundation of the Nature tree were meant to work as a cohesive whole. There was a lot to unpack in that, starting with the idea that working with nature magic required a holistic understanding of nature itself, but that was something I preferred to experience and explore rather than ruminate upon.

With two skill points left, I decided to get one I'd been itching for. You know, as a treat.

Caidreabhas—This skill is a foundational one in the Tàthadh tree, but it is not one to be used lightly. Caidreabhas, like Tàth, forms a consensual bond with an animal companion, but unlike Tàth, this bond is permanent and will persist until your death or that of your companion.

Many animals in an ascended world stretch past their

previous limits, often ranging from sentience to outright sapi-
ence, in time. Caidreabhas encourages such growth in your
companion, bolstering the animal's natural strength and adapt-
ability as well as their intelligence.

Unlike most active skills, Caidreabhas will not level, as for it
to do so would cause first bonds to eventually lose their appeal
with the ability to form more complex bonds. Instead,
Caidreabhas evolves—with each animal you bond, your rela-
tionship with your companion will shift depending entirely upon
what you invest in it.

Your current abilities allow you: 1 companion

Then came the hard part: the final skill point.

As much as I wanted to look at the Wild tree and the
Arcane tree again to see what lay ahead there, letting my
leg heal the long way was *not* ideal. And if we were going to
take on the optional part of the quest and escort a bunch of
level-one adults and likely children the rest of the way to
Oban, I wasn't willing to risk having only one option to heal
one person of one injury once per day.

Even moving slowly with kids, we were only eight or
nine miles from Oban, which should be doable in a day. But
as each and every day so far had taught us harshly, a *lot*
could go wrong in twenty-four hours. A lot could go wrong
in twenty-four minutes.

I moved over to the Slàinte tree.

Beannachd Shlàinte hovered in the trunk, and I hadn't
even really examined the root-level skills, so I did that now,
which brought immediate relief.

. . .

Slànaich—A basic healing spell, Slànaich provides a general increase to inherent healing in both speed and duration. While it will not stave off death in the event of a mortal wound, it will both refresh tired muscles and soothe smaller injuries, which may make the difference between life and death even if it feels less dramatic.

I knew already that was going to be the one, but I wanted to be more thorough this time and look at the others.

Dìon-Slàinte—This spell provides a temporary barrier to a single target and can be cast on others to shield them from a debilitating blow. It can absorb the equivalent of 1 killing blow, 2 maiming strikes, and 5 negligible hits, though once it has been struck, it will no longer protect fully against a mortal wound.

Increased experience with Dìon-Slàinte can allow the caster to use it with greater efficiency and complexity, including the ability to cast it on multiple targets.

Pian-Sgiath—While this spell does not actively heal or protect the target from injury, Pian-Sgiath is a necessity in any healer's repertoire. Casting this spell acts as an arcane analgesic, freeing the target from pain to make them more comfortable. While it can be used for everything as simple as migraines to broken bones, Pian-Sgiath is a mercifully palliative spell that can bring peace to someone when all other routes to healing fail.

Duration: 5 hours

Oof.

I'd known that they'd be tempting, but I hadn't realised they'd all seem so necessary.

Regardless, needs must.

I put my final skill point into Slànaich—that was where it would be most immediately useful.

While none of my affinities had levelled up, it seemed a few of my spells had.

Cumhachd had reached level two, as had Tairm.

Tairm (Level 2)—This spell calls upon the land around you to respond, which it will, based on your affinities and your own intent. As this is wild magic, the results are difficult to anticipate for the caster, though if that is true, it is all the more confounding for the targets.

Be clear in your need, and nature will respond to your call.

Your use of Tairm for both distraction and offence has increased its efficacy. While this spell will never become predictable due to its very nature, at Level 2, you are capable of calling upon aspects of the land. This direction is more suggestion than aim, but your will as a mage can, for instance, call upon the trees or the rock beneath your feet or the clouds in the sky.

Results may vary.

That wasn't terrifying at all.

FORTY

By the time I snapped out of it, I was alone in the classroom.

Well.

Almost.

Alison was there with me, sitting in a corner and reading a book, facing slightly away.

She started when I moved.

"God, that's weird," she said, voice breathy. "I saw the others doing it too, but it's just bizarre watching people so still. Even sleeping people move more."

"Where's Eilidh and Rhona?" I asked, slightly unnerved to have just been zoned out in front of a total stranger. "And where's the kitten?"

"Rhona said something about 'chasing down the fucking violets,' and Eilidh went with her. She took the cat. She's a bit . . . odd, isn't she?"

"Eilidh?" For some reason, the thought of a stranger making that comment about Eilidh made me bristle.

Alison shook her head hastily. "Rhona. Eilidh's just terrifying."

I blinked. She wasn't exactly *wrong*, but I wasn't going to confirm. "Rhona is . . . spirited. She needs the violets for a quest."

"There's quests?" Alison's big brown eyes grew even larger.

"Aye, though they only seem to trigger for fairly momentous things."

"Monster carnivorous sheep aren't momentous?"

I took a deep breath and let it out my nose. "Guess not."

"I'm so glad you showed up," Alison said after an awkward pause. "I don't know what we would have done without you."

I had the strangest feeling she was *not* talking about Rhona and Eilidh, and while she was very pretty, I kind of couldn't shake the discomfort of having someone look at me like I'd done something heroic when all I'd done was punch through some sheep with a needle made of brambles.

To avoid my own confusion, I changed the subject. "Do you know anything about what might have been notable about Lord Bawbag's dealings before the ascension? Specifically in Argyll?"

Alison blinked at me as if I'd made a hairpin turn and she'd have expected me to go on about Boris Johnson's hairstylist before asking the question I did.

But she recovered quickly. "Not . . . much? I'm from Oban, though, and my uncle stays in Taynuilt and said that Sackington Incorporated was trying to buy up land. There were a few holdouts up at the north end of Loch Awe, last I heard, but that's about all I know."

I winced. That . . . might be enough. Sackington's corporation was an umbrella, under which most of the worst news stories festered but the law seemed to just slide right off like water off a corrupted duck. They were known for being aggressive, but last I'd heard, they weren't trying to expand in the highlands. Guess that had changed.

"Thanks," I said.

"What's going on with him?" Alison asked.

"No idea, aside from the usual 'all plebes should lick my boots' shite, anyway." My notifications hadn't flashed, so I assumed Alison's information wasn't enough to complete that bit of the quest objectives. "I'm going to get up and stretch. My feet are asleep."

Naturally, that reminded me of my leg. The pain wasn't as bad, but it certainly wasn't back to normal, either.

Time to give my new spell a go.

Grimacing, I cast Slànaich to heal myself.

I braced myself for incoming pain. I'd had enough stitches and breaks over the years to know that sometimes the treatment could be as bad or worse than the moment of injury, but the pain never grew.

Instead, cool relief spread through me, starting in my core. It washed away the impending pins and needles from my blood-deprived feet, and it sank into my quad where that sheep's horrid beak had nearly ripped through the muscle and into my femur.

I let out a deep sigh, my lungs expelling breath they'd apparently been stockpiling for the occasion.

"Did you—did you just do magic?"

Alison's eyes practically went anime sparkles.

"Erm, aye, a healing spell," I said, waggling my left foot side to side. The pain was still there, but it felt weeks old instead of hours. Bliss.

"That's amazing," Alison said. "Can you teach me to do it?"

What?

"I wouldn't know where to start," I said, gingerly rising to a one-legged crouch before I could decide if I was brave enough to put weight on the foot. "But once you level up, you'll get skill points, and the knowledge sort of . . . seeps into your brain by osmosis."

"Osmosis is only the diffusion of water through a membrane," she said, a twinkle in her eye. "But it's still a cool metaphor."

"Erm. Right." Science teacher, I presumed.

"Guess we'll have to find a way to get me to level up, then," Alison went on.

"I'm sure there'll be an opportunity for you to do just that," I said.

Just then, the door behind me opened, and I swivelled awkwardly in my one-legged crouch, testing the bum leg as Eilidh breezed into the room. A waft of woodsy air seemed to cling to her, and as I hastily rose into standing position—the leg bore the weight!—for a moment all I saw was a woodland warrior haloed by the red-brown glow of her auburn hair.

Her gaze floated right past me, landing on Alison and turning to flint.

Or maybe that was for me, because almost immediately, she shifted to look at me. She had one hand in Sailean's carrier, and I could hear the kitten's little rumbling purr.

"You're on your feet," she said without preamble.

"He just healed himself!" Alison said.

This time, the flinty gaze was for sure *not* for me.

"He does that," Eilidh said blandly, then turned back to me again. "Rhona found her violets. She wanted me to give you one."

"That's . . . very thoughtful of her?" I said, bemused.

Had everyone been drinking while I was in screen-time mode?

"To eat, jackass."

"Oh. Wait. What?"

Eilidh rolled her eyes, holding the little purple flower out to me. "She gave one to me, too. Apparently they are magic sweet violets. Rhona was very excited. They give a nice wee buff."

"Oh. That's lovely, then," I said, taking the slightly bedraggled violet.

It was small and purple, with two petals—or maybe just split petals—pointing up and two down, both at a diagonal. It looked a bit like a pansy, which I vaguely remembered were also edible. It was slightly floppy and oddly charming, for something most considered a weed.

Since we were safe and not in imminent danger of attack, I cast Keen Eye on the flower.

Ascended Sweet Violet

This little flower has been used in confectionery when sugared or to flavour liqueurs and cocktails for ages. With a sweet, floral taste and a heady aroma, you can see why this violet evokes a sense of sumptuous luxury.

While it can be used in culinary endeavours, it is also a powerful alchemical ingredient as an analgesic and an anti-inflammatory as well as a source of vitamins C and A, which makes them excellent additions to health potions and poultices, but it is their magical properties that truly elevate this sweet and common flower.

Transformative and restorative, the violet is also hardy, with a keen ability to bridge the gap between worlds and strengthen spirit. It is also used in advanced alchemical infu-

sions along with other herbs to induce dreams that may benefit the dreamer.

The ascension has strengthened these properties, making this plant widely described as a weed into something of great value to the discerning mind.

Well, then.

I popped it into my mouth without further thought. My spirit had taken a ten-percent dip—the bonuses from the sheep seemed to have dulled the bite of Keen Eye some-what—but as the fragrance of the violet rose through my airways and its light, sweet taste burst on my tongue, my spirit began to replenish far faster than I'd seen it do before.

You have been granted a buff from: Ascended Sweet Violet.

Spirit regeneration increased by 20% for 10 hours. Bonus to the following skills for 24 hours: Connection, Fuaran.

Whoa.

No wonder Rhona had wanted us to eat one now.

"She got enough for the quest?" I asked Eilidh, whose chin dipped once in affirmative.

"Gu leòr," Eilidh said, using the Gaelic phrase English stole: galore. She seemed to war with herself for a moment and then sighed. "Thig cò' rium, a Chaluim."

I had no idea why she'd switched to Gaelic all of the sudden, but when she beckoned, I followed her with some relief—Alison was nice, but my brain couldn't really take being stared at adoringly right then.

Eilidh led me outside of the school rather than farther

into it, and she seemed to relax—insofar as she ever relaxed —when the cool breeze hit our faces, bringing with it the earthy scent of petrichor.

The rain had blown over, leaving only scudding clouds, but the fragrance calmed me, too.

"Carson a' Ghàidhlig?" I asked Eilidh, nonplussed.

She blinked at me like she had no idea why I was asking her why she'd spoken Gaelic to me, but her cheeks turned ever so slightly pink.

"I need to give you your armour," she said, ignoring my question entirely. "And I need to make sure it fits."

Oh. That . . . would have been helpful pre-sheep.

My trousers were torn almost into jorts above my left knee, which was not delightful. I looked dubiously downward at them.

"There's—ugh, here. Get changed. I'll be back."

Eilidh had materialised a bundle of clothing and armour, and at my sideways glance as I took it from her, she shrugged. "We had a *lot* of wool. Don't worry. It's not scratchy."

My doubt increased.

"Just tell me when you're decent," she said, walking determinedly around the front of the school.

The last thing I wanted to do was flash a bunch of kids, so I quickly stepped around the back corner, checking for windows. I put my back against the wall to be safe, quickly stripping out of my soiled clothes and running threads of Purifire over my entire body to rid it of dried blood. It worked, but it left behind a lingering odour of burnt iron.

I really needed to figure out a better way of getting clean. Thank the gods I had clean pants in my inventory, because cleansing the other pair with Purifire did not convince my brain it would get rid of swamp ass.

The wind blew away the less-than-pleasant smell after a moment, and I looked at the pile of things Eilidh had handed me.

Time to give Keen Eye a workout, I guessed.

Sturdy Wool Trousers
   These trousers were created from the fleece of ascended sheep and infused with ascended oak bark to colour them black. They will stay warm even when wet.

Sturdy Wool Shirt
   This shirt was created from the fleece of ascended sheep and infused with ascended oak bark to colour them black. It will stay warm even when wet.

I was beginning to see how Keen Eye functioned—the simpler the item, the less spirit it took to identify.

Next were the bulkier items, and I had to marvel. Eilidh'd made *boots*. They smelled of leather, honey, and . . . fish?

Sturdy Leather Boots
   Made from the hide of ascended sheep and lined with fleece, these calf-length boots have been infused with ascended oak bark to colour them black and waterproofed with a blend of brown trout oil and beeswax.

· · ·

I didn't care if they smelled of fish—my feet were only not covered in blisters due to the ascension-assisted healing. They practically screamed to get inside these supple, miraculous boots. Pulling the trousers and shirt on, I had to wonder at how Eilidh hadn't been taking the piss out of me. They really didn't feel scratchy, like she'd somehow managed an impossibly fine weave of cashmere instead of monster sheep. Or maybe the monster sheep were all beaks and blood but their fleeces were silky smooth? Who knew.

I practically kicked my old shoes into a bush and swapped out my socks.

The boots fit perfectly—like broken-in, moulded-to-my-weird-wide-soles perfectly.

Giving each foot a wee flex to test the boots, I almost moaned with how comfortable they were. Was this what it was like to have shoes that were made precisely for one's feet?

Next came the armour.

I'd certainly never worn armour before, unless you count the time I was Iron Man for a fancy dress party in high school, which was all fake muscle suit and plastic.

I didn't think that counted.

The chestplate came first. It looked like the hardened version of leather from my boots, but it was overlaid with something I couldn't identify. My spirit was about a quarter gone, so I had enough to use Keen Eye on it, too—but I winced when it took another quarter all in one go.

Hardened Leather Chestplate (Set Item 1/4)
Fashioned from oak-dyed ascended sheep leather, this chestplate is cured and treated with brown trout oil and beeswax for water resistance and reinforced with giant centipede chitin and

blackthorn to add greater protection against ranged and melee attacks.

As a set item, you will receive bonuses for combining the pieces of the set.

2 pieces: Strike your enemy with 10% of whatever damage they inflict upon you.

3 pieces: Generate 50% spirit for every point of damage you take.

4 pieces: Armour will actively channel spirit from your surroundings to keep you dry.

They didn't have to tell me twice.

On it all went.

While it was a little awkward trying to get into it alone, I almost felt like the armour helped me, as if it moulded to my shape until it fit like a second skin but barely inhibited my range of motion. And the moment the fourth piece was on, it was like I could feel something click together around me. I glanced up at the sky—the one time in Scotland I wanted it to rain, and the clouds were holding out on me.

Without confirmation of my new magical waterproofing, all that was left was to allow Eilidh to inspect it.

Why did that make me more nervous than if she'd come round the corner while I was naked?

CHAPTER

FORTY-ONE

When I called out to Eilidh that I was ready with a Gaelic "Tha mi deiseil!" that sounded far more confident than I felt, she came around the corner after a slight pause and a crunch of gravel.

She had something else in her hand that looked like a charcoal-grey . . . blanket?

"Here," she said, holding it out to me, and at my raised eyebrow, she gave an exasperated huff, adjusting the kitten carrier to take up the space the blanket thing had vacated. "It's a cloak. Also can double as a blanket. Or a tent. Or a pillow. Or a bag, in a pinch, I guess."

"Oh! Thanks," I said, taking it from her.

She stood back after she handed it over, eyes narrowing as she scrutinised me. "It actually fits."

"Did you expect it to not?"

"I just made three sets of magical armour essentially by thinking very hard at a pile of wool and untanned sheep-skins." Eilidh, to my surprise, gave a nervous chuckle, scrubbing one hand through her hair, which made it fall into her face, which then made her try to blow it out of her eyes, which didn't work. "I don't know what to expect from anything anymore."

I had the sudden—probably suicidal—urge to push her hair back from her face myself, but instead I just looked away.

"Turn around," she ordered.

I obeyed. When my back was to her, I said, "You really didn't need any tools or anything?"

"For simple stuff, no. There are apparently crafting tiers, but as I understand it—which is barely, so don't ask me to elaborate—using tools is less about the effect of the tools themselves and more about the . . . hm. Meditative state of the process that focuses the crafter on the work."

By the time she finished, I was back to facing her, and I nodded slowly, wracking my woodcrafting knowledge to see if it was the same for me. Images and memories flooded my mind with a thought: a woodcrafter painstakingly etching a complicated, unending knot-work design into her staff; a carpenter sanding away the rough edges from a door that, through his labour, would be stronger than steel; an architect drawing unfamiliar runes and sigils into the beams and girders in his blueprints.

Beyond that, they actively chose which woods to use for their inherent properties. The protective rowan, the flexible willow, the strength of the oak.

When I said that aloud, Eilidh nodded again, this time thoughtfully. "It's easy to do the simple things that are in line with a material's structure and nature without tools. It's the blackthorn in your armour that causes the thorns damage"—she paused there to give me a wry smile at the video game term—"but that also adds protection. If I wanted it to work with something else in a more complex fashion, though, it would need coaxing."

The only word I could think of to describe what I saw on her face was *hunger*. She wanted to try it—just like I was itching to experiment myself.

For a moment, there was no confusion or animosity between us, just a pause where we both marvelled at the possibilities and potential magic of this new world.

"Eilidh, are you out here?" Rhona's voice bellowed, and though Eilidh and I were a solid two meters apart, we both sprang back farther as if we'd been caught with our trousers round our ankles.

That was not an analogy I wanted to think about too much.

"We're right here," she said, turning away from me immediately.

I followed, and Rhona met us just on the other side of the corner.

"Oh, you're both here," she said. "You should come inside. I think you'll want to hear what Ronald has to say."

"Say that again," I said to Ronald.

Only a few minutes had passed, but I felt like the world had shifted under my feet again.

We were in the same classroom where I'd woken, and someone had cleaned my blood off the floor, so the room reeked of bleach despite the open window sending a swirl of fresh air through the place.

Ronald and Mairead were with us, but Alison was not— I presumed she was with the kids, and that was a niggling relief.

"Before this all happened, Lord Sackington was trying to buy up most of the land around Loch Awe," Ronald said.

"I got that part. The other part." I hoped I'd heard wrong.

"His plan, ostensibly, was to create an exclusive resort and renovate Kilchurn Castle, but the people who owned the land adjacent his holdings didn't want to sell. Most of their families have lived there for generations—some even through the Clearances." Ronald cleared his throat, his prominent Adam's apple bobbing. "Sackington, Incorporated had started using intimidation tactics when bribes didn't work—not that they'd offered more than a bare nod above market value."

"And who was in his sights?" I asked, dread pooling in my belly.

"Heaps of people, but he was primarily focused on Kilchurn Suites—they're a house on the north side of the—"

"We met them," Eilidh said quietly, stopping Ronald in his tracks. "He sent a simulacrum that killed one of the owners and the man's adult daughter."

Mairead stared at us.

"Did you know them?" I asked.

"No," she said. "Not personally, anyhow. My husband and I stayed in one of their guest rooms last year for a couple nights. Lovely people."

"Diana and Andy—that's Diana and Donald's grandson—escaped and went to my seanmhair's," Eilidh said.

"That explains why the simulacrum was there," I said slowly. "It wasn't looking for us."

"It could have been also looking for us, but aye, it had another reason to be there." Eilidh's pale face had gone a bit paler.

"I think we can safely say Lord Bawbag is no longer planning an exclusive resort," I said with a sharp smile I could tell did not reach my eyes. "But since he's clearly pursuing the same goals he had before the ascension, we'd be stupid to assume whatever he decides to do once he consolidates his hold on Loch Awe won't go farther."

"You did say he'd sent his goons towards Craobh Haven. Why would he do that?" Ronald asked.

"The marina," I said immediately, just as Eilidh said, "Port control."

Rhona had been silent all this time, but now she spoke up. "I remember hearing him talk about Craobh Haven when I was waiting on him. He's got a couple yachts there."

"With a little luck, they're as buggered as cars," I said, and she shook her head.

"At least one of them is a proper sailing vessel, and he knows how to use it," Rhona said stubbornly.

I happened to be looking in Eilidh's direction when that sank in, and our eyes met, hers widening enough that I could see my own wide-eyed expression reflected in her irises.

I suddenly wished *I* had Sailean so I could pet her and feel her comforting little warmth. Eilidh had her own hand in the carrier again, and I had to resist the urge to ask for her back.

"He's preparing to come at Oban from land and sea," I said, the sudden flash of gold in my peripheral vision making that pool of dread in my belly turn to lead. That was all the confirmation I needed. When Eilidh's eyes went distant, her answering wince just made it worse. "It has to be. If he can even bring one or two boats full of his people in from the sea, and they're levels nine or ten or higher?"

"Without knowing how Oban's getting on, we have to assume they'd be caught almost completely unawares," Eilidh added.

Grim silence settled over the room.

I took a deep breath and let it out again. Oddly, Eilidh did the same as I said, "Oban's the gateway to the Western Isles, not to mention the open sea. He won't be able to do much with a couple small sailing vessels, but Oban's harbour is much bigger and deeper, and he could—"

"He could build a fleet," Eilidh finished.

"Fuck," Rhona said succinctly.

Looking around the room, it seemed she had spoken for all of us.

Things moved very quickly after that.

The adults from Kilninver sprang into teacher mode, leaving the three of us to check our notifications, which were flashing.

The Hills Have Eyes: Part II

While you discovered the source of the simulacra and the tip of the proverbial iceberg of Lord Edwin Thomas Sackington's plans for Argyll, you know of more threats, including the mysterious beast, and you are learning that Lord Sackington has his eyes on sea access.

Furthermore, you came upon the village of Kilninver and rescued fifty-three of its inhabitants from a herd of ascension-twisted sheep.

Remember the prime directive of the ascension and take time to recover and regroup yourselves.

You will need to prepare.

Objectives:

-Create a weapon (Calum Green only.) (Complete)

-*Craft the following items:*
-*Basic armour x3 (chest plate, greaves, boots, bracers, pauldrons, helmet) (Complete)*
-*Basic upgraded daggers x3 (Complete)*
-*Basic upgraded claymore (Complete)*
-*Basic sheaths x3 (Complete)*
-*Forage food*
-*Nettles x10 (23/10 Complete)*
-*Alexanders x10 (27/10) (Complete)*
-*Dandelions x20 (34/10) (Complete)*
-*Sweet Violets x10 (18/10) (Complete)*
-*Velvet Shank Mushroom x10 (11/10)(Complete)*
-*Wild Garlic Leaves x10 (13/10) (Complete)*
-*Defeat the horde of ascension-mutated sheep (Complete)*
-*Escort those who choose to leave Kilninver to Oban (Optional)*
-*Ask Kilninver's adults about Lord Sackington's pre-ascension activities in Argyll (Complete)*
-*Reach Oban safely*
Rewards:
-*Experience (commensurate with current level progression)*
-*Unlock The Hills Have Eyes: Part III*
-*1 item (ascension dependent)*
-*All cooldowns reset*
As this is a shared quest, it cannot be completed alone. You must work together if you are to have any hope of successfully progressing. Remember the ascension directive.

Our duty was now to get to Oban—whether the residents of Kilninver came with us or not.

And that wasn't all.

. . .

You have discovered a quest!

Defend Oban

In your travels, you have pieced together a danger that threatens not only the immediate vicinity of Loch Awe but, more widely, the town of Oban.

With no knowledge of the town's current status or of how quickly Lord Sackington's plans are progressing, you are now in a race to not only reach Oban with vulnerable people in tow but also to communicate the threat to the townsfolk and prepare for a violent invasion.

You have already observed that Lord Sackington employs ruthless measures upon those he deems a nuisance or a threat—but even his brute strength can be neutralised by those working in the spirit of the ascension directive.

Objectives:

-Reach Oban

-Seek out the following inhabitants who are most likely to believe your story:

-Catrìona and Iain Whyte and Farid "Meeksy" Meeks

-Ross and Jo MacIntosh

-Ruaraidh and Ciorstaidh Smith

-Jack Miller

-Tina Dunlop

-Convince at least twenty fighters of level five or above of the threat

-Formulate a plan to defend Oban

Rewards:

-Experience (commensurate with current level progression)

-1 item (ascension dependent)

-1 skill point

-5 attribute points

-???

. . .

This had to be serious—the system had given us a second quest, and it definitely didn't do that lightly, from what we'd seen.

That was about all I had to look at, so I closed out of my notifications to find Eilidh and Rhona both still zoned out, but Eilidh snapped out of it a second later, swallowing as if she'd just tasted something bitter.

"Hey-ho, I guess," she said after a beat. "This escalated quickly."

"Maybe the system's wrong," I replied, though I didn't mean it and was pretty sure Eilidh knew that from her answering snort.

"There's no way it's wrong," Rhona said, startling both of us.

Her own voice sounded strangely distant. Whatever her usual bravado and silliness, she was still barely an adult, and this couldn't be easy for her.

Eilidh's face softened, and she went over to the young woman and put a comforting arm around her. I had to force myself not to stare—I didn't think I'd ever seen Eilidh affectionate except with Susanna, and that always felt different. Habitual. Not cold or anything, just like it was expected of her, so she did it. Cheek kisses and hugs, letting Susanna drape herself across her lap in taxis when we were all drunk, that sort of thing.

"We'll get through this," Eilidh said, steel in her voice despite the gentleness of the way she gave Rhona's shoulder a squeeze.

"Aye, we will," I said.

"You're both full of shit," Rhona replied, though her voice had a bit of its old spark to it. It faded again as she took a shuddering breath. "You didn't see—you didn't see what he's capable of."

I thought of how Rhona had unlocked the Stealth tree, how she must have learned to stay silent and observe as a way to keep herself safe in that house. Why anyone in her family had agreed to let her work there was beyond me. The man's reputation as a sex pest was enough even without the well-documented trail of human exploitation and ruthless pursuit of self-interest no matter who it hurt.

"Well," I said, "not entirely, but since his goons beat us up and locked us in a shed—"

"'Locked.'" Eilidh made sardonic air quotes around the word.

"—and were probably planning on gutting us in front of Lord Bawbag when he returned, I think we've got some idea. And we got out of there, right? Even with only two of us, we managed. Now there's more of us."

Rhona managed a tremulous smile, then brightened. "At least if he comes to Oban, I'll have another chance of making his head explode with my banshee scream."

"That's the spirit," I said, and even Eilidh laughed.

CHAPTER
FORTY-TWO

The school had become a beehive of activity—or maybe a kicked anthill.

When we opened the door on the way out, the first thing we saw was Alison, heavily laden with several flats of Fruit Shoot and a few sleeves of biscuits precariously close to rolling right off the edge of the armload.

She squeaked when she saw us, and one of the sleeves —dark chocolate digestives—did tip over the edge.

I snatched it out of the air without a thought, and Alison jumped at that, too.

"You could just put all that in your inventory," Rhona said, nonplussed. "It'd be easier than juggling."

Alison's milk-pale face flushed pink at that, her eyes darting to me.

I shrugged. "Takes some getting used to—just concentrate on your intention of putting it in your inventory."

The sleeves of biscuits popped out of existence one by one, followed by the Fruit Shoot.

"You can also do it all at once," Rhona said helpfully, the

helpfulness marred only slightly by her exasperated sigh. "The inventory will sort it out for you."

"I don't know how any of this works," Alison confessed. "Sorry."

"No need to apologise," I said. "We've had more practise."

I felt a slight warmth as Eilidh slipped behind me, and I turned to see her heading down the corridor to my left without a word.

"Erm," Alison said, "want to help me get the rest? We're trying to make sure everyone's ready."

"What else do we need?" I asked.

Some of Alison's embarrassment slipped away as she sidestepped into teacher mode. She rattled off a list of items from the canteen as well as the fact that a couple of the adults—Ronald among them—had gone off to nearby houses to mobilise the villagers, either to get parents to join their kids or simply to let them know people were evacuating to Oban.

"Which way did they go?" Rhona asked suddenly.

Alison, having been in the middle of a sentence, stopped. "Oh, erm, they went north, mostly. In pairs," she added hastily. "Nobody went alone."

"I'm going to try to help them," Rhona said to me. "I'll either scout from a distance or just knock on doors if I need to."

"Want me to come?" I asked.

"Nope. You should get everyone ready here," Rhona answered, and then she gave me a lopsided grin. "Besides, I'm sneakier than you."

With that, she was off, practically a blur that breezed through the door and vanished.

"Right," I said to Alison, who looked spooked at Rhona's quick exeunt. "Show me what we need to get."

She nodded, leading me through the small building in the direction she'd been coming from. Down the hall, I could hear children's voices for the first time. I did not envy the adults, teachers or parents, for having to deal with kids in this situation. First the ascension and then a possible evacuation? Would their parents even believe us?

"How many people do you think will come with us?" I asked Alison as she showed me to a pantry full of snacks and tins.

"I don't know," she said, reaching for a small box of individual apple sauces.

"Wait." I did a quick search around the room until I found some bin bags. "Load each of these up. If you do it one at a time, each separate item will take up an inventory slot, but if you put everything in a bag first, the bag just takes one."

Alison's eyes widened. "Got it."

We worked in silence for a few minutes. I had four inventory slots open, so I utilised those as well. There were digestives and more juices, some boxes of oats, long-shelf-life milk that could be used for hot porridge or fuarag in a pinch—a simple cold porridge of oats and milk or cream—and anything we could find that would be high calorie but easily portable. I winced at all the empty carbs. There wasn't anything wrong with carbohydrates, but nutrition-wise, without other and more diverse foods, it was a bit lacking.

The deepening light coming through the window added an air of urgency to our work. Some people would likely balk at leaving tonight, but every hour was precious.

Even *if* Lord Bawbag didn't attack immediately, every

day we weren't in Oban was now a day that could either save lives or condemn them.

The sheep had been bad enough; anyone here who'd seen them had gotten a firsthand glimpse at new dangers. Adding human intelligence and malice?

Aye, that was a recipe for motivation if I ever saw one.

Once Alison's inventory was chock-a-block full of food, we headed back down the corridor to the biggest of the classrooms, where the door was just swinging shut.

Ronald was in there, talking to a few people I assumed were parents, judging by the young kids who clung to their legs. One little girl gnawed on her bottom lip as she stared wide-eyed up at her father and Ronald.

Almost every child in the room turned and stared at me, and I heard a different little girl mutter, "He's got *armour*" in an awe-struck voice, followed by a breathy, "Coooooool."

The skinny teacher looked up at us when he heard that, and he frowned. "Where's the food?"

"Inventory," I said, "but we'll need to spread it around as much as we can. Do the kids have inventory?"

When all I received was a blank stare in response, I gritted my teeth, taking a calming breath.

"Can everyone listen for a moment?" I said loudly. I wasn't one for talking to groups of people, but right now I didn't have time to be precious about it.

A couple of the parents' eyes narrowed, but they did turn towards me.

"I hope by now people have walked you through how to navigate this system's information and your inventory as adults." I glanced around at the kids, who ranged from around five to ten or eleven. "Have yous explored yours? Like, look."

At that, I pulled my rucksack out of my inventory and

heard a few of the kids gasp and more than one additional "Cool!" and "Wicked!" filter through the air.

I put the rucksack back. "Grab anything you've got handy, a book, a shoe, whatever—hold it and concentrate on putting it away in your inventory."

There was a confused rustle among some of the younger kids, but after a moment, one of the older boys crowed.

"Did you see that?" he squealed. I hadn't, but a moment later, an empty Fruit Shoot bottle materialised in his hand only to vanish again.

One look around the room showed other kids disappearing and reappearing small items, and I suddenly remembered that I didn't think anything living could go in there.

"Make sure you don't try to inventory anything that's alive," I said hastily. "You don't want to hurt anything or anyone by accident."

All the adults in the room swivelled to eye me askance for not, you know, leading with that.

"Sorry," I mouthed to them.

"It won't let you, anyway!" one of the kids chirped, a wee girl probably about seven. "I tried it with a spider."

"That's . . . good to know," I said with some small bit of relief.

To change the subject, I started unpacking the supplies from my inventory, and Alison did the same.

A couple of the other adults came over to help us sort things, and one produced a stack of smallish paper bags, into which we began to sort a few meals worth of food that could easily be distributed to the kids in case of an emergency. Each of them could take two bags, so they'd always have something to eat on them in a worst-case scenario where they got separated from adults.

I didn't know where Eilidh'd gone, but when we were about halfway through the distribution of apocalypse lunchables, she came back through the classroom door, arms piled high with woollens.

Her eyes tightened when she saw me, and I immediately felt tired.

"Whichever of the kids are coming with us, they'll each get one of these," Eilidh said, looking to Ronald. "They're not much, but they'll keep them drier and will double as blankets. I couldn't do the same bonus I did for myself and Calum and Rhona, because I just didn't have enough materials, but—"

"It's more than enough," one of the parents said, cutting Eilidh off mid-sentence. "We'll find some way to make it up to you."

Eilidh flushed, shifting uncomfortably, then strode over to one of the desks that had been shoved up against the wall, depositing her pile of crafted cloaks.

"You're sure you want to leave tonight?" Eilidh said in a quieter voice, drawing Ronald aside.

"I don't see how we can afford not to," he said. "It's about time for the kids to be picked up anyway, and as soon as we know who's coming and who's not, we'll get on the road."

"What about the ones who don't want to come? Or who want to go home first to pack?" I asked.

One of the pairs of parents drew closer. "We were thinking we could volunteer to stay as a second group. Leave in the morning with whoever needs to take the night to think."

"Do the others who went off knocking on doors know

that?" I asked.

The mother, a slight woman with hair as pale as thistle-down, gave a perfunctory nod. "All of us have tried to organise outings before," she said, her voice bland. "We knew there would be some resistance to the idea. It's hard enough wrangling children, let alone all their parents, and I'm sure some of them are hoping that whatever this is will just blow over and life will go back to normal."

I had to stifle a laugh at that. It was a bitter laugh, one I saw reflected in other faces around us. What even was normal anymore? First plagues and war, now magical apocalypse from a big cosmic whoopsie-daisy.

This *was* normal for this new generation.

That thought sobered me—most of the kids in this room knew nothing before COVID. It'd just been one thing after another since then; it was the adults who remembered times that weren't so tumultuous.

"When are the kids due to be picked up?" I asked. "I'm pretty sure the system can tell us the time, but that counts on people knowing that."

"Sun's on its way down," someone said. "They should be showing up by now."

"Got it," I said. "Might be a good idea to have a familiar face outside to greet them. I'm not sure seeing me and Eilidh will be ideal. She and I can work on . . . marching orders, for lack of a better term."

"I'll go outside," Ronald said. "Alison, will you stay here with the kids and make sure all the food is distributed?"

For a moment, I thought the young woman was going to protest, but she didn't, only nodding and darting a glance at me and Eilidh.

"Join me in the other classroom?" I asked Eilidh herself.

She didn't answer for a second, then shook herself. "What? Oh. Aye, good thought."

The two of us headed back down the corridor with Ronald, and just as we reached the classroom we were aiming for, another thought struck me.

"Ronald," I said, keeping my voice low. "I think we need to be prepared for the eventuality that some parents might not show up to get their kids."

He stopped in his tracks at that, his face going pale. "You think—you think they could have gotten hurt?"

Eilidh was watching me with an unreadable expression on her face, blue eyes unblinking.

"It's a distinct possibility," I said. "But in a community this small, hopefully neighbours have been checking on each other, or someone will know where to look, at least."

"Right," he said. Ronald's voice sounded very far away. "Right. All right. I'll let you know."

"Stay close to the door," Eilidh told him. "If you so much as see a rabbit acting unusually, come get us."

He nodded, mouth moving wordlessly, though I think as he got out of earshot, I heard him muttering something about wishing he had a holy hand grenade.

FORTY-THREE

Eilidh and I ran over the map with Sailean pouncing a ping-pong ball we'd found in a box of stuff in the back corner—her tiny kitten paws were still clumsy, and her pouncing was distracting, but it was a much-needed dose of levity. Calculating to the best of our ability the pros and cons of the most direct route to Oban and the likelihood of shelter along the way, we managed to hash out a Plan A, a Plan B, and a Plan C, if we needed it. It was only about eight or nine miles now, an easy jog for us in an hour or so, but the kids were kids.

We guessed it would take four to five hours at best, and that was without any inevitable pitstops. Plus, it'd be dark for most of it. Looking out the window, the weather threatened more rain, which would slow us further and truncated our chance to have any daylight. It was going to be a long walk, and probably a wet one. No one functioned perfectly when cold and wet in the dark in a scary world where things literally wanted to eat you. But I couldn't do much about that. Just mitigate the dark and the wet bit. A few of the kids had wellies, but most were in trainers. Eilidh's cloaks wouldn't do much to keep feet dry.

Though Rhona wasn't with us, we decided she'd be our rear guard. She was quick, silent, and virtually invisible when she wanted to be. She could keep an eye on our flanks to make sure nothing nasty snuck up on us.

I'd do the same at the front, taking point, and with Eilidh's speed, she'd cover everything in between, checking in every so often. My ranged spells would buy us time if we got attacked from the front, and Rhona's banshee scream could do the same from the rear, with Eilidh joining the fray wherever the threat was the worst.

Some of it would depend on how many people ended up joining us, but assuming there was at least one parent per pair of kids, we would do a buddy system, making sure there was an adult present every few children. Of course, it would help if the parents had any levels yet, but maybe staying put and being somewhere without any fighting just hadn't afforded them the opportunity. It was moot; we had to work with the resources present.

"Reckon we'll see how it goes," Eilidh said with a wry smile. "No plan survives contact with the enemy, et cetera."

"Do you mean monsters or parents?" I asked her just as wryly.

"Yes." This time the smile did reach her eyes for the barest breath of a moment, and for that moment, it lit up her entire face.

Then it was gone—I wondered if it'd been a mirage.

"Fair play," I said after an awkward pause. "I mean, we're a couple child-free thirty-somethings waltzing into a primary school with weapons and slaughtering an entire herd of mutant sheep. Not sure I'd want to take marching orders from me either."

"Alison would probably follow if you told her to march to Mull from here, never mind the water in the way," Eilidh muttered.

"What?" I'd heard her, but oof. I did not want to think about that, and I'd been hoping I was wrong. Why, I didn't know. It wasn't like I was seeing anyone. "I wouldn't tell her to march to Mull."

That was the wrong thing to say. Eilidh's eyes turned flinty again, but it passed quickly. She straightened from where she'd been leaning on the desk we were using to look at the map.

"I'm going to go check on Ronald. You good with Sailean?" she said abruptly, and just as abruptly when I nodded, she was gone.

She was acting *weird*.

Her friend was the one who'd cheated on *me*, not the other way around, and besides, I was single and had been for months. If anyone had earnt the right to look elsewhere, it was me. And I wasn't even looking at Alison, anyway. To say this was bad timing was the understatement of the century.

I did not need that headache.

Maybe another one would suffice.

If Eilidh had managed to put together cloaks for the kids, maybe I could do something to help as well.

It might get me in trouble.

I made sure the door was shut and that Sailean was still nearby—I could feel her back under the shoved-together student desks against the wall, probably pouncing a dust bunny, since the ping-pong ball lay forgotten in the middle of the classroom floor.

She'd be fine while I worked.

I didn't think staves would be helpful for all the adults, though a couple might not go amiss as walking sticks, if absolutely nothing else. But having some sort of weapon, even a simple club, would be helpful.

Most of the desks in the room weren't wood—or if they had been at one point, the wood had been so mixed with plastic and fibreglass and other materials so as to be unidentifiable. But the teacher's desk?

That was another story.

I didn't think they'd thank me for dismantling the enormous desk, but it was solid hardwood, and that would help us tremendously. I'd make them a new one if we ever lived through this mess. By then, I'd probably be able to get it to grade papers by itself or something. Everyone would win.

I wove spirit together and cast Keen Eye on the desk.

Simple Maple Desk
A teacher's desk. Heavy and cumbersome, but well-crafted. It may not be much to look at, but the hardwood it's made from is a protective influence on the area around it.

Interesting. Maple, then. I sifted through the knowledge the woodcrafting book had instilled in my brain.

Maple
A common hardwood, this beautiful tree is known mostly for the sweetness of its sap and the stunning vibrance of its autumn

foliage, but its boons have been recognised across the world for hundreds of years.

Some peoples put a piece of maple over their thresholds to guard against demonic incursion; others insist maple is tied to the moon. But one thing is for certain: the maple tree's seeds soar upon the wind, their delicate wings propelling them away from their mother tree to find fertile soil to grow into their own patch of sunlight. As such, maple is an excellent wood for undertaking travel.

That was all I needed to read.

The drawers were probably full of all sorts of things, but I figured that wouldn't matter too much, since worst-case scenario, I'd just end up dropping it onto the floor if I transmuted the surrounding wood into a club.

I mentally moved through the different options with maple. It would likely be best as blunt force, but if we had anyone with archery skills, it would also make an excellent bow, if we could find something to string it with.

Touching the desk, I triggered Connection, concentrating on what I could feel within the wood, how it would work with me, what shapes it felt most naturally drawn to. The flows of spirit were less active in the wood, but its structures remained; all wood was once alive.

Across the Irish Sea, there was a particular type of walking stick and cudgel called a shillelagh, which came from the Irish "sail éille," which meant *strap willow*. Traditionally, they were made from blackthorn or oak, despite the name, and they were frequently cured over months or years either by being placed up a chimney or in brine, but I didn't need a chimney, and I didn't need months or years. Not with my Purifire.

I knew people's heights varied, and I thought I could adjust the shillelaghs if necessary after they were done. I started with just one.

My skin broke out in gooseflesh as my magic literally prised the wood apart from the desk on a cellular level. I left a bulb at the end, the bit that would most often come from a root when made from blackthorn, and then, with Connection still active, I began to thread Purifire through the length of wood, willing it into a shape that would help a walker and provide a solid thump of a mallet if necessary.

The Purifire twisted around the stick forming in my hand, turning the pale wood darker and darker as it travelled up and down it in swirls that followed the paths of the grain.

Perspiration beaded on my forehead from the sustained effort, but after a few moments more, it was done.

The desk looked as if I'd removed a shillelagh-shaped puzzle piece from its long edge, and when I examined my creation, holding it by the bulb end, I almost gasped.

The yellowish maple had darkened everywhere to black, but when I turned it this way and that, the raised bits of the swirling grain pattern along its length gave off an iridescent blue-green shimmer, almost like the colours of a raven's wing.

I cast Keen Eye on it, wincing as my spirit dipped ten percent.

Purified Maple Shillelagh
A traditional Irish walking stick and cudgel, the shillelagh has been used in combat as long as it's been used to steady one's step. Versatile and strong, this particular iteration is made from non-traditional maple rather than blackthorn or oak, bringing

with it a 7% bonus to movement speed and a protective error with a 10% chance to repel would-be foes from attacking at all.

This weapon has been infused with Purifire, and as such, it will not burn. It grants the wielder 15% fire resistance and every 10 strikes, on the next strike, it will have a chance equivalent to the fire resistance to cast Purifire upon the targeted foe.

Oh, my fucking god.

I could feel sweat dripping down my left temple, but my lips curled up in an outright grin.

Sure, fire resistance in Scotland was not precisely the most useful thing, but adding Purifire to a bonk on the head absolutely made up for it!

I waited a minute or two for my spirit to recover—the crafting hadn't taken *too* much out of me, but it was tiring —and then I started again.

This time, I was more prepared for the process, and I directed my spirit with more intention. The wood seemed almost eager to perform, and as my Purifire twined about the second shillelagh, I felt how it moved, how it woke up the dormant wood cells and brought them back, if not to life, to *purpose*.

When I examined the second one, my grin returned. I'd increased the bonuses by a couple percentage points each. This time I didn't wait for my spirit to recover, simply dove into the third.

I was so caught up in my work that I didn't hear anyone come in until I finished the ninth shillelagh, and I dropped it with a clatter when someone's hand landed on my shoulder.

Alison jumped back, eyes wide. "Sorry! I'm sorry! It's just"—her gaze darted back and forth between the line of different-sized shillelaghs on the floor and the desk, which now looked a wee bit like someone had taken an ice cream scoop down the length of it—"everyone is ready to go. Everyone who's coming, anyway."

"Got it," I said, wiping the back of my gauntleted hand across my forehead. I could feel my curly hair sticking to my skin with sweat. "You should take one of these. They're for the adults, just in case."

"You made . . . walking sticks?"

"They're more than that," I told her. "They're shille-laghs, and they're protective, just in general and especially if using them in combat. Every tenth hit there's a chance it'll cast a fire spell on whoever's on the business end. Should be good in case of an emergency."

I looked somewhat forlornly at the desk, then sighed, gathering up the shillelaghs, including the one I'd dropped at Alison's jump-scare moment.

"I was going to make more, but hopefully this will be enough for the adults who are coming with us," I said dubiously.

"It will," Alison said, still staring at the pile of blackened, magical sticks I held to my chest. She seemed to shake herself. "Only five adults are coming with us, and about twelve kids. Some of the parents who came to get their kids are going to make their way north with Ronald tomorrow, but . . ."

She trailed off.

"But they either don't see the need or think it's too much of a risk," I said.

Her chin dipped in assent.

"Then we'll take five of these and leave the other four to whoever's coming tomorrow."

I selected one that I thought would be an appropriate

length for Alison and handed it to her. She took it with a mix of awe and trepidation. My instinct had been right; it was the perfect height for her.

"Thank you," Alison said softly, gazing up at me through her eyelashes.

I shifted my weight, remembering what Eilidh had said. "It's fine," I said, trying to keep my tone neutral. "I just really hope whoever stays doesn't end up regretting it."

After a week in this new world, though, I couldn't help but believe they would rue the day they chose to stay.

CHAPTER
FORTY-FOUR

In the end, there were five adults—not including myself, Eilidh, and Rhona—and thirteen kids going with us.

The one "extra" child was already in tears asking where Mummy was, and none of us had an answer for him. He was also one of the youngest, just barely in primary school at all, which made it worse.

Alison immediately went with him and two others who were more sanguine—they were going with us early, ahead of their parents who would join Ronald in the morning, and they were doing an admirable job of stiff-upper-lipping it. One of them, a ten-year-old boy, held the younger boy's hand and was talking to him comfortingly.

Of the others going with us, there was Mairead—who took the smallest shillelagh I'd crafted with grim determination—a pair of parents I didn't recognise called Saoirse and Ben, and a man and woman called Andy and, somewhat unfortunately, Susanna. Not a common name, but definitely one I knew would make me jump with that old, unpleasant pang each time someone used it. Ouch. No, please.

I did my best to squash it.

Rhona was a good distraction. She looked windblown but exhilarated when she came up to me, giving me an affectionate—I thought—punch to the deltoid in greeting.

"You'll be happy to know that everyone who went chapping doors gained at least a level," she said. "Anyone tell you that yet?"

"Nope," I said, relief spreading through me. None of the adults with us had been part of that group, and it lightened my worry significantly knowing that tomorrow's group would have at least a few people who were not level one. "That's brilliant. What'd you run into?"

"Another stoat," Rhona said. "And a ptarmigan the size of a bloody *mastiff*."

She shuddered, but then a grin split her face. "That thing alone put the fear into them—I think what's-his-face thought we were exaggerating, but he went full evangelical after the birdbrain. Like, literally, he went berserk on the thing's head with a rock. Bird brains everywhere."

I winced. "Thanks for *that* visual."

"I see you made a bunch more sticks," Rhona said approvingly. "Good for you! That'll be useful for the tomorrow people. Too bad we don't have an actual mastiff handy you could throw the sticks for in the meantime."

"Careful what you wish for," I muttered.

The sun had officially hit the tops of the surrounding hills, and daylight was wasting.

"Is everyone ready?" I called out. "We need to get moving!"

I got a lacklustre chorus from the adults, but the kids all chirped out yesses, except for the wee boy whose mum was unaccounted for.

"Lead on, MacBeth," Rhona said to me.

"It's 'lay on, MacDuff,'" I said with a chuckle. "But you got the play right at least."

Rhona looked me right in the eye long enough to be sure I saw it when she dramatically rolled them, but she was grinning as she headed to the back of our small column of vibrating children and anxious adults.

Eilidh caught my eye from the centre of the group, giving me a nod.

"That's us, then," I said to Ronald, who stood at the front of the school with a couple of the others who would be coming along tomorrow—that included a man still spattered in blood and, I suspected, ptarmigan brains. I moved closer to him and spoke quietly. "Remember, run if you need to. There's no shame in hiding from something bigger and badder than you. And if you can practise with those shillelaghs even a little bit, who knows if the system will reward you. At least get a feel for them."

When he nodded, it was bleak. "We'll see you in Oban tomorrow."

I swallowed. "You will."

I wish I'd had the confidence to believe it.

The light left us almost completely within an hour of starting off. The clouds hung low in the sky, a thick, grey barrier between us and any glimpse at the sunset, and mist settled over us.

Despite the danger in creating a beacon for anything out there to home in on, I kept a consistent thread of Puri-fire running through my own staff to light the way. I kept it dim, more of a glow than a beam, just enough for us to see by but not so much that it would wreck our night vision completely.

I kept Connection almost constantly active, sending threads and tendrils of spirit out into the surrounding trees and fields. They were alive with the diurnal and nocturnal animals and their gloaming business, but they all scurried away from us rather than towards us, even the time or two my tendrils lit upon a massive hare the size of a boar and another time a bat with the wingspan of a gannet that flapped above our heads. The bat sent a jolt through the group—its wings beating the air sounded like the snap of sailcloth catching the wind with every flap—but the creature paid us no notice as it winged its way out over the sea loch to our left, Loch Feochan.

We made it through the first hour of walking without incident.

Rather than filling me with relief, though, it set me on edge. It felt like I was walking along the top of a wall that had been moderately wide at the start and gradually narrowed until I could barely put one foot in front of the other.

Eilidh moved back and forth between me and Rhona with the kind of focused purpose that made me truly glad she was on our side. Every so often, she'd murmur to me about something Rhona saw—a badger that watched us for five minutes and apparently decided we weren't worth the risk, a pack of field mice the size of small cats who scurried away at our approach, nothing alarming.

The second hour passed much the same, except then came the rain.

I put up the hood of my cloak at first, but I quickly realised it obscured my peripheral vision too much to trust. I'd have to deal with a wet head.

Behind me about twenty yards, I could hear the plaintive sounds of children fussing. I couldn't blame them. Some of them had seen the sheep; they knew monsters were suddenly real. Most kids didn't love the dark, and here we were trudging through the hills in the pitch black and mist, the only light a blue-green glow ahead of them. Even that was partially obscured by the drizzle, diffusing the illumination and casting the entire procession in muted dread.

We finally stopped for a snack in the carpark at the head of Loch Feochan.

Mairead came up to me once the children were situated with something to eat, and I was half eating from a packet of oatcakes and half concentrating on feeding Sailean her bottle.

"We're not making very good time," Mairead said. "And they're getting tired."

"I've got a spell that should help," I told her. "It should restore some of their stamina and refresh them. We're doing better than you think—we're not quite halfway to Oban yet, but we will be soon."

"I've also got a spell that should help," Eilidh said from beside me.

I jumped. I'd not even seen her approach. Maybe she'd also picked up a stealth spell when I wasn't looking.

"What's it do?" I asked.

"It's called Tapachd," she said, and at Mairead's blank stare, hurriedly translated. "It means courage or hardiness. The willingness to persevere. It's a buff that lasts for a couple hours, and it draws from the party's sense of community. Since we all have a common goal, it should help."

Mairead nodded. "I never thought I'd see a day where I

had to approve of casting spells on children, but their safety comes first, and keeping them focused for a couple more hours will help with that."

"Rhona still has those sweet violets, right?" I asked suddenly. "I mean, enough for the quest and then some?"

Eilidh's eyes went distant. "Aye, she's got eight left. What are you thinking?"

"See if she'll give one to each of the adults."

"What do those do?" Mairead asked dubiously, wiping a drip of water from the tip of her nose.

"They increase spirit regeneration," I said, "and they also boost certain skills. If anyone else has unlocked the Nature tree and has Connection, that's one it boosts. It's what I've been using to sense potential threats."

Mairead nodded again, and out of the corner of my eye, I saw someone beckon her over. With a hesitant look at me, she left.

I spent a couple minutes going around to the groups of children and seeing how they were doing. The adults were taking them off in twos to pee—mostly behind a bush— and a few were resistant to go anywhere outwith the small circle of light from my staff.

Most of them were excited to peer into the carrier at Sailean, who was sleepy after her feeding, her little kitten muzzle milk wet and her belly round. A few, though, didn't even look up at me. I guessed they were among the kids who were sent ahead of their parents, from the lost looks in their eyes and the way they wouldn't raise their gazes above the level of the cat carrier.

The little boy whose mum had never showed up to get him seemed to be in the worst shape. He clung to Alison's leg, staring vacantly at the loch. I could sense Alison wanted to speak with me, but I extricated myself and instead kept moving, checking on the kids, occasionally making a wee flare of magic if I thought it might spark their interest, and by the time I'd made a circuit, Rhona and Eilidh had distributed the sweet violets to all the adults, and it was time to get back on the road.

"Everyone come close for a minute," I said to them, beckoning them towards me. "I'm going to cast a spell that all of you should be able to feel. You know how your parents talk about coffee or tea in the mornings? Like it helps them wake up?"

There was a smattering of nods, most of them listless, except for one girl, who proudly affirmed, "My mum says she wants to inject it into her *veins!*"

This broke a little of the tension as the lass's mum chuckled and ruffled the kid's hair. "Aye, it's true. I admit it."

I grinned at them, feeling some of my own tension abating ever so slightly. "Well, this spell doesn't need an injection, but it should help you all perk up. Eilidh's got one too, and we're going to help you so you don't feel so tired and we can get to Oban. Okay?"

This time, the nods were a little readier, though the parents looked a bit uneasy.

With a glance at Eilidh, I moved to the centre of the circle and began to draw on my spirit and cast Fuaran, focusing it with my staff like the weapon was the centre pole of a tent and the spell could simply fan out around it, making a dome of magic. I wanted it to be visible, but I wasn't prepared for the way it spun off the globe at the tip of my staff like fractals from a fountain of fresh, clear water in rippling streams. With the light of the Purifire suffusing the air, they glittered and shimmered, and some of the weans looked up in wonder, the web of the spell reflecting back at me in their eyes.

I wasn't prepared for what happened next.

Eilidh stood in the outer rim of the circle, and when I felt the dip of spirit that told me she was casting her own spell, threads rippled out from her like a summer's breeze lighting the cold, late-February night with gold like molten sunlight. When they touched the threads of my magic, it was like what happened if you laid a square of kitchen roll next to a puddle of water. My magic seemed to soak up Eilidh's, her threads of gold rushing from where she stood and racing across the dome until everyone was covered not only in the web of Fuaran, but also Eilidh's Tapachd.

Gasps rippled through the group, and it felt as if no one dared breathe for a long moment.

Slowly, the spells faded, leaving me with a glowing gold afterimage imprinted on my eyes.

Or maybe that was just my notifications flashing.

There was a moment of stunned silence.

I felt like every single eye was on me, even though a good half of the people present were staring at Eilidh—and rightly so. Her auburn hair was haloed with an ethereal golden glow that sank back into her a moment later. For a long moment, she and I simply stared at each other, unblinking.

"We should go," said a voice.

Alison.

The moment snapped like someone had broken a stick over their knee, and I cleared my throat.

"Aye, we should," I said, just as Rhona's breathless voice spoke up with, "Incoming!"

FORTY-FIVE

My brain had just enough time to process what she'd said before I moved.

"Get the kids back! Not too close to the water, just away from us," I said. "Any adults who can fight need to be ready."

I cast Connection, feeling out behind us in the direction we'd come from.

They hit something I had never wanted to see again. My spirit was recovering quickly, so I cast Keen Eye.

Steven Brown
 Level 11 Amhasg
 Affinities: Broadsword, Grappling

"Fuck," I said. "Rhona, are there more?"

"Just him for now," she said from right beside me, though when I looked towards her voice, I could barely see a shimmer in the air. Her stealth was getting *good*.

"Eilidh, it's the broadsword bloke, the one whose class I think is supposed to mean reaver." I glanced at her where she stood with her claymore already drawn and ready.

"Has he seen us?" she asked in a low voice.

"I don't think so," Rhona replied.

I turned to the group of adults and children. "Get back on the road and go, as fast as you can towards Oban. We'll catch up—I don't want this man to see them if we can avoid it. We'll distract him."

Mairead seemed to hesitate, and Alison's mouth opened and closed a few times as if she were about to protest, but something about the way all three of us had readied ourselves to fight seemed to stop her from voicing it.

It was Saoirse who moved first, Andy right behind her as they bustled the kids towards the road. They'd have no light without me unless one of the adults could figure out how to cast one, but that was for the better.

"He's coming," Rhona said just as I cast Connection again and felt him, that horrid puppeted hart beneath him like a maggot-infested wound.

"I feel him," I said. "He's level eleven now, but there's three of us and one of him. When I say now, look away from my staff and cover your eyes."

"What are you—" Rhona started, then I could almost feel the dawning understanding even though I couldn't see her face. "You're going to blind him."

"Hopefully," I muttered.

I let the light in my staff die as I felt this Steven Brown come closer. Connection told me that our charges were moving away at the fastest clip little legs could manage—I only hoped this would be enough.

He was on the road, and we still stood in the carpark, and I slowly built a weave of spirit thread by thread, adding in will and pathos. The will for this cleansing fire to act like a beam of pure, painful light in his eyes. The will built from my rage that this man would threaten anyone in Argyll, but especially this group of vulnerable children.

Even if he'd not seen them, I didn't care. He was on his way north, which meant he wasn't scuttling back to Lord Bawbag.

Which meant he was still on some sort of mission.

I heard the sound of hooves on the road, moving at a steady lope. A hundred yards. Eighty. Sixty. Fifty. Forty. Thirty.

"Now!" I said to Eilidh and Rhona.

When he hit twenty yards away, I brandished my staff, and the carpark lit up like midday.

Even trying to protect my own eyes, I was momentarily blinded, and I heard the hart scream as the beam hit it.

It wasn't just light I'd created, but Purifire, and while I'd been aiming at Brown, the beam also caught the stag he rode, which filled me with guilt I couldn't afford to entertain.

It wasn't the deer's fault; he'd been taken over by magic that shouldn't exist, stripped of his agency.

As the brightness faded, the hart snorted and bellowed again, and there was an angry accompanying yell as Brown crashed to the tarmac.

Eilidh held her claymore in one hand, seeming to ignore the weight of it as she brought it together with her free hand in front of her chest with a pulse of magic like a struck bass drum. It reverberated out from her. I'd attacked with light; she'd attacked with sound, and even as Steven brown scrambled about on the ground, I could hear him roar to respond to her challenge.

She didn't wait. Eilidh charged him, closing the distance with long strides that ate up the intervening yards.

But he was *fast*.

Despite being caught by surprise and thrown from his mount, Brown leapt to his feet, drawing his own broadsword in time to meet Eilidh's devastating downward strike that would have cleaved him from shoulder to hip, had it connected.

The clash of steel striking steel rang through the air like a bell.

I pulled on my spirit, casting Cumhachd as I thought of the dark waters to my right, salty sea mingling with the river delta that capped the loch, brackish and cold.

A missile of bitter saltwater exploded out from my staff, and for the first time I got to see in action what the system had meant by no friendly fire. I'd had a clear shot when I released the spell, my every fragment of will intent on Steven Brown, but he and Eilidh circled as Cumhachd sped towards them, until it was her unguarded back facing me.

The spell curved midair.

It flitted around Eilidh and struck like a devastating right hook that caught Brown in the jaw with an audible crack of bone.

And the man barely *flinched*.

Rhona was nowhere to be seen, and I both hoped for and dreaded her banshee scream. It had been shown to hurt even Lord Bawbag himself, but in the middle of the night, who knew what it would draw to us?

Even as I thought it, there was a grunt, and this time Brown more than flinched as a blood-wet blade flashed away from his side.

I drew more spirit into me, casting Spèird to try to

throw the man off balance while he was injured, but he parried Eilidh's next strike and then bellowed with rage.

A wave of pure energy hit me, sinking into me with the dark cold of a trench far beneath the surface of the sea where teeth lurked, ready to devour.

It staggered Eilidh even harder.

Close as she was to the brunt of the attack, she reeled back, the force of Brown's magic and the multiple levels he had over Eilidh combining into a juggernaut of force. Spèird seemed to bounce right off the man, who cast about, looking for his mount.

The hart still staggered nearby, lines of Purifire coursing over his hide, his antlers, the lines of his nose, which flared in the light. I'd no idea what was happening there; all I knew is Brown could not be allowed to remount the stag and get away. We'd likely never get another shot at him where we had an actual chance.

As fast as my spirit could regenerate and more, I spooled threads of it into Tairm. The way the brambles had impaled sheep after sheep still haunted me, as did the eruption of roots the first time I'd cast it as a distraction.

Eilidh was now on the defensive.

Though he'd yet to strike her, his overpowering strength and levels showed through his every move. Each sweep of his blade caught upon her parries a little more frantically; each step she took backwards came with a little less surety and balance.

Where was Rhona?

I couldn't afford to wait.

With a swirl of spirit, I cast Tairm.

At first, nothing happened.

Except for the sudden dearth of spirit that left me gasping, that is.

And then a shriek rent the air.

Unlike the other times I'd seen Rhona use her banshee scream, this didn't seem to cover the whole area we inhabited. Instead, it pierced like an awl, and a flicker of movement showed exactly where she was: right at his shoulder, her mouth to Brown's ear.

It bought Eilidh a pair of precious seconds as she danced backwards away from Brown's fumbled swing, her own blade batting his aside.

Around us, wind rose.

It started as a swirling breeze that lifted my shaggy curls and spun one into my eyes. I shook my head to dislodge it, only for it to land right back.

Eilidh's hair whipped up around her, and the wind began to whistle through the nearby trees, bringing with it something else.

The sound of rushing water.

I turned to my right, towards Loch Feochan, and I saw what Tairm had wrought.

In the dark of the night, the wind whirled in a cyclone, and great gouts of water lifted from the surface of the sea loch, spinning and spinning until they formed a water spout fifty yards high.

It made landfall almost before I could register it, tearing towards the melee fighters where they stood.

I had a feeling this spell did *not* come with a friendly fire waiver.

"Eilidh!" I bellowed. "Down!"

For the rest of my life, I thought I would remember how, without so much as a dubious glance at me, she dived to the floor and rolled away from Steven Brown, whose blade then encountered empty air—and the funnel of my chaotic cyclone.

Rhona materialised on the other side of Eilidh, yanking her away from the miniature hurricane even as it wrenched Brown's sword from his hand and sent it arcing wildly across the carpark.

Eilidh stumbled to her feet, spinning back to face Brown. Caught in a torrent of wind and water, his enraged face showed through in flashes, visible only in the flickering light of magic.

I felt as Tairm began to wane. My spirit was down to twenty-five percent, but I had enough for Cumhachd. I delved deep into myself and the surrounding ambient spirit, thinking of the strength of the bedrock, the boulders, the force of the water.

As the cyclone died, I let it loose.

Rhona and Eilidh moved back into action, both making a beeline towards Brown, but his resistances must have been *phenomenal*; even as he stumbled, released from Tairm, and even as Cumhachd slammed into him like a stone fist, he didn't fall.

Instead, he gathered his muscular legs beneath him and leapt directly at his sword where the wind had flung it.

Even with his strength and speed, Rhona was faster.

She intercepted him only a few steps away from his blade. He reacted instantly, swinging at her with an uppercut that would have been an instant KO—except she was already gone, dancing back, one foot scooping under the hilt of his broadsword with breathtaking dexterity and agility both.

With a delicate kick, she sent it soaring end over end like the world's smallest and weirdest caber toss, and then, as Eilidh closed the distance, something green materialised in Rhona's hand.

A long, green stalk with spade-shaped serrated leaves.

With a Zorro-like flourish, Rhona slapped the stinging nettles back and forth across Brown's face, and he instinctively snatched them from her hand, flinging them to the floor.

He moved faster than I thought possible.

Brown took Rhona with a brutal backhand to the face. She went sprawling, and he lunged for his sword.

Even with my bonuses of spirit and my regeneration, I barely had enough left to do anything. I felt powerless as the man smirked, his hand closing around the hilt of his sword.

All of this had happened so quickly that by the time Eilidh reached them, he was ready for her.

Rhona lay still on the gravel of the carpark, her brown hair covering her face.

Eilidh circled Brown warily. I had to hope he didn't have many more tricks up his sleeve, but that was nearly impossible. He was level eleven, which meant at least eighteen skill points. Some had to be passives, but others, like that bellow of his that had nearly stunned us all, had to be active ones.

Even as I thought it, he triggered one.

Like the bellow, it pulsed out of him like an underwater boom, but unlike that, this one hit me with physical force.

I flew backwards, only my Agility allowing me to move Sailean's carrier so that I didn't crush her when I landed flat on my back, the air gusting out of me with a sharp gasp.

She let out a terrified mew, and I couldn't breathe enough to reassure her. I should have sent her with the others, but there'd barely been time to think.

I scrambled to my feet only to find Eilidh with blood

running from a cut on her cheek, Brown's blade at her throat.

"If you so much as twitch, I'll hole punch her artery and drink her blood in front of you," Brown said conversationally.

If I'd had any doubt whatsoever that this man deserved to die, that dispelled it.

"I'm not moving," I said after a beat.

"Drop your weapon," he said.

I obeyed.

Eilidh's eyes burned with pure hatred as she stared up at him, her throat moving as she swallowed against the indent of the blade in her pale skin.

"You're the one who's been causing so much trouble," Brown said. "And if you're here, I suspect it was you who pulled the little trick down the road earlier, was it?"

"Maybe," I said. "Depends on the trick you're referencing."

My heart gave a wild beat; I could no longer see Rhona.

"Don't play dumb, wanker." Brown raised his gaze from Eilidh to me, contemptuously deciding he didn't need to even pay attention to her since she was cowed.

"Well, let's see," I said. "I came across a trio of sentient turds earlier, but I certainly didn't play any tricks. Maybe if the road rises up to meet you and slap you down, you should reconsider some of your life choices."

"Careful," he said, pressing his blade a little tighter against Eilidh's throat.

I shut up.

"You're going to tell me what you did to my stag," he said. "And then you're going to undo it."

The air rippled behind him.

I caught Eilidh's eye, and with every fibre of my being, I willed her to understand me. *Be ready to move, be ready to move, be ready to move.*

One twitch and she'd be dead. One move of his arm and her blood would water the carpark. One mistake, and outnumbered or not, Steven Brown would kill her—maybe even all three of us.

"I don't know what I did to your stag," I said honestly. "But the spell is a cleansing fire. Once it's gone, it does what it wants when it senses something unclean."

My staff lay at my feet, but I'd gone days without it when we started.

I only hoped Brown didn't realise I didn't need it to cast.

The air rippled behind him again, and I threaded together my meagre spirit, remembering what I'd done once with the simulacrum and how the fire had leapt to Eilidh's claymore.

"Not good enough," Brown said. "You're going to fix it, and then you're going to die."

Now, I thought, using every ounce of my self-control to keep my body still as I loosed Purifire. Two flaming blue blades flared into existence on either side of Brown's body, and just as quickly, they plunged into his kidneys even as Rhona—their stealthy wielder—threw her entire weight backwards to yank him off balance.

He didn't have time to thrust with his own sword, and Eilidh gasped and scuttled backward, scrabbling at the gravel as she shoved herself to her feet. A trickle of blood ran down her throat, but I'd take a trickle over a fountain any day of the week.

But I wasn't ready for his attack.

Despite the smell of burning flesh, despite the dual

daggers embedded in his torso, Brown wrenched himself sideways, grabbing hold of Rhona before she could vanish into stealth again.

Before either Eilidh or I could react, he lunged at her, sinking his teeth into Rhona's neck.

CHAPTER
FORTY-SIX

N*o.*
It was a cliché, a tired one, but it was a cliché for a reason. My entire body seemed to *scream* out my rejection of what was happening.

Eilidh was closer, and she was moving even as blood spurted from Rhona's neck.

I hadn't thought the word amhasg would mean vampire, for fuck's sake.

Even as my brain struggled to process, my feet churned into a run. Some distant presence of mind had me slip out of Sailean's kitten carrier, setting it lightly off to the side. I'd never forgive myself if something happened to her.

I'd never forgive myself if Rhona died with this monster's teeth in her throat.

As I ran, each step seemed to take an hour. Each thud of my heartbeat seemed to count down to the young woman's death.

And in my desperation, something in me opened.

I'd had Freumhan for what felt like ages now, the word for roots, for root systems, the channels of spirit within me that allowed magic to flow through me, and as my pulse pounded in my veins, I heard another rhythm.

I *felt* another rhythm.

I *breathed* another rhythm.

It felt like light kissing spring's first leaves, and I seized it like they would to nourish long-dormant channels that had slept through the ice of winter.

This time, when time stretched and slowed, it wasn't out of terror.

Every hair on Steven Brown's head seemed to come into focus. Every spatter of blood and spittle flying from his ravening mouth shone like rubies.

My roots, my Freumhan, connected every part of my body with spirit—and spirit connected me to *everything*.

The world narrowed to a single point of focus.

I could see Eilidh, her sword poised to swing, like a vengeful comet.

More, I could feel her awareness of me, her reaction times as I wrapped ropes of pure spirit around Brown's chest and *pulled*.

His mouth came free of Rhona's throat with a sickening, squelching pop of broken suction, and he flew backwards—directly onto Eilidh's blade.

In a flash, I'd spun to face them both, seeing the length of steel protruding from his torso. His entire face dripped with blood.

Weaves of spirit and will formed in the palm of my hand, and when I heard Rhona's body hit the floor beside me, I slammed my palm into Steven Brown's chest.

His heart detonated.

It exploded with a crunch of ribs, and he collapsed further onto the claymore, but I was already falling to my knees beside Rhona, already harvesting Brown's manipulation resources to fill my well.

I served as a conduit, bridging the gap between killer and would-be victim, using the energy he'd stolen from her to heal the wounds he'd torn into her flesh.

For the second time in two days, I triggered Beannachd Shlàinte, and Rhona jerked where she lay, her eyes flying open with a gasp.

The next minutes passed in a blur.

All three of us slumped to the carpark's rocky surface, the only sound Sailean's pitiful mews that were more like *mew*sic to my ears. It meant she was fine.

Unlike the rest of us.

Rhona was the first to struggle to a sitting position, her hand going gingerly to the unbroken, unblemished skin of her neck. She shuddered visibly, her mouth slightly open as her breath still came too fast through her lungs.

Blood was drying on Eilidh's cheek. She lay splayed out on the gravel, claymore beside her with its own blooded blade akimbo, both her arms clasped over her forehead as she drew breath after shaky breath.

"We need to go," Rhona said hoarsely.

Her voice still bore a brittle edge of panic. Who could possibly blame her? She'd been torn open by two monsters in two days, first claws, now teeth. Dragged under the water to drown. It was a miracle she wasn't fucking catatonic.

She also happened to be right.

I pushed myself to my feet, wobbling. I felt different. It was as if water was sloshing through me, filling my inner ears like after swimming when you can hear it moving in there. Disconcerting.

The moment I stood, I saw the hart.

He wasn't where we'd left him, strangely frozen and flickering with blue-green fire.

And he didn't look like he had when we'd first seen him.

His eyes were clear, all traces of that terrifying, watery rheumy glaze gone as if they'd never been there at all.

In the minutes—ages?—of the battle, the horrid, mangy patches that littered his coat had healed, and he now stood taller. He wore a saddle, and as I watched him, he took a step towards me.

My spirit reserves were all but full after my instinctive harvest of Steven Brown, and I cast Keen Eye.

Purified Hart

This stag was taken over by Lord Edwin Thomas Sackington and puppeted for the use of his minions. Through the ingenious use of Purifire, you have cleansed this stag of Lord Sackington's influence, and moreover, you have freed him from the resulting torment.

Puppeted creatures are an abomination. To imprison them in their own minds is torture—and it is something few survive.

As a result, this animal owes you a debt. He will repay it.

Perhaps you should free him from his more mundane burden.

I blinked at that.

That was more personal information than Keen Eye had given me before, and I wasn't about to discount it.

"Can one of you get the kitten?" I said absently.

"I've got her," Rhona said. Her voice still sounded a bit rough and husky.

The hart watched me, uneasy but not bolting.

I could feel the others' eyes on me as I took one step, then another.

"Ciùinich thu fhèin," I murmured to the hart to soothe him. "It's okay."

He snorted and tossed his head, but he took a step closer to me.

In two more steps, I'd reached him, and I held out a hand for him to sniff, which he did, surprising me when he then nudged me. I continued to speak in Gaelic under my breath to him, my own language coming more naturally to me—or perhaps it was the force of habit. My mother always spoke Gaelic to the animals in her care.

I placed my hand on his shoulder, which was nearly at the height of my face.

And then I realised I'd miscalculated. I hadn't the faintest idea how to remove a saddle, let alone how to do it properly—and this was no horse.

"Eilidh," I said softly, and then I asked her for help. "An cuidich thu mi?"

Without a word, she came to my side, and the hart didn't so much as blink when she extended her own hand to him.

"Mar seo," she said. *Like this.*

I watched as she carefully unfastened the buckles on the right side of the stag's belly, and then she walked around his head to the left side, carefully grabbing the dangling belts and placing them together atop the saddle. She came back around to his right side and lifted the saddle from him.

Then she chuckled lightly to herself, shaking her head.

"What?" I asked.

"I'm acting like he's a horse out of habit, but he's not been trained to wear a saddle. He doesn't even have a bridle or reins."

I had a horrible moment of imagining Steven Brown using the stag's antlers like handlebars.

The stag himself shivered, his skin twitching as his hackles rose, and he pawed at the ground a few times.

Both Eilidh and I backed up quickly.

"Siuthad, ma-tà," she said to him to shoo him away, but the stag hesitated, dipping his head.

I had the oddest sense of being perceived, as if the hart had cast Keen Eye on *me*, but it might have been no more than a fancy.

After a moment, it passed, and he turned and trotted away across the road and toward the hill that rose up there, invisible in the dark.

Eilidh gave the hart's retreating back an inscrutable glance and then turned towards Rhona.

I followed, wondering how on earth a deer could pay a debt.

And if I could somehow free the others, too.

It took very little time for us to catch up with the ragtag group of primary-school pupils and their gaggle of adults. Once we were healed and mobile, the three of us were at least three times as fast as they were at a sedate walk, let alone the jog we set. Plus, we'd left them without any light.

Rhona was very quiet on that jog, and out of the corner of my eye, I kept seeing her swallow, her hand going unconsciously to the side of her neck where Steven Brown had dug into her with his teeth.

Gods, I hoped we would find Oban in some semblance of order. Rhona deserved a quiet week. Hell, a quiet *day*.

When we sighted the ragtag group of weans and adults, I called out in a low voice. "It's Calum—we're back."

They still all startled in the dark like frightened rabbits, and though Eilidh'd scrubbed the blood off her face in the loch, the dark stain on Rhona's cloak gave her own injury away.

"I'll get back to scouting," Rhona said quietly to me, and between one step and the next, she slipped into the shadows out of sight.

Alison was craning her neck around to see us, and the group stuttered to a stop before both Eilidh and I gestured at everyone to keep moving.

"We're fine," Eilidh said to Alison as we passed. "It's taken care of."

I hurried back to my place at the front of the wee column, feeling almost twenty sets of eyeballs boring into my back. Mairead gave me a nod. Though she didn't ask anything straight away, the deep crease in her brow belied her discomfort.

About fifteen minutes later, she cleared her throat, and I turned to look at her, slowing my pace a tiny bit and casting about with Connection to be sure there wasn't any partic-ular danger lurking in the darkness.

"What level?" she asked.

"Eleven," I told her. "Up one from earlier today."

Had that really been today? Gods, this day was lasting forever.

"On a scale of one to ten?" She phrased this question

even more delicately, both of us all too aware of the pair of nine-year-olds on either side of her.

"If ten is by the skin of our teeth?" I said. "Or not at all?"

"The former," she replied after a moment's thought.

"Then ten."

The crease between her eyebrows grew deeper, and her lips parted involuntarily. After another few steps, she gave me a terse nod. I saw the way she took a deep breath, her eyes fluttering closed while she held it for a mere moment, and they opened again when she let it out.

I went back to my vanguard duty.

My notifications really wanted my attention, but there was no way I could do that and walk at the same time. Walk, read, and make sure I wasn't sending a bunch of kids into the maw of some hitherto impossible beast?

Yeah, no.

The night dragged on. And on. And on.

Some of the kids started crying when we stopped briefly for a snack and then had to start walking again. Never had three and a half miles felt so interminable.

Twice, Rhona called Eilidh and me to take care of a low-level threat—which we tried to do where the kids couldn't see us. One was a rabbit that made me rethink my previous metaphor of our little group jumping like frightened bunnies, because the formerly adorable wee fluffer almost took Eilidh's right arm off like the goddamn killer rabbit in *Holy Grail*.

And that made the kids scream, because naturally, that was the one they did see—and their screams caught the attention of a pair of giant voles that were so fat and cylindrical, it was a bit like fighting a giant pair of furry sausages.

Those ones we had the adults come smack a few times

with a shillelagh for some easy experience, but that left Rhona with the kids, and I desperately hoped we wouldn't come back to find them more traumatised.

Eventually, after the sixth hour of our trudge up the coast, the kids stopped crying.

That was worse.

Part of my heart crunched at that. I wanted to believe they were just tired, but I couldn't. Kids cry because it gets them help. It gets them comfort. Because it stops whatever is hurting them.

When they give up on crying, it tends to mean they've learnt no comfort is coming.

Just when I thought *I* might start crying myself, I saw something familiar—a large building that housed United Auctions.

And NFU Mutual.

I heard the adults heave breaths of relief as familiar landmarks came into view.

Houses.

Candlelight flickering in windows.

Oban.

We'd made it to Oban.

CHAPTER
FORTY-SEVEN

I t wasn't long before there was a flicker of lace curtains backlit by golden light as we passed a row of terraced houses.

First one door opened, and then another.

"Oh, my goodness. They've bairns with them," a middle-aged woman said, wrapping her dressing gown more tightly around her. "Where have you all come from?"

"Kilninver," I said. "There's meant to be another group coming in the morning."

"Where're ye fae?" called a man in Scots.

"Glasgow for me," I said, which set everyone on their doorsteps to murmuring. "I've friends I'm trying to get to in the city centre."

Another woman called out from across the street. "Do yous need somewhere to stay?"

Behind me, I heard Mairead choke back a sob.

When I turned to look at her, she'd already composed herself for the most part, but her voice cracked slightly when she answered. "Aye, we've thirteen weans with us and eight adults."

"Oh, you poor dears—you've walked what, eight miles?" A man I presumed was the husband of the woman in the dressing gown squinted at us.

At that, a few of the kids burst into tears.

That was all it took.

The first people we'd encountered since Loch Awe who weren't trying to kill us or capture us. The first people we found in Oban—they showed us what Highland hospitality meant.

Within minutes, they'd organised and figured out where to house everyone. Some of them had bustled back inside to get food ready; others surrounded us with hugs and kisses on the cheek and murmurs and benedictions. Before long, despite the hour, a few of our new friends brought their own children down, which served to perk up the baker's dozen we'd brought with us.

One of the older men took me aside as everyone was heading off to their night's lodging. He told me his name was Angus—he was a rangy man a bit taller than me and had a bit of a stoop to his shoulders, but his eyes were clear like the sea in the harbour.

"Yous face any trouble on the way here?" he asked me carefully.

The question alone told me he knew what kind of trouble we might have run into. Maybe.

"Aye, we did," I answered just as carefully. "A couple voles the size of corgis and a rabbit that acted more *rabid* than rabbit."

"That all?" Angus looked at me sideways.

For some reason, this made me glance to Eilidh, who wasn't far away. She stood watching the conversation, as usual with that impassive expression on her face. She gave me an almost imperceptible nod. If she, with her class abilities, thought it was safe, I'd trust that.

I guessed we had to start somewhere when it came to convincing people of what was coming.

"No, that's not all," I said to Angus, and I quickly related what we'd discovered about Lord Bawbag.

If I'd still doubted the Oban man, the way he spat at his feet at the mention of the name Sackington would have assuaged any nerves I had.

"Level eleven, you say?" He eyed me grimly once I reached the bit about Steven Brown.

I gave him a curt nod. "I'd assume the other two I saw are at least that by now as well. You don't seem surprised."

"You're not the first to come straggling into the town," he said, glancing over at Eilidh for the first time. "Just the ones in the best shape."

I did not like the sound of that.

"Tell me," I said.

And tell me he did.

Some time later, Eilidh and I were settled in Angus's lounge with Rhona, the women on a pull-out sofa together and myself on a pile of sofa cushions on the floor.

"What are we going to do?" Rhona asked after a long silence.

"Fuck if I know," I said, scrubbing a hand through my hair.

We all looked a bit like *we'd* been plucked off the ground by my little chaotic cyclone and dumped a few miles away. The house had running cold water, and we'd all cleaned up as best we could, shoving our armour and underthings into inventory and pulling them back out again since none of us thought we could manage to sleep without being ready to fight if someone sounded the alarm.

Angus's tale had put the fear in all of us.

Oban had escaped the initial ascension with relative ease—what we'd seen was pretty much par for the course: people helping people. Being human. But as he'd said, people had been trickling into the town from the hills.

Brown and the other two stooges we'd seen weren't the only ones who had been on little adventures for Lord Bawbag. Where he'd *found* all these people, I'd no idea, but it seemed the people we'd seen at his manor house were only a bare fraction of his actual force. That he'd apparently just had a bloody militia lying around when the ascension hit felt like someone had poured liquid nitrogen into my spinal column.

Where we'd been up at Kilchurn had been hit hard not long after we'd left. Bawbag's modus operandi appeared to be to strike quickly while people were still reeling from the ascension and then either force them into service or kill them outright, which explained the leap in his goons' levels.

No one had made it to Oban from Kilchurn.

That had made Eilidh's fists clench so tight, her knuckles went whiter than even her already-pale colouring usually allowed.

Someone from Inverinan on the opposite side of Loch Awe to Lord Bawbag's manor had made it as far as Taynuilt with a septic wound even the system's healing couldn't touch, and the only person with a healing spell nearby had gone out hunting. The injured man had died with the grim news that everyone in his village was either dead or had been pressed into working for Sackington.

The speed with which the man had moved beggared belief.

Something told me we weren't going to have to do much convincing here in Oban.

I could tell the others were mired in thought like I was.

There were people here who were climbing in levels—according to Angus, who was himself level five, there were at least a couple of level tens in the town centre and someone was level nine up in Connel, with most people hovering around level three. Most of those who were higher had fought something bigger and scarier than a vole, and when we'd mentioned the giant seagull, the tightening of Angus's lips said they weren't strangers to the bastards here in Oban, either.

Rhona looked like she was either about to vomit or fall asleep—or possibly both at once.

"Give me a plan," she said, swallowing hard. "I need a plan or my brain is going to run on a fucking hamster wheel all night."

"First thing tomorrow, we start finding our people," I said. "We'll make sure we keep a line of communication with Angus and the folks here so we hear when the next group from Kilninver arrives tomorrow, but we've got to get moving on that quest."

Rhona shut her eyes tight for a moment and exhaled sharply through her nose.

Eilidh reached out an arm and put it around the younger woman's shoulders. "Hey. We made it this far, and now we're not alone."

Opening her eyes again, Rhona gave Eilidh a tight smile, which faltered after a moment. "You're not going to leave me, are you?"

"Absolutely not," I said. "I think after the few days we've had, you qualify as family at this point."

"Calum's right," Eilidh agreed. She didn't even add a snarky *for once* at the end of it. "We're not just going to abandon you."

"Or each other, right?" Rhona said. "I know you don't like each other much—or so you *act*—but you're a good team."

"I solemnly swear to stick around until you two give me the boot," I said, shunting the "*or so you* act" off into the recesses of my brain to deal with later. "And I'm sure once you meet Iain and Meeksy and Catrìona, they'll want to adopt you too."

None of us voiced the underlying thread—that our people, the ones we'd trekked across half of Argyll for, might not even be alive. For all the system had told us to find them, none of us knew whether that meant they still lived or if we'd find them dead.

FORTY-EIGHT

A s much as I wanted to just dive straight into sleep, like Rhona, my mind was racing, and if nothing else, the notifications were like a sodding strobe light inside my head.

My arse kept sliding down between two of the sofa cushions on the laminate flooring, anyway. After several nights of sleeping in the great outdoors, I was thankful for a pillow and a blanket, but jeezo. I felt like I was trying to get comfortable on a slip-n-slide.

I figured while I was awake, I might as well start with the big ones.

Quest complete!

The Hills Have Eyes: Part II

You have reached Oban with the refugees from Kilninver, and with the help of some locals, you have discovered that Lord Sackington has been terrorising Argyll to a degree that surprised even you.

Your small group has been surprisingly successful—

. . .

I had to stop and snort at that. Thanks, awfully, system dearest.

—and as such, you are well suited to the tasks that shall follow.
  Objectives:
  -Create a weapon (Calum Green only.) (Complete)
  -Craft the following items:
  -Basic armour x3 (chest plate, greaves, boots, bracers, pauldrons, helmet) (Complete)
  -Basic upgraded daggers x3 (Complete)
  -Basic upgraded claymore (Complete)
  -Basic sheaths x3 (Complete)
  -Forage food
  -Nettles x10 (23/10 Complete)
  -Alexanders x10 (27/10) (Complete)
  -Dandelions x20 (34/10) (Complete)
  -Sweet Violets x10 (13/10) (Complete)
  -Velvet Shank Mushroom x10 (11/10)(Complete)
  -Wild Garlic Leaves x10 (13/10) (Complete)
  -Defeat the horde of ascension-mutated sheep (Complete)
  -Escort those who choose to leave Kilninver to Oban (Optional) (Complete)
  -Ask Kilninver's adults about Lord Sackington's pre-ascension activities in Argyll (Complete)
  -Reach Oban safely (Complete)
  Rewards:
  -Experience (commensurate with current level progression)
  -Unlock The Hills Have Eyes: Part III
  -1 item: Freumhan: Understanding Spirit and the Mind-Body Connection

Remember the ascension directive.

Quest updated: Defend Oban

In your travels, you have pieced together a danger that threatens not only the immediate vicinity of Loch Awe but, more widely, the town of Oban.

You have succeeded, and not only have you reached Oban with vulnerable people in tow but also you have learnt that some here already know of the threat of Lord Sackington's seemingly imminent violent invasion.

You have already observed that Lord Sackington employs ruthless measures upon those he deems a nuisance or a threat—but even his brute strength can be neutralised by those working in the spirit of the ascension directive.

Objectives:

-Reach Oban (Complete)

-Seek out the following inhabitants who are most likely to believe your story:

-Catrìona and Iain Whyte and Farid "Meeksy" Meeks

-Ross and Jo MacIntosh

-Ruaraidh and Ciorstaidh Smith

-Jack Miller

-Tina Dunlop

-Convince at least twenty fighters of level five or above of the threat (2/20)

-Formulate a plan to defend Oban

Rewards:

-Experience (commensurate with current level progression)

-1 item (ascension dependent)

-1 skill point

-5 attribute points

-???

. . .

It seemed that Angus and his wife Eliza were both level five and counted towards the quest total. That was a relief.

I wanted to laugh at the title of the book I'd received as a reward for completing the second stage of the Hills Have Eyes quest. It was so . . . self-helpy.

But at the same time, I was itching to get my little synapses into it. We'd been on the move since the battle. I'd not had a chance to think through what I'd done, how I'd somehow broken through my own spirit limits and pulled arcane energy from all around me to a degree beyond Cumhachd. Cumhachd hinted at the possibility by its mere existence, but what I'd done? That was something else. I hoped that somewhere in the mire of my notifications, there'd be some sort of answer about that.

I was a little disappointed that my personal quest showed no real movement except for my days of practise having increased to two out of three. The quest still wanted me to name my staff, which sounded like a euphemism for something else entirely, and the twelve-year-old in me was tempted to call it something like Bod nan Gleann—Dick of the Glens—or something equally loaded with double or triple entendres.

I resisted the urge. Since this was the first living weapon globally, I reckoned I should probably treat it with a little gravitas. The name *Brac-Meanmna* still echoed in my mind.

Couple more fights like tonight, though, and all bets were off.

I gave myself till tomorrow to settle on a name for certain, since I'd need to practise with my staff one more day anyway.

Then came the deluge.

. . .

Through physical exertion, you have gained a permanent +3 to Agility and +5 to Stamina. Please note that such increases have diminishing returns as your base statistics grow.

Through arcane exertion, you have gained a permanent +7 to Spirit, +1 to Pathos, and +3 to Will. Please note that such increases have diminishing returns as your base statistics grow.

You have increased your affinity: Nature (Level 5)

You have increased your affinity: Nature (Level 6)

You have increased your affinity: Healing (Level 4)

You have increased your specialised affinity: Wild (Level 2)

You have increased your specialised affinity: Wild (Level 3)

You have unlocked an affinity: Synthesis. Continue to explore the melding of arcane techniques to increase your affinity and your abilities. This affinity does not unlock a skill tree, but it allows for new branches on your existing trees.

. . .

That got my attention. Apparently my experimenting had paid off—I hoped.

Through diligent use, you have increased the level of your skills: Connection (Level 5), Purifire (Level 6), Keen Eye (Level 3), Spèird (Level 2), Cumhachd (Level 3), Beannachd Shlàinte (Level 3), Slànaich (Level 2).

Holy hell.

I guessed I'd spent the last twelve hours casting Connection almost continuously, but I was still surprised to see the gains.

Connection (Level 3)—You gain a deeper affinity to the earth and its needs, and it whispers to you.

Increased use of this skill enables you to take in an entire scene at a glance and appropriately assess its secrets. Additionally, the skill will allow you to ascertain the needs of the natural world, giving you the power to aid creatures and plants that may one day return the favour—this has been proven through your rescue of the puppeted hart.

Your use has granted you a bonus to clarity. Your ability to see and identify patterns has increased, and you are now 12% more likely to spot items of import, foes in stealth, and escape routes.

Purifire (Level 3)—This skill is most used in combat, instilling basic fire with the power of the arcane, making it burn hotter and brighter than typical flame—and all within the mage's control. This fire is not friendly fire in more than one way. Magic is will and intent, and it will strike only your foes. While a staff is needed for advanced use, this skill can be wielded without need for a weapon.

You have discovered the utility of this offensive skill in using it not only against your opponents but also to control your environment. As such, you have gained the upgrade Ring of Fire, which you can use to encircle your foes.

Increased use of Purifire allows for more complex use. Your use of it has been diverse, from illumination to cleansing to combat, and you are only scratching the surface of its potential. At its heart, this skill moulds itself to its wielder, and only the mage can decide its limits.

Keen Eye (Level 3)—This ability allows you to examine an item, foe, or location, and in conjunction with Connection, it can reveal secrets or vital clues that will push you towards helpful information. Keen Eye comes with a one-time bonus to Mind of +1.

Continued usage will improve the complexity and usefulness of the information Keen Eye provides. As your knowledge of its uses has grown, you have discovered the boons to this subtle skill. As with many worthwhile things, you get out of it what you put into it.

Spèird (Level 2)—Often the first spell a mage learns, Spèird is a blast of force that can be used to fling projectiles and foes alike to buy the wielder precious time or space to manoeuvre.

Increased use of this skill allows for more targeted applications and, with the power of a true proficient, can be as lethal as a martial arts' master's fists. Your use has tapped into *the potential of Spèird, including its synthesis with other spells and abilities. Continued experimentation could provide further illumination.*

Cumhachd—This spell is one of the most versatile in the hedge witch's arsenal. By tapping into the ambient spirit that surrounds you to augment your own, you are able to form missiles based upon your environment. Not only does this spell shift dramatically from mage to mage, but it also enhances your acquisition of points in Spirit. This ability is bolstered by and best used within your existing affinities, but it also rewards creativity.

Continued use may unlock additional benefits and upgrades. As you are beginning to understand, Cumhachd—Power—is aptly named. Most people lack the holistic under-standing necessary to access this particular spell at higher levels, but you have taken the first steps on the path to true synthesis. As with all things in an ascended world, the limits are your own imagination.

Beannachd Shlàinte (Level 3)—This skill can be used once per twelve-hour period to heal a severe injury of tissue trauma and infection. You gain an increased affinity for Healing, allowing you to intuit what is necessary to save lives of humans and animals alike.

Increased use of this skill allows for more complex healing, including but not limited to: internal haemorrhaging, progres-sive disease, antivenin formulation, purging toxins, and limb regrowth. Additionally, greater knowledge of the body's anatomy and physiology makes you more effective in combat.

Through your growing Synthesis affinity, you have

combined this spell with others to great effect, and your increasing understanding has cut the cooldown time by 50%.

Slànaich (Level 2)—A basic healing spell, Slànaich provides a general increase to inherent healing in both speed and duration. While it will not stave off death in the event of a mortal wound, it will both refresh tired muscles and soothe smaller injuries, which may make the difference between life and death even if it feels less dramatic.

Your increased usage has increased the efficacy of this spell by 10%.

My brain reeled with all the new updates. And that wasn't even all of it.

You have reached Level 8! You have three attribute points and two skill points to distribute.

You have reached Level 9! You have six attribute points and four skill points to distribute. You may now access: class specialisation or reallocation!

Two levels again? And I'd hit level nine? Fucking hell.

I guessed with both finishing that quest and the fight against someone who had multiple levels on us did something—or maybe I'd just been close to level eight to start with. I'd take it.

With that many attribute points plus the natural gains

I'd gotten from exertion both arcane and physical, this felt like a level up indeed.

A thrill went through me at the thought of class specialisation. I decided to do my attribute points first, since I already knew I couldn't place those in any of the Manipulation categories.

After a few minutes of thinking, I knew what I needed to do.

I put three points in Mind, continuing to prioritise that stat. I was a magic build; that much was obvious. While it rankled that my Strength would remain low, if we ever got to stop moving for more than a day or so, I could always work on my push-ups or something.

The thought of Eilidh or Rhona walking up on me doing squats was one that lent itself to a certain amount of hilarity—at my expense—but I reckon they'd understand that I didn't want to skip leg day. Pathetic hamster I may be. No need to be a pathetic hamster with chicken legs.

Ultimately, Strength was something I could commit to increasing the old-fashioned way. Or the new-old-fashioned way? Either way, it wasn't worth borking my build to use my attribute points to hulk out.

I divided the remaining three between Agility—two—and Dexterity. The latter was a thought about my woodcrafting and a long-game plan. If I was going to continue it, I wanted to be set up for intricate work. Something Eilidh had said about crafting with tools had appealed to me, a meditative state of focus that could allow me to do more complex work. Part of the reason I had gotten into IT was because I enjoyed working with my hands. It just ended up that there was much higher demand for coding, so I'd lost touch with the hands-on side of things. Maybe this was my chance to pick it back up.

After allocating my new stats, my character sheet looked . . . well, formidable.

Name: Calum Green
    Age: 36
    Level: 9
    Class: Hedge Witch (Further class available!)
    Affinities: Nature (Level 6), Healing (Level 4), Synthesis (Level 1)
    Specialised Affinities: Wild (Level 3)

Alteration:
    Strength: 12
    Dexterity: 17
    Agility: 19
    Mind: 39

Regeneration:
    Constitution: 18
    Stamina: 26

Manipulation:
    Spirit: 40 (+443 capacity for 24 hours)
    Pathos: 22 (+324 capacity for 24 hours)
    Will: 31 (+115 capacity for 24 hours)

Boons: Blessings

CHAPTER
FORTY-NINE

That was looking . . . really good.

At least to me. Maybe it was totally fucked and I had no idea.

I'd waited enough—it was time to look at my level-nine class specialisation options.

At Level 9, you may choose to continue within your existing class, to choose an entirely new class, or to specialise within your current class.

-Keep existing class: This option will unlock the Hedge Witch skill tree and the Witchcraft affinity, and while you will have a further chance to access these paths at Level 27, they are exclusive to those with the Hedge Witch class.

-Find new class: You will retain access to all existing affinities and skill trees, but depending on your inclinations, this option could require a significant amount of work to be effective. You should only choose this class if you truly feel your current class is a poor fit.

-Specialise (Recommended): You will receive three speciali-

sation options, each with its own skill tree and affinity. These are tailored to your personal experience and choices.

Would you like to keep existing class, find new class, or specialise? Until you have selected and confirmed a new class, if you choose the latter two, you may still return to this choice. Choosing to keep your existing class at this stage is final.

That thrill continued within me, like a buzz beneath my skin. While I liked my hedge witch class, I wasn't sure I wanted to go further down that path. That said, I knew I didn't want to completely redo my class. I was thankful for the option, but I remembered what the system had said way back—an entire week ago!—about choosing things that suited what I wanted to be.

That meant specialising.

I selected that option, and a wave of relief went through me. That was the first time I'd seen the system recommend something, and I wondered if it would further do that with the various specialisations. Only one way to find out.

Your class specialisation options are as follows:

Arcane Warrior—Able to fight at range and in the thick of things, an arcane warrior is a master of versatility. You can draw on your existing affinities to meld a fighting style that will confound your enemies and prove invaluable to your friends. You will receive an immediate bonus of +3 to Strength, Agility, and Dexterity, as well as a permanent +9 to Spirit.

Arcane Warriors are as diverse as they come; no two are alike. You may use your magic to shroud you from notice, striking with exquisite precision from the shadows with enchanted weapons or pure spirit. You may channel your spirit into bladed weapons and fight at melee range—or you may create powerful projectile weapons with the elements or with bows. Or you may fight with a staff or polearm, able to flow between casting and blade-to-blade combat as necessity requires. An Arcane Warrior is always an enigma at first glance, but they will soon show that they own the battlefield.

That sounded interesting, but not quite for me.

Harbinger—The forerunner of a battle's trajectory, the Harbinger chooses what to bring to the field. Adept healers, they know the body inside and out—something enemies forget at their peril. Those who can put a body back together are also eminently skilled at taking bodies apart. You will receive an immediate bonus of +3 to Mind, Dexterity, and Stamina, as well as a permanent +3 to Will.

Harbingers are feared across the Ascended Alliance. Always a wild card on the battlefield, they have been known to swiftly redirect the outcome of the battle, either by healing themselves and their allies or by unleashing devastating and deadly attacks upon their foes. A Harbinger is a dual-edged sword that cuts both ways—they are equally adept at surgery and dismemberment.

Jesus.

The Hannibal Lecter of an ascended world, I guess, though without the cannibalism.

Probably without the cannibalism.

Probably.

I wasn't hugely enthused with that one, though I could

definitely see the benefit, and I knew I wouldn't have vibed with an outright healer, either.

I was starting to feel a bit apprehensive about my final option. Would I end up deciding to just go back and double down on the hedge witch class? With trepidation, I looked at the last one.

Draoidh—An ancient class, this is one native to Earth and indigenous to your personal homelands. The Draoidhean often comprised the few humans who were sensitive to spirit even before the ascension, and as such, they drew power from the natural world and their people alike. You will receive an immediate +9 to Mind and a permanent +3 to each Spirit, Pathos, and Will. Please note that this is a Pathos-based build, and as such, it is recommended that hopefuls meet the minimum threshold of 30, as all but the foundational spells in the Draoidh skill tree require this minimum, with prerequisite Pathos increasing by 3 with each progressive unlocked spell.

Revered and remembered across aeons, the Draoidhean have been memorialised—often romanticised—in human culture all over the world, but it is in the ancestral lands of Scotland, Ireland, Wales, the Isle of Man, Cornwall, and Bretagne on the European continent where these traditions were rooted. There is an immense power in connection to your world, but to tap into it requires a harmonious self and deep connection to one's own spirit and emotions. Few are willing; fewer are able.

It felt like my heart stalled in my chest.

For a long while, I just lay there uncomfortably on my raft of cushions. I felt like I was floating through an eerily calm sea.

Pathos was my weakest link, and unlike Strength, I couldn't see a clear route for increasing it. For all my joking with Eilidh about having exactly one emotion, that wasn't true for anyone, least of all me.

Ever since my mum had passed away, I'd locked away my emotions. Susanna hadn't helped. She'd greeted any emotion I showed other than passion with stoicism at best, if not outright scorn.

That she'd left me for someone so emotional he couldn't stop sending me angry text messages was a mystery I didn't care to solve.

Our recommendation is to use them not according to the life you have led thus far but according to the life you wish to lead.

I remembered what that text had said back in my flat in Hyndland that now felt so distant. I pulled it up again just to read it.

Our recommendation is to use them not according to the life you have led thus far but according to the life you wish to lead.

According to the life you wish to lead.

Something in that description called to me. I knew I could take the easy way out; I could back out of the specialisation menu and confirm myself as a hedge witch. My skills were good so far, and they were getting better. The Synthesis skill tree would only help.

It occurred to me that the system might have been pushing me in a particular direction—the use of the Gaelic draoidh over the English druid was telling enough. It seemed when this system wanted me to really grasp something, it used my mother tongue.

But that number felt impossible. I'd gotten as high as I

had with Pathos only because of the fuath and that reaver, both of which were fuelled by emotion: rage.

I had a feeling that if I were to reach thirty, it would require more than a single-sided approach. Anger was an emotion; it just wasn't the only one.

From Connection to Freumhan to the Synthesis affinity, there was a message hidden in plain sight. The ascension directive simply built upon that—the will to survive was one thing, but no one could do it alone.

Even Lord Bawbag knew that. He only forced connections rather than building those freely given.

A year ago, I might have taken the easy way out.

Maybe it was my existing increases in Pathos that had unlocked something in me, or maybe it was seeing Rhona almost die twice in twenty-four hours. Maybe it was the sound of those children crying or the swell of pride I'd felt when the people of Oban surrounded us, embraced us, welcomed us home.

Just like Gaelic and Scots were our indigenous languages here in Scotland, the system had offered me a class that was too. Something connected to this earth, to this home of mine.

I knew what I had to do.

Congratulations! You have unlocked your first class specialisation: Draoidh. You have unlocked the Draoidh skill tree. You have unlocked the specialised affinity: Draoidh.

As an indigenous class, this has been first offered in its own homeland. There is no blood requirement to be offered this class, only attunement with the land. You are the third human to take the Draoidh class, which is called Derwydd in Wales and Draoi in Ireland. Both of the others are in Wales.

Welcome to the ascended world, a Chaluim Uainich. Make your place in it.

You have four skill points to distribute. At Level 9, you may also use your skill points to manually increase the level of existing active skills. Adding skill points to existing passive skills or skills excluded from standard level increases will not boost their efficacy, but it can increase the likelihood of evolution.

From Level 10, you will receive three skill points each level instead of two.

Use them wisely.

I almost groaned.

Part of me was delighted that I could now manually up the level of my skills, but because that was something I could do organically to great effect, I figured that was best left for emergencies. As for the second half of that paragraph, that was a long-game plan if I ever saw one.

First order of business was to look over my newest skill trees: Synthesis and Draoidh.

Though Draoidh was burning a hole in my proverbial pocket, I tried to open Synthesis . . . but there was nothing there, because I was a numpty and had bloody forgotten it would only add leaves to the existing trees.

The thought of going through all of my skill trees right this second was too daunting. My brain was decisioned out.

I opened Draoidh, and my breath caught, even in the system-induced catatonic state.

While the other trees were beautiful, this one was a work of *art*.

It reminded me of a bur oak in Kelvingrove Park, a massive arboreal specimen that reached both outward and skyward, shading a solid thirty-yard radius around its trunk under the branches of its canopy. Its massive boughs were polished smooth in places from centuries of people finding footholds to ascend into its arms. Its trunk and branches were gnarled, knobbly, and most of all, alive.

The foundational root-level spells of the Draoidh tree were *nine* in number. I remembered that the next class specialisation was not till level twenty-seven, so I'd plenty of time to get comfortable here. Decision paralysis tried to set in . . . until I realised there was only one unlockable skill anyway.

Phew. That made things easier. At least for skill point one of four.

Tursa—The ancients moved twenty-tonne slabs of rock hundreds of miles to build their monoliths. From this we have gleaned not only their technological capabilities but also their astronomical understanding. Many of these ancient monoliths were built with an intimate knowledge of the stars in the sky and the movements of the sun's path.

This skill is the bedrock upon which the Draoidh builds their power. In unlocking it, you will gain an instinctual knowledge of astronomy and its relationship to you. While this may not seem like much, it will root you in time, in the seasons, and upon the surface of the earth itself. For what is more constant than the stars for navigation? To get anywhere, you need to know where you are.

Both a passive and an active skill, Tursa will allow you to carry an instinct of time and the turning of the wheel, but upon casting, it will give you an innate understanding of your envi-

ronment, a precious glimpse that can allow you to strategise in the heat of battle or work your way out of natural obstacles when you can see no escape.

Damn.

I wasn't sure what I expected, but this seemed to be both everything and nothing. I unlocked it, thinking it would unlock the roots on either side of it, but it didn't. The three-dimensional tree only had the first lit up, the eastern root, and only the one immediately behind it pulsed as unlockable. It seemed it would move in a sunwise circle around the base of the tree.

I wondered if all of these would be similar. On one hand, I could see the benefit of layering in such fundamental knowledge and understanding. On the other, I just hoped it would prove to be applicable. The threat of Lord Bawbag was too great. It wouldn't do me much good to be able to slap a giant YOU ARE HERE sticker on my own forehead if he wiped out everything and everyone I loved or turned them into zombified automatons like those puppeted stags.

That thought was less than helpful.

Next spell. Ability. Whatever.

Òran na Cloiche

I got as far as the name and had to stifle a snort, my brain immediately going into the vocable chorus of the well-known Gaelic song with the same title. "'S i u ro bha ho ro hilli um bo ha / Hilli um bo ruaig thu i hilli um bo ha/ 'S i u ro bha ho ro hilli um bo ha . . ."

The words were mostly nonsense syllables, a common thing in traditional Gaelic song.

It'd been one of Mum's favourites. It meant *Song of the Stone*, and she'd sung it in her Gaelic choir when I was in high school. I doubted this new spell had much to do with it.

Then again, who knew at this point?

Òran na Cloiche—When the Draoidhean speak, the people listen. And when the Draoidhean sing, the people weep. With this passive skill close to your heart, your words will reach receptive ears. Once per week, you may also find inspiration to weave words into song, and those songs will ring out through your lands to touch all those who hear them. Friend or foe, the listener will not remain unmoved—for better or for worse.

I could feel my frozen face turning red at the thought of that. It wasn't that I didn't enjoy singing; I just hadn't done it in years. Not since Mum died.

Already I could feel the increasing understanding of what I'd done in choosing this class worming its way deeper into my soul. It had warned me that Pathos was the primary lynchpin of the class. I shouldn't have been surprised that it was stirring feelings I would have preferred to leave buried.

Mum had always loved when I sang. When my voice dropped into an uncertain baritone and the bottom fell out of my range, she'd dragged me along to her choir with her. They were short on basses. We'd gone together all throughout her illness, and I'd found comfort in that, at the time.

After she was gone, I couldn't bear going back.

And now this skill wanted me to sing.

I took a long, shuddering breath.

So be it.

I unlocked it.

And then I exited out of my notifications, unable to continue peeling back the layers of my skin.

My breath was quick, heavy, and none too steady. Rhona snored quietly on the pull-out bed next to Eilidh, and in the dim unlight of the wee hours of night, I had the strangest feeling I wasn't the only one who couldn't sleep.

CHAPTER
FIFTY

I must have drifted off at some point, because I had to deal with the ignominy of waking the fuck up, which was unpleasant.

Blinking felt like someone had gone up to Ganavan Beach, stripped it of sand, and come back and dumped it all into my eyeballs. Every. Single. Grain.

Post-ascension humans needed less sleep, but apparently we still needed *some*.

Eilidh was already awake, perched on the edge of the mattress and looking like she might sway right off it.

"All right?" I asked her quietly.

"Sat up too fast," she said. "Dizzy."

Rhona groaned. "It's too early."

"That's rich coming from the one person among the three of us who actually slept," I muttered.

"I'm a growing girl," she said, but it came out muffled because she'd flung Eilidh's pillow over her face. "I need my beauty sleep."

"What are we, ugly ducklings?" Eilidh asked.

Rhona retorted with something undecipherable that I presumed was an affirmation but couldn't really be sure.

A door somewhere in the house opened and slammed, and heavy footsteps stumped across the floor, followed by low, urgent murmuring.

That set my tail tingling.

Eilidh seemed to have had the same thought. "I think that's our alarm going off," she said softly.

Another groan from under the pillow.

Sure enough, the heavy footfalls came closer until there was a knock at the door, and Angus called, "Sorry to bother you, but we've got a problem."

"We'll be right out," I replied. "Rhona, come on."

Eilidh's pillow flew through the air and smacked me in the face. When I pulled it into my lap, scowling, Rhona gave a long-suffering sigh.

"I know, I know, apocalypse, et cetera," she said.

Just like that, we were moving, and Rhona even quickly got the sofa bed put back together within about twenty seconds of getting up, stacking the pillows neatly at the edge of it and even managing to fold the fitted sheet.

Ascension superpower, it must have been.

We found Angus and his wife Eliza, a lovely English woman whose southern accent had given way to hints of an Argyll burr over the years, in the kitchen with the smell of coffee thick in the air.

They'd put out three cups for us, and upon our arrival, they moved aside so we could get to them.

"There's not a lot of time," Eliza said, "and it's just instant. We're trying to save the tea."

It was such an absurd thing to say, but also it wasn't. Hanging on to small comforts in an apocalypse didn't feel stupid.

"We'll be quick," Eilidh promised. "What's wrong?"

"Not entirely sure yet," said Angus as I dumped sugar and powdered milk into my coffee and stirred. "There's an old woman down the way who had the second sight even before this mess, and she was offered a rare class right out of the gate—she's a seer, and she said there's a threat coming in from the west."

Rhona had her cup halfway to her lips, and she froze. "Like from Connel?"

Eliza and Angus exchanged a glance. "Yes."

"My family's in Connel," Rhona said, her voice almost a whisper.

All the air seemed to have been sucked out of the room. Without a thought, I gulped down my coffee, burning the shit out of my tongue and not caring. Let the system deal with that minor injury. It felt like liquid fire going down my oesophagus, but I let it ignite my tired body to ready it for action.

I saw Eilidh do the same; she grimaced at the pain but just as quickly ignored it as I had. Rhona just stood there with her cup in her hands.

"Let's go," I said. "We can be there in twenty minutes if we run. Can we leave the kitten here?"

Angus nodded with a wave of his hand as if that weren't even a question. He'd set up a little tray of sand in the guest bathroom the night before, though I wasn't entirely sure Sailean knew what to do with that.

Eilidh gently took Rhona's cup from her. "We'll do anything we can to make sure your family's okay."

Rhona had been the definition of a trooper through all of this. She'd been hurt worse, lost more, and still, she'd kept going. But right then, standing in an unfamiliar kitchen, her hands clawed in front of her as if they still thought they were holding the coffee cup, she looked very lost and very small.

It lasted about five more seconds, and right in front of my eyes, that sense of smallness folded in on itself until it vanished, and all it left behind was a hardened young woman with brown eyes like peat embers that would burn anything that got in her way.

"Fine. Let's go."

"There're fighters gathering at the harbour," Angus said. "You can go with them."

"They'll only slow us down," Rhona answered sharply, but then she wavered. "Sorry. I'm—"

"Don't apologise, lass." Angus clasped her shoulder, and Eliza nodded from where she leant against the worktop.

As if those words cut a cord, Rhona spun on her heel and was off.

Though I'd spent the last week in a feverish attempt to reach Oban, now I barely saw it. Familiar buildings flashed by as we moved, the hills rising up around us like the embrace of a friend.

We saw people. They pulled back when they saw the speed of our approach, the weapons we carried, and the singleminded fervour that had gripped us. And as we ran, I saw the subtle changes Tursa had wrought in me. I took the lead, my brain charting out the most efficient route north through the town. We avoided the harbour entirely, though even from the side streets we took, we could see other fighters moving in that direction. Some of them noticed us —a couple called out—but we merely waved them off.

Our strides linked as we ran, Rhona somehow matching us step for step despite being shorter and needing to take two for each of ours. I pulsed Connection, and the first time I did it, it nearly threw me off balance.

The spell combined with Tursa to not only reveal threads of spirit and their eddies but now to show them in relationship to where we were. Where before I would have a general sense of "that way" when I sensed a creature, now it was as if my mind had been overlaid with a perfect rendering of the topography, anything it lit upon high-lighted in exquisite relief.

But in the town, it was nearly overwhelming. Threads and flows of spirit layered on top of one another, sifting through the houses and streets, levels upon levels of inter-twined energies. Either I'd have to learn to filter out humans or be limited to using Connection when we were in the hills—I truly hoped it wouldn't be the latter.

Each mile our strides ate up pushed us farther. Faster. We picked up speed to the point where even my ascension-strengthened legs burned from the exertion, and while I'd thought we could make the five miles in about twenty minutes, when we were about a mile out of Connel, it had only been ten minutes since we left Angus's house.

Only ten minutes and we were almost too late.

FIFTY-ONE

We saw the first people fleeing just as we reached the outskirts of Connel. They ran with nowt but the clothes on their backs, often carrying babies and younger children, sometimes even older children who simply couldn't run as quickly. Their eyes were all wide and frightened, some streaming tears.

And after that first wave, we started seeing people whose skin was red with spatters of blood.

Though I couldn't see Rhona, I knew without looking that she was frantically scanning every face, every pair of terror-struck eyes, for a glimpse of her family.

Then, suddenly, she let out an anguished sound.

"Ricky!" she yelled, skidding to a halt at the sight of a teenage boy who half-stumbled as she appeared in front of him like a spectre.

"Rhona," he gasped, throwing his arms around her. He was thankfully free of blood himself, but he had the dazed look of someone in shock. "What are you—you're alive!"

"My family," she said without further preamble. "Are they okay?"

"They were right behind me," he said, turning. But his eyes avoided looking back as if he were afraid of what they'd find.

Rhona frantically looked where he feared, and I could *feel* the jagged waves of agitation pouring off of her. "I don't see them."

"They were right there—they got me away from that— from that *thing*."

"I don't *see them*." Rhona's voice now carried the edge of panic, and I went to her before I could stop myself, placing one hand gently on her back.

"Ricky, thank you. We'll find them. Go to Oban as fast as you can. If the fighters there haven't left, tell them to hurry. *Now!*"

My voice came out with a startling resonance like the remaining vibration of a guitar's bout after the strumming has stopped but the sound carries on.

That was when I felt Òran na Cloiche take hold for the first time. My words seemed to calm the boy, and his eyes cleared. He nodded. He darted in to give Rhona a fluttering hug. And then he turned and ran.

"We'll find them," I said again, this time just to Rhona. "We will."

Eilidh was staring at me like she'd never seen me before, but she shook herself and took off running without a word.

Both Rhona and I followed, and if our pace had been quick before, now it was as if we'd hit a turbo button somewhere. Perspiration beaded on my forehead and dripped into my eyes. More and more people passed us, splattered with blood that seemed to make no sense. I couldn't see anything beyond minor injuries, but the terror? It seeped through the air like poison, diffusing through the tiny village of Connel like it planned to permeate every stone, every branch, and every body within its sick circumference.

I knew without casting Connection what it was.

It was the beast.

I'd seen what it could do to a couple of individual human beings; it had left them in pieces in the middle of the road, their body parts cooling in the highland mist.

But now I saw what it could do to a village.

At first, it looked like footage from a disaster film—houses seemed like someone had picked up an ancient redwood and slammed it down onto roof after roof. As we moved, we got glimpses into bedrooms, into kitchens, into bathrooms, one with the shower still running and blood in a pink-red smear across white tile.

This thing—had it *grown*?

We traced its path, but it seemed like it had no straight movement. The trail wove to and fro like a drunken snake —or at least I thought so until Rhona gasped beside me, a blur of motion as she shot ahead.

There, next to St. Orans Church, was the monster.

When we'd seen it before, it had been merely a suggestion of a beast, a ripple of distorted air and a thrum like drums in the deep.

It was all that now. And it was more.

My first guess at *mutated adder* fell so far short it was like I'd hypothesised an anaconda was an earthworm.

I knew Keen Eye would absolutely destroy my spirit, but I also knew that if we didn't know what we were fighting, we had no chance of beating it. None.

More than half of my spirit vanished as I cast it, and I swayed on my feet, focusing on the text in front of my eyes. My stomach acid curdled my hastily drunk instant coffee and its sludge of powdered milk.

. . .

Beithir

A mythological creature and one of the many iterations of the fuath, the beithir is a creature of the corries and glens. It is a monstrous serpent, sometimes called a dragon, but where a dragon has breath of fire, the beithir stings like a scorpion. Its tail is tipped with a venomous, brutal spine that it uses to immobilise its prey before devouring them.

The only cure for this venom is to get the victims to the nearest body of fresh water before the beithir itself can reach the shore—if the beithir wins this deadly race, the victim's fate is sealed.

A famed beithir in Islay once devoured seven horses as it made its way overland to Loch-in-daal, and those who destroyed it only did so with great preparation of barrels filled with spikes and cannon fire.

This beithir has broken free of an attempt at control, and it is confused, having fulfilled part of its orders. Its confusion will not last long, and a cornered beast is a dangerous beast.

The beithir is a creature of storms and hunger; it is drawn to lightning and cannot be harmed with the same.

Beside me, I felt the crackling of spirit as Rhona drew on her lightning.

"Rhona, no!" I cried out. "That'll attract it!"

"I know it will! It killed my parents!"

It was only then I saw the bodies that lay half hidden behind a hedge.

Venom.

The gears in my mind spun into overdrive. The beithir

would eat them alive, not dead. They were only immo-bilised.

"They're not dead!" I almost tripped over the words as they fell out of my mouth, and Rhona spun to me. "The beithir is venomous—it stung them with its tail. It wants to eat them, but if they were dead, it wouldn't! Its prey needs to be alive!"

Rhona's eyes widened, and for a moment, I thought my words had done the trick and she wouldn't release the spell, but then she turned her gaze on me. The sky darkened above us, purple-black clouds like a bruise.

"How do you fix it? Can you heal them?"

"The only cure is to get them to the nearest freshwater before the beithir can reach it," I said.

"Good. Do that," Rhona said, and she released her spell.

"Rhona, no!" This time it was Eilidh who cried out, but it was too late.

Lightning split the sky, and both Eilidh and I were thrown away from the younger woman as a jagged fork slammed into Rhona's body like she was a lightning rod.

I *felt* it as the beithir's attention snapped onto her small form, a Goliath to her David, and she'd just hit it between the eyes with a pebble from her sling.

I scrambled to my feet, trusting more than seeing that Eilidh was doing the same, and as the beithir surged into action, I launched myself at the prone forms beneath the hedge.

Something told me that the second we started towards the loch, the beithir would have eyes only for us, the people who wanted to steal its prey.

But that didn't matter.

Eilidh was indeed right behind me, and we reached the

two bodies only a heartbeat apart. Without asking, she grabbed the man, who must have been Rhona's father. He was easily twice the size of her mother, a pot belly taking up his sizeable midsection, and though he had the look of someone who would be the jolly man down the pub, right now his skin was pale with a jaundiced, yellow undertone and a froth of green spittle dripping from the corners of his mouth.

Without a word, I scooped up Rhona's mother. Even though my Strength was not great, I thought I could run with her. Eilidh was off like a shot, and I followed, amazed at the way she'd managed to get that much-bigger man into a fireman's carry over her shoulders in the space of a couple seconds.

The loch was maybe fifty meters away. We didn't have to go far. But then something horrifying struck me. Here, so close to the sea, Loch Etive wasn't freshwater—and the freshwater burn just over the road lay down a steep embankment.

On top of that, the beithir had indeed reacted.

Its bellow was like an earthquake. I heard Rhona's shriek of fury as the beithir turned its away from her and onto the interlopers who had stolen its victims.

I did the only thing I could think of.

I cast Ring of Fire, the upgraded version of Purifire.

It stretched out as far as I could around me, and I could only pray it was far enough to encumber the beithir and allow Eilidh and me to reach the water.

And not the loch—the stream that ran alongside the street. Lusragan Burn.

My body burned as if I'd cast it inside of me or as if I'd again swallowed that scalding coffee in two gulps. Sweat poured from me as my feet churned the tarmac.

The sorry irony was that Lusragan Burn ran alongside

us, but for a moment, I thought my Ring of Fire didn't allow us to reach it. As I ran, I prayed to every lucky star that the beithir would be singleminded enough—or confused enough—to simply follow, rather than diving off to the side into the freshwater burn itself. And I had to hope that I hadn't already buggered us by casting Ring of Fire at all.

A screech rose behind us that wasn't Rhona.

Ten meters.

Eilidh vaulted over the low stone kerb and vanished down the steep bank of the small burn. My stomach plummeted at the sight of how far down it was.

There was a splash as Eilidh literally *threw* Rhona's father at the water, followed immediately by a spluttering gasp.

It worked. *It fucking worked.*

There was no way I was going to be able to vault that far, and Eilidh spun and leapt back up the incline to meet me, using the branches of trees to pull herself up.

She grabbed Rhona's mum's limp body from my hands and dropped back to the water, this time plunging straight into it herself. My Ring of Fire covered half the burn—it was enough.

The older woman came to with a flailing splash and a yelp, her eyes wide and rolling.

"It's okay," I called from above. "You're okay. Stay inside the circle of fire."

Now that I could see what I'd done, I almost collapsed in relief—the Ring of Fire extended maybe two yards into the burn. That was it.

Eilidh heaved a breath, turning to me and beginning to climb back to me.

"We need to get back to Rhona," she said.

"Rhona—my daughter! Is she okay—is she—"

"She's alive, but she won't stay that way unless we go help her," I said. "We'll explain later if we're not dead. Do *not* leave this circle of fire or the beithir will get you again!"

With that, we were off again. Eilidh's strength awed me as she clawed her way back up the steep bank. I desperately wished we'd had time or the presence of mind to eat something, because the exertion was getting to me—and with my Stamina where it was, that was impressive.

The beithir had slammed up against the barrier of my fire with an enraged shriek, and now it bucked and turned first one way to look for a gap, then the other.

"Rhona!" Eilidh yelled.

There was no answer.

"Fuck," I said.

"How do we kill this thing?" Eilidh turned to me as she lurched onto the road again, dread in every line of her face.

"I don't think we do," I said. "We were outmatched back at Lord Bawbag's, and we're outmatched now, new levels or not."

"And if the fighters from Oban get here?"

"We might have a shot then."

"Then we need to hold it off until they do."

"Rhona!" I bellowed her name, feeling it resound through the village with the force of Òran na Cloiche. "Your parents are alive! If you can hear me, get inside the Ring of Fire and cast your lightning to distract the beithir!"

For a moment longer, there was still no answer, but then a bolt of lightning struck the far side of the road near the wall of the church, directly opposite the bank where we stood.

"She's alive!" I yelled triumphantly as the beithir spun itself towards the lightning. "Come on, Rhona. You can do it. Get in the circle."

I couldn't see her, but with Rhona, that didn't mean she wasn't there. All that mattered was that she was alive and fighting.

Now that we were closer and protected by my Ring of Fire, I finally got a good look at the beithir—if seeing the thing could be called good at all.

Its bizarre camouflage worked through shifting, snake-like scales that rippled and changed as it moved, reflecting colours and textures from the world around it. It was at least twenty yards long and at its centre was as thick as a car. The tail curled back like a scorpion and lashed in turn, and when it flexed, a glistening, translucent spike protruded.

The deadly stinger was at least as long as my forearm, and when it emerged from the sheath, droplets of clear venom gathered on it, a slight golden shimmer the only thing that kept it from looking like pure water. I hadn't seen any puncture wounds on Rhona's parents, but then again, I hadn't exactly been looking. I wondered if it also contained something that would close up the wound around the venom after it injected.

The thought was as horrifying as the rest of the monster.

With it facing away, I couldn't get a proper look at its head.

My spirit recovered enough for me to cast Ring of Fire again, and just as I could feel the previous one faltering, I did just that at the same moment Rhona hurtled into the circle.

She was limping, but other than that and a fresh shiner already turning yellow-blue on her cheek, she seemed fine. Rhona darted straight over the stone kerb with a sob, prac-tically falling down the embankment to her parents, who had pulled themselves out of the burn and were sitting, dazed. I could barely see them when I peered over the side from the road, but I saw enough.

Her mother let out a gasp, throwing her arms around Rhona so tightly I was afraid she'd crack a rib or three. Rhona's dad pushed himself to sitting, lurching over to hold them both.

"Thank you for saving them," Rhona said once she caught her breath.

"I wouldn't thank us yet," I murmured, eyes on the beithir.

It was still casting about for Rhona where she'd thrown the lightning.

Just then, it seemed to realise it had been tricked.

Its screech split the air and worse as it threw its enormous body against the road, its dripping stinger plunging into an innocent clump of heather as if the beast were trying to take out its frustration. The tarmac cracked under its weight with a sharp report.

With that, it wheeled about with another piercing screech coupled with a thrum of a rumble we all felt in our bones—and slammed directly into my Ring of Fire.

FIFTY-TWO

I felt the reverberation of the impact in every thread of spirit that connected me to the ring.

"How long can that hold?" Eilidh asked urgently.

"I don't know," I said.

"Can you attack it from here?" Rhona clambered back up over the stone kerb, leaving her parents where they were, though her mother reached out a hand like she wanted to pull her daughter back despite the solid fifty feet between them.

"My only real attacks use spirit, and it takes a lot to cast a ring this big," I told her. "If I use up all my spirit, I won't be able to cast it again."

"Shit." Eilidh shifted her weight. "I wish we knew if the fighters from Oban were coming."

"Me too." I wracked my brain, trying to think of a strategy, any strategy, that could make this survivable.

Keen Eye had shown the beithir's strengths but not its weaknesses—or had it?

In Islay, they'd managed to lure it onto barrels full of

spikes. Which meant it was vulnerable to piercing damage, at the extreme least.

The beithir slammed itself against the Purifire barrier again. At this rate, I'd need to cast it again any minute, and that would take me down to probably twenty percent of my spirit reserves. As it was, I was just ticking over seventy percent.

"Look," Eilidh breathed, lifting one hand to point at the beithir where it had struck the Purifire.

Its scales changed colour so much that it was hard to see any consistency, but when she pointed it out, I saw it: the point of impact no longer changed. It turned a sickly green-brown, slightly mottled, but now that I saw it, it made the entire beast more visible. A target.

I grimaced and cast Connection, which only made my spirit dip a little. At level six, Connection had upgraded significantly; I only hoped it was enough.

The spirit that formed Ring of Fire spun in a maelstrom around us, licking upwards and outwards from the circle.

The beithir knew we were in here; it raged against that fact, and through the haze of my own Purifire, I could see the way the monster's spirit flowed. I could see how it flowed *around* that point where it had struck the fire.

"I think I know what to do," I said. Bile tried to creep up my throat. "It's dangerous."

"More dangerous than sitting in here without attacking until that thing kills us?" Eilidh asked.

"It might kill us faster this way, but at least this way we have a chance to take the bloody thing with us," I said.

"Then let's do it." Rhona's hands lingered on the hilts of her daggers for a moment before she pulled them free of their sheaths.

"Just promise you won't hate me if we die," I muttered.

I went over the plan as quickly as I could, watching both of their faces war with competing hope and grim resolve.

Without knowing whether the fighters would come our way, without knowing if my harebrained idea was even viable, all we could do was try.

I thought of Iain and Meeksy and Catrìona—part of me wished we'd gone to see them straight away last night, just run to their house to see if they were alive. I knew why we hadn't; at the end of the day, none of us could have taken bad news. But even so, if we didn't make it through this fight, I'd always regret it.

The beithir thrashed in anger, its massive tail flexing and extending. Great drops of venom dripped from the stinger onto the Purifire ring, vaporised by the heat on contact. It filled the air with acrid smoke that made my eyes water, and I didn't think that would be healthy to breathe outside of my protective flames.

Focusing on the spirit around me, I tried to ground myself in my body. I could feel the channels throughout, the flows of spirit that moved in me, ready to be used. Freumhan was a subtle passive, but it was there, like points of power ready to receive more. I took a breath, imagining I was drawing more spirit into me, letting the air out and willing that extra to stay to release only air.

The beithir slammed once more against the flame wall, and I felt the magic begin to falter.

"Be ready," I said to the others. "Rhona?"

She held her daggers on guard, and I could almost feel her crackling with contained electricity.

"Here we, here we, here we fuckin' go," Rhona murmured, shooting me a sardonically quirked eyebrow as she used the classic Glaswegian chant in a whole new context.

We all held our breath and watched as the beithir, riled into a near frenzy by its inability to get to us, pulled back to strike again.

This time, I let the barrier fall just as it was about to hit.

The monster flung itself into a nonexistent wall, the weight of its body throwing it off balance. Immediately, Rhona let loose her lightning.

It struck near the beithir's head, and the beast roared. The sound it made was horrible, at once a high-pitched hiss and that low, bass rumble that simultaneously made my eardrums pang and my every internal organ vibrate.

My spirit was still not as full as I wanted it, but it was good enough for the next stage of my plan: I poured Purifire into Eilidh's claymore and into Rhona's dual daggers.

As the beithir righted its massive bulk to strike at Rhona, Eilidh struck with speed akin to the lightning itself, her sword wreathed in blue-green flames as it plunged into the dull, matte block of scales where the monster had struck my Ring of Fire.

Now the beithir screamed in earnest.

In a flash, Eilidh jerked her claymore free, moving to the side even as Rhona practically flew in to take her place.

I cast Fuaran to give them each a boost of stamina for the fight ahead, grimacing as Rhona's daggers widened the hole Eilidh had carved in the beithir's side.

This part of the plan had gone off without a hitch, but one thing we hadn't counted on: the beithir began to heal before our eyes.

With my spirit barely over forty percent, we couldn't afford to have that wound heal. I poured as much as I dared into Cumhachd, bolstering it with whatever threads of spirit I could pull through the environment, channelling the flames of Purifire into a missile I aimed directly at the now-gaping wound.

It struck with an audible splat and a splash of blood that immediately sizzled with the heat of the fire. Eilidh and Rhona dashed out of the way of the thrashing beithir. Its massive tail whipped through the air above it, and a drop of venom landed only a hairsbreadth away from Rhona's leg, where it steamed and hissed upon the tarmac.

And then it lashed out, flinging the tail sideways instead of downward. Whether it was out of desperation or pain was anyone's guess, but it struck Eilidh in the side, throwing her into the air. She sailed all the way across the road and struck the guard rail separating the street from the loch with a clang.

Eilidh slumped to the ground, dazed. Somehow, she'd held onto her sword.

The beithir whipped around at the sound of her impact.

Its movement took us out of range of the wound in its side, and Rhona skittered backwards towards me as quick as she could.

My spirit was barely fifteen percent. Barely enough to do anything, but as panic surged and the mahoosive snake reared back, its tail now a controlled weapon above our heads with a stinger that pulsed in and out of its sheath as if it was hungry, I had to do *something*.

I threw myself forwards with as much energy as I could muster. My ascension-enhanced Agility practically let me take flight. In three light steps, I was at Eilidh's side, scooping her up in my arms as I launched myself away again. My staff clattered against her hardened leather breastplate and smacked me in the face, but I didn't care.

Out of the corner of my eye, I saw the tail descend.

Instinctively, I grabbed what spirit I had and flung it away from me in a wave of Spèird.

"I'm okay!" Eilidh said as we lurched to a halt. She untangled herself from me and my staff, the dazed look slowly clearing from her eyes.

The wave of force had again set the beithir off balance, and now it flailed sideways, hissing.

My Purifire missile had done something unexpected.

It was like launching it directly into its body by blades and magic alike had gotten the flames into the beithir's bloodstream. Where before it was a swiftly shifting mass of camouflage like an octopus changing colours before my eyes, now tendrils of that unchanging, matte scale pattern slowly spread over the zenith of the beithir's back and reached over onto the side we could see.

The monster struck out at us with its head this time, and I got a whiff of acrid breath as all three of us leaped out of range.

Then something soared through the air above our heads with a faint rush of air and smacked into the beithir's face.

In almost comical slow motion, all three of us watched the rock bounce off and fall to the floor.

Someone had . . . hit the monster with a rock.

And then came a second. This one missed, hurtling past the creature and striking the metal guard rail with a resounding clang.

"People are coming," Rhona said urgently. "People are coming!"

Without enough spirit to trigger Connection, I didn't dare turn my back on the beithir to look, but then I heard it —the sound of footsteps and panting.

And a veritable hailstorm of rocks.

The beithir started to turn towards this new threat—the flying stones were likely little more than an annoyance to a creature of its size, but they got its attention anyway.

Eilidh planted the point of her claymore against the ground, and I felt the draw as she pulled on her spirit.

"Over here, you glorified earthworm!" She yelled the insult at the thing as if it could understand her, and for a moment, I didn't think her taunt was going to work even as her power burst from her in a golden glow.

Just as the first of the barely armed villagers came into view in my peripheral vision, though, the beithir wheeled its head around to look at Eilidh. Rhona was gone again, vanished into the shadows, but I pinpointed her a heartbeat later as she planted her daggers right in the still-healing wound on the far side of the beithir.

Eilidh sprang forwards, slashing out with her claymore even as the giant snake-scorpion brought its stinger down precisely where she'd been standing. So close, as it was, that I felt the strange heat of its tail and the wind it made in its movement, and I spun my staff at the place where the stinger met its sheath.

It was little better than hitting the creature with a stick, but to my utter surprise, the impact of wood against stinger made a startling crack, and the beithir roared.

More rocks flew through the air.

My spirit was just over half, and I lurched away from the tail, which had spasmed. The beithir drew it back up as if to strike again—or perhaps just to remove it from the danger of the stinger getting hit a second time—and I could see the mottled, clearly visible scales spreading across its back.

People were here.

Most of them carried buckets of rocks, which they

continued to throw at the beithir, but a few were armed with garden spades, one with a pickaxe, and another with a katana that looked like it'd been bought at comic con, but it *was* at least a blade.

My staff felt alive in my hand, alive in a way I hadn't sensed it before. With a surge of spirit I felt up from the ground and through both me and the weapon, I suddenly knew what to do.

"Aim for the mottled parts you can see, not the bits that look invisible!" I called to them, and I pulled spirit into me. "Don't drop your weapons—I'm going to enchant them with blue fire! It won't hurt you!"

Even with the warning, as I triggered the Purifire again, I saw at least three people drop their rocks like hot potatoes with a blur of blue-green fire, but soon there were missiles of Purifire flying through the air.

Eilidh ducked under the snake's swinging head and neck, scoring a line of flame across the creature's throat, and it bucked, surging backwards and slamming into the guard rail. The metal bent as if it'd taken a car at full speed. Crunching metal broke the air, and then the brave villagers with their garden implements were running at the snake, spades blazing blue.

I continued to pour Purifire into their weapons, feeling as again, my spirit drained below thirty percent. In my hand, my staff flared as if in triumph.

The beithir was weakening against the combined onslaught.

It was.

And then a battle cry pierced the air.

CHAPTER
FIFTY-THREE

At first, I felt a surge of hope and triumph.

The fighters from Oban had finally made it. They swarmed through the crowd of villagers with their makeshift weapons, aiming straight towards the beithir with single-minded resolve, but I quickly realised they had no idea what they were up against.

There were mages among them, and while I saw some flashes of Purifire, it was lightning that lit up the junction—lightning that drew the beithir's attention like flame for a moth.

And as the first forks of lightning touched the beithir's hide, I saw something horrifying.

This was a creature that loved storms, and this was why.

Everywhere the lightning hit it, those mottled, visible patches of scales I had been painstakingly growing throughout this whole fight began to fade.

"No!" I yelled, the resonance of my voice pouring out over the din of the fighting. "Lightning heals it! Don't use lightning!"

But it was too late.

The beithir roared, renewed, as all visible traces of our handiwork were erased from its left side. A sick feeling coated the inside of my stomach—I knew, I just *knew* that on its right side where it'd had that gaping wound, the wound was now healing.

Too late.

I didn't dare use the rest of my spirit for another bout of Purifire, and all I could do was watch, helpless, as our relief contingent swarmed over the beithir, strengthening it instead of hurting it.

People began to call out in dismay, and some of the villagers scattered—I couldn't blame them. Voices yelled out not to use the lightning, but one mage in particular wasn't listening. He continued to throw bolt after bolt at the beithir, his hands crackling with electricity.

And as Rhona, Eilidh, and I had learnt already, that was like pouring honey on yourself and lying in a berry bush in bear country.

"Look out!" I bellowed.

The beithir's tail came down.

I'd thought it would be bad. I had not been prepared.

Rhona's parents had gotten off easy. Either they'd barely been clipped by the stinger or it had struck fleshy areas.

The stinger hit the hapless mage head on—literally.

Barely three yards ahead of me, that pulsing, hungry sting punched through the lightning mage's skull.

There would be no frantic run to the loch this time. When the tail jerked back again, the tip of it was coated in blood and brains, and the beithir drew it back to strike again.

Fuck it. I triggered Connection, leaping out of the way

as the spell initiated just in time to predict the likely downward arc of the next strike. The Purifire had damaged it. It hadn't yet completely healed—if we could reignite it, maybe we'd have a chance. Maybe. There were no open wounds to throw it into this time, but . . .

"Hit it with Purifire!" I yelled. "The eyes! Hit it in the eyes with Purifire!"

I heard a woman's voice yell out this time as the stinger came down with a sick squelch, but I couldn't turn to look.

"Purifire!" Eilidh echoed me, her own voice ringing out. "Aim for its eyes!"

It seemed only two of the Oban fighters had the spell, but at least they still had spirit to use it.

Purifire arced through the air. Their aim wasn't as precise as Cumhachd would have made it for me, but the beithir took two blue-green fireballs to the face, and it reeled back, wrenching its stinger free of its second victim in a spray of blood that painted a line through the fighters who tried in vain to score hits on the massive snake.

The beithir screeched.

Everyone flinched, including me, and several people screamed.

The monster's tail whipped round once more, this time in a wide arc that threw the entire bulk of the fighting force into one another like a snow plough, clearing a wedge of the junction.

I leapt out of the way, but most weren't so lucky, and people fell like dominoes against one another, landing in a heap only a yard to my right.

And then, so quickly I could only track it by the flaming glow of Purifire at its head, the beithir spun and fled.

Anger and disappointment warred in me. We'd been so close to killing it. We would never see it this weak again.

"Fuck. Alison."

Rhona's words seemed to come out of nowhere—my focus was still on the retreating monster—but my head snapped around to see Alison's slumped form on the road, just out of the wedge where people were scrambling to their feet.

She'd come along with the fighters. And she was the beithir's second casualty.

I was moving before I could think.

"Get out of my way!" I shouted, and despite the clumsiness of it, people lurched away from my path.

Eilidh was beside me, and together, we reached Alison, lifting her in one movement without needing to coordinate.

If the beithir had gone into the loch, if it had already reached the water . . .

I couldn't think of that. We'd know in a moment.

Rhona's parents were still cowering only half visible on the edge of the burn, but they quickly got out of the way when they saw us coming. Eilidh stepped over the stone kerb half a second before I did. Only our hugely enhanced strength and agility kept us from tumbling arse over tit as we slid down the embankment into the cold water of Lusragan Burn, tree branches whipping us in the face the whole way down.

We lowered Alison into the rushing stream. I stubbornly tried to keep my eyes off the bloody hole in her torso. The beithir's tail had punched straight into her stomach, and I didn't have Beannachd Shlàinte to be able to use on her. I didn't dare before the water revived her, anyway.

For a moment, I thought we were too late.

The beithir must have gone straight to the loch, I thought, bile rising in my throat.

But then Alison stirred.

Her eyes fluttered open, and she gasped, flailing against my arms and Eilidh's that held her.

"We need a healer!" I called. "Now!"

My spirit would be enough to cast Slànaich soon, but it would leave me with nothing.

I heard someone clambering down the embankment, and then there was a breathless middle-aged woman wading into the water next to us.

I felt the pull of spirit as she cast a healing spell on Alison, but all I could see was Eilidh's eyes locked with mine.

And then I heard Alison's voice, pulling my gaze away.

"You saved me," she said.

Then she passed out.

The trackers from Oban told us the beithir had headed up Loch Etive, probably to nurse its wounds, but they didn't think it would come back our way. They seemed baffled that it had at all, but considering it had made a beeline for Rhona's parents, I wasn't willing to think that was a simple coincidence. Not even a little bit.

When we got back to Oban, Eilidh and Rhona split off, Rhona with her parents and Eilidh ostensibly to find her family members, which left me one task.

I was sweaty and covered in splatters of beithir venom and loch water, salt from the sea loch leaving little white lines on my trousers where they'd dried. I guessed the anti-water properties of my clothing didn't extend to submersion.

I didn't give a fuck.

Oban wasn't very big, but every step I took towards the

familiar house seemed to come at the expense of leaden legs.

I didn't know what I'd find—I'd asked a couple of the fighters if they knew Iain and Meeksy, but they'd just shrugged and said they weren't from around here.

The beithir had gotten away. That stung more than I wanted to admit. I guess we'd won, but it was a bittersweet victory despite the flashing notifications telling me it had progressed *something*.

That was something to think about later.

Suddenly, there it was in front of me.

It was a typical semi-detached, stone-front house on Ardconnel Road. I'd spent what felt like half my childhood in this house—Iain's mum and mine had been close, and Iain had been my best mate for as long as I could remember.

I walked up the stairs on unsteady legs. It felt so normal —and at the same time, it felt anything but.

They'd painted the door blue since the last time I was there—I had a vague memory of Iain telling me about it.

Somehow, part of me would have rather faced the beithir alone and devoid of spirit completely than knock on the door and not have them answer.

I raised my hand anyway and knocked hard, three times.

Again, time stretched out into nothingness. My brain tried to fill in the gap with every horrid thought it could imagine, from the giant gulls tearing them apart to a monstrous seal or an each-uisge dragging them into Oban's harbour to drown.

Footsteps.

The door clicked as the lock disengaged and opened.

Iain stood on the other side of it.

"Holy fucking shit," he said. "You're late, you wanker."

The next few minutes were a whirlwind of hugs. Despite Iain's rude-sounding greeting, when I stepped over the threshold, he threw his arms around me in a crushing embrace I half expected to break my spine.

Iain was slightly shorter than me, but where I was lanky, he was pure muscle from years of martial arts. His usually short blond hair had grown a bit shaggy, and he sported a couple days of stubble and had the beginnings of bags under his eyes—he looked tired, but his expression was jubilant.

He bellowed at his mum and Meeksy after that, and I was soon treated to just how much of a bear hug a man could give when he'd been a bear *before* the bloody apocalypse, let alone after chucking a bunch of points in Strength. Farid "Meeksy" Meeks was six feet two inches of Iranian-Scottish bulk, and his long black hair didn't have so much as a whisper of silver in it yet. He kept it clubbed back from his face, which was also covered in hair. Meeksy took great pride in his beard; I wasn't sure I'd ever seen him without it. He truly *looked* like a bear of a man, which was both true and hilarious, all things considered.

Catrìona wasn't much better—if I'd thought I'd get off easy after having the innards squeezed out of me by my best mate and his partner like a goddamn tube of toothpaste, I was dead wrong.

Iain's mum had grown up on fishing boats with her family, and she had the muscles to prove it. For the first time in I didn't know how long, my eyes started to prickle as she hugged me.

"We were so worried about you, a ghràidh," she said, pulling back only to brush a couple windblown curls off my face and then throwing her arms around me again.

I was a grown-ass man, but this was the closest thing to family I had left.

When she finally let me go, my eyes were wet. I couldn't believe they were just . . . here.

Catrìona quickly bundled us all into the cosy kitchen, giving me a wee jolt when she heated a kettle for tea with magic like it was nothing.

At my startled look, Meeksy grinned at me, giving Iain's hand an affectionate squeeze. "World may be pants, but we're adapting as best we can."

That spurred the requisite storytelling hour as we had our tea. They described how they'd immediately started working with the town to make sure Oban was safe and the nearly inhuman efforts at organisation that had taken hysterical panic down to a more manageable simmering unease, mostly by leaning in hard to the ascension directive, though they didn't say that in as many words.

People had been helping each other—Iain was a fourth-dan black belt in tae kwon do, so he'd started training people who were interested in hand to hand, and Meeksy, as a nurse, was a natural for a healer class. Catrìona was much the same with her herbalism and knowledge of the sea. It seemed they'd gambled on knowledge as power, and while the three of them were just a hair above level six, they'd managed to give people something to do rather than sitting around panicking that the telly wouldn't work.

For my part, I recounted my journey as best I could, and their expressions all grew darker as I related Lord Bawbag's actions and apparent plans, though I didn't think they were surprised.

The reason they'd not been with the fighters in Connel was that they'd been out all night supporting another group of stealth-based fighters—Iain as a hand-to-hand-based brawler, Catrìona as an alchemist, and Meeksy as a hedge healer—and they'd managed to lay out a series of crafted wards around the perimeter of Oban. Which was, incidentally, how we'd gotten the warning about the beithir.

"You think it'll be back?" Meeksy asked, giving Iain a worried glance.

"Honestly, I'd been afraid that Lord Bawbag had taken it over like he did the stags I mentioned," I said. "I'm not entirely sure he didn't try—Rhona used to work for him, and that monster went straight for her parents."

"That sort of revenge does sound precisely like something he would do," Catrìona said, holding her teacup without sipping it. An errant swirl of steam fluttered around the rim with her exhale, vanishing into nothingness.

"I've not had the chance to look over my notifications yet," I said. "There might be something in there to give us a hint. Eilidh might have some thoughts on that too."

"Who is this Eilidh?" Catrìona asked.

"Susanna's best friend," I said sourly at the same time Meeksy said, "I went to school with her."

I did a double take. I'd completely forgotten about that. For fuck's sake, that was even how I met her and Susanna in the first place. I ought to have remembered.

"Well," Catrìona said, "I hope her friendship with Farid here is more indicative of her character than her friendship with Susanna."

"She's a hundred times the person Susanna is," I said without thinking, and every eye in the room focused on me.

My face began to warm. "She hates my guts, but she's a very good person."

"I don't think she hates your guts," Meeksy said, looking nonplussed.

"Tell her that," I muttered. "Anyway, she's got a class that gives her some good insights into the truth. I told her and Rhona we'd meet back up at the harbour tonight, but I've also got to run back up Soroba Road to get the kitten."

"I can't believe you kidnapped—kit-napped?—Lord Bawbag's cat," Iain said, shaking his head. "Illegal endangered cat, no less."

"Neither can I, mate. Neither can I."

FIFTY-FOUR

The rest of the day veritably flew by. The relief I felt being around my friends and family relaxed something in me that had been tense and tightly wound since that night in my Hyndland flat. Not without reason, but part of me had started to believe I would never relax again. Which wasn't to say things weren't still going to get hairy with Lord Bawbag.

Pretend I didn't put the word "hairy" with "Lord Bawbag"—I was going to give myself nightmares with that image.

Iain and Meeksy came with me to Angus's house to pick up the kitten, and while the walk there was uneventful other than our usual banter, the moment we got there, I could see trouble seeping out of the street.

It was Eliza who greeted us at the door, at first looking concerned to see a pair of burly men—and the gangly one behind them, yours truly—at her door, but the moment she recognised me, she let out a breath.

"I'm glad you're back," she said. "I heard what

happened today, and it's good you're okay, but there's something else you need to know."

That did not sound good.

"Can we come in and get Sailean?" I asked. "You can tell me whatever I need to hear—I take it you've not yet seen Rhona or Eilidh?"

Eliza shook her head, a curtain of straight silver hair rippling with the movement. "Angus has gone to find them, but you've only just missed him, so he may be a wee while yet. But yes, come in."

We stepped inside and all took off our boots before going in much farther, and as we did that, I made introductions, which was interrupted by the skidding sound of tiny claws on hardwoods and the blossoming of a warm little presence in my mind as Sailean came half galloping, half sliding around the corner from down the hall.

"Sorry," Eliza said. "I had the door open because I was playing with her."

Sailean got to my trouser leg and decided that was no obstacle to a mighty kitten, giving a little hop and proceeding to climb up the side of my leg—much to the dismay of the integrity of my skin. I winced as her little claws found purchase in wool and flesh alike and plucked her off my thigh to hold her.

I could practically see Iain and Meeksy itching to give her a pat, but their restraint was admirable.

"What happened?" I asked once Sailean was settled on my shoulder and Iain's hand twitched towards her as if it was reflexive.

"The second group from Kilninver never arrived," Eliza said. "We sent some scouts out that way at midday, but none have returned."

My decent mood evaporated, and it felt like someone had touched hoarfrost to my veins.

"What?" I said. "Should the scouts have been back by now?"

"Aye," she said. "If they're not back by sundown, we'll have to either send someone else after them or post more sentries on that side of town just in case."

"Shit," Iain said. "Who was leading the scout group? Was it Benji?"

Eliza blinked at that. "Yes, I think so. You know him?"

Iain and Meeksy exchanged a glance with me. "He's one of the few level tens we have. Absolute monster in a fight—he took down a fuath singlehandedly two days ago in Loch Etive."

From Eliza's confused look, I didn't think she knew what a fuath was, but I definitely did. "And we know the beithir was in Connel, so this Benji probably didn't run into that, but it could have been the other two of Bawbag's henchmen—they would have been almost impossible for him to face alone."

"We stay near the harbour in Ardconnel Street," Meeksy said to her. "I think we should head back there and see if we can regroup with Calum's friends—from what it sounds like, they're now among the top-level fighters we've got in Oban, and we're easier to get to there."

Eliza nodded. "I take it those things you mentioned are difficult enemies."

"They're literal monsters," I said, suppressing a shiver at the thought of the fuath. "Like straight-outta-folklore monsters. Terrifying doesn't even begin to scratch the surface."

The older woman blanched, but she recovered quickly, nodding as if ticking off boxes on a mental checklist. "I know where my Angus will be going, so I'll find him and bring him back to the house. You should all try to find Eilidh and Rhona, and we'll all discuss then what to do. The few people who did make it here from Kilninver with you last night are beside themselves."

"I don't blame them," I said bleakly. "I just wish more people had come last night."

Sailean's tiny claws dug into my shoulder as if to punctuate my sentence.

No sooner did we get back to the Whyte house—that was always a wee joke with us growing up—than Meeksy and Iain left me to look over my notifications.

"We can find Eilidh and Rhona," Meeksy assured me. "We'll bring them back here—you need to find out anything you can from this system in the meantime."

That's how I found myself in my old guest room upstairs, lying on the bed with Sailean on my lap.

"Here goes," I said to her. She simply purred, kneading away at my stomach.

Quest updated: Defend Oban

In your travels, you have pieced together a danger that threatens not only the immediate vicinity of Loch Awe but, more widely, the town of Oban.

You have driven off the beithir, which seemed to go right for Rhona's family members—an eerie coincidence and one you have rightly deduced to not be a coincidence at all. While Connel is safe for the present, the beithir is not dead, and as long as it lives, it is a threat.

In Oban, you have found the first of your people and discovered what they have been doing throughout the early days of the ascension. They will be strong allies in the coming days.

You have already observed that Lord Sackington employs ruthless measures upon those he deems a nuisance or a threat—but even his brute strength can be neutralised by those working in the spirit of the ascension directive.

Objectives:

-Reach Oban (Complete)

-Seek out the following inhabitants who are most likely to believe your story:

-Catrìona and Iain Whyte and Farid "Meeksy" Meeks (Complete)

-Ross and Jo MacIntosh (Complete)

-Ruaraidh and Ciorstaidh Smith (Complete)

-Jack Miller (Complete)

-Tina Dunlop

-Convince at least twenty fighters of level five or above of the threat (5/20)

-Formulate a plan to defend Oban

Rewards:

-Experience (commensurate with current level progression)

-1 item (ascension dependent)

-1 skill point

-5 attribute points

-???

That told me that we were on the right track, but I really couldn't be sure.

Hadn't we also unlocked the next stage of the Hills Have Eyes quest? I thought we had when we finished the second stage.

Even as I thought it, it popped up in my vision.

You have discovered a quest!

   The Hills Have Eyes: Part III

   While defending Oban is personal to you, there is more at stake than simply the town itself. You have seen with your own eyes what is possible to do in an ascended world when the ascension directive does not yet hold weight with the people.

   But it is clear you still hold the attention of Lord Sackington —every time you thwart him, his hatred of you grows.

   Continue on your path of ascension. Do not grow complacent. More than lives depends on your actions.

   Objectives:

   -Complete your personal quest (Calum Green)

   -Complete your personal quest (Eilidh MacIntosh)

   -Complete your personal quest (Rhona Smith) (Complete)

   -Work together to craft infused armour (6 sets) (Calum Green, Eilidh MacIntosh)

   -Create alchemical solutions to aid your party (6 sets) (Rhona Smith)

   Reward:

   -1 skill point

   -5 attribute points

   -1 item (ascension dependent)

   -All cooldowns reset

That reminded me—I had to have gotten to completion range of my personal quest. And I thought I knew what I wanted to name my staff.

   Brac-Meanmna.

   I couldn't have translated it to English if I tried, not

with the nuance it required. In Gaelic, it alluded to imagination, to mac-meanmna. In my mind, it was a wave of spirit. It was the clash of antlers in autumn, the strength of an arm. It was the spark of imagination, spirit, heart.

It brought to mind the hart I had purified, his antlers strong and proud. He had survived and come out stronger. It felt fitting for a living weapon.

Even as I thought it, something dawned on me. *Yes.*

Hart's Heart. That was the English I needed for it. It was no literal translation, not even close, but it fit. My notifications flashed again, slightly brighter as I was learning they did when there was something new.

Personal quest complete!

Having created Earth's first living weapon—two others have since joined you in this distinction, one in Kenya and one in Thailand—you as yet have little comprehension of what you have done.

Myriad factors contribute to the creation of a living weapon, not least of which is luck. But most ascended worlds agree that the ability of a crafter to create a living weapon increases with experience not because the experience itself increases the likelihood but because, through experience, the crafter must by necessity learn to connect with their crafting materials.

This means understanding, intuiting, and actively forming a relationship with the world around them, something that is an insurmountable feat for many or most people, even in traditional ascended worlds.

Some believe living weapons respond to need; others believe it is the soul of the crafter. The statistics with which we describe the chances of creating a living weapon are, therefore, not the same for everyone—they are merely the most logical expression of what we find in ascended worlds across the known universe: that the ability to connect with one's world is precious and rare.

Yours is the first in your world. As such, it is already a legend, though it is new and untried.

You must get to know it the way you would any other mind: with diligence, patience, and an open heart.

Objectives:

-Commune with your living weapon (Complete—You listened to your weapon in the heat of battle. Continue to do this, and you will be rewarded.)

-Practise with your living weapon for three days (3/3) (Complete)

-Name your living weapon: Brac-Meanmna (Complete)

Rewards:

-2 items (ascension dependent): The Flow of Spirit: A Mind-Body Connection. Rooted Between Realities: Foundational Staff Technique

-Affinity: Staves

You have unlocked an affinity: Staves

Those *books.* I couldn't afford to waste any time—I mentally reached for the staff technique manual first, bracing for the onslaught of information.

I was nowhere near prepared.

Before, the information I'd absorbed had only been a bit of muscle memory. But this? This was combat technique.

My body seized up like every single muscle I had went into spasm at once. Dimly, I was aware of Sailean's startled mew as she vaulted off my lap and onto the bed, but beyond that, I couldn't focus on anything but the sudden pain.

It was as if ten thousand hours of practise took effect at once, and as I lay there, muscle fibres screaming in agony, I wasn't sure I'd ever move again, let alone fight.

Time bled together as images and memories wove into my own. The centrifugal force of a spin, the feeling of successfully stopping a strike before impact. Feet learning step by painstaking step the need for proper balance and grounding. The way two staves meeting in combat sent vibrations ricocheting up one's arms.

And beyond learning how to use a staff as an actual physical weapon, there was the magic. Oh, there was the magic.

A thousand thousand memories of movement with spirit and breath, each and every one taken with deliberation and care over and over to ensure that, in the moments it counted most, they would flow like water down a hill. They would become their own gravity that pulled me back to the right way.

By the time the rush abated, my entire body still screamed, but I felt elated. Before, I'd basically been using my living weapon as a glorified walking stick. I'd barely considered how to use it, let alone tried to be intentional about it.

Now I would.

Against my own better judgement, I went for the second book too.

This one was less intense physically, but what it lacked in simulated—or real—lactic acid, it made up for in mental strain.

I was thankful I had already unlocked Freumhan,

because without that, it might have actually given me a stroke.

My brain throbbed with the torrent of knowledge; the book seemed to tear open new pathways by brute force, and even more, when it reached the aspects of mind-body practical connection, I could feel where it lit up the pathways from the book on staff technique.

I was covered in sweat by the time it was done—which, naturally, was when everyone else turned up at the house.

D ownstairs was crowded when I arrived, and I was relieved to see both Eilidh and Rhona. Eilidh was sitting in easy comfort with Meeksy, every so often leaning over to bump her shoulder with his, which gave me an odd sense of . . . jealousy? Meeksy and Iain had been together for years, and besides, Iain was the bi one. Meeksy had zero interest in women—well, to tell the truth, in anyone but Iain.

I wasn't sure what rubbed me the wrong way about her affection. Maybe it was what we'd been through in the past few days, literally seeing the raw meat of her chest before the system healed her.

Rhona, though, she was in fine form.

I could already tell Catrìona wanted to adopt her, though I wasn't sure what Rhona's parents would have to say about that. Angus and Eliza both didn't quite seem to know what to do with Rhona.

"We're just waiting on a couple other people—Mairead and Ronald are due any minute," Angus said to me when I went up to him. "I know a couple of the MacIvers are gathering a second team to go out to Kilninver. They'd gotten that started before I even got into town, so the real question is if you'll send anyone with them."

"Got it," I told him.

Just then, there was a knock at the door, a hesitant one.

"I'll get it," I called to Catrìona, and I excused myself to Angus, moving back across the house to answer the door.

Alison was on the other side.

She looked so uncertain, I immediately felt terrible for her.

"Come in," I told her. "Are Mairead and Ronald with you?"

She stepped through the door, tripping over someone's shoes. "They're on their way. I—erm. I wanted to talk to you, actually."

With a quick glance around, she motioned towards the empty lounge, which connected with the dining room through a double glass door, which was closed, shielded from the dining room's line of sight with a flimsy lace curtain.

"Okay," I said, following after Alison.

She moved to sit down on the loveseat, so I sat on the sofa, but before she lowered herself, she came over and sat by me instead.

"I needed to say thank you," she said. "You saved my life."

"It wasn't just me," I said automatically. "Eilidh—"

"You saved my *life*," she repeated. "I thought I could be brave and fight that thing, but it—it was horrible."

"It was," I said, shifting uncomfortably.

"It killed that other bloke like it was nothing," Alison said, shuddering.

To my chagrin, her eyes were full of tears. I glanced

towards the dining room, but that stupid lace curtain was in the way, so I couldn't see anyone. I didn't know why I was so uncomfortable—Alison was a perfectly nice, very pretty young woman.

But the way she was looking at me made me feel like I was about to be gilded and set up on top of a giant fucking pedestal, and that was the last thing I needed right now.

Almost as if she'd heard me, she threw her arms around me.

I returned the hug awkwardly, trying to pull away after a moment. She smelled like sea air and leather, and I couldn't for the life of me figure out why that sparked resentment in me.

"Calum," she said when I finally managed to extricate myself, "you have no idea how thankful I am."

"It's all right," I said. "I would have done the same for anyone."

This, apparently, was the wrong thing to say.

Alison burst into tears and flung herself into my arms again.

I did not know what the fuck to do.

She was clearly experiencing some sort of post-traumatic something or other, but I was neither a therapist nor a friend, not really. But I guessed I could be a shoulder to quite literally cry on. I would just need to have a long talk with Iain about how to set some bloody boundaries after this.

He and Meeksy were always good at the communication stuff. I'd joked for ages that they should start their own advice column.

I lost track of how long I sat there, awkwardly patting Alison's shoulder every so often as my own got wetter and wetter. I guessed my set bonus also didn't really work on tears and snot.

At some point, the front door opened and slammed, but since no one came to get me, I figured it wasn't Mairead and Ronald. The sky started to darken outside the window, and finally, I had to gently push Alison away or I was going to have a crick in my neck worse than absorbing the knowledge from the bloody ascension-given book.

"You must think I'm disgusting," she said through sniffles as I reached out and grabbed a box of hankies for her.

"I think we're all under a lot of stress right now," I said. "Will you be all right now? I need to go find out what the deal is with the others."

Alison gave me a tremulous nod. "Come back when you're done?"

"I'll try," I said, dread pooling in my belly.

I made my way back through the house, where everyone—including Mairead and Ronald—were gathered.

"What the fuck happened to your shoulder, mate?" Iain muttered when I walked up to him.

"Long story," I replied under my breath. I looked around the room and realised it wasn't actually everyone. "Where's Eilidh?"

"Oh, she went off with the MacIvers," Eliza said. "She's going to help them look for the scouts and the Kilninver people."

"What? When did they leave?" I asked.

"About forty minutes ago?" Ronald said, glancing at his watch, which was analog and I guess still worked. "You were . . . occupied."

"Fuck, I should go after her," I said, looking around for Rhona, who was staring at me with an odd expression on her face, halfway between a scowl and confusion. How the hell had it been forty minutes of me sitting there since I heard the door slam?

All at once, I realised that the door slamming had to have been Eilidh leaving, and I hadn't even *heard* the others coming in. My face warmed at the implication in Ronald's tone. *You were . . . occupied.*

"I'm going after her," I said. "Rhona—"

"Yeah, yeah, I'm ready, and I was here for the briefing, so I know the route they're taking."

"Calum, love," Catrìona began, frowning.

"It's not safe out there. None of us know what they're walking into better than me and Rhona," I said, interrupting her before she could go on. "I—"

I broke off, suddenly feeling like a buoy with no rope attached, floating pointlessly out to sea.

"We'll go too," Meeksy said with a glance at Iain. "Give us two minutes."

"What if we need you here?" Angus challenged me. "If you're best equipped to deal with a threat that comes, what happens if you don't make it back?"

"If she doesn't make it back, I'll be useless anyway," I said flatly, the sting of truth in my words like getting slapped in the face with a bushel of nettles. "Meeksy and Iain, meet us outside. Sailean's upstairs—she'll need a bottle and—"

"I'll deal with it, a ghràidh," Catrìona said, an unreadable expression on her face. "Go."

Alison wasn't in the lounge when Rhona and I exited, for which I was grateful, but I hadn't heard her leave either. I did not have time to think about that.

Outside, the wind was brisk in the falling dark.

"You two are absolutely bizarre," Rhona said, peering at me. "You know, I should have figured it out sooner."

"What are you on about?" I asked her irritably.

"At first I thought maybe she really did hate you, but that's bullshit. This, though?" Rhona waved her hand in the air, gesturing vaguely at the house. "Now I get it."

"What. Are. You. On. About."

"Eilidh doesn't hate you, you muckle bam of a man," Rhona said. "I think it might be herself she hates. But you? She's in love with you."

I just stared at her.

True to their word, Meeksy and Iain came out the door just then, and I could barely tear my gaze away from Rhona to look up at them.

"What just happened?" Iain said, peering down at me.

"I told him Eilidh's in love with him," Rhona said breezily. "Let's go!"

With that, she spun on her heel and slipped into a shadow, out of sight in an instant.

"Oh, that." Meeksy looked at me sideways. "Aye, that's why she bolted when she saw you and that bird making out in the lounge through the door."

"*What?*" I said. "I absolutely did not make out with her—she practically threw herself into my lap crying. I was trying to escape that whole time without being a total dick, and—"

"Mate, no judgement either way," Iain said, eyeing Meeksy askance.

"Some judgement," Meeksy said to me. "But that's only because Eilidh's one of my oldest friends, and if you hurt her, I will personally chuck you into the harbour next time a mutated basking shark shows up."

Mutated—no, not getting sidetracked.

"Are you three going to sit there all day with your mouths hanging open or are you going to help me make sure our two twitterpated frenemies don't end up Romeo and Juliet-ing themselves out of making out?" Rhona called from somewhere up the street. "Because I know where my vote is. I've always shipped them."

"How did you put up with this for days on end?" Iain asked, stepping into gear and lengthening his stride to catch up with Rhona.

"Honestly, I don't know. It got worse each time I saved her life," I said.

"I heard that!"

"We're family—if you're going to dish it out, you better take it!" I called back to her.

Her answering giggle was like a peal of bells.

"Forty minutes' head start," Meeksy said. "Can we close that gap?"

"Depends," I replied. "You gotten any better at running?"

Meeksy let out an explosive breath through his nose, making his beard ripple.

Despite every warring emotion in my chest, I laughed, a brittle laugh. "No time like the present."

An hour later, we'd seen no sign of them.

It was as if they'd vanished right off the map.

Despite Meeksy's huffing and puffing, we'd made amazing time, and we were already back to Kilninver— which had become a ghost town.

There wasn't a light in a single house we passed. Not one.

"Fuck," said Iain. "I do not like the looks of this."

"You're telling me," Meeksy muttered, wheezing slightly.

We turned south with the A816, and after another minute of jogging, I saw a light.

Even as it registered, Rhona appeared, and all memory of her previous mirth had vanished.

"The school" was all she said.

I burst into a run.

The end of the school facing us was covered in dark smears, and without even a thought, I poured spirit into my staff, illuminating it with pure, white light.

It wasn't dark—it was red.

Like someone had finger-painted with blood.

There was a crude drawing of a woman, with special care given to her long, red hair.

And beside it was what looked like two hastily done eyes with an equals sign between them.

The message was clear enough.

They'd taken her.

Eye for an eye—Eilidh for Rhona.

An exclamation from Meeksy followed by a moan of dismay told me all I needed to know. The rest of the team Eilidh'd come with lay just around the corner. Iain went to see, and a moment later, I heard him retching into a hedge.

"Calum," Rhona said in a small voice. "This is my fault. I shouldn't have run away from him."

"Don't ever say that again." The tone in my voice made her freeze, and I tried to soften it when I turned to look at her. "You didn't do this. This was not your fault. This is *his* fault. This is all his fault."

Iain came over, wiping his mouth with the back of his hand. "He's right."

Meeksy put his hand on Iain's shoulder.

"Calum?" Iain said.

The staff in my hand was glowing, but I wasn't doing it. It pulled at me, asking me for something I couldn't quite understand. My anger, my guilt.

That was it. Guilt.

I hadn't been able to articulate what I felt for Eilidh until she was gone, and now there was a hole I'd filled in with guilt.

The staff's resonance picked up in frequency, thrumming through me, through the carpark beneath my feet, through the threads of spirit that flowed in and around me.

"Calum," Iain said with more urgency. "What are you doing?"

"People aren't possessions," I said through gritted teeth, and my staff *sang out*, lighting the air with swirls of blue-green magic.

Just as I was about to let it loose, I saw something else, and my magic faltered.

It was something simple, a mere inkblot in blood, like someone had purposely pressed a bleeding wound against the wall once, twice, three times. Each slightly less bloody, like when we were kids and dipped potato halves in paint to make stamps. I remembered a certain conversation I'd had with Eilidh all too well.

Who the fuck would make an inkblot on the side of a building next to a distorted pictogram of themself?

Someone who wanted to send a message, all right. One message. For one person. It's not that often that Rorschach tests come up in casual conversation.

"She's not out in the wilds with the bad guys," I said, barely above a breath. "They're stuck out there with *her*."

"What?" Iain squinted in the direction I was looking, his face screwed up in confusion.

"I said she's not out there *with* them." The more I looked at the triune blot of blood, the more it looked deliberate. Fast, but effective. Incisive. Hell, I wouldn't have put it past her to methodically press her own wound up against that whitewashed wall to get this point across. "She left us a message so we'd know they didn't take her. She got away. And she went after them."

"How exactly do you know this?" Meeksy asked dubiously.

"When we were captured together at Lord Bawbag's, we had a moment where we talked about a comic series where an antihero gets locked up in prison with all the guys he put there," I said, watching comprehension dawn on Meeksy's face. Iain, though, just turned to look at me.

"Explain," he said.

To my surprise, Rhona sauntered over and gave him a hearty smack on the back.

"Eilidh's saying that *she's* the dangerous one—not whoever's trying to trick us into thinking they've captured her," Rhona said. "I didn't take Eilidh for a comics fan. She's full of surprises."

"Look who's talking," I muttered, then cleared my throat to speak more audibly. "Eilidh knew we'd see this and think they took her—hell, I bet that's what they wanted us to think so we'd rush after her. But she's saying they didn't get her. She's saying she got away . . . and she's not going to lose their trail."

"Have I ever mentioned how absolutely *terrifying* Eilidh is?" Iain said under his breath to Meeksy.

"Wait'll you see her with her claymore," I told him. A lopsided grin took hold on my face. Hell.

"So what are we going to do?" Iain asked, staring at me as if he'd never seen me before.

Now I let my magic gather again, but this time it wasn't pure fury fuelling it. It was something brighter, something far more powerful. It was the resolve of knowing Eilidh could and would handle herself but that together with the rest of us? We'd be unstoppable.

Blue-green fire lit the length of my staff, spirit pouring into me in waves. I felt it suffuse my channels, moving throughout my body in ever-expanding rivulets that turned into a torrent.

I looked at my friends—friends who were the only family I had. "We're going to find whoever she's hunting, and we're going to help her with whatever made her tear off after them alone, and then we're going to help *her* serve them justice however she sees fit."

I grounded my staff in front of me, where it struck the surface of the carpark with a sub-audible *boom* that I felt more than heard.

There was a gargantuan creak and a groan from the school, and the horrid finger-painting, the hedges around it, the bodies behind it—all of it began to shake.

I couldn't tell where the spirit was coming from; my personal well did not deplete. But as Iain and Meeksy scrambled back in alarm, tugging Rhona with them, the walls collapsed inward with a sharp report, sending a wave of dust in billowing clouds outward from the impact.

And something at the centre of that downward movement broke through, not going down, but climbing up, up, up.

I didn't need to see it. I cast Connection, drawing as deeply as I could upon my memories of Eilidh—her smell like herbs and lilac, the tang of her sweat after a fight, the flash of her blue eyes, her rage and her exhaustion and her rare, beautiful laugh.

I could have pointed to her on the other side of the galaxy.

But she was far, far closer than that, and I had my family beside me.

"That way," I said, raising my arm to point to the south.

I didn't wait to see if they were following. I didn't need to.

Behind us, from the rubble of Kilninver Primary School, an enormous oak sprang free of the earth, reaching for the sky.

AFTERWORD

Thank you so much for reading *The Transcendent Green*! Keep reading for a sneak peek of the next book in this series, *The Ascendent Sky*—the first chapter is right after this wee note.

If you've come here via *Terra Incognita*, a mahoosive thanks for following me north to Scotland. Will's journey will return this winter, first at my Patreon and a few weeks later at Reddit Serials. If you've not yet read *Terra Incognita*, you can find that here! It was written as part of the Inkfort Press Publishing Derby, and as such, it's quite short, but I originally intended it as a prequel . . . and it grew legs on me. How very dare.

If you're new to LitRPG, there are some great places for you to get your fix! Try the LitRPG Books group on Facebook to chat with fellow readers and authors!

I've had an absolute blast writing in this world, and I really wanted to bring LitRPG to my homeland. Figured it'd be good craic, and I think that proves true. Calum isn't so much a pathetic hamster now, I reckon—I'm stoked to see where he goes from here.

Speaking of which, you won't have to wait too long to find out. Turn the page for the first taste . . .

SNEAK PEEK AT THE ASCENDENT SKY

A sneak peek at the next instalment of Calum Green's story, The Ascendent Sky.

I had to hand it to Eilidh.

How she'd been so certain I would come after her was a question I'd need to ask as soon as I caught up with her, but that was moot for now.

The intricate glyphs of spirit she'd laid out like bread-crumbs for us to follow, though? *That* was not moot. That was art.

I'd travelled with her for days on end, fought side by side with her in life-or-death battles gu leòr, and she knew for a fact that I used Connection almost constantly. More than that, she was familiar with the signature of my spirit. She knew I'd be the one looking for her.

She'd counted on it.

Every time I cast the spell, tendrils of spirit caught her golden glyphs. On tree trunks, on the winter-browned bracken just starting to give way to spring growth, on boulders—Eilidh had thoroughly and meticulously given us a path to follow, keyed specifically to me and me alone.

I wasn't ready to unpack that, so instead I just stayed glued to her trail like a goddamn magical bloodhound.

For three days we'd trekked away from Oban after working so hard to reach the town in the first place. We'd made it into the depths of a pine forest after skirting the northern edge of Loch Avich, and once we came out the other side, we'd once again be on the edge of Loch Awe, though this time on the western shore.

The forest would have felt oppressive, dense evergreens crowding in on us as we frantically searched. I had a vague memory of a deciduous forest on the western edge of Loch Awe, where at least the lack of leaves on the March trees would let more sunlight filter in, but for the present, that didn't matter. Instead, it just felt eerily quiet—all that mattered was that I knew there was a thread of magic connecting me to who we sought. I would have been tearing my hair out if Eilidh had actually been captured by Lord Edwin Thomas Sackington's arsehole thugs, but Eilidh was as canny as she was dangerous.

Which is to say *very*.

A fact that my best mates' banter behind me was trying to diminish as they cartoonishly argued over what her D and D class would be.

"Cleric," Iain was saying stubbornly.

"With that strength stat?" Rhona snorted, somehow right behind my ear, making both Iain and Meeksy jump—the teenage girl hadn't hit her second decade of life yet, but her own class was wraith, and none of us could ever really be sure where she was if she hadn't chosen to be visible.

Meeksy craned his neck to look for Rhona but gave up

quickly, tossing his shiny black ponytail of hair over his shoulder. "The kid's right—"

"Not a kid!" came Rhona's voice, from farther away that time.

"—Eilidh's a paladin or I'm a block of tofu," Meeksy finished.

"She's neither," I said. Irritation threatened to overtake me. "She's a dìonadair. And Lord Bawbag's goons are going to drop the forest on our heads if *you* goons don't shut yer gobs."

"Well, chuck me in the steamer and call me edamame," Meeksy muttered. "How come she gets the Gaelic class?"

This was going to give me a migraine.

"If I ever encounter someone from the Ascended Alliance, I promise to ask them how they make linguistic decisions," I said. "Now, if we could—"

I didn't get a chance to finish my sentence because Iain's arm cracked me across the sternum, stopping me in my tracks.

Ow.

Armour or no, my oldest mate had an arm like a bloody steel girder.

By now, we'd all learnt the rules of this ascended world.

Number one: if someone stops you in the wilds, shut up first, whinge later.

Number two: anything is possible.

As I followed Iain's gaze through the dense forest's tree cover, I immediately saw why he'd brought my talking and our movement to an abrupt halt.

Spunkies, as they'd be called in Scots. Sionnachain in Gaelic. And in English, glowing lights in the wilds were usually best known as Will o' the Wisps. And Jack o' the Lantern, before that got co-opted by the Americans as something you make with a pumpkin and a candle. My mum had still kept to the traditional turnips.

But the bluish light through the green of the dim forest afternoon was neither pumpkin nor turnip related. No, this was just a glow, aloft where it shouldn't be, drifting like thistledown on a nonexistent breeze.

Not just one, either.

A ragtag line of them led off into the woods, in the opposite direction to where we were tracking Eilidh's glyphs.

After a moment, Rhona appeared, looking exasperated. Her brown hair was plaited back from her face, but there was a bit of moss clinging to a spot just behind her ear. What on earth had she been doing?

"Why'd you stop?" she asked, then simply looked in the direction all of us were staring. "Oh. Never mind."

We all stood there, watching the wisps float through the darkened woods.

"Reckon we have two options," Iain said. "We can follow them and either wander pointlessly all night or run into some ascended monster out of nightmare itself, which could bite us in the arse . . . or we ignore them and go on our merry way and possibly leave something to flank us, which could more literally bite us in the arse."

Knowing it might be futile for decision-making purposes, I cast Connection, expecting only to see Eilidh's glyphs . . . except the one I'd found last was nowhere to be seen. I turned to seek out the last one—she'd been diligent about keeping them in easy line of sight. But it was as if they'd never been there at all. Not even so much as a spark of spirit lit up gold.

"Shit," I said.

"Uh-oh." Meeksy shifted his broad shoulders and turned to eye me askance.

"I think the decision might have just been made for us," I said slowly. "Whatever this is, it seems to have somehow erased Eilidh's glyphs."

Rhona's eyebrows drew together in worry, and she opened her mouth, pausing before she seemed to think better of speaking altogether and shut it again with the click of teeth.

My entire midsection wanted to revolt at the very thought of losing Eilidh's trail, but if I let that take me over now, we might never make it out of these woods.

"Whatever those wisps are, it's too much of a coincidence to presume they're acting independently of the disappearance of the glyphs." Correlation wasn't causation, but it would be a muckle leap to think two bizarre occurrences out of the blue had happened at the exact same time without being related. When the others nodded, I went on. "Which means something wants us to follow the wisps. Whether they want to eat us or talk to us, though—that's the question."

"Calum," Rhona said, as if she were speaking to a thick-headed toddler, "have you met *literally anything* yet that just wanted to talk to us and not eat us?"

"Sailean," I said promptly. "And the stags, and the horses. The pigeon that flew our message back to Oban."

"You're stretching the definition of 'talk' to breaking point there, mate," Iain muttered. "But fair play. Not everything wants to eat us."

"If this whatever-it-is wanted to eat us, it could probably think of a more fun way to go about it than sending us on a wild goose chase through the woods," Meeksy agreed. "Though mythologically speaking, I guess plenty of monsters thought that was a cracking good time, so who knows?"

Feeling like it was probably as in vain as the first attempt, I cast Connection again, this time focusing more on the wisps themselves. I tried to keep myself from panicking about losing Eilidh's trail.

The others' bickering faded into a hum as I quieted my mind, breathing with the flows of spirit around me. My new affinity was called Synthesis, and I could almost *feel* it as it worked in the background of my Nature affinity's passives. Gu h-Ìosal. Gu h-Àrd. All things below, all things above.

Taobh a-Muigh. Taobh a-Staigh.

Inside. Outside.

Spirit connected me to all of it.

And through that, a burning ember of pathos, almost too faint to see in the glowing wisps of . . . will.

Will.

I almost laughed when it clicked—*Will o' the bloody Wisps* indeed.

Gingerly, I felt for that thread of spirit that was my spell, prodded it until it came in contact with the nearest wisp.

The moment it did, I lost my breath.

Connection dropped away, leaving me dumbfounded as the patter of my pals' banter swam back into focus in my ears.

"Hey," Rhona was saying, looking at me even as she waved an impatient hand in Iain's face. "I said *hey*!"

At that, both Iain and Meeksy halted their back-and-forth bickering about the nature of ascended creatures' motivations, and they both turned to stare at me.

"Well," I said, clearing my throat when my voice

cracked awkwardly on the word, "I guess every day's a school day."

"What the hell is that supposed to mean?" Iain asked, exasperated.

"It means we've just stumbled across the first ascended being who *does* just want to talk to us." I pointed towards the line of wisps, the certainty of that brief contact with the creature's will filling me with both eagerness and trepidation. "We'll find Eilidh's trail again afterwards."

"You're sure," Meeksy said. "Because if this thing tries to eat us and we end up dying and abandoning Eilidh to Lord Bawbag and the parade of sphincters he calls flunkies—"

"Believe me." I interrupted him before he could get farther than that. I did not want to think about Lord Bawbag or sphincters of any kind. "If I thought that was going to happen, I would be high-tailing it in the other direction."

"What exactly did it . . . say to you?" Rhona said, peering at me with an uncomfortable amount of trust in her brown eyes.

"It didn't say anything—I felt their intentions." I swallowed, shaking off the sense of just how daft that sounded and how hard everyone here would have laughed if I'd said such a thing a month ago. More to the point, everything in me screamed that I should trust this instinct. "All I know is that we don't want to ignore this invitation."

With that, I straightened my shoulders and started off towards the nearest blue glow, which gave a sudden surprised hiccough of movement, followed by a whirl that looked suspiciously joyous.

Brave new world, was it?

What on earth were we going to encounter now?

CALUM'S STATS AND SPELLS

Name: Calum Green
Age: 36
Level: 9
Class: Draoidh (Further class specialisation at: Level 27)
Affinities: Nature (Level 6), Healing (Level 4), Synthesis (Level 1), Staves
(Level 1)
Specialised Affinities: Wild (Level 3)

Alteration:
Strength: 12
Dexterity: 17
Agility: 19
Mind: 39

Regeneration:
Constitution: 18
Stamina: 26

Manipulation:
Spirit: 40
Pathos: 22
Will: 31

Boons: Blessings

* * *

*Beannachd Shlàinte (Level 3)—This skill can be used once per day to heal a
severe injury of tissue trauma and infection. You gain an increased affinity
for Healing, allowing you to intuit what is necessary to save lives of humans
and animals alike.*

*Increased use of this skill allows for more complex healing, including but not
limited to: internal haemorrhaging, progressive disease, antivenin formulation, purging toxins, and limb regrowth. Additionally, greater knowledge of
the body's anatomy and physiology makes you more effective in combat.*

Through your growing Synthesis affinity, you have combined this spell with others to great effect, and your increasing understanding has cut the cooldown time by 50%.

Affinity: Healing

Skill Tree: Slàinte

Caidreabhas—*This skill is a foundational one in the Tàthadh tree, but it is not one to be used lightly. Caidreabhas, like Tàth, forms a consensual bond with an animal companion, but unlike Tàth, this bond is permanent and will persist until your death or that of your companion.*

Many animals in an ascended world stretch past their previous limits, often ranging from sentience to outright sapience, in time. Caidreabhas encourages such growth in your companion, bolstering the animal's natural strength and adaptability as well as their intelligence.

Unlike most active skills, Caidreabhas will not level, as for it to do so would cause first bonds to eventually lose their appeal with the ability to form more complex bonds. Instead, Caidreabhas evolves—with each animal you bond, your relationship with your companion will shift depending entirely upon what you invest in it.

Your current abilities allow you: 1 companion

Affinity: Nature

Skill Tree: Tàthadh

Connection (Level 5)—*You gain a deeper affinity to the earth and its needs, and it whispers to you. With this skill, you are able to see how things around you interact, be it the tracks of a deer hunted by paw prints of a stalking cat or the passing of a band of hunters.*

Increased use of this skill enables you to take in an entire scene at a glance and appropriately assess its secrets. Additionally, the skill will allow you to ascertain the needs of the natural world, giving you the power to aid creatures and plants that may one day return the favour.

Your use has granted you a bonus to clarity. Your ability to see and identify patterns has increased, and you are now 12% more likely to spot items of import, foes in stealth, and escape routes.

Affinity: Nature

Skill Tree: Nature

Cumhachd (Level 3)—*This spell is one of the most versatile in the hedge witch's arsenal. By tapping into the ambient spirit that surrounds you to augment your own, you are able to form missiles based upon your environment. Not only does this spell shift dramatically from mage to mage, but it also* *enhances your acquisition of points in Spirit. This ability is bolstered by and best used within your existing affinities, but it also rewards creativity.*

Continued use may unlock additional benefits and upgrades. As with all things in an ascended world, the limits are your own imagination. (ch23)

Affinity: Synthesis, Nature

Skill Tree: Arcane

Fuaran—*Like its name, Fuaran is a skill that brings with it a wellspring of refreshment. This skill increases your spirit regeneration by a base of 20% for 3 minutes, and if comrades are within 10 meters of you, it will also do the same for them.*

Increased use of this skill will increase its efficacy and area of effect and may also bestow other boons that can benefit you and your party. (ch23)

Affinity: Arcane

Skill Tree: Arcane

Gu h-Àrd (Passive)—*You gain an understanding of all things above the earth: the currents of the air, the patterns of the clouds, and those that make their home therein. You receive an immediate +2 to Mind and a bonus to calling upon the powers of weather, wind, and creatures of the heavens. With experience, you may also summon the storm.*

While Gu h-Àrd will not increase in levels as active spells will, your understanding of magic will, on occasion, trigger evolution.

Affinity: Nature, Synthesis

Skill Tree: Nature

Gu h-Ìosal (Passive)—*You gain an understanding of all things below the earth: the waters that flow, the roots that grow, and those that make their home therein. You receive an immediate +2 to Mind and a bonus to calling on the powers of flora and earth-bound fauna. With experience, you may also free the forest to do your bidding.*

While Gu h-Ìosal will not increase in levels as active spells will, your understanding of magic will, on occasion, trigger evolution.

Affinity: Nature, Synthesis

Skill Tree: Nature

Keen Eye (Level 3)—*This ability allows you to examine an item, foe, or location, and in conjunction with Connection, it can reveal secrets or vital clues that will push you towards helpful information. Keen Eye comes with a one-time bonus to Mind of +1.*

Continued usage will improve the complexity and usefulness of the information

Keen Eye provides. As your knowledge of its uses has grown, you have discovered the boons to this subtle skill. As with many worthwhile things, you get out of it what you put into it.
Affinity: Synthesis
Skill Tree: Arcane

Purifire *(Level 6)—This skill is most used in combat, instilling basic fire with the power of the arcane, making it burn hotter and brighter than typical flame—and all within the mage's control. This fire is not friendly fire in more than one way. Magic is will and intent, and it will strike only your foes. While a staff is needed for advanced use, this skill can be wielded without need for a weapon.*
Increased use of Purifire allows for more complex use. Many mages utilise it with metal weapons to great effect, adding burning damage and spirit damage to physical. Others prefer a staff's elegance and the advanced precision a mage finds therein. At its heart, this skill moulds itself to its wielder, and only the mage can decide its limits.
You have discovered the utility of this offensive skill in using it not only against your opponents but also to control your environment. As such, you have gained the upgrade Ring of Fire, which you can use to encircle your foes.
Increased use of Purifire allows for more complex use. Your use of it has been diverse, from illumination to cleansing to combat, and you are only scratching the surface of its potential. At its heart, this skill moulds itself to its wielder, and only the mage can decide its limits.
(upgrades: Ring of Fire, Fist of Flame)
Affinity: Nature, Staves
Skill Tree: Arcane

Slànaich *(Level 2)—A basic healing spell, Slànaich provides a general increase to inherent healing in both speed and duration. While it will not stave off death in the event of a mortal wound, it will both refresh tired muscles and soothe smaller injuries, which may make the difference between life and death even if it feels less dramatic.*
Affinity: Healing
Skill Tree: Slàinte

Spèird—*Often the first spell a mage learns, Spèird is a blast of force that can be used to fling projectiles and foes alike to buy the wielder precious time or space to manoeuvre.*
Increased use of this skill allows for more targeted applications and, with the power of a true proficient, can be as lethal as a martial arts' master's fists.

CALUM'S STATS AND SPELLS

Affinity: Staves
Skill Tree: Arcane

Tairm—*This spell calls upon the land around you to respond, which it will, based on your affinities and your own intent. As this is wild magic, the results are difficult to anticipate for the caster, though if that is true, it is all the more confounding for the targets.*
Be clear in your need, and nature will respond to your call.
Affinity: Wild (Special)
Skill Tree: Wild

Taobh a-Staigh *(Passive)*—*You gain an understanding of the intrinsic qualities of all life and its relationship to spirit. Rooted in Connection, this skill grants a permanent +1 to Mind and +1 to Pathos, and you receive a bonus to all spells and skills that deal with things internal: healing, buffs, and your understanding of your own spirit.*
While Taobh a-Staigh will not increase in levels as active spells will, your understanding of magic will, on occasion, trigger evolution.
Affinity: Nature, Synthesis
Skill Tree: Nature

Taobh a-Muigh *(Passive)*—*You gain an understanding of the relational qualities of all life and ecosystems as well as their place in the web of spirit. Rooted in Connection, this skill grants a permanent +1 to Mind and +1 to Will, and you receive a bonus to all spells and skills that deal with things external: bonds, brawls, and anything that acts upon the outside world.*
While Taobh a-Muigh will not increase in levels as active spells will, your understanding of magic will, on occasion, trigger evolution.
Affinity: Nature, Synthesis
Skill Tree: Nature

Tàth *(Level 2)*—*This ability allows you to form a consensual bond with an animal, giving you the power to see through the animal's eyes and guide the creature's movements where necessary. These bonds, once created, will bring a consistent drain on spirit until released, but the benefits far outweigh the sacrifice. Tàth comes with a one-time bonus of +1 to Pathos.*
Continued usage will improve the usefulness of these bonds, providing a symbiotic balance for both you and your companion. You gain eyes and ears and mobility—they gain intelligence, protection, and, in rare cases, special abilities. (Ch 18)
Affinity: Nature, Synthesis

CALUM'S STATS AND SPELLS

Skill Tree: Tàthadh

Tursa—*The ancients moved twenty-tonne slabs of rock hundreds of miles to build their monoliths. From this we have gleaned not only their technological capabilities but also their astronomical understanding. Many of these ancient monoliths were built with an intimate knowledge of the stars in the sky and the movements of the sun's path.*

This skill is the bedrock upon which the Draoidh builds their power. In unlocking it, you will gain an instinctual knowledge of astronomy and its relationship to you. While this many not seem like much, it will root you in time, in the seasons, and upon the surface of the earth itself. For what is more constant than the stars for navigation? To get anywhere, you need to know where you are.

Both a passive and an active skill, Tursa will allow you to carry an instinct of time and the turning of the wheel, but upon casting, it will give you an innate understanding of your environment, a precious glimpse that can allow you to strategise in the heat of battle or work your way out of natural obstacles when you can see no escape.

Affinity: Nature, Synthesis

Skill Tree: Draoidh

About Mati

Mati Ocha is a Scottish author of LitRPG and progression fantasy. He likes scrambling up mountains, jumping in cold lochs, and generally making mayhem in Gaelic and English. When he's not being chaotic in the wilds, he can usually be found ruining his characters' days or grinding yet another seasonal character in Diablo III.

His social media game is less than ideal, but you can follow him if you really want to on Facebook, Reddit, or Twitter.

LOVE LITRPG?

To learn more about LitRPG, talk to authors including myself, and just have an awesome time, please join the LitRPG Group!

MORE FROM ROBOT DINOSAUR

•ᐧ ᐧ(⟨⟩⟨⟩)ᐧ ᐧ•

R.J. Theodore's Peridot Shift:

(Swashbuckling Science Fantasy)

Flotsam

Salvage

Cast-Off

The Worlds of Novae Caelum:

Magnificent (A Superhero Novella)

The Throne of Eleven (Epic Fantasy)

The Truthspoken Heir (Epic Space Fantasy)

The Many Marvels of Merc Fenn Wolfmoor:

Wolf Among the Wild Hunt

Friends for Robots

These Imperfect Reflections

Monster Girls Don't Cry

Robot Dinosaur Press
robotdinosaurpress.com